Finding Hope at Hillside Farm

Rachael lives by the sea in the north-west of England
with her husband, six children, two dogs, two cats,
three chickens and two guinea pigs. She is very grateful
to the inventor of noise-cancelling headphones.

Rachael writes for adults and teenagers – her books
include *Sealed with a Kiss*, *Coming Up Roses*, *Wildflower
Bay*, *The State of Grace* and *My Box-Shaped Heart*.

Keep up to date with Rachael at rachaellucas.com. You
can find her procrastinating on Twitter @karamina and
at Instagram.com/rachaellucas.

Also by Rachael Lucas

Wildflower Bay
Sealed with a Kiss
Coming Up Roses

The State of Grace
My Box-Shaped Heart

e-novella
Sealed with a Christmas Kiss

Rachael Lucas

Finding Hope at Hillside Farm

PAN BOOKS

First published 2019 by Pan Books
an imprint of Pan Macmillan
20 New Wharf Road, London N1 9RR
Associated companies throughout the world
www.panmacmillan.com

ISBN 978-1-5098-8275-5

1 3 5 7 9 8 6 4 2

A CIP catalogue record for this book is available from the British Library.

Typeset by Palimpsest Book Production Ltd, Falkirk, Stirlingshire
Printed and bound by CPI Group (UK) Ltd, Croydon, CR0 4YY

Visit **www.panmacmillan.com** to read more about all our books
and to buy them. You will also find features, author interviews and
news of any author events, and you can sign up for e-newsletters
so that you're always first to hear about our new releases.

To Archie, with love

Chapter One

Ella

'It was a little girl.'

'I should think it was a stray tourist.'

Ella was certain it had been a little girl. Haunted dark brown eyes in a pale, dirt-smudged face, framed with long, dark hair. When she'd moved towards the hedge, calling hello, the child had started and ducked out of sight.

Her aunt Bron lifted a saucepan from the top of the Aga and clattered it down on the slate worktop. She turned around, brushing a thick lock of grey hair from her face with the back of her arm. Ella couldn't remember it happening – just that one day she'd noticed the thick plaited rope that hung down her aunt's back had somehow shifted from deep auburn to a uniform steely grey. Bron had aged by stealth – the laughter lines that crinkled in the corners of her eyes growing longer, the furrows between her brow deepening over time. Ella watched as her aunt put her hands in the small of her back and stretched, arching her spine with an audible crack.

'I checked the village page, just in case one of the kids from school had wandered off,' Ella said. The laptop lay open on the battered pine table in front of her. It floated on a sea of discarded post and days-old newspapers, forage bills and junk mail. Ella and Bron lived in what they liked to refer to as comfortable chaos.

'And?'

'Nothing. It just seemed so strange. I couldn't get her face out of my head. She looked so sad.'

Bron looked across at her. 'I'm sure there's a perfectly rational explanation.' She shooed the cat out of the way with a wave of her hand.

'I rang Lissa to check in case she'd heard anything.'

'And?' Bron pushed up her sleeves and ran her hands under the hot tap, lathering them with the cracked bar of soap that sat in the seashell dish by the sink.

Ella shook her head. 'Nothing.' Lissa was her best friend, and a teacher at the village primary school. There wasn't much that went on in the village that she didn't know about – partly because she was party to all the goings-on at the school gates, but also because her nose for gossip was particularly sharp.

'Well then,' said Bron, as if that was the end of that. She put the soap down on the dish and rinsed her hands under the hot tap. It seemed to Ella that the never-ending green bar of soap had been sitting there for decades. She could remember turning it round and round in her hands as a little girl when they'd visited the farm, back when a week in the summer holidays helping out with the sheep and the chickens and the goats was the highlight of her year. Back then, she could only have dreamed that the farm would become home.

Ella headed back out to the yard to finish off the final checks for the evening. A flurry of whinnies started up as soon as the horses heard her footsteps on the gravel – the high-pitched squeal from Blossom, the nine-month-old filly, and the low whicker of anticipation from the pregnant Sweetbriar. As the oldest mare of the herd, she presided over the yard from her box, which was set apart from the others. This was more for practical than hierarchical reasons. Left to her own devices, she'd snake her neck forward and take a warning bite out of any of the others who dared come too close. Right now, though, the other eight horses were still grazing the last flush of grass which had grown in the warmth of the autumn sunshine, and so Sweetbriar's only charge was her fiery little niece in the stable opposite, who shared the same deep chestnut colouring, white blaze, and flaxen mane and tail.

'Get back, you,' Ella laughed as Blossom reared up, her tiny hooves waving in the air. Her mother, up on the hill, would have given her a warning nip on the neck, telling her to get back in line. Ella lifted a finger, which was enough to send Blossom skittering to the back of her stable.

It was the last day of October, and the nights had suddenly turned chilly – the clear, bright, sunny afternoons giving way to evenings that were cold up on the hill. The clocks had changed, giving them a brief few weeks of extra light in the evenings, but that would be over soon. Then night feeds would be done in darkness, freezing fingers wrapped around the handles of icy cold feed buckets, the horses clouding the air with dragon-puffs of warm breath. This was the week when autumn took hold – the last few years, October had been a treat of a month, with afternoons which warmed up after misty cold mornings. Down the valley, Ella noticed smoke curling from the chimneys of the cottages below. Some of them were holiday lets, which often sat empty for the six colder months of the year. The town always quietened down as the temperature dropped. She rubbed her hands together, trying to warm them up, then slid the lock back into place.

The farmhouse was warm and welcoming, and the two dogs lay snoozing in a tangle of legs and tails in front of the Aga. The temptation to collapse on the sofa with a large glass of red and the remains of the box of chocolates was strong. But the prospect of Lissa's wrath was more terrifying . . . Ella had promised that she'd be at the Hallowe'en party at the Lion. And she'd promised again when she'd spoken to Lissa on the phone earlier that evening – no, she hadn't forgotten, and yes, she was definitely going to be there.

She reached down and rubbed Cleo, the spaniel, behind her long floppy ears, and ran a hand over the snoozing wire-coated Jack Russell, Bob. He opened one eye, checking for treats. Realizing none were forthcoming, he dropped off to sleep again.

'All right for you two,' Ella laughed, turning away.

She dragged off her long, brown outdoor boots, kicking them under the table, and turned for the bathroom, picking up a heap of roughly folded towels from on top of the Aga. They were deliciously warm. She wrapped her arms around them, feeling the heat rising under her chin. It was half five already, and she had to transform herself from practical equine therapist into something suitable for a fancy-dress party. Or at least suitable to be transformed by Lissa, because – Ella shook her head, smiling to herself – she knew that the second she arrived at her friend's house she'd be attacked with eyeliner pen and about a ton of make-up.

Grasping the towels tightly, she headed to the stairs.

'Ella, have you got a minute?' Bron called through from the sitting room just as Ella put her foot on the first step. She hovered, the other leg in mid-air, towels balanced precariously under her chin.

'Just going to have a shower. Lissa's expecting me.'

'I know.' There was a pause. Bron cleared her throat and Ella stepped back, feeling a strange, uneasy sensation in her stomach. She pushed the door open. Bron was sitting, her fingers steepled together, her brow furrowing.

'What's happened?'

'Nothing's happened –' Bron chewed on her lip and leaned forward, straightening the wine glass that sat in front of her on the coffee table.

Ella inclined her head, inviting her to talk. 'Come on.' She put the towels down and balanced herself on the arm of the sofa, her long legs tucked to one side. She noticed a hole in her sock and bent forward, pulling it off.

'The thing is . . .' Bron sat back, and sighed. 'I don't know how to tell you this. I've been trying to find a way for – well, for ages.'

Ella swallowed. Her throat felt tight and as she spoke her voice sounded quiet and somehow distant. 'Tell me what?'

She could feel the adrenalin response beginning to take effect. Heart thudding against her chest, blood rushing in her ears. She took a deep breath in, calming herself as she did her clients, holding the inhale and then slowly letting the air out of her lungs. It didn't work.

Bron began to speak. 'The thing is, my love, I'm not getting any younger.'

'You're always telling me seventy is the new forty,' Ella said, leaning towards her. She scanned her aunt's face properly for the first time in she didn't know how long. She looked thin, and her face was weather-beaten and worn. Why hadn't she noticed she was ill? She'd been so wrapped up in herself, thinking about work, worrying about bills . . .

'I need you to take on a bit of help with the horses. I'm going to be away for a bit.'

I knew it, thought Ella. Visions of Bron, pale and out of place in a hospital bed, rushed into her mind. She'd never cope with something like that. She was an outside creature. Hospital would be the end of her.

'I'm sorry –' Ella began. She could feel the prickling on her cheeks that meant tears were on the way. She rubbed at her face again, shaking her head. 'I should have noticed. It's OK. I'll look after everything. We don't need to take anyone on.'

'You can't do that, love.' Bron shook her head. 'The thing is, I'm not going to be here –'

Oh, please no. Please, please, please. Anything but that.

'It's Isobel. She said she didn't want to worry me, but –'

'Oh –' Ella let out a breath and squeezed her eyes shut for a moment before opening them wide, and looking at Bron once again. 'You're not ill?'

'Healthy as a horse,' said Bron, looking slightly indignant.

'But I thought –'

'No need to be thinking about me. I'm fine. It's Isobel who's having problems, not that she'll admit to it, the stubborn old mule. She hasn't changed since we were children.'

Ella's memory of her aunt Isobel, who had emigrated to Australia when she was a young nurse in her early twenties, was of the energetic woman who'd flown over to visit when Ella was a little girl. It had been a summer holiday where the sun shone endlessly, and Ella had spent it in shorts and T-shirt, her limbs tanned and her hair swinging in a long ponytail. They'd lived on barbe-cued sausages and she'd roamed the hills every day with the dogs, exploring until she knew every track through the tall bracken and each tumbling waterfall that poured down through the woods.

'She's not doing well at all. Let's face it, to even let on to me that things aren't quite right is a sign that things must be pretty bad.'

Ella chewed on the inside of her cheek, closing her eyes. The family had always been very much of the stiff-upper-lip, just-get-on-with-it persuasion. That brisk attitude had been just what Ella had needed when she'd arrived here years back, and it would take something pretty major to shock either Bron or her aunt Isobel into admitting they weren't doing well.

'It's not all bad.' Bron reached over and gave Ella's knee a pat. 'Every year I say that I'm going to take some time out and go travelling. I've been saying it since I was thirty. Now thirty years have passed and if I don't go now, it's never going to happen.'

Ella picked at a loose thread that was hanging from the edge of her shirt, worrying it until it was long enough to pull.

'It won't do you any harm.' Bron's expression was serious. 'You'll be better off here without me cramping your style.'

Ella pulled at the thread and watched, mesmerized, as the hem of her shirt unravelled with the tug of just one loose thread. It left a pattern of tiny little holes.

'I don't *have* a style.'

'That's part of the problem.' Bron chuckled. 'Living with your seventy-year-old aunt is not exactly doing wonders for your street cred, is it?'

There was a moment of silence. Ella listened as the ancient farmhouse groaned and creaked with the same end-of-the-day noises she'd heard a thousand times. It was safe, and familiar. She was more than happy with safe and familiar.

'I didn't want to tell you today, of all days, but in a way maybe it's a good thing. There's never a right time.' Bron squeezed Ella's knee again. 'But it's been ten years. Maybe it's time for us to move on a bit.'

Ella looked up at the photograph on the dresser of her father with his arms around Bron and his other sister-in-law, Isobel, taken one long hot summer. The picture was bleached from years of sitting on the dresser in the morning sun. In it, her father's hand was shading his eyes from the same sun, standing on the wall outside the cottage, beaming with love and happiness, the family all together for once. It had been taken the last time Isobel had visited, the final time. The thrombosis she'd suffered on the plane back had put paid to further flights and she'd been lucky to survive. Bron, tied to the farm and the animals and the hill, had managed a couple of short visits – paid for by Isobel, who had worked for years as a specialist nurse in Sydney. But plane fares were expensive, and money was tighter now. It had been years since they'd seen each other.

'Won't you miss the horses?'

'Less than I ought to, I suspect.' She chuckled. 'I've been here for thirty years, remember. I suspect I'll enjoy the break.'

Ella had done more and more of the work around the stables as the business had begun to grow. Initially, her equine therapy business had been a small sideline to Bron's breeding programme. But she'd sold on several of the broodmares, and that side of the business had dwindled away until the focus was on Ella's therapy work. She'd used the inheritance from her father to build a big covered school where she could work with clients and horses all year round, protected from the Welsh rain – or liquid sunshine, as they liked to call it, rolling their eyes as it fell incessantly all summer. And there was a little arena outdoors too, floodlit and surfaced with springy, weatherproof material, sheltered on each side by high thick hedgerows to break the harsh Welsh winter wind. Two of the stables had been converted into a sitting area and a waiting room, where clients could help themselves to coffee from a machine, sit on the comfortable leather armchairs and watch the tank full of tropical fish flitting back and forth. Business wasn't booming, but they managed to wing it each month, bringing in enough money to keep afloat. And – Ella looked down at her cheap, scruffy jeans and battered fleece covered in straw – she might not be dressed in designer clothes, but the horses didn't want for anything. If Bron was brave enough to set off to Australia for an adventure, she'd have to step up and deal with it.

'Now you get yourself off and get ready for your night out,' Bron said, reaching forward for the remote control. 'We can talk about this more in the morning.'

'Well, yes,' Ella said. 'We've got plenty of time.'

'Mmm.' Bron made an odd noise, then cleared her throat. 'About that.'

Ella's dark eyes darted to meet her aunt's blue ones. Bron looked slightly uncomfortable.

'I've been trying to pluck up the courage to tell you for a while.'

'Oh-kay . . .' Ella frowned. 'So we don't have plenty of time after all. What've we got? Weeks? A week?'

Bron shifted in her chair and looked at the coffee table instead of meeting her eyes.

'A week.' Ella shook her head. 'Are you joking?'

Bron gave a small shrug and pulled a face. This was typical of her – she hated confrontation, or uncomfortable conversations.

'I thought it might be easier if we just ripped the plaster off.'

'OK. We can deal with that. I can manage.'

'It's not quite a week, though,' Bron said quietly. 'My flight leaves on Monday afternoon.'

Ella stood up and shoved the towels under her arm, picking up a brown envelope which was sitting on the coffee table as she did so. She felt a bit wobbly, but didn't want to show it. She took a deep breath, turned back for

11

a moment, and looked at her aunt steadily. 'I think –' she ripped open the envelope and pulled out the contents – 'you're doing the right thing.'

She headed out to the hall and stood for a moment, trying to catch her breath.

Bron had always been there for her, and perhaps it was time to let her get on with her own life. The sitting-room door swung shut with a gentle click, and Ella shook out the paper from inside the envelope. IMPORTANT was stamped at the top, and the contents were ringed with a box of red. That only ever meant one thing. They'd balanced a financial tightrope for long enough that she recognized the seriousness of a final demand straight away. She sat down on the stairs and looked more closely at the letter.

Further to our repeated attempts to contact you, it began. Ella felt a familiar churning in her stomach. Neither of them were exactly hot on paperwork. They shoved a box full of receipts once a year at Glynn, the accountant, who shook his head and sighed, before working his magic and sending off the details to the tax office. In between times, with the animals and the business taking up their days from dawn to dusk, things were quite often missed, mislaid or forgotten. It always worked out, somehow.

This is a final demand for payment of building rates. Unless a payment of £4,000 is received within ten days . . .

Ella looked up at the calendar and down at the stark wording of the letter.

'Ella?' Bron called through from the sitting room. 'You all right out there?'

'It's nothing. Yes. I mean, I'm fine.' She shoved the letter back in the envelope, the page crumpling at the corner as she did so.

Bron had taken thirty years to pluck up the courage to do something for herself. The least she could do now was let her aunt go, and deal with this without giving her a reason to hesitate.

God, she was going to have to sell a kidney or something – and fast. She'd been drifting for far too long, managing to squeak by from one month to the next, and she'd always pushed the nagging worry that she should have something put away for a rainy day to one side. The bottom had fallen out of the horse market, too, so even if she wanted to sell one of them – which she couldn't bear to think of – there wouldn't be any point. She knew of breeders who were giving their horses away.

Horses were an expensive business, and she'd been happily complacent, not getting out of her comfort zone – ironically, given she spent most of her therapy hours gently encouraging her clients to do just that. The little website she'd had designed years back brought in a gentle trickle of enquiries, and the clients she already had passed on a steady supply of word-of-mouth recommendations. But this bill was in a different league altogether.

Biting her lip, Ella pushed herself up to standing. She

still had to get ready to go out. Whatever was going to happen would have to wait until tomorrow, at least. She shoved the letter into the back pocket of her jeans and climbed the stairs.

Chapter Two

Jenny

Despite being old enough to know better – old enough, she thought to herself, to be his mother – Jenny couldn't help admiring the removal man's bottom as he bent over, dropping the crate with an alarming thud on the flagstone floor of the cottage. She was a girl of twenty not that long ago – only . . . forty-five years? Good God. She was old enough to be his *grandmother*. It was amazing how age crept up on you when you weren't looking.

She slipped past the removal man and stood for a moment, looking at the cottage as it stood in the low afternoon sunlight. It was whitewashed and timbered, the low roof sheltering windows that were set deep into thick stone walls, protecting the inhabitants against the wind, which must blow fiercely through the valley. She wrapped her arms around her chest, realizing that despite the warmth she felt from all the rushing around, out here there was a chill in the air. A couple of pale climbing roses were still blooming bravely on the bush that grew up the side of the back door, and in the wooden planters some hardy pelargoniums were holding on, warmed by the late October sunshine they'd had across the country. Through the open stable door she could see the removal men stacking the last of the boxes neatly against the ancient wood of the staircase. The cottage was hundreds of years old, and full of history. And now they'd landed here to add their voices to the ones that echoed through the walls – Jenny smiled at the thought. It had been a crazy idea, and the last-minute panic had set everyone on high alert, but she had a feeling everything was going to be fine. Later she'd nip down to the little supermarket in the village. Maybe the bakery would have some bread left over – dinner could just be cheese and bits and pieces – Hope's favourite, and hers too. No cooking was always a plus, especially after a long day like today.

'Nearly done, love.' One of the removal men – the cheerful one, she'd already named him in her head – carried in a box. 'What have you got in this? Gold bullion?' He chuckled.

'Books.'

'Blooming heavy ones!'

She smiled and headed back inside, curling her hand around the bundle of keys in her cardigan pocket, feeling their comforting, familiar weight. Car. Ancient keyring from Sarah's school ski trip to Austria. Big Yale key from the storage place where they'd left the majority of their furniture. And home – well, not any more. Not for the next six months. It had been the most impetuous thing she'd ever done – and Lou, still recuperating from a major heart operation, had gone along with it. They'd rented out their big, airy Georgian house in Norwich to a couple who were new to the area, house-hunting for a place of their own to bring up their two small children. It had been the perfect solution for both families.

Jenny pulled the set of keys out and slid the cottage keys onto the ring. There were so many now, she'd look like a gaoler if she emptied her handbag.

'Oh, bloody hell!'

There was a thud from the room next door.

'Grandpa, you've broken the lamp.' A small, shrill voice carried through the hall, echoing off the bare wooden floorboards and the rough whitewashed plaster.

'That's us off,' said the less friendly removal man, thrusting a clipboard in Jenny's direction. 'If you can just sign –'

'Two seconds.'

She waved it away and hurried through, ducking her head to avoid banging it on the low, beamed doorway. The cottage was a complete contrast to their high-ceilinged house in Norwich, and it was going to take some getting used to.

'What on earth is going on?'

Lou was on his hands and knees, picking up pieces of china that had scattered over the floor. A wooden crate lay on its side on the flagstones, the contents spilling out. Hope was inexpertly stacking the books which had fallen over into a toppling pile and Jenny could only stand and watch as they slid, slowly but inexorably, from the arm of the still-not-in-place sofa to join the muddle of broken vase pieces on the floor.

The removal man poked his head around the door. His eyebrows shot up as he took in the scene.

'Breakages?' He sucked his teeth. 'I'm afraid we only cover the goods in transit . . .'

'It's not ours, it belongs to the cottage.'

Jenny suppressed a sigh of irritation. They'd paid an absolute fortune for the removal company so they could make the cottage feel like home for a few months, and they'd done exactly what they were paid to – and not a thing more. Lou's recovery regime meant he was supposed to be taking things easy, not crashing around unpacking boxes. Perhaps she should have paid for them to sort that out as well. She chewed on the side of her lip for a moment, wondering just how big a tip and how many cups of tea might swing it.

'If you're all right to sign this, then –' he waggled the clipboard again – 'I need to get this truck back before it gets too late. We're running behind as it is.'

'Oh.' That's that, then, she thought. 'It's fine,' she said, reaching across and swiping the clipboard from his hands. 'No real damage done.' She signed her name and handed it back, absent-mindedly pocketing the biro he'd given her.

'That's great.' He ripped off a pink duplicate copy and handed it to her. 'Can I have my pen back, please, love, and I'll get out of your hair.'

*

'Thank God that's over,' said Lou, closing the door as the removal lorry trundled over the brow of the hill. 'Now, why don't I make you some tea, and then I'll sort out some of this unpacking. Go and put your feet up for a bit.'

He made a shooing motion. Even after the weeks of recuperation, it was still strange to have her husband around all the time. They'd spent all their married life with very firm boundaries: him out at work – long, unpredictable hours which hadn't changed even when his job as DCI became more office-based.

'No.' Jenny was firm. She blocked the doorway to the kitchen and stood in it, not moving, so he had no choice but to duck through the low-ceilinged hallway and into the whitewashed sitting room. She motioned to the plumply stuffed sofa. Hope had already removed the cushions and piled them up on the armchair, where she was now sitting, Princess and the Pea style, reading a tourist information leaflet about Wales.

'You sit. *I* will make tea.'

The advantage of a holiday rental cottage was that everything they needed was already in place. All they'd had to do was bring along the bits and pieces they needed to make the place homely – only somehow that had extended from a couple of boxes in the car boot, as each of them staked a claim on belongings they couldn't possibly do without. The kitchen was spotless, if a bit dated, with brown wooden cupboard doors and a fake marble worktop. But the Aga made the room warm and welcoming, and the window looked down the valley towards Llanidaeron itself. Jenny opened the wooden door of the larder and found a wicker basket, filled with everything that the holiday visitors would have needed. There was tea, coffee, and someone had delivered two packs of freshly baked Welsh cakes. Inside the fridge sat a fat roll of local butter wrapped in gold paper and a pint of organic milk from a local dairy, as well as a bottle of wine ('by way of apology', the note tied to the neck explained).

When the holiday cottage company rang to say that they'd *had a bit of a mix-up*, and the cottage they'd signed up for on a special six-month offer for the winter had been taken off the books, she'd almost shot through the roof of their Citroën Picasso with fury. Only the presence of Hope on the back seat, her headphones clamped over her ears but her ever-watchful eyes taking everything in, stopped her from exploding. Instead she'd been completely calm. Or near enough, anyway.

'We're incredibly sorry,' the manager had said, sounding harassed. The reception was terrible – he sounded like he was calling with his head halfway down the loo. 'This isn't something that's ever happened before. But the owners have sold the property – quite unexpectedly – and as it happens we have an absolutely beautiful cottage available in Llanidaeron which is only five miles away, as the crow flies.'

'We are currently driving towards Llanover,' Jenny

said, through gritted teeth. Lou shifted slightly in the passenger seat, emitting a quiet snore. It was a miracle that he was actually relaxing. If she started losing the plot now, he'd get stressed, and that was the last thing any of them needed.

'Surely there are clauses? They can't just withdraw the property without a notice period?'

'There are, yes – but we'd have to turf you out after a month. This seemed like the best option.'

Why is it never easy, Jenny thought to herself, gritting her teeth.

'Right. Fine.' It was only a few months, after all. And the whole point of this was to take them out of their routine a bit. Hope had said she didn't want to see the cottage before they arrived. So she decided to try and be calm about it. She took a deep breath in. How bad could it be? 'What's this new place like?'

'Absolutely charming.' She heard the manager's voice shift, relieved, into sales mode. 'The most adorable thatched roof, beams everywhere, an old-fashioned iron range in the sitting room, and a master bedroom with a beautiful en suite.'

'But it does have three bedrooms?' Jenny flicked a quick glance at Hope in the rear-view mirror. She was chewing a lock of hair, her dark eyes lost in thought.

'Yes, three and a little office, in fact. I just know you're going to love it. I'll come out to meet you myself if it helps – I've got a Hallowe'en party for my daughter tonight, but we can swing past?'

'No need.' Jenny was firm. The last thing they needed was *more* people and more stress. Hope had been relatively calm and happy so far and everything – apart from the minor detail of a new house – was going reasonably well. Ish.

'Are you absolutely sure?' Despite the terrible line, she could hear the obsequious tone in his voice.

'Completely.' The last thing they needed was to deal with the manager of Hideaway Holidays on a charm offensive. 'If you could just message me the postcode.'

And so – having called the removal driver, who was on the road somewhere behind them – they'd typed the new postcode into the satnav, and both Jenny and the driver wondered how *five miles as the crow flies* managed to add on an extra forty minutes to the drive.

Of course – Jenny lifted the kettle and poured boiling water into two mugs – that had become clear when they'd driven past the sign for Llanover and up a hill. And down another. And back round the side of another hill. Eventually they'd found themselves in Llanidaeron, the pretty little high street nestled in between the shoulders of the green hills on either side of the valley, and driven up, up, along a narrow lane flanked on either side by the bare branches of hawthorn hedges, and pulled into the gateway of Robin Cottage, their home for the next six months.

'Here you –' Jenny stopped herself mid-sentence as she opened the door. Lou was sitting, legs stretched out and crossed over, head back against the plump cushions of the armchair. His mouth hung open and for the briefest second she felt her stomach dropping to her feet. Time stood still for a moment. And then he gave a walrus-like snort, waking himself up.

'What?'

Jenny gave a peal of relieved laughter. 'Tea.'

She wondered if that feeling of panic would ever go, or if she'd feel a flicker of fear every time she saw him motionless and silent. Losing people – or almost, in Lou's case – just made you more aware of how precious and fleeting life could be. She passed him the steaming mug, and gave his shoulder a brief, gentle squeeze.

He gave her an odd look but said nothing. She sat down opposite him on the armchair by the fire. It wasn't the most comfortable thing she'd ever sat on, and she lifted off a prickly woollen rug from the arm and tossed it across to the little wooden coffee table.

'Here we are then,' Lou said. 'Are you pleased with it?'

'I will be once I've got this lot sorted.'

The room was stacked with boxes – a surprising number considering they were only supposed to be bringing the bare minimum – and it all needed to be sorted.

'What's Hope doing?' She'd disappeared from her pile of cushions, leaving a heap of leaflets in her wake.

'Upstairs,' Lou said. 'She's unpacking, I think.'

Jenny knew what that meant. Chaos. She plonked her mug down on the table and pushed herself out of the chair, suppressing a groan. Her back was protesting after the long drive and she'd have liked nothing more than to collapse in front of the sofa, have a long bath, and deal with everything else tomorrow. But she was responsible for Hope, and eight-year-olds didn't slow down just because their grandparents were feeling frazzled.

'I might just check. She's suspiciously quiet.'

'Probably drawing or something.' He reached forward and picked up the remote control. 'How do you think this thing works? I don't understand why they can't all be the same. Where's the on button?'

The narrow staircase had been there for centuries and the stairs were surprisingly steep. She popped her head in the door of Hope's bedroom, but she wasn't there.

'Darling?'

There was a pause as she waited. Sometimes Hope liked to play hide and seek – usually at the most inopportune times. They'd waited half an hour once when she was four, searching behind the clothes on the hangers in M&S, knowing she'd tucked herself somewhere. The security managers had manned the doors, convinced she'd been abducted, but Jenny had stayed surprisingly calm. Eventually one of them found her, cocooned inside the warm fleece of a dressing gown, apparently unconcerned by the rising panic of every adult in the shop.

And now there was no sign of her under the bed, or – thankfully – in the wardrobe, which seemed quite unstable. It was a beautiful piece of old walnut furniture, but swayed alarmingly when she pulled open the door to check inside.

'Lou?' she called down the stairs, 'No sign of Hope here.'

The responsibility of bringing up her granddaughter weighed heavily. She felt a pang of guilt, thinking about her promise to Sarah to bring her up and give her the security she needed. If Harry was here a bit more, she thought, it wouldn't be so bloody – she shook her head, feeling guilty for even thinking it. She had to tell herself that he was doing the best he could. They all were. She had to believe that, even if sometimes it felt like she'd pulled the short straw in everything.

'She said something about seeing horses. Or drawing them?'

No sign of any art equipment where normally it would be strewn across the floor – Hope liked to lie on her stomach, propped up on her elbows, colouring in pictures she'd created. She could spend hours like that.

The first chilly fingers of fear sneaked into Jenny's stomach. She took an instinctive breath in, feeling her chest rise, closing her eyes for a moment, remembering the words of the grief counsellor she'd seen for so long after Sarah's death. Not everything is a calamity, she reminded herself.

'Hope?'

Her voice sounded breathy and high-pitched. She strained her ears, listening for the rustling that would indicate a small child hidden somewhere.

'She's here.'

Thank God.

At the bottom of the stairs she paused again for a moment, watching as Lou caught Hope by the waist and pulled her in for a cuddle, taking her by surprise. 'You smell of fresh air,' he said. 'Have you been in the garden?'

'Darling . . .' Jenny bent over to pick up the wellington boots – white stars on a blue shiny background – left strewn across the flagstones of the hallway. She placed them on top of the stack of cardboard boxes and looked at Hope. 'Can you tell me or Grandpa if you're going to play in the garden? Just so we don't worry?'

'I wasn't in the garden,' Hope said, standing on one leg, one striped sock hanging off the end of her toes, the other rolled over her jeans. She cocked her head to one side, thoughtfully, her dark eyes dreamy, long hair hanging in curtains on either side of a face smudged with mud. 'I was looking at the horses. I'm going to go and draw them now. Did you know there's a desk in my room? And I can see the horses from the window if I stand on tiptoe . . .'

'Please don't go leaning out of any windows,' Jenny said to Hope's back as she scampered out of the room.

'How are you feeling?' she asked Lou.

'Fine, darling.' She could see her husband doing his best not to roll his eyes. 'Don't fuss.'

'I'm not fussing.' Jenny pursed her lips. 'I just prefer you alive to hooked up on a million machines.'

26

'I've no intention of letting that happen again.'

A fleeting image of Lou, covered in monitors which had beeped and whirred alarmingly, popped into her head unbidden. She shook her head slightly as if to scare it away.

'Good.'

'Fine.'

He smiled at her for a second, his eyes twinkling, and something in his look reminded her of the boy he'd been when they met. Maybe this place could be a chance for them to remember who they'd been, before – everything.

Chapter Three

Ella

Each of the trees that lined Llanidaeron High Street was wrapped with a thousand tiny orange lights, glowing in the evening dusk like fireflies.

Ella stopped to look in the window of the post office, out of habit. She was still thinking about the little girl she'd seen earlier. She'd probably been out walking with her family, wandering up to look at the strangely compelling sight of the wind farm that stretched out along the top of the hills, filling the air with an unceasing, mysterious hum which spoke of ley lines and magic and not, more prosaically, of renewable energy and the town's contribution to the National Grid. A surprising number of visitors made their way up the hill just to stand and watch the huge arms spinning. It was a contentious subject in the village – most of the locals had been positive about it, seeing it as an obvious way to bring much-needed money into the town, the population of which was slowly dwindling away, year on year. There was still a tattered poster hanging on by two rusted drawing pins to the announcement board, advertising a protest meeting. It had been arranged by one of the incomers. Ella had somehow bypassed incomer status and been accepted into the fold, probably because she'd moved in with Bron – so she'd been accepted over the last ten years as one of the locals. She'd attended more than her fair share of village improvement meetings and watched as many of the little businesses struggled to keep afloat. There were always people – floating out to the country-side to live the self-sufficient life, dressed from head to toe in ethnic-printed organic cotton – who were deter-mined to keep the quaint nature of the village sacred, unaware that the village they imagined, sadly, no longer really existed. Teenagers left in search of university or jobs as soon as they could, the shops closed as the owners retired, and sometimes it felt like one day Llani would be nothing more than a ghost town.

But they'd still have the Lion, of course. It was a per-manent fixture. Ella paused for a second to check her reflection in the shop window. Her dark hair was already wind-ruffled and in the blue-white glow of the shop light her face looked pale, her freckles standing out even more than usual. She pushed a strand of hair behind her ear and ran a finger along her lower lip, wiping away a smudge of lipstick. Behind her a gaggle of tiny ghouls tottered past, their faces painted white, high on artificial colours and squealing with delight.

'All right, Ella?'

It was Susan from the art shop, hair covered with a black wig, cloaked in a voluminous black garment threaded with trailing silver ribbons. She was mummy to two of the tiny ghouls who'd just passed – Ella had no idea which, disguised as they were by the darkness and their elaborate costumes.

The sea of tiny people stopped, connected to Susan by some psychic link, and as one, swirled back, an ever-moving black cloud of energy and excitement, and surrounded them.

'You going to the party at the Lion? As soon as I've filled this lot with as many sweets as they can eat and sent them to bed to dream of the dentist, I'll be joining you. Lissa said you were coming out.'

Ella nodded. There were a million emotions swirling around inside her and, like a child, she felt an urge to rush home and cling on to her aunt. What if Bron never came back? What if the flight was too much for her and she suffered the same fate as her sister? Ella chewed on her lip, realizing as she did so that she'd probably taken off half of the plum-coloured lipstick she'd so carefully applied.

One of the children tugged at Susan's sleeve. 'Can we go now? Mrs Evans said if we came to her house she'd be doing hot dogs and party games and grown-up drinks.'

Susan brightened slightly at this.

'Grown-up drinks?' She waggled her eyebrows at Ella. 'Are you thinking what I'm thinking?'

'We might get *Coke*!' said a small boy.

Both adults laughed.

Ella recognized him as one of the children of the couple who owned the health food shop. He'd probably been dreaming of this night all year long. Coke and sweets weren't allowed the rest of the time. The children were treated once a week, his mother had informed Ella recently, to a bar of carob on a Friday – *if* they'd done their meditation every morning.

'I'm not sure that's the kind of grown-up drink she meant, Danny.' Susan caught Ella's eye with a conspiratorial wink. She lowered her voice to a whisper. 'Bloody hope not, anyway. I'll see you later.'

Ella trailed up the high street to Lissa's little cottage. The curtains were not yet drawn. The lit window framed a picture of pre-party disorganization. There was an ironing board set up in front of the outsize television screen which was showing one of the music channels, half-naked girls gyrating in front of an unappealing-looking singer in too-tight leather trousers. A bottle of wine stood on the floor, half empty already. Behind the sofa Lissa was standing in a dressing gown, face mask on, drying a pair of tights with a hairdryer. Lissa seemed like the sort of person who'd escape Llani for the exciting lights of the city as soon as she could. She had, in fact, when she was eighteen – heading to Manchester University to study politics, determined to make her mark. But the lure of the Welsh mountains had been so strong that following a postgraduate teaching qualification and a few years ('absolute bloody hell, it was') teaching in a grim, failing

31

inner-city primary school she'd found herself drawn back to the village and now taught at the local primary school. As a senior member of staff, she prided herself on her professional standards, maturity, organization, and the certainty that the parents knew that while she was teaching she was a model of decorum, even if she was downing pints at the bar with the rowdier half of the PTA on a Friday night.

'You going to stand out there all night?' The front door was wrested open as Ella went to knock. 'There I was, blow-drying my tights, and I look up and you're staring in the window looking like you've seen a ghost.'

'I was dreaming,' said Ella, taking off her coat and hanging it on the end of the banister. She dodged two huge crates of schoolbooks, which Lissa would have to mark tomorrow with a hangover.

'Here,' said Lissa, pouring a glass of sparkling wine. 'Get that down you.'

By the time Lissa had got herself dressed and Ella's make-up had been redone ('Let's make you a bit witchy, like. Here, I'll do your eyes'), the bottle was finished and another one had been opened. Lissa shoved it under her coat as they headed out into the cold night and pulled the door closed behind them. Ella, concerned, peered into the empty house through the window.

'What you doing?'

'Just checking you haven't left the iron on, or the hair straighteners, or any of the other things you do when you're distracted.' Ella nudged her friend, teasing.

'I checked them all, I'll have you know.'

'Right,' said Ella. 'Let's get this over with.'

'It's not a bloody torture session, Ell, it's a night out at the pub. And it's Hallowe'en. Everyone loves Hallowe'en –'

There was a tiny beat of silence and Lissa tipped her head slightly, looking at Ella as if she'd just remembered something.

'Oh, honey. I know this is a shitty time of year.'

Ella shook her head. 'Pass us that bottle,' she said, reaching across. She took a long drink and handed it back to Lissa, wiping her mouth. She put the thought of the enormous bill, Bron leaving, and everything else to the back of her mind. There was nothing else to do with it.

They walked down the hill towards the old Victorian hotel which stood on the road that skirted the edge of Llanidaeron. A handful of young teenagers ran past, prompting Lissa to shove the wine bottle, previously waving about as she made a point, back underneath her long purple cloak.

'You out trick or treating, Miss?' one of the boys shouted back over his shoulder.

'Bloody hell, that was close.' Lissa pretended to mop her brow.

Their footsteps echoed in the empty street. An owl hooted overhead in the silence, and a rumble in the distance could be heard, as the lights for the level crossing started to flash. There was a creak and a metallic clanking as the arm of the barrier groaned into life.

'Shit, the bloody Aber train. I was stuck here for ten minutes the other day. I swear there's something wrong with the timer on it, or something.'

Crossing when the lights were flashing and the alarm beginning to sound might be Lissa's style, but that kind of risk wasn't Ella's usual sort of thing. But –

She grabbed Lissa's arm and pulled her on. They hurtled across the metal railway tracks to the other side.

'Duck,' she shouted, and they bobbed underneath the barrier.

'Bloody hell,' Lissa bent over, puffed out and laughing. The huge floodlight that illuminated the crossing cast a pale white glow on her face, emphasizing the black shadow that formed sharp, witchy peaks at either side of her huge dark eyes. The alarm continued to sound, beeping repeatedly in time with the three red lights that flashed a warning in the darkness.

'Cutting it a bit close there, girls. You off to the Lion?'

Looming out of the darkness, Alan from the post office approached. He lifted an arm in greeting.

'Yes we are,' Lissa indicated Ella with a nod of the head. 'If Ella doesn't get us run over by a bloody train first.'

Ella, exhilarated and feeling the wine going to her head, grinned.

There was a faint metallic hum as the train approached the little station platform behind them.

Alan shook his head. 'Don't think it's my thing, girls. I'm a bit old to be out partying in my Hallowe'en outfit. I'm away off home with a pie from Rhian.' He lifted the paper bag he was holding from the fish and chip shop.

'Are you sure you can't be tempted?' Lissa waved the wine bottle in the air in reply.

'Absolutely not.'

The lights of the train loomed out of the dark fields that lay beyond the village and drew closer. In a moment it had passed, pulling with a squeal of brakes into the little train station, disgorging its cargo of weekend tourists, students home for the weekend from university, and the late-night commuters who worked each day in Shrewsbury. It was another world – Ella couldn't imagine it. Leaving this beautiful place every day for traffic and noise? There might be downsides to living in the middle of nowhere, but she wouldn't swap life here for the bright lights now, not for anyone.

The warning lights blinked off and with a groan the hydraulic arm was lifted up again, pulling the barrier back. As Alan passed, his normally deadpan face broke into a rare smile.

'You're looking very glamorous tonight, Ella,' he nodded. 'Nice to see you out and about and out of your work clothes.'

Ella and Lissa opened the door to a wall of noise and the heat of countless bodies crammed into a tiny space. The air was thick with perfume and the damp, hoppy smell of spilt beer. A werewolf, a zombie nurse, three vampires and a mummy, his bandages already drooping, were hunched over the wooden stools that circled one of the beer-barrel tables just behind the door.

'Ella!' The mummy raised his glass in greeting. She peered forward through the half-lit room and recognized Mick from the grain stores, lifting a hand in a half-wave of recognition. It was busier this year than ever, with everyone having dressed up for the occasion. Like a masked ball, she thought, nobody quite knew who anyone was – and it meant that this night, of all nights, was the one when misbehaviour was at its peak. Even Adelaide Evans, owner of the little village bookshop, who normally presided owl-like over her desk like a Victorian schoolmistress, was standing by the bar with a glass of cider in one hand and a broomstick in the other. Her hair, still in its neat little top knot, was sprayed silver and a cobweb – complete with spider – hung from her round-framed metal spectacles. She was deep in conversation with a black-clad shape wearing a ghoulish rubber mask.

Sally behind the bar gave them a wave, rolling her eyes and lifting palms upward in mock despair, as if she couldn't believe what was going on. She was the architect of the yearly Hallowe'en party, instituted years back when her children were much younger. 'Why should they get all the fun?' she'd said, telling everyone at the school gates and along the river when she met them out dog walking. 'We can bloody well have our own Hal-

lowe'en celebration once we've got our lot off to bed.'
And so she did – Gareth and Charlotte, her twins, were
at university now, no doubt causing mischief wherever
they went, but the tradition continued. Now whichever
parents had drawn the short straws – Susan was one, this
year – would be trailing over-excited children around the
village, looking for the lit-up carved pumpkins that indicated a welcome while the others would be back home,
preparing for a much-anticipated night out. The children
would be delivered home and teenagers bribed into
babysitting with money and vast buckets of trick-or-
treating leftovers.

Ella stood for a moment, letting the sounds wash over
her. The music was almost drowned out by the clamour
of voices and the clatter of glasses. She ran a hand along
the wooden carving on the panelled wall. A hundred
years or so ago, someone had lovingly created each of the
ornate wooden oak leaves which ran along the edge of
the panel, detailing each one with the finest miniature
branches of veins, each one different, all beautiful. Over
the years, the edges had become smooth and rounded
with all the hands that had touched them over a hundred
years. The things the hotel had seen years back, when the
traders were making their way across the country to and
from London. And now here they stood, the place filled
with ghouls and gargoyles, the light dim, skeletons and
ghosts hanging from the ceiling.

She lifted her gaze and scanned the room. Lissa had
already managed to duck under the heaving throng of

people waiting to be served at the bar and could be seen waving a twenty-pound note at one of the young, good-looking barmen. With her dark hair curled and her old-fashioned, bosomy figure cinched into a drawstring corset, Ella wasn't completely sure what her friend was supposed to be, but she looked like she'd been poured into her dress and the effect was dazzling. Lissa wasn't having any trouble attracting attention. A second later and she'd exchanged the money she was waving for two pints and two shots of something alarmingly purple in colour. Ella waited as she managed to part the sea of people and make her way back out, beaming triumphantly.

'Here you are.' She handed two of the glasses over.

'Should I ask what it is?'

'Haunted horror, it said on the poster.' Lissa raised her glass, clinking it against Ella's. 'Something purple and –' She took a mouthful, pulling a face. 'Well, it looks nice, anyway. I reckon Andy behind the bar made it up off the top of his head.'

Ella sniffed cautiously, threw her head back, and downed it in one. She placed the glass on a nearby table, feeling quite pleased with herself. This was more like it. Maybe Dutch courage was what she needed.

It was hard to move through the bar to get to the function room at the back of the hotel. They sidled, stepping sideways, glasses held high.

'I can't believe Bron's off to Australia.' Lissa took advantage of a break in the music, turning to Ella, her dark eyes thoughtful. 'How are you feeling?'

'Fine. Good.' Whatever was in the drink was definitely going to her head. 'I'm going to make some – *changes.*'

'Really?' Lissa looked impressed. 'So what's the plan for the new and improved Ella?'

Ella took a deep breath, and another large mouthful of her drink.

'I'm going to talk to Nick tonight.'

Chapter Four

Ella

'Oh.' Lissa's eyes widened. 'I'm not sure that's –' She stopped midway through a sentence, looking at Ella briefly, then across the sea of black-clad bodies. The music had been turned up and was thumping so loudly now that Ella could feel it reverberating through her body, shaking her bones, waking her up. It brought back memories of long ago – nights out clubbing, dancing under ever-changing coloured light, staggering exhausted into the hazy half-light of an Edinburgh dawn at four in the morning. Back in uni days they'd stayed out all night. It was a far cry from the life here in Llanidaeron, where the sounds most likely to wake her at that time of the morning were a ewe calling for a stray lamb, or the milk tanker chugging past on the way to start the first collection of the day over on the coast.

'But I'm not ready for him yet,' said Ella, grabbing Lissa's hand, pulling her onto the already-packed dance floor. They were folded immediately into a throng of bodies, twirling and thrusting and moving with the beat, which was hypnotic. The lights pulsed in time with her heartbeat and Ella threw her hands in the air, losing herself in the music.

Lissa, when the music dipped temporarily, grabbed Ella's hands with a beaming smile, her dark eyes bright.

'This is bloody brilliant, isn't it?' She spun around, knocking into a green-clad zombie who nodded his head in acknowledgement, pointing both fingers and dancing backwards, inviting her to join him. 'That's – oh my God,' she yelled, only just audible as the ancient, familiar sound of Michael Jackson's 'Thriller' came through the speakers, 'Gerry, you've got the moves, boy.'

She turned away, laughing, taking the hand of Gerard Lewis, head of the secondary-school science department, normally seen in a white lab coat looking thoughtful or reading the paper over a coffee in the bakery on a weekend. This was a departure for him. Ella laughed aloud, finding herself shoulder to shoulder with a row of ghouls who clearly knew every step of the dance from the song. She didn't have a clue what she was doing, she was surrounded by noise and chaos, and she was having fun – for the first time in bloody ages, she was letting her hair down. She'd even managed to – almost – forget the slight matter of a bill she had no idea how to pay.

Extracting herself from the grip of an over-excited Mrs Evans who, clearly brightened by several sherries, was determined to drag everyone into a conga, Ella headed for the loos, buffeted and bumped by countless half-recognizable fiends along the way. At times like this, living here in Llanidaeron felt like being part of a huge, unruly family. She pulled open the door to the green-tiled bathroom and leaned back against the wall, waiting for a loo to become free.

'All right, Ella? Haven't seen you for ages, love.' Hannah, another horse owner from the village, looked up, catching her eye in the mirror.

'Work,' said Ella, by explanation. 'You know what it's like.'

'God, tell me about it. Nice to get out though, hey?'

Hannah rubbed her hands dry on her zombie suit – after goodness knows how many years, the hand dryer still wasn't working properly unless you –

Ella gave it a sharp wallop on the side with the flat of her hand and, startled, it whooshed into life. Hannah laughed.

She pulled the door open so the sound spilled into the bright white light of the toilets. Turning back, she touched Ella on the shoulder as she left.

'Don't be a stranger, all right? You know you can always pop round for a coffee any time, lovey.'

Ella smiled back. It was easy, as winter came in, to go into hibernation mode. If it wasn't for Lissa dragging her to the pub, she could have stayed up on the hill for weeks on end. When Bron went, she'd be up there by herself. Even thinking about it felt a bit lonely. She gave an involuntary shiver.

'I will,' she said. 'Promise.'

Hannah blew her a kiss and was swallowed by the

crowd as the door slowly shut, leaving Ella standing looking in the mirror alone.

She hadn't seen Nick yet. There was no way he would be missing tonight, though, and she knew it was only a matter of time before they found each other. It had started as a flirtation at work – he'd turned up in town, having taken over one of the old units in the converted barns, where he'd set up his farriery business. Old Tom – who had been known by that name for as long as Ella could remember – had finally given up the ghost and retired, almost bent double after a lifetime of shoeing the horses that lived and worked in the valley. He'd been more than happy to hand over his business to the charming, young and – Ella had acknowledged to herself when he'd arrived in his red van, swinging himself out with an easy manner that could tame the most recalcitrant and awkward of horses – pretty bloody good-looking man.

'All right, my lovely,' he'd said to Bella. Bella had, Ella swore, telling Dion later that afternoon, actually melted slightly, batting her long eyelashes and gently nuzzling his back as he trimmed her hooves. Ella hadn't been able to tear her eyes away from the strip of skin that Bella's inquisitive muzzle had revealed. He was tanned and muscular under a battered grey marl T-shirt, with the strong arms that came with his profession. But where Old Tom's arms were grizzled and scarred with countless injuries, grey-haired and twisted, Nick's were – well, Ella had to look away. She'd spent years not even thinking about men, or sex, or anything, so it was a complete surprise – and one she hadn't shared with Bron, who up until then had been party to Ella's deepest secrets – that she'd found herself accepting his offer of a drink that night.

They'd headed to the tiny little tapas bar that had recently opened by the canal bank – the most exotic thing that Llanidaeron had to offer – and spent the night drinking red wine and flirting until Ella took matters into her own hands and invited herself back to his cottage, where she stayed the night. The next morning, still amazed at the fact that she'd been basically overtaken by nothing more than overwhelming lust, she'd marched the long, hungover walk back through the village and up the hill to feed the horses, arriving back in the kitchen to put the kettle on and jump in a shower before Bron had even risen for the day.

She hadn't – she insisted to Nick, who seemed as matter-of-fact about this as he did about pretty much everything else – wanted a relationship.

'That's fine,' he'd grinned. 'How about we leave it as – well, you can't deny we're pretty compatible . . .'

Ella had felt herself going pink, remembering their night together. She didn't want a relationship with anyone – life was too complicated for that, and despite Lissa's protestations that life was short and she ought to grab it with both bloody hands (and Nick, for that matter, whom Lissa had pronounced 'a damn fine specimen') she didn't want complications. So they kept it very loose – if she was at the pub, they'd hook up. If he was shoeing the horses, she'd catch a lift down to the village in his van and they'd go for something to eat and inevitably end up staying the night.

But she'd kept a cautious distance. And so over the next few years she and Nick had danced back and forth, not committing to anything, sleeping together once in a while, sharing a laugh. They were both happy with that.

Until now, that was. Ella looked at herself in the mirror and ran a finger under her lower lashes, smoothing the deep black liner that Lissa had used. It emphasized the darkness of her eyes, making them sparkle against her pale skin, which was flushed from the heat of the party. She pulled a comb from her bag and ran it through her hair, pulling it back and shaking it out against her shoulders. She pulled up the sweetheart neckline of Lissa's velvet dress, took a deep breath and headed back into the party.

A few drinks later, having danced until her feet were killing her, she collapsed on a bar stool. Lissa – who seemed to have the stamina of a marathon runner – waved from the middle of Mrs Evans' conga line, which was now snaking the full way round the tiny dance floor of the hotel, out the fire exit, and apparently all the way round the old Victorian building and back in the front door. At least half the partygoers were involved, the others grabbing a spot at the bar to order a drink while people were occupied, or hiding in corners and taking advantage of their disguises to misbehave. Ella averted her eyes as one of the ghouls she'd seen earlier ran a hand up the back of a racy-looking, blood-splattered French maid and guided her into the darkness of the space underneath the fire escape. There was a giggle, and then silence fell.

Ella watched the line of people skipping through the front door, realizing that Nick might well be part of it. There was Lissa, holding on for dear life to the bear-like, bearded form of one of the fathers who helped with the PTA, and behind her, arms clamped tightly round her waist, looking particularly pleased with himself, was George, deputy head at the school, who had a well-documented crush on her and was clearly delighted to have this opportunity to make contact. Ella shook her head, laughing.

She stood up, realizing the noise and stuffy atmosphere of a hundred sweating bodies was making her head start to swim. Not to mention, of course, the mixture of goodness knows what that had been in the purple drinks they'd been knocking back all evening.

'There you are!' Lissa escaped the conga line and tucked her arm into Ella's. The dancing had worn everyone out slightly and the place seemed calmer and less frantic. Gary, the DJ (and school caretaker by day) had changed the tempo of the music, filling the rooms with a low, thrumming beat. She peered across the bar, trying to work out where Nick was. Normally by this time of night they'd have found each other, magnetically attracted with the help of a few glasses of something and the knowledge they'd be falling in the door of his little cottage on the outskirts of the village . . .

'Have you seen Nick?'

Ella turned to her friend. Lissa was busily re-tying the laced bodice of her costume, which had come undone with all the racing around. Her eyeliner had smudged down one rosy cheek and her black curls were wild, spiralling out, the clips that had held them back long gone. Ella reached out a finger and smoothed away the mark on her friend's cheek. Lissa's eyes, she noticed, were darting slightly from side to side as if she too was looking for something.

'Nick?'

'Nick – you know, tall, handsome, bit too charming for his own good?' Ella raised an eyebrow. 'Nice arms?'

Lissa took a step backwards, putting a hand on the bar to steady herself. The heat of the room was turning her pinker by the moment. She shook her head, repeating herself.

'Nick? No, haven't seen him all night, actually. Maybe he's working or something.' She pulled her purse out and fiddled with the remaining notes inside. 'Shall we get a drink? Let's get a drink.'

'I'm fine,' said Ella, watching as Lissa's mouth twitched sideways and she peered over her shoulder, moving sideways slightly. She rubbed her nose. 'Nope, he's definitely not here. In fact, let's go to the loo.'

'I don't need the –' Ella protested, as Lissa pulled her by the arm towards the toilets. Inside she made a huge show of dabbing moistened loo roll on her cheek to rub off the now-invisible smudged make-up, running wet hands through her hair to try and tame the curls which were springing out, clipping it back from her face with her never-ending supply of hair grips.

Ella reapplied her lipstick and closed the lid with a decisive snap.

'I bet he's here somewhere. Probably hiding in a corner playing some awful rugby drinking game with the boys.'

She rolled her eyes at the thought. There was a fairly strong seam of the rowdy, tray-banging, rugby-song-singing lad in Nick, and it drove her mad. Usually when she found him in that state she'd wave to him from one end of the pub but give him and the lads a wide berth – but God, nobody was perfect, were they? She'd need to learn to live with it – and him.

'Hold on, can't find my bloody phone.' Lissa rummaged in her bag. They'd been in the loos for what felt like ages.

'Come on, I'm on a mission.' Ella shook out her hair and looked at her reflection. Alan was right – she did scrub up all right. It was time to stop spending her whole life in jodhpurs, hair tied back and a polo shirt with 'E. J. Equine' embroidered on the front. There was more to life than work.

'Thing is, Ell,' Lissa began, as they headed out of the loos, 'I think you need to –'

She put a hand on Ella's arm just a fraction of a second

too late. Ella stood, transfixed, eyes wide open in shock. Leaning with one casual arm against the wooden beam of the hotel bar, the other lazily caressing the waist of the tall blonde woman he was kissing, was Nick.

'I was trying to say –' Lissa started again, stepping in front of Ella. She wasn't tall enough to block her eyeline. Ella remained fixed to the spot until Lissa pushed her backwards, into the bright, exposing light of the toilets.

'Nick's here,' Ella said flatly.

'Yeah. I was trying to say he's here, and I – God, Ell, I just wanted to shield you from him.'

'It's fine.'

'It's not fine. He's a bloody dickhead.' Lissa shook her head in fury, hair flying everywhere again.

There was a creak as the door of the loos opened and – of course, Ella thought, who else – the blonde girl Nick had been kissing walked in, smiling at them politely.

'I'm going to have a word,' said Ella, pushing past Lissa, leaving her with her mouth half open in protest.

'Hi,' said Ella. Nick stood in the shadow of the fire escape by the back door. His cheekbones were sharp, accentuated by the brightness of the light that shone up on his face from his phone. She nodded towards it.

'Just updating everyone with your latest news, are you?' said Ella, her heart racing dangerously fast. She couldn't hear anything but the sound of it whooshing in her ears as she stood in front of him, her hands balled into fists. How bloody dare he.

'Ells, I—'

'You what? You wanted to let me know you were seeing someone? You forgot to give me a shout and tell me?' She motioned to the phone in his hand. 'Don't tell me, you were just firing off a quick text to let me know whilst she was in the loo.'

Nick shook his head, a confused half-smile on his face. He reached out, putting a hand on her shoulder. It was such a brotherly, matey thing to do that Ella recoiled, turning to look at his hand as if it was one of the Hallowe'en spider decorations come to life.

'Look, Ella.' Nick removed his hand. 'You're a lovely girl. But I thought we had an arrangement.'

It was never anything official, but she'd thought – well, she'd assumed – that he'd certainly have had the good manners to at least let her know there was someone else.

'What kind of –'

'You, me, a few beers – it's been a laugh and that, but –' Nick shrugged again. She was beginning to think if he did it one more time, she'd clobber him with the carved wooden lion that stood on the bar opposite.

'Right.' She took a deep breath. Bloody hell. She wasn't going to be humiliated in public with half the village doing the Macarena in the background.

'Ells.' Lissa was behind her, a voice in her ear.

'The thing is, Ella, I really like Nell.' Nice. 'Like – properly.'

'It's fine, Nick. It's not like we were going out or anything. You're right, it was just casual.'

She drew herself up to her full height, pushing her shoulders back. As she did, she noticed Nick's brand new blonde girlfriend slipping though the door of the loos, smiling shyly at him as she did so. He lifted his hand in a coy little wave, and Ella rolled her eyes.

'Don't worry,' Ella said, watching the future she thought she'd planned vaporizing before her eyes. It wasn't until later that she admitted to herself that she'd only been planning it for a matter of hours.

'Have a good night,' she said, giving a bright smile to Nick's new love.

She turned to Lissa.

'I'm sorry, sweetheart.' Lissa's face was a twist of concern.

Ella shook her head. 'No matter. I've got enough going on without dealing with washing some bloke's rugby shirt on a Sunday when I could be sitting by the fire reading the papers and eating toast.'

'That's the spirit,' said Lissa, pulling her towards the bar.

Several dodgy cocktails later, Ella marched up the hill to the cottage. She'd insisted to Lissa as they'd said goodbye at the bottom of the road that no, she didn't want to stay and yes, she'd be fine. But the walk home was a lot bloody longer half-pissed and in heels. She pulled them off, walking barefoot on the frozen single-track road that led out of the village to the farm. It was sharp and clear and freezing cold, the full moon lighting her way. The lights of the cottage – left on by Bron to guide her home, as they always were if she went out for the evening – glowed softly through the trees. Soon Bron would be gone, and she'd be all on her own. Well, bollocks to it. She didn't need a man to sort out her life. She'd proved that already.

*

She stands leaning on the kitchen counter, aware of Mac's physical presence directly behind her, the heat of his body radiating through his shirt. She longs to take a step backwards, knowing if she does she'll meet the warmth of his arms wrapping around her as they've done so many times before. Instead they stand on the opposite side of the kitchen island whilst her aunt Bron, sleeves rolled up, flour dusting the work surface, gives them a lesson in how to make shortcrust pastry for her famous mince pies. Ella, who normally craves them above all else, is shifting from one foot to the other with impatience. Bron has left the animals in the care of an agricultural student and come to stay with Ella and her dad for the Christmas holidays, bringing boxes of her home-made fruit cake and filling the house with the smell of baking scones and a sense of motherly order that is missing from the military precision of their home. Her dad keeps life organized because it's the best way, he says, to make sure nothing is forgotten. As a single parent he's done the best he can, but Bron's influence brings colour and warmth and a delightful chaos, which Ella treasures. Having her mum's sister there for Christmas gives the little house a feeling of home which is often missing. This time is even more special, because Ella has brought Mac home with her. She is determined that her family will fall in love with him just as she's beginning to realize she has . . .

Ella sat up in bed. The only thing she didn't have control over was her dreams. They were stubborn and consistent, taking her back to a past she'd rather forget. She closed her eyes and tried to sleep, but the memories had been stirred up. They danced in her head until she fell asleep again, exhausted.

When they'd arrived, they'd pulled down the battered old cardboard boxes of decorations from the attic, telling her dad they'd organize everything. They'd festooned the tops of the kitchen counters and all around the windows with fairy lights and the place was glowing. Mac had thrown his things in a rucksack and rather than returning home – where he'd spent years being handed like a parcel from one parent to the other following their bitter divorce – he'd opted to spend the first part of the Christmas break with Ella. His parents were, for once, united in their outrage. But Mac loathed Christmas and longed for the grey chill of January. Ella, who loved the jolly, relaxed Christmases she'd had every year, had insisted he come and join in.

Ella and Mac were inseparable from the moment they met, introduced by mutual friends one night at a bar in town. Their university was so huge and impersonal that their paths hadn't crossed once until their third term, and they were determined to spend every moment they could together. After months spending each night together tangled in the sheets, eating toast in bed and falling asleep amongst the crumbs, it was hard to be back home in the strange halfway world. Not quite a child, not quite an adult. Her father had made up one of the spare rooms for Mac, and Ella, feeling shy, hadn't known how to say to him that they'd be happy with just one.

'So the secret is you mustn't roll the pastry too thin.' Bron looks up, holding a pale disc of pastry in her hand. She places it carefully in the baking tin. Ella turns, watching Mac nod solemnly. She catches his eye and he winks at her, his eyes twinkling with amusement.

'Would you like to have a turn?' Bron bends down, clattering around in the kitchen cupboards, searching for more baking tins. He quickly leans forward, whispering in her ear. She feels tiny hairs rising on her arms in reaction to the words that whisper on her skin.

'Let's sneak away when she's not looking.'

He looks at her sideways, making her laugh.

'Shh.'

Ella suppresses a giggle. He turns, putting a hand on her hip, pulling her in close to him. All she wants to do is grab him by the hand, pull him upstairs, tear off his clothes . . .

He drops a kiss on the top of her head, wrapping his arms around her. They stand for a moment as Bron continues pottering in the kitchen.

'You young things aren't the least bit interested in making these pies, are you?' Bron turns around to look at them, her hands full of curls of green apple peel. She raises an eyebrow. Her sharp eyes are twinkling with amusement.

'We are, look.' Ella picks up the rolling pin and brandishes it in the air. He catches her hand from behind, spinning her round, unable to resist. He leans down, brushing a smudge of flour from her cheek, and kisses her. Ella blushes scarlet in front of her aunt, who bursts out laughing, pushing her long plait back over her shoulder.

'For goodness' sake. Get off with the pair of you. I need double cream.' She reaches into her battered brown handbag, which lies on the kitchen worktop, pulling out her purse and handing Ella a twenty-pound note. 'And pick me up a bottle of Irish Cream while you're at it. Can't have mince pies without it.'

They pull on coats and mismatched found gloves from the dresser in the hall. As she opens the door, the blast of cold air sends Ella back to find the snowflake-printed red bobble hat she wears to the stables, balancing it on top of her dark curls before they head out into the darkness of the December evening.

The cobbles on the narrow road are slippery with the beginnings of an evening frost and they step cautiously down the hill, passing the ancient timber-framed houses, their windows glowing yellow in the late-afternoon dusk. The air smells of the woodsmoke that curls up from the chimneys.

'Come here, you.' Ella catches the ends of his scarf, laughing at the wide-eyed look of surprise on his face. She pulls him into a gap in the laurel hedge outside the church. Reaching up, she feels the cold of his cheek against her face as she hooks her arms around his neck and kisses him. His fingers tangle in her hair, pushing the woollen hat backwards so it lands on the frozen cobbles beneath their feet. She feels his mouth curling into a smile against hers.

'Lost your hat.'

'Don't care.'

Her hand reaches around his back. She slides it inside the back of his sweater, reaching beneath the shirt, which is hanging loose, untucked as always. His skin is burning hot and her hands are –

'Bloody hell –' Mac steps back, bursting into laughter. 'Your hands are freezing.'

'Sorry.' Ella looks up at him through innocently lowered lashes.

'You are not.' He reaches down, picking up the red hat and putting it back on her head, pushing back the curls that are caught half inside the collar of her winter coat. His hand strays down her cheek and his tone is teasing. 'You're not sorry at all.'

'Not a bit,' she says, catching his hand, trying to pull him back onto the street. 'Come on, we'd better get to the shop before it closes.'

He doesn't move, an expression on his face Ella hasn't seen before, and her heart thuds out of time in her chest.

'I love you,' he says, for the first time, and all time is forgotten as he kisses her again.

Chapter Five

Harry

'I'll have a coffee, please.'

Harry, waiting to be served, loosened his tie. He twisted open the top button of his shirt with a sigh of relief.

'Actually, no.' The woman standing beside him flicked him a shy glance and then stood a bit taller, clearing her throat. 'Make that a mojito . . . in fact, make it a double one.'

She pulled her purse out of her handbag and started rifling through it, muttering to herself.

'I'm sure I had a tenner in here – oh God, I gave it to Joe for after school club . . .'

There was a clink of ice as the barman paused in his work for a second and looked at her. Harry watched as she flushed with embarrassment and pulled an awkward face. Her linen tunic was almost the same shade as her cheeks – rose-pink, and crumpled, as if she'd been travelling for ages. She probably had – this place was the same as a hundred others just off motorways all over the country. The bars were full of consultants in suits that sagged at the knees after a long week of working away from home, the restaurants populated by *table for one, please* diners who knew the laminated menu offerings by heart.

She was becoming more flustered with every second.

'I'm *so* sorry,' she said, turning the purse upside down and shaking it, quite hard, as if there was some money clinging on somewhere in the depths and she could scare it out. 'I'm afraid I haven't got any cash on me at all.'

'You're staying here, right?' The barman looked at her, patiently.

She nodded, messy tendrils of blonde hair falling loose around her face. She bit her lip and for a second he thought she was about to burst into tears. Her chin wobbled.

'What's your room number?'

'Oh!' She flushed even pinker and dropped her purse on the floor. By the time she'd scrambled off the high bar stool Harry had bent down, and – still halfway between the bar and the carpet – he handed it to her, looking up at her with what he hoped was a comforting sort of smile. She must've had a bad week. Her hands were trembling.

'I'll charge it to your room,' said the barman when they stood up. With a few more deft movements he'd created a mojito worthy of a beach bar in Jamaica, which was all the more impressive given they were in a faceless chain hotel somewhere in Cheshire.

'I'm so sorry,' she said, taking a sip. 'Ooh, that's lovely. It doesn't taste alcoholic at all.'

'It's double strength, like you asked,' said the barman defensively.

'I don't mean –' She began another round of apologies, and then stopped herself.

'It's room fifty-four. And thank you.' She turned to Harry and gave him another smile. She was sweet, he thought, watching as she wended her way across the hotel foyer before tucking herself into a corner and pulling out her phone.

The barman gave him a knowing look.

'And a coffee for you, sir, was it?'

Harry nodded.

Half an hour later, having caught up on some emails from work, he closed his laptop and sat up, stretching his arms with a groan. Working hunched over the table in a hotel foyer wasn't doing his back any good. He checked his watch – almost half seven. Maybe he could just grab his stuff and do a quick half-hour run in the gym to blow the cobwebs off. He rubbed his jaw, which was jagged with stubble. He'd left Paris at five in the morning, which was actually four their time, driven from Heathrow, stopped in at the Birmingham office on the way. Tomorrow he'd a meeting in Chester, and then he'd be heading home. Only it wasn't home. He had to make his way to a village in Wales where Jenny, his mother-in-law, had shipped the whole family in some completely insane mission to rebuild their relationships. How the hell it was going to make any difference, he had no idea.

'Hello again,' said a slightly familiar voice.

The woman from the bar stood for a moment, hovering by his table. She looked as if the alcohol had taken the edge off her day.

'Busy day?' she asked.

'Busy week, more like.' Harry shook his head ruefully. The prospect of the gym wasn't appealing – he was completely knackered.

'Me too.'

She gave a half-smile and put a hand to the string of brightly coloured beads she was wearing. They hung almost to her waist.

And then she took a breath, as if she was about to say something – but then stopped herself. It was a fleeting moment, but – he realized afterwards – there was always that split second before a decision is made that changes everything, where possibility crackles in the air. He always remembered a girl he'd locked eyes with on a tube escalator when he was seventeen. She'd looked directly at him and he'd wondered if he should jump off when the got to the top and follow her back down through the maze of tunnels and say hello. In a movie, of course, he would have. But instead when he got to the top he paused for a second, contemplating it, before a man with a briefcase knocked into his back and sent him sideways, and that was that.

She was older than him, maybe forty at the most?

Scandinavian colouring, bright blue eyes and prettily flushed pink cheeks. Most of the women he saw in the evenings in business hotels were dressed in functional, dark-coloured work suits. They carried briefcases like his and spent their evenings hunched over their laptops, waiting for the weekend to come.

She was in a pair of dark, cropped trousers and her linen tunic didn't disguise an hourglass figure. The neckline was low and he could see the beads hung between softly swelling cleavage – not that he should be looking, he realized instantly. He averted his eyes.

She wore a plaited friendship bracelet around her wrist.

He found the words – realizing as he did that they'd been inevitable since their meeting at the bar.

'I was going to head upstairs, but –' he looked down, briefly, fiddling with the button on his shirt cuffs, feeling for a second like his seventeen-year-old self – 'd'you want to have another?'

She beamed. 'I would *love* to.'

'I found a seat by the fire,' she said, half getting up as he returned with the drinks. 'Well, the fire – ish.' She motioned to the artificial flames, which flickered safely behind a wall of thick glass.

'Here you are.' He passed the drink to her – another mojito, as requested, 'but a single this time, please'.

'I'm Harry.'

She laughed. 'Like the prince.'

He nodded, taking a sip of beer. 'Everyone says that.'

'Sorry. It must get old pretty quickly.'

'It's fine, honestly.'

There was an awkward silence, and they both took a sip of drink. He looked across the room, seeing another couple of workers who'd paired up for a drink laughing and chatting comfortably. At the bar, he'd seen a woman in unfeasibly high heels slip onto a chair alongside a couple of men who had announced they'd arrived for a conference the next morning. They were flirting pretty hard by the time he'd picked up their drinks and left.

This was what happened, Harry thought, when you left a load of bored, lonely people in an anonymous, faceless, corporate hotel night after night. It was almost inevitable that anonymous, faceless, corporate pairings would be the result.

'Oh God,' she said, putting a hand to her mouth. 'I'm Lucy. Sorry. I forgot that bit.'

'Hello, Lucy,' he said, smiling back at her.

'. . . And that's why I'm here,' she concluded, some time later.

Harry watched as the couple who'd been sitting opposite him ordered another drink. They were on the same couch now, having started off on separate chairs. When the woman had returned from the loo she'd sat down, casually, as if it was completely natural or as if she'd forgotten quite where she was supposed to sit.

The guy had now loosened his top button and discarded his tie, removed his suit jacket and rolled up his sleeves to reveal tanned arms, in a clear attempt to make it clear that he might spend his *days* sweating over a hot laptop, but his evenings were spent on more physical pursuits.

Harry didn't suppose that the man opposite was listening patiently as his female companion explained in breathy gasps between sobs (mopped up with napkins from the bar with the hotel logo on) that she had run away from home, leaving her three children with her husband, because she'd discovered he was having an affair.

Other people had hot, uncomplicated, anonymous hotel encounters. He, on the other hand, ended up being agony aunt to a middle-aged woman having a breakdown.

Lucy blew her nose with a loud *parp*.

'God, I'm sorry.' Her eyes were red-rimmed, and her cheeks were streaked with the tracks of the gallons of tears she'd shed.

He shook his head.

'Don't be.'

'You're *so* sweet and lovely.' She reached out a hand and squeezed his knee. 'If Marcus was more like you I bet he wouldn't even have thought of doing what he's done to all of us.'

'I'm not really,' Harry protested, thinking of the past.

He wasn't sweet or lovely – in fact, he was a complete

shit. It served him right that he was here right now, and not – he watched the man across the room stand up – heading upstairs with a woman who had thrown caution to the wind for an evening.

'You really are lovely. You've listened to me banging on about *him* for hours –' she blew her nose again – 'and you haven't spoken about yourself at all.'

There hadn't really been space to. He'd heard all about Marcus and how he'd taken to working away four nights a week and how he'd started off being lovely and charming and buying her extra presents and seeming jollier and kinder than normal, and how over the last six months he'd become more and more distant and withdrawn, glued to his phone ('when he wouldn't even have *Facebook* before') and then – clearly consumed by guilt and shame – had confessed to an affair with his boss.

So that was the story of why Lucy had run away.

'I didn't know what else to do. I thought I'd get my revenge on him by coming to one of these places and – and – and doing what *he* did.'

He thought of her inexpert attempts to order a drink at the bar earlier.

'So you were . . .'

Lucy nodded, her eyes round. 'I had sort of chosen you.' She giggled.

He didn't quite know what to say. Random hook-ups had never exactly been his style in the past, and it looked like they weren't in his future, either. It was probably safer to just stay single forever, given his history.

Lucy took a large sip of her third drink. The ice had melted and it had been sitting in a slowly gathering pool of condensation that had dribbled down the sides of the glass and onto the table as she'd alternately raged and wept.

'Ugh,' she said, before drinking some more.

'Perhaps I could get us a coffee?' Harry made to get up and head for the bar. He watched the all-seeing barman polishing glasses, his eyes scanning the room. They must see all sorts of things going on in this place, night after night.

She shook her head and pulled his arm, so he missed his footing and landed on the sofa beside her.

'Oops.'

She seemed a bit giddy now, as if pouring her heart out had lightened it, somehow.

'Why don't you get another drink?'

'I—' he began.

'No!' She stood up suddenly. 'Ooh, that might've been all watery but it's definitely gone to my head. I'll get us one. I'll charge it to my room. It's all going on Marcus's work account, anyway. He can blooming well explain *that*.'

Lucy headed to the bar. Harry leaned forward, elbows on his knees, and sunk his head into his hands. This was not exactly the evening he'd planned. He had a difficult meeting first thing where he had to explain to a supplier why they were taking business in-house, and the sale of his parents' house to arrange in the meanwhile, now that probate was sorted. His head was pounding.

'I got you a mojito too!' Lucy said cheerfully. She sat down with the two drinks. 'I'm so grateful to you, Harry. You're a prince.' She rolled her eyes. 'Sorry, couldn't resist that.'

He shook his head and laughed despite himself. Lucy was sweet, and this Marcus was an idiot. By all accounts they had a lovely life, with a cottage in Buckinghamshire, and a house full of children and dogs.

The drink was disgusting – it tasted like too-sweet, alcoholic mouthwash. Plus it was full of pieces of mint leaf and the pith of a lime that had seen better days, judging by the half-dried slice garnishing the edge of the glass. He placed the drink on the mat. Perhaps she wouldn't notice if he didn't drink it.

'So.' Lucy turned to him, her head cocked to one side. 'Tell me about yourself, Harry. Is there a Mrs Harry at home?'

He shook his head.

'No.'

'My goodness,' Lucy raised her eyebrows. 'But you're so lovely and handsome. Why haven't you been snapped up?'

He took a breath. This conversation always went one of two ways. He either lied, which meant dealing with people trying to fix him up with someone lovely they knew who was just perfect for him, or he told the truth and had to go through the performance.

'Are you divorced?' Lucy continued probing, the rum having taken the edge off her natural politeness.

He took a breath and paused, bracing himself for the inevitable response. 'No, my wife died.'

'Oh my God.' Lucy's hand flew to her mouth. Her nails, he noticed, had been painted pale pink but half the varnish had chipped off.

'It's fine, honestly.' He shook his head. 'I mean – it's not fine.' It didn't matter how many times he tried to handle this, he always managed to mess it up. 'It was five years ago.'

'And no children?'

'One.'

'Oh, the poor darling.' Always the same response. 'Boy or girl?'

'A girl. Hope. She's eight.'

'Where is she now?' Lucy cocked her head, thoughtfully.

'Oh.' Harry rubbed his chin. This part always felt slightly uncomfortable – probably, if he admitted it to himself, because he felt uncomfortable about it, too. But there didn't seem to be any way of changing the status quo. 'She lives with her grandparents. Well, we both do, really. I travel a lot, and they have a huge house, so we're not under each other's feet when I'm home. And Hope has family around her.'

Lucy nodded 'Gosh, yes, and that's so important. You must spend a lot of time making up for the loss of her mum.'

Harry looked down at his feet.

'We do,' he said. She didn't have to know it wasn't strictly true.

Nipping to the loo, he couldn't help thinking that it was as if people were given a conversation script as soon as they became adults. *This is what you say when someone dies. This is what you say when you find out someone has lost a partner. These are the words we think you want to hear.*

Almost from the moment Sarah had died, he'd found himself having to counsel everyone from school teachers to total strangers in their grief. He was a widower – that tragic archetype, beloved of romantic films. But the reality was far more complicated, and because of that he couldn't ever really let anyone know what he felt. And the truth was, he knew that working all the hours he did was his way of escaping from home, escaping from the complications of family life.

Sarah had been gone for five years – longer than they'd been together. Sometimes it felt like he wanted to divorce her ghost and get on with living his life, but that sounded impossibly callous and didn't begin to cover the feelings he had about it all. It just seemed – impossible. And that was before he even began factoring in Jenny and Lou.

When he got back Lucy was standing up, her bag over her shoulder.

'I'm so sorry, I shouldn't keep you,' she said. 'You've probably got work first thing, and your whole evening's been listening to me rabbiting on about my tiny little problems.'

He shook his head, smiling. 'It's fine. I'm glad I helped.'

'I'm so grateful.'

'It's nothing.'

He picked up his laptop bag and shouldered it, pausing for a moment. What did one do in these circumstances?

'Are you going to the lift?' Lucy flicked a glance towards the three metal doors.

'Yes.'

There was another split-second moment – this one of awkward indecision. Should he make an excuse and let her go on? Should he just make a move? He'd had his share of anonymous encounters like this in the past, but they left him feeling slightly grubby and uncomfortable – and as if something was missing. But perhaps –

'Finished with these?' the barman said, breaking the moment. He lifted the two half-drunk glasses with a questioning expression.

'Yes,' they said, as one.

'Right, well, let's go,' said Lucy, decisively.

He pressed the middle button, she pressed the one on the right-hand side. Both lifts slid open at exactly the same time. He stepped forward, thinking she was going to get into the other one, but instead she joined him with a strange sort of half-hop and an awkward laugh.

'This is very British,' she said. He pressed the number 4.

They stood in silence as the lift whirred upwards and slid to a halt.

'Well, this is me,' he said.

'Me too.' Lucy stepped out and as the doors closed behind them she paused for a moment and turned to look at him.

'Harry?'

'Yes?'

'Can I –' she said, and took a step towards him and coiled her arms around his neck. She smelled sweet, of mint and a floral perfume and of apple shampoo. Her mouth was on his and she was kissing him and . . .

'Oh God, I am SO sorry.'

She leapt back, covering her mouth with her hand. Her cheeks were scarlet.

'Oh God, oh God, I'm so sorry.'

The correct response, presumably, was *don't worry, it's fine, it happens to me all the time*. The easy response would be to sweep her into his arms, kiss her again, and head for the hotel bedroom. He'd be lying if he said Lucy's unexpected passionate kiss hadn't had an effect. In fact, after a stunned moment, he'd responded in kind, dropping his bag and allowing a hand to slip around her waist. The same hand was now hanging by his side, and his mouth was parted as if waiting for words to come out. But there weren't any, it seemed. Not from him, in any case.

Fortunately Lucy had quite enough for both of them.

'I'm so sorry,' she said again. 'Oh God, I'm just as bad

as him. And I didn't even *ask* you. I just leapt on you like some sort of maniac. I didn't mean to, it's just the rum and you're so sweet and tragic and –'

The aphrodisiac qualities of the widower were a never-ending source of amazement to Harry.

'Truly,' he said, picking up his bag, 'It's fine. I mean it was lovely. I mean –'

'You are lovely,' Lucy said, putting both hands to her still flaming cheeks. 'But I am forty-three and you are – not. And whatever the hell is happening with my life, I shouldn't be kissing strange men in hotel corridors '

And for some reason, this made them both burst out laughing. A man put a head out of the room door opposite and peered at them, perplexed. From inside the room the sound of a crying toddler – cross and tired, Harry could tell – was increasing in volume.

Somehow this galvanized Lucy into action.

'Let me –' and she went to shake his hand, before leaning forward again and giving him a hug. 'I'm so sorry for being such a complete clot, and I'm so grateful to you for being a good Samaritan when I needed one.'

'I'm not sure good Samaritans buy cocktails,' he said, rubbing his chin again.

'Well, they blooming well should, in my book.'

'What are you going to do now?'

'I dunno.' Lucy fished her phone out of her bag. It was vibrating, as it had been for quite a lot of the time they'd been talking. 'I might agree to talk to him.'

'Really?' He'd thought Marcus was definitely for the chop.

She nodded vigorously. 'Believe it or not, the thought of you being – of you – of your –'

'My wife being dead.' It was almost impossible for people to say. It was another one of those things that you learned after the event. Not only were you a counsellor for other people's feelings, but you had to help them find the words to talk about it.

'It made me think about how I'd feel if something happened to – to –'

Lucy waved the phone in the air. MARCUS, the screen said, flashing to indicate he was calling, and not for the first time.

'That's always worth thinking about.'

Running on the treadmill with a stomach full of sickly sweet cocktails wasn't his wisest move. He'd chucked on his kit and headed down, planning to clear his head with a half-hour blast. The music on his headphones drowned out the sound of the pop music that was being piped through the speakers, and the noise of the blood rushing in his ears. He ran through a stitch in his side, and when his legs started to burn he upped the incline instead of easing off.

If only running and music could drown out the thoughts in his head. They kept circling, though. Round and round they went, keeping pace with the steady thudding of his feet on the treadmill. He had the house sale to sort out. His mum was gone, and now his dad, too. Her place had been left to her sister and Harry had inherited the money, which now sat in his bank account, gathering interest and dust. He imagined it there – guilt money.

His parents had used him as a pawn in the years after their divorce, their love-hate relationship far more important to them than his feelings about how it felt to be passed back and forth like a parcel on Christmas Days and birthdays. And now, with probate sorted, he had the big old house where he'd grown up to sell. It would go to a family moving out from London, who could exchange their one-bed flat in Islington for a house in the country. They were welcome to it.

When he pictured the house in his mind, it was as grey as the flat skies that surrounded it, reflected in the still waters of the Broads that bisected their land. And the only good memories of that place were from another life – one he tried not to think about.

The counter showed seven miles and he hit the stop button, letting the machine run down to walking pace. Sweat poured down his face and his heart was pounding in his chest, but he'd chased away the demons for now. He'd sleep well tonight.

Showered and rubbing his hair with a towel, he emerged from the lift on the fourth floor to see Lucy once again. She was carrying an overnight bag, and her face was washed clean of tears. Her pale blonde hair was brushed, all the flyaway strands swept back up into a neat twist on the back of her head. She'd swapped her crumpled linen tunic for another one, pale grey, with the colourful string of beads still in place. She looked much brighter and her face lit up when she saw Harry.

'Oh, what luck. I was going to leave you a message at reception, just to say thank you.'

He nodded his head, indicating the bag she was holding.

'Everything OK?'

'Better than that.' She beamed. 'Marcus is coming to pick me up. We've had a long chat, and we're going to sort everything out. Starting with a holiday to Mauritius at Christmas.'

She made it sound incredibly simple.

He smiled and watched as she headed into the lift.

The last he saw of Lucy was a happy wave as the metal door of the lift slid closed. Her life was sorted – short-term, at least. Meanwhile, he was still clueless as to where he was going and what he was doing. All he knew for sure was that somehow, thanks to a whim of his mother-in-law, tomorrow morning he had to find his way to Wales if he wanted to see his daughter.

Chapter Six

Ella

It was a relief to be outside, even if the weather had changed for the worse. The crisp sunshine had been replaced with an oppressive grey blanket of cloud that hung over the hills, obscuring their peaks, hiding the valley. Her head was throbbing with hangover and regret from the night before. She knew trying to push things with Nick had been a mistake, but it still hurt.

The mist that still hadn't lifted left everything with a clinging layer of damp that sneaked under layers of clothing, leaving Ella freezing cold within moments of being outside. Tor, a checked stable rug keeping him warm, leaned an inquisitive head over the stable door as Carol arrived.

'Hello, beautiful.'

Carol, a tiny, fine-boned woman, climbed out of her car. She smiled at Ella, but her affection was for Tor, her favourite horse. She pulled the door of the car closed and headed straight for his box as Ella crunched across the gravel to close the yard gate behind her.

'How are things?'

Carol ducked her head. With her quick, darting movements and dark, bright eyes, she reminded Ella of a sparrow. She'd arrived at the yard, referred by a friend who'd worked with Ella to overcome PTSD after an accident in the workplace, and who suggested that perhaps working with the horses might help her to get over the trauma of her divorce.

'Good.' She reached up, holding a hand out for Tor to sniff. He ran his velvety muzzle across her fingers, searching hopefully for a treat. 'None for you until afterwards.'

She took the head collar and opened the stable door, using the signal she'd been taught to get Tor to step back politely. She unfastened his rug and slid it off, folding it neatly and hanging it on the edge of the hay rack. He ducked his head down low, allowing her to fasten the head collar around his neck before she led him out into the yard. Ella smiled at this.

When Carol had first arrived, hunched and defeated, she had taken half an hour to build up the courage to approach Tor's box. Ella, who loved watching the relationship between horse and client reveal itself, had been interested to discover that she'd been instantly drawn to the beautiful chestnut rather than one of the quieter, smaller horses in the yard. But the connection between horse and human was different every time, and each one brought the clients exactly what they needed.

'Who knew I'd end up taking half a ton of horse for a walk on a lead,' Carol smiled. She slid open the latch on the stable door and Ella stepped back, watching as the pair walked steadily, side by side, towards the indoor arena. She followed, sliding the door closed behind them, and flicking on the lights against the midwinter gloom. With a buzz and a click the long yellow strip lights illuminated the arena. The air was filled with the sweet, sawdusty smell of the all-weather surface they'd had delivered last year.

Ella stood by the side of the arena, watching as Carol led Tor around the perimeter. She had one hand on the rein, another draped casually across his neck, walking in step with him as they made their way round to meet her.

'It's a shame you can't marry a horse, really.'

'Oh believe me, teenage Ella would have done it in a snap if she could.'

Tor tossed his head up, mane flying, snorting as if in agreement.

'I had a date last night,' confided Carol. She ran a hand underneath the heavy tangle of Tor's mane, combing it out with her fingers, expression thoughtful. 'I never thought I'd do that.'

Carol's ex-husband had systematically destroyed her self-esteem. He'd spent years convincing her that she was worthless, driving away the friends and family who had always been an important part of her life. Piece by piece he'd dismantled everything that meant anything to her until she'd been convinced that she was to blame when he disappeared off on long work trips. Her lack of belief in herself meant that when she discovered he was sleeping with a number of different women, a part of her brain was truly convinced that it was her own fault for not being good enough. It had taken the death of her mother – and almost missing the funeral through Mick's furious jealousy that someone else should mean so much to her – to change things for good. She'd fled, returning home to the village of Llanidaeron where she'd grown up, staying with her sister, who wouldn't let Mick within fifteen metres of the front door. When the police had eventually been called – after one drunken night when he'd staggered up the front path, having booked himself into the Lion for the night – they'd put a restraining order in place, keeping him well out of reach. Only after six months of counselling had Carol felt brave enough to turn up at the yard, telling Ella how, as a child, she'd dreamed of having a horse of her own. And now here they were, months later, and Carol's transformation had been wonderful to see. She'd cast off the drab, dark clothes she used to wear and was clad in a vibrant purple fleece with a bright floral scarf at her neck. Her hair had been highlighted with subtle red tones, and her cheeks were flushed with the possibility of new romance.

'How did it feel?'

Carol's face lit up. 'Amazing. I met him through that online dating site we were talking about last week. He likes all the same things as me, we talked for hours . . . I'm seeing him again tomorrow night.'

Ella beamed at her. She remembered Carol's first visit, talking through her feelings with Ella as they'd gently introduced her to the horses, the years of hurt and anger pouring out. Spending time in the quiet, non-judgemental company of Tor, she'd cried into his mane, allowed herself to lean against his huge muscular shoulder, and over the weeks discovered that as she grew stronger and more confident in his company, it was having an effect on her daily life.

It was a magic which Ella never tired of seeing. All her childhood she'd loved spending time in the company of horses, but it had been the riding that had been her primary goal. Now – during the years that had passed – she'd learned that their wise, silent companionship could be the most effective tool for healing that anyone could experience. She didn't miss the riding part at all – at least, most of the time. On clear, crisp winter days, when the sun backlit the hills and the bracken on the moor was tipped with frost, she sometimes wished she could jump on Tor's back and canter off into the quiet space where nobody could find her and just soak up the beauty. But then there was always walking, and the enjoyment of seeing how working with the horses transformed people.

Carol turned expectantly, waiting to hear what today's session would involve.

'Would you like to do some loose schooling with him?'

'I'd love to.'

Carol unclipped the head collar rope and – giving the signal she'd been taught, telling Tor to wait until she'd reached the centre of the arena – stepped back. He flicked an ear backward, aware of Ella's presence. She hushed him with a hand to his shoulder, feeling the warmth of his skin through the fluffy winter coat that had grown over the last couple of months. He was such a character. She'd trained him well over the years, and could guarantee that he'd always behave. Carol raised an arm in a sweeping motion and he set off around the outside of the arena, circling in a trot.

Ella walked across to join her, watching as she lifted a finger to steady him, before calling the command which sent him across the diagonal, his long legs stretching out, hooves landing with precision.

'I never thought in my life I'd be doing something like this.' Carol's big dark eyes were sparkling with excitement. 'All those years living with Mick, doing what he said, feeling like I was worthless.'

'But you're amazing.' Ella turned to her, reflecting the smile that was plastered over Carol's face. 'You know Tor wouldn't do this unless he trusted you – you've built up a bond, and he recognizes how confident you've become.'

When Carol had first arrived they'd spent time just working in the close confines of the stable, grooming Tor and handling him in the safety of a smaller space. As a herd animal, Tor relied on the sensory input he received from the people he was with to judge how safe he was. Carol's nervous, jerking movements would have startled a horse which was less well trained, but Tor had become accustomed to unpredictable behaviour over his years of training. The first day that Carol had taken him into the arena and led him around had been a breakthrough: the time when she took him off the lead rein and controlled the behaviour of a huge, 500-lb animal with her own body language had made her burst into tears of happiness and relief.

'Look what you have accomplished.' Ella pushed her hands into the back pockets of her jeans, turning to follow Carol's gaze as she watched Tor moving around the arena.

'Not bad for a waste of space.'

'Don't even say it in jest.' Ella lifted a finger in warning. 'You're strong and powerful and you can do amazing things. Would you have believed a few months ago that you'd be standing here doing this?'

Recognizing what was needed, Ella beckoned Tor in towards them. He slowed to a walk and made his way across, coming to stand at a rest in front of Carol. She dropped her head for a moment, looking down at the rope in her hands. Tor moved his head in gently until it was leaning softly against her chest and she placed her hands on either side of his face, resting them on the broad flat planes of his cheekbones.

She gave a deep sigh, closing her eyes.

'I feel like he can read my heart, sometimes.' As she opened them, Ella saw her lashes were wet with tears. 'I'm still trying to make myself believe I'm worth something.'

'That's understandable.' Ella reached a hand out,

touching Carol's arm gently. 'You've been through so much. How does it feel with Tor there?'

Overhead in the eaves there was a flurry of wings and the sound of the birds who roosted there each winter scuffling around, their song clear in the silence. Carol looked at Ella, her gaze level and proud. She'd come so far. Each session had brought some kind of breakthrough, and taking the step to go out into the world and risk a relationship was a huge one. She was so brave.

'Like I'm being supported. Like I deserve to be supported.' Carol smiled. It wasn't the hesitant, nervous one that had flitted politely across her face when Ella first met her.

'You do.' Ella reached a hand across, running it along the ruffled hair of Tor's mane.

'I deserve this.' Carol took a deep breath and straightened her back. 'I deserve to be happy with someone else.'

Ella watched as she clipped the lead rope back onto Tor's head collar and led him back onto the track. The irony wasn't lost on her. All these years fixing other people's lives, yet she was no further forward with her own.

Chapter Seven

Harry

'I need to give you directions. I know I said the cottage was in Llanover,' the voice said, 'but there's been a bit of a mix-up.'

The rain was absolutely teeming down and even with the wipers on full speed, Harry was having trouble seeing what was in front of him on the motorway. The bluetooth connection in the car was useless at the best of times.

'I can't hear you very well.'

There was a crackle as the person on the other end of the line did something.

'Is that any better? I've taken it off speakerphone.'

He tried to turn up the volume, fruitlessly – it was already at maximum.

'SY18 . . . something. Oh God.' There was a pause and the voice increased slightly in volume. 'What's the bloody postcode, Lou?'

Harry shook his head. The rain was getting worse, and he really wanted to concentrate on getting there in one piece. He pulled out into the middle lane to overtake a slow-moving lorry.

'It's breaking up, Jenny,' he shouted. 'I'll ring you in an hour or so.'

Something was happening. In the dim light of the storm, even through the grey sheets of rain, he could make out a blurry blue flashing ahead. He braked carefully and flicked a glance in the rear-view mirror. The lorry behind him was closer than he'd like. The wipers crashed on through the deluge. It looked as if someone was sitting on top of the car pouring a bucket of water onto the windscreen.

As he drew closer he realized the blue lights were stationary, and that they were surrounded by a flickering sea of orange hazard lights, warning of an obstruction in the road. He clicked his on and slowed the car further. He drummed his thumbs on the steering wheel as the vehicle drew to a standstill, surrounded in moments by cars on either side of him. In the distance he caught a glimpse of the high-visibility jacket of a police officer who was gesturing to one of the drivers ahead. His stomach knotted, thinking of the people up ahead. It looked like a crash. Even after all this time, seeing a crash could bring the past right back into the present moment. He looked down, realizing he'd gripped hold of the steering wheel so tightly that his knuckles were whitening. He released them, shrugged his shoulders to try and release the tension, and rolled his head back, hearing the tension crackling in his spine as he did so.

'*Major problems on the roads,*' said a cheery voice, as he switched on the radio.

'You're not bloody joking.' His irritation was mixed with worry for whoever was in the accident in front. He turned his phone over, thinking that he could probably get away with checking it as he cut the engine. It looked like they were here for the long haul.

'*A lorry has overturned . . .*' the voice continued. '*Diversions are being put in place, but in the meantime if you're heading that way, I'd suggest taking an alternative route.*'

Harry looked out of his window and saw the man in the car next to him lighting up a cigarette, sliding his window open the smallest crack. He met Harry's eyes and shook his head in a despairing fashion.

'*Let's hope there aren't too many of you out there tonight stuck in that delay,*' said the DJ, cheerfully.

'Thanks for that,' said Harry. He reclined his car seat slightly and leaned his head back, feeling his neck clicking again. God, he was stressed.

Half an hour later, they hadn't moved. The rain had eased off slightly. A stream of rescue vehicles and transport police 4x4s had made their way along the hard shoulder, and people were beginning to hop out of their cars and down to the verge. Rain-soaked men could be seen relieving themselves in the not particularly concealing scrubby woodland. The car in front was steamed up and the children in the back seat were drawing funny faces in the condensation on the window. One of them grinned at him, the gap in her tooth reminding him of Hope, and he smiled back at her. She covered her mouth in delighted laughter and ducked out of sight. If this bloody traffic queue would just get moving he could get there and pick his daughter up, spin her round in the air, and hear all about the move. He hoped it would be what she needed. Something had to be . . .

The phone rang again. He picked it up.

'Harry?'

'Hi.' The line was much clearer. Jenny's voice echoed in his ear.

'You're not driving, are you? I'm just ringing to let you know there's some sort of accident on the motorway, so you might want to avoid it.'

He caught a glimpse of his expression in the rear-view mirror. If his eyes had rolled any further, they'd have fallen out the back of his head.

'Definitely not driving, no.'

'Good, because you know what Lou's like about that. Once a copper, and all that.'

Harry knew. His father-in-law was a stickler. He'd been in the police all his life, and his retirement – which had come a year early, due to ill health – hadn't sat well at all.

'Yes, I know.'

There was a shriek in the background.

'Daddy?'

His heart swelled with love, hearing Hope's voice.

'Can I have a word with her?'

'As long as you promise you're not driving. You know that hands-free thing is just as dangerous, apparently . . .'

'Hand on heart, Jenny.' He laughed. 'I'm not on the hands-free, and I am absolutely, positively not driving.'

'Good. I just worry.'

'I know.' (She didn't need to know he was parked on the motorway.)

'Hello?'

The little voice was hesitant, after her initial shriek of excitement.

'Are you coming today? Grandma said you're coming today?'

'I am, my darling, just as soon as I can get there.'

There was a long silence. Long enough for Harry to feel the familiar niggling discomfort of guilt. He loved Hope, he wanted to do the best for her – so why was he never there?

'Darling?' Maybe she'd hung up by mistake.

There was a scuffling noise.

'Sorry, I went to get you a picture I drew this morning. I wanted to tell you about it.'

'Go on then, honey. What's in the picture?'

'It's got three horses in it. One is brown and one is whitish grey and – what time are you going to be here?'

He glanced at the clock on the display. The plan had been to make it for seven, in time to do bedtime stories, watch *Strictly* together (Hope loved the dancing and the brightly coloured outfits) and hear all about how they were settling in.

'I'm not quite sure now, sweetheart.' He didn't want to build her hopes up, knowing that over-excitement could easily spill over into tears. 'Soon.'

Silence.

He could imagine her face falling and he felt another stab of guilt. When he got there, he was going to sit down with Jenny and have a serious talk about what they were going to do. Something had to give, and right now it felt like it was Hope, right at the time when she needed him.

'How about I promise that the very second I get back I'll come directly to you and read you a story, even if I have to wake you up?'

'No.' The tone was firm. 'I will stay up. Now the other horse is sort of orange and it has really long hair and when I went to the field this morning I climbed through the hedge and stroked it and—'

'Sweetheart, if you don't let Harry get going he will be even later,' Jenny said gently in the background.

'I'm staying up,' repeated the small voice.

'I'll just tell him that, shall I?'

There was a bit of a scuffle and a small howl, and then Jenny came back on the line.

'She's a bit over-excited about you coming. It's been—'

'I know.' He stopped her before she could start the sentence. 'I'm sorry, it's just been ridiculous with work and everything going on.'

'Mmm.'

Saved by the bell. There was a low growl of engines

as they were switched on – he hadn't realized just how *quiet* it could be sitting parked on a motorway.

'I'm going to get going now,' he said. 'Remind me of the second half of the postcode?'

He typed it into the satnav and waited as it calculated the distance.

Estimated journey time: 2.03 hrs.

He might just make it on time, after all.

They filed past the overturned tanker. Harry was relieved to see the driver standing by the cab, distinctive in a uniform that matched the livery of the HGV he had been driving. There were no ambulances, but a couple of fire engines still stood by the scene of the accident, their lights blaring.

He put his foot down, glad the rain had passed, and decided against stopping at the services for a coffee to keep him going. There was bound to be another one on the way, and if he got another hundred miles or so under his belt he'd feel more confident about making it to – what was the name of the place again? – Llan-something – in time for bedtime stories.

The roads were half-familiar. In another life, long ago, he'd visited the same part of Wales. He shook his head as if to change the picture in his mind. He thought instead about Sarah, and the day they'd met.

Chapter Eight

Harry

Before

'Watch yourself there, my love,' said the nurse, as the doors swung open. Harry's nose and throat filled with the all-too-familiar scent of disinfectant and cleaning products and for a moment he thought he might throw up. He pressed himself to the wall and let the hospital porter push the bed past him, the nurse bustling at his side. The patient in the bed was fast asleep, attached to a drip.

He took another breath, which caught in his throat and turned into a sob.

'You OK?'

Outside, sitting on the edge of a wooden tub filled with pansies, Harry had gathered himself. Or at least he thought he had.

'Fine.' He looked up. 'Yeah, I'm fine.'

A dark-haired young woman, her hair cropped in a gamine style, looked at him thoughtfully. She was wearing a very small baby on the front of her chest in some sort of rucksack carrier.

'You look like you could use a cuppa.'

'This place is run on cups of tea, isn't it?'

'I think you're probably right.' She gave the head of the baby a gentle pat. 'Come on, this one's just been fed, she'll be asleep for ages. The hospital shop does a killer scone.'

In the end she didn't stay asleep for very long at all. As soon as they walked back into the brightly lit, noisy atmosphere of the hospital the baby seemed to sense something was up, and she started screaming loudly. Harry bought a cup of tea for the young mother, instead, and a coffee for himself. He set them down on the table, not quite knowing where to put his eyes.

'Don't worry, it's only a boob,' she said, cheerfully, waving a hand in the general direction of the baby's head. It was making surprisingly loud gulping noises for such a small creature.

Harry nodded and tried to look as if he sat opposite women breastfeeding every day. This whole week had been – well, it was as if someone had turned everything upside down.

'So what's the problem?' She motioned to the teapot. 'Can you just – ?'

Realizing what she meant, he poured the tea. 'Milk?'

'And two, please.'

He ripped open the little packets and tipped in the sugar, stirring it before sliding it across the table so she could reach it.

'I know I said you could do with a cup, but my God, I was dying for one.'

It felt a bit odd watching her drinking tea over the top of another human being. He was slightly concerned that she *might slop some on the baby and burn it, but she carried on, looking quite content.*

'I'm Sarah.'

'Harry.'

'Ooh. Like Prince Harry.'

Normally this would have elicited an inward sigh of irritation, but not today. 'Yes.'

His mum, a fervent royalist, had been convinced that calling her son after the prince born the month before him would be a lovely tribute to the newest member of the Royal Family. Instead it meant he was one of about twelve in his year at university, and had spent the entirety of his school year being known as Harry M., to differentiate him from Harry B., Harry P., and a whole flotilla of other Harrys.

He swallowed a mouthful of too-hot coffee, along with another sob which was threatening to make its way, unbidden, out from deep inside him.

'So what's up?' Sarah fixed him with a direct gaze, which seemed to look straight inside him.

He took another sip of coffee and pressed his teeth together, feeling the strange rigid sensation again in his cheeks. It was as if his face was made of slowly setting concrete. Everything in the world seemed to have shifted slightly, and he didn't know what to do with it.

'My mother. She just – died.'

It sounded ridiculous. The words someone else would say about another person. His mother. Gone.

'Oh my God.' Sarah reached over the top of the now-

sleeping baby and squeezed his hand. 'I'd hug you, except '
She motioned to the little figure in the snowsuit.

He shook his head. 'It's OK.'

'No, it's not,' Sarah said firmly. And she didn't let go of his
arm.

'You said seven o'clock,' said a small, cross voice, from underneath the covers. 'It's now eight fifty-two and forty-five seconds. Forty-six.'

'I'm sorry, darling.' Harry patted the lump under the covers. 'There was an accident on the road. A tanker was overturned – it fell over sideways, I mean.'

Two dark eyes and a tangle of dark hair appeared from underneath the quilt.

'Was anyone killed?'

'No,' he said, firmly. 'Nobody was killed, everyone is fine.'

'Because I was watching a thing on YouTube about accidents, and it said that 1,713 people are killed in car accidents in the UK, every year. I looked it up before you came home.'

He felt a twist in his stomach at the word. It wasn't home. He should be glad, he supposed, that Hope felt that way. Glad that for her, wherever he and her grandparents were meant home. He reached out a hand to stroke the hair off her forehead.

'Sorry I was late.'

'S'OK,' she said, pulling the covers down so her whole face could be seen.

They sat in silence for a moment. Harry took in the bedroom, which was already swamped with the detritus of small-girlhood. Toy horses lay on the floor in a sea of paper and pencils. There was a desk where she'd set out her collection of fossils and assorted bits and bobs she'd rescued along the way – you could never quite tell with Hope what was going to catch her magpie eye, and it was never what you'd expect. A stack of coloured plastic bottle tops in a glass jar, surrounded by a circle of blue Lego pieces. He'd learned over the years not to touch anything – what looked like mess to him was almost always something of significance. His heart swelled with love and he put a hand on her head, running it down the back of her ruffled hair.

'D'you want me to brush that for you?'

'Uh-uh,' her head slid under his hand. 'It's fine.'

'OK.'

It was worth a try. Some days she'd sidle up to him like a cat, set herself down at his knee and instruct him to brush it 'like a horse's tail, please' and he'd sit, listening to her chatter, smoothing the long dark locks. But tonight wasn't one of those times.

'Shall I read you this story, then?'

'Yes please.' Her mouth stretched the words out as she yawned, despite herself. 'I'm not tired,' she added, out of habit. Hope was never tired, she maintained. She definitely needed less sleep than most children, springing out of bed at five every morning. At least now she would sit with her drink and a snack and look at her iPad – most of the time. Harry heard the familiar clattering and mumbled chat of Jenny and Lou downstairs, and the comfortable sound of a bottle of wine being opened.

'Same one as always?' He lifted the book she loved from the bedside table, and she snuggled down, pulling the covers up to her nose.

'Same one as always.' The reply, despite her protestations to the contrary, was fuzzy with sleep.

A quarter of an hour later, he crept downstairs. Perhaps Jenny was right and the country air was good for her. Or perhaps her escape to the horse farm up the road was the key to her exhaustion. She'd told him how she'd sneaked out to look at the horses in the field next door and watched a woman bring them buckets of food. He paused for a second on the landing, looking out of the window.

The stars were crystal bright, and up on the hill he could see the lights of a farmhouse, and another house a distance away. But that was it. They were completely in the middle of nowhere, with virtually no mobile phone reception. One of those lights must be the horse place Hope loved so much.

Maybe tomorrow he'd take her up to say hello to the horses in the fields and let her show him her favourites. She'd told him, very solemnly, that she'd chosen names for them all.

*

'Glass of red?' Lou made to get up from his armchair. 'Let's get you settled in. You must be knackered.'

Harry shook his head. 'You stay where you are. I'll get it.'

'Bloody hell, you're not going to be fussing over me as well, are you?' Lou tutted, and sat back down in the chair.

'I'm not,' said Harry, unscrewing the lid of a bottle of red, which still had the price tag on it. £4.99 from Spar, it said. He took a mouthful and disguised his wince at the taste as a cough.

'Everything all right with you boys?' Jenny appeared from the kitchen, a tea towel in hand.

'I'm telling Harry I've got enough on my plate with you fussing over me, without him starting as well,' said Lou, gruffly.

Jenny perched on the arm of his chair and flicked her husband playfully with the tea towel. 'I'm not fussing. I just want you in one piece. That's why we're here.'

'I don't know why we had to move to the bloody depths of Wales for me to stay in one piece,' Lou grumbled, but he chuckled as he spoke. He shifted in his chair and gave a heavy sigh.

'Because *you* weren't going to recover from a major heart scare by spending every waking moment on the phone to the office finding out what was happening.'

Lou shook his head, but put a hand on his wife's knee. Until his retirement, he had been a DCI in the police force in Norwich when he'd been felled by a severe heart attack. After he was rushed to hospital, it transpired that only 25 per cent of his heart was still working, and only the IED they'd placed in his heart was keeping him alive. Rest and recuperation were the orders, and after a second scare saw him blue-lighted to hospital, Jenny had put her foot down.

She'd always talked about wanting to move out of the city – but neither Lou nor Harry had expected her to come up with the idea of renting out their house and moving to Wales for six months, in winter. But Hope had been struggling at school, and her grandma had decided to take things into her own hands. Yes, they would move to the hills of mid Wales, where she'd spent her child-hood holidays. Hope – who had missed so much school due to tummy aches, headaches, and *just not feeling right* that the teachers agreed that perhaps the change would be as good as a rest – had been transferred to the tiny little village school, and would start after half term. And Harry – well, he would carry on doing what he'd been doing since Sarah died.

Harry looked at the picture on the mantelpiece. The hall was still full of cardboard boxes, but he knew that Jenny would have lovingly unpacked the picture of her daughter from the tissue-paper wrapping first and placed her there to look over them all.

What Harry hadn't known, back then when he met his future wife, was that there was a reason she'd bumped into him coming out of the oncology wing. He always wondered, afterwards, at how grief had blinkered him so he hadn't realized. Sarah had discovered her cancer two years earlier, when she was twenty-eight. She might have looked like a teenage mum when he'd met her, but she'd just turned thirty, and tiny Hope was only three months old. Hope's father wasn't on the scene, and it seemed as if Harry had fallen into the arms of Sarah's family just when he needed them most. And yet, just when he thought he had a chance at the happiness that had eluded him so far, Sarah's cancer had returned. This time it took no prisoners. It hit her so fast and hard that the whole family was left reeling by the side of her grave, seemingly moments after they'd tried to understand the kindly consultant who'd told them that there was nothing she could do.

'I've made a chilli.' Jenny broke through his thoughts. 'I've just got to finish off the bits to go with it and we can sit down.'

'Or we could have it in here,' said Lou, picking up the remote control and looking at it, pressing a few buttons before the television switched on. 'The news is on at nine, and I'd like to see what's going on in the world.'

Harry knew what was coming next. Lou was an insatiable consumer of news – without the politics of the workplace to keep him busy, he'd moved on to become obsessed by the world's political happenings. Lou leaned forward as the headlines flashed up on the screen.

Jenny shook her head. 'You're supposed to be switching *off*, not on.'

'If you don't let me keep my brain active, it'll shrivel away. And they don't have an IED for that.'

'Fine.' Jenny pulled a face, recognizing that she'd been outfoxed. 'Harry, don't you get up. I'll do this. Rest after that long drive.'

She pulled the door shut behind her.

'There was accident on the road, then?' Lou said, muting the weather. 'Rain, and more bloody rain. We don't need a forecast to know that. She's moved us to the wettest part of Wales, if that's possible.'

Harry closed his eyes for a second, pressing the heels of his hands against them in an attempt to wipe away the memories that lurked, ever-present. 'Not an accident – well, a lorry overturned. Nobody hurt.'

'Good.' Lou gave a nod and turned the sound back on.

'So how did she escape?'

'You make her sound like an animal from the zoo,' Jenny chided, as he stacked the dishes beside the sink. The meal finished, Harry had insisted he help with the tidying up. Lou had returned to the sofa. Jenny rummaged in a cardboard box. 'I knew I put dishwasher tablets in here. Here you go.'

She pulled the door open and popped in the tablet before starting to stack the plates.

'Let me do it.'

'You've had a long drive.'

'So have you, yesterday,' said Harry, putting a hand

down, barring her way. 'You sit there and talk to me, if you won't go and settle. I'll wash this saucepan.'

Jenny sank into the chair, and he could see how grateful she was. Bringing up an eight-year-old wasn't easy at the best of times, never mind when you were supposed to be enjoying retirement. It wasn't surprising that Hope had managed to give them the slip.

'I didn't hear a thing, you know.' Jenny picked up the mats on the kitchen table and stacked them as she spoke. 'She must have just slipped out.'

'I suppose we should be glad she headed up the hill towards the horses and not down into the village.' Harry had a vision of Hope meandering across the high street of Llanidaeron – the village seemed small enough, but even when he'd got there earlier that night, there had still been a reasonable stream of cars trundling through, not to mention the screech of a couple of boy racers in a souped-up Corsa. And then there was the train . . .

'We just need to keep an eye on her. Lock the gate.' Jenny frowned in thought.

'I suppose –' Harry rinsed soapy water down the drain. The chilli was welded to the bottom of the pan. 'I'll leave this to soak.'

'I shouldn't have taken my eye off her.' Jenny pushed her chair back and made for the sitting room.

'It's not your fault,' Harry said to her retreating back.

He rubbed his hands up and down his face. He was exhausted, but it was nothing to how Jenny and Lou must be feeling. Things were going to have to change somehow. This had been brewing for a while and the truth was – he caught a glimpse of himself in the dark of the kitchen window, noticing the dark shadows and darker stubble – he needed to sort himself out. Sort all of this out. One way or another.

He lay in the bed, staring at the whitewashed ceiling. It was bisected by a heavy wooden beam, knotted and dark-stained. How many other people had lain here, tossing and turning, unable to sleep, over the years?

The situation was unusual, he knew. His friend Holly, who knew him better than almost anyone, had been on at him for ages to sort it out. He picked up his phone and slid a finger across the screen, unlocking it, looking at her messages.

> Speak to J and L when you're there at the weekend, she'd said. You've got six months to work out what to do from there.

> It's not that easy, he typed. How do I broach the subject? How do I tell them I think they need to step back and let me make my own mistakes bringing up Hope, when they don't think I'm capable?

But there was no mobile signal – no way of asking the question. He hit the delete button and watched the cursor travel backwards, letter by letter, until there was nothing there.

Sarah would have known what to do. She'd have dealt with it perfectly. The trouble was, if she'd been there, none of this would have been a problem in the first place.

She'd been so bright and open and direct. Her taciturn dad Lou had been silent on the subject of her death, pretty much from the moment they returned from the graveyard that day five years ago. He'd let himself have one morning where the tears had poured unchecked down his face, and then returned to work and to normality. He softened whenever he dealt with his darling granddaughter, and Harry knew that he could see Sarah in her – they all could.

Meanwhile, Jenny had thrown herself into caring for Hope, which was just as well. Harry had been pretty useless then – the death of his partner had brought back long-buried feelings from previous losses. By the time he recovered from grief and started to move on, Jenny – a natural organizer – had taken over. And now his dad was gone, too. The complicated sort of love he had felt for his parents was something he couldn't articulate. He looked at the screen-saver photo of himself and Hope wearing mouse ears at Disney – Hope wrapped in his arms, beaming with happiness – and smiled to himself. When his dad's house was sold, he'd have enough money to spend all summer there if they wanted to. But how would Jenny feel about that, even if it was an option?

He put the phone down on the little wooden stool that served as a bedside table, and lay in the darkness, thinking.

Chapter Nine

Ella

Ella woke with a start. She turned, pulling the clock to face her. The glowing face informed her that it was – as she would have known, if she'd been awake enough to think – 3.45 a.m. She pushed it back across the battered oak chest of drawers that stood by the side of the bed, knocking aside a heap of unread books, narrowly missing a half-drunk cup of coffee.

It was always the same time when she woke. The dreams, when they came, were always the same. She lay flat on her back, pulling the covers up against the chill of the evening, watching the slip of the moon between the curtains. The hills were dark shapes against a bright sky.

She took a deep breath in, holding it for a moment, releasing slowly. She knew that the adrenalin would disperse, that her heart – currently thudding wildly in her chest – would settle, and in moments she'd be fast asleep again. She had trained herself well, using the same techniques that helped her to tame the fears and anxieties of her clients. The therapies worked – in conjunction with , the calming nature of the horses, who could intuitively sense the feelings that lay behind the words, the anxieties and anger.

The next morning when she got up – groggy from the middle-of-the-night disturbance – she found Bron already in the kitchen, making lists.

'What are you up to?'

'I'm just working out the things I do that I might forget to tell you.'

'I am a functioning adult, you know.' She gave Bron a nudge and then, smothering a yawn, pulled out the box of cat food and tipped biscuits into a bowl.

Over the last few months she'd had several emails from an over-enthusiastic new journalist from the local paper, desperate to fill space with a feature on equine therapy. Her name was Miranda. Ella had been putting her off with vague, polite responses about lack of time and the horses being unwell. If she got some extra publicity, though, she might be able to cover the rates bill . . .

'What're you doing?'

'I'm thinking that I'll get Miranda Whatsit from the paper to do the article she wants.'

'But you said . . .' Bron looked dubious.

'*Absolutely no way was I having a journalist sniffing around the place.* Yes, I know. But things have to change. I can't keep ticking over, bringing in just enough money to cover the bills and no more. By the time you get back from Australia, you won't recognize this place.' Scrolling through her emails, Ella scribbled down Miranda's number on the edge of a discarded envelope. She felt surprisingly determined and businesslike. 'And I'm going to need someone up here to give me a hand – we can kill two birds with one stone and save ourselves a job finding someone. I'll see if she'll mention it in the interview.'

Bron nodded thoughtfully. 'Good thinking.'

'I'll ring her this morning.' Ella caught a glimpse of herself in the mirror that hung on the wall by the stable door which led out to the yard. She looked exhausted – purple shadows beneath her eyes, her hair an untidy rats' nest of tangles from tossing and turning on the pillow. And of course she'd refused to let herself think about what had happened with Nick.

'Have you fed Sweetbriar and the baby?'

'I let them out first thing. The dogs were nagging for a run up the hill, so I took them up before it was even properly light.'

Realizing that someone like Miranda was probably attached to her email 24/7, she typed a quick reply to Miranda's most recent, breezily enthusiastic message. *'Sorry for not getting back to you sooner,'* she lied, *'but I've got a bit of time today if you're free?'*

The laptop beeped with Miranda's response as Ella was pulling a dry towel out of the airing cupboard in the hall.

Wonderful! Delighted to hear. Don't suppose you're free at 1 pm?

'*Perfect*,' typed Ella, and looked at the clock. Maybe she'd better get the horses down from the field and looking halfway respectable first, then have a shower. She pulled on an old lambswool fleece and a bobble hat and slid her feet into wellies. Breakfast could wait.

Unfortunately for Ella, what she hadn't factored in was that the herd, determined to binge-eat the final flush of autumn grass growing on the hill, were not in the mood for being caught. One after another they slipped just out of reach, their eyes bright with mischief. Ella almost managed to get a hand on the head collar of Muffin, the naughtiest little Welsh pony, before he dodged away with a snort and a whinny of triumph. His little hooves thudded hollowly on the mossy ground.

You swine, Ella thought to herself, feeling her feet slipping on a patch of mud. Before she could stop herself she lost her footing completely and thudded to the ground with a squelch. Bloody brilliant. Now she was freezing cold and soaked through. She pushed herself up, putting one hand down in something unspeakable left by the sheep that roamed the hillside. The horses stood just out of reach, ears pricked forward in polite interest, expressions innocent.

'You little sods.'

Ella turned her back on them and headed for the gate. Sometimes if she played it cool they'd follow her down and if she could get one caught, the others would traipse along behind, always worried they'd miss out on treats or something interesting. Horses were intrinsically nosey – it was that part of their nature that made them so perfect for the therapy work. If she and a client laid out a trail of wooden blocks, whichever horse they'd chosen to work with would trundle along behind, sniffing each one with interest, following the humans instinctively.

Sure enough, as she meandered down the hillside Ella could sense – the huffing of breath and the jostling for position being the giveaway – that she was being followed. She put a hand in her pocket, pulling out a handful of grain almost as if surprised. She looked at it in her open palm and laughed as Tor's chestnut nose appeared over her shoulder. She looped the rope of the head collar around his neck and led him through the gate, guiding him to step back with one pointed finger, watching as the others all processed through, in pack order.

First came little Muffin. A grey Welsh Mountain pony, he was a native of the hills and therefore seemed to claim natural dominance over the others, wheeling round the young Arabs and nipping at their hocks, keeping them in order when the colts threatened to get above themselves and start messing about.

Echo was next. He was old and stiff, his back leg damaged after an injury in the field a few years back. His coat was thick and white all year round, a side-effect of the Cushing's disease they'd discovered a few years back. But he was kind and patient, and one of the characters the quieter clients were often drawn to – there was something in his eyes, a sense that he knew how it felt to be at the bottom of the heap, which Ella suspected drew them in. She ran a hand over his back as he passed, feeling his muscles move beneath the thick waterproof rug that kept off the worst of the Welsh mountain weather. He felt thinner than she'd like – she made a note to up his feed that evening.

There was a skirmish as Lido and Lily, brother and sister, both strikingly beautiful with their chestnut coats and four white socks, shoved and squealed their way through the gate. Tor gave a snort of surprise and stepped back, pulling at the rope.

'Watch it,' warned Ella. Her expression and body language was enough to settle them and they dropped their heads in polite submission, walking nose to tail down the long path that led back to the stable yard.

Last of all came Bella, Sweetbriar's sister, who gave Ella an apologetic look. If Ella had a favourite mare (although she told herself over and over again that she loved them all equally, like children), it would be Bella. Her coat was darker – a deep chestnut brown. Her huge brown eyes were fringed with long dark lashes, and her mane and tail looked as if they'd been into London for an expensive colouring job – the ends highlighted a beautiful caramel gold.

'Go on, then, beautiful.'

Ella let her through and pulled the gate shut behind them. She ran a hand down Tor's mane, praising him for waiting patiently. He nudged at her pocket, hoping for an extra treat There were a few crumbs there and he took them gently from her outstretched hand, nodding his head in thanks.

With the horses installed safely in the outdoor school, standing nose to tail, waiting for instruction, she pulled the gate shut and checked the time on her watch. Miranda had said she'd be there by one.

'Do you want me to iron this polo shirt?' Bron shouted from the depths of the washing basket. Clothes had a tendency to make it from washer to tumble dryer and then into a pile on the worktop in the boot room, where they'd be hauled out in a tangle of socks and winter long johns. Often they stayed there, the plastic washing basket acting as a makeshift wardrobe. There wasn't much time at either end of the day for sorting out domestic stuff, and Ella had loved Bron's cavalier attitude to housework and laundry when she was a child. Having grown up with her father's military organizational skills, she was drawn to her aunt's comfortable chaos. Her mother, Bron said, smiling reminiscently, had always been bloody untidy as well. It was in the genes.

'Iron?' Ella laughed as she buttered some toast. 'We are going to town, aren't we?'

'If you're going to be in the *Mid Wales Argus*, I want you looking respectable. I can do that for you before I go, at least.'

'Do we even *own* an iron?'

From the boot room came a clatter, the sound of some cardboard boxes falling over, and several swear words.

'Yes. I knew it was in here somewhere. Hope it still works.'

'I'm going to go and give the horses a bit of a brush, make them look half decent in case she wants a photo.'

By the time she had taken advantage of the unseasonably warm sunshine to take off the waterproof rugs of every horse – apart from tough little Binnie, who grew a thick enough coat that she could survive a winter on the mountains by herself – Ella was covered in a layer of dust and horse hair.

Taking a brush, she groomed each of the horses quickly, running the bristles through the silken strands of mane, smoothing the hair of their winter coats where the rugs had left it ruffled. They all looked beautiful. She, on the other hand, looked like she'd been rolling on the dusty all-weather surface of the arena.

'Hell's bells, girl,' said Bron, who was folding a reluctant, squeaking ironing board. 'What happened to you?'

'Eight horses.'

'I should go and get in the shower if I were you.'

Ella kicked off her boots with a resigned sigh, taking the neatly ironed polo shirt from her aunt.

'Not bad, considering neither me nor the iron have done anything like that in blooming years.'

'Maybe you could earn a few bob in Australia, get yourself a holiday job?'

'Don't push it.' Bron pursed her lips in mock-warning. 'You get yourself cleaned up. I'll go and give the office and waiting room a bit of a sort out.'

Ella stood in the shower, washing the dust and dirt out of her hair, trying to convince herself that the interview wasn't a terrible mistake. She and Bron trundled along quite happily, except – she upended a bottle and squeezed out the last of the conditioner – they didn't have a bean in the bank for contingencies. One unexpected bill and she was screwed. She'd spoken to Maddie, her mentor, about a pioneering scheme that was being offered by some NHS trusts. If she could get approval for that, and get referrals . . .

Maybe that could work. But it was a massive leap out of her all-too-safe comfort zone. She ducked her head under the hot water of the shower and tried to clear her busy mind.

Stepping out of the shower and drying herself, she looked out of the window and across the hill. There were a fair few people in the village who thought she was up to something akin to witchcraft – using horses to help people overcome emotional issues was a new, and at the same time very old, form of treatment. Back in the desert past, the Arabian ancestors of her own horses would have lived in the tents with their Bedouin owners, and a bond, once made, was made for life. That special connection, Ella was sure, was why her horses worked so well with people.

In the far distance she could see the tiny white speck of a cottage across the valley. If the inhabitants of the cottage had binoculars, she realized, they'd be able to see right into her bathroom window, which had never had any kind of blind or covering. It was lucky that people didn't come round that side of the cottage as a –

Ella pulled the towel around herself with a start. She looked down, catching a glimpse of what looked like the same dark-haired little girl she'd seen before, standing at the gate at the back of the garden, looking straight up through the window.

'Bloody hell.' Ella stepped back out of view, feeling herself blushing scarlet. When she looked back again, there was no sign of the girl. At least Ella knew now that she hadn't imagined her earlier sighting. She'd have to find out who the girl was, somehow.

She looked into the toothpaste-splattered mirror and noted the dark shadows under her eyes. She rinsed her mouth with water and patted her face dry, taking a moment to rub in some of the expensive face cream she'd bought ages ago but always forgot to use. One day, if she wasn't careful, she'd look into the mirror and see Bron's face looking back at her. She peered more closely, checking her parting for any signs of grey hairs.

The crunch of gravel and the sound of a car alerted her, and the metal yard gates squealed a warning. It must be Miranda – early, and in typical journalist fashion no doubt making herself welcome by wandering around all over the place where she wasn't wanted. Ella felt her stomach sink with dread and old, familiar memories, and took a deep breath.

Not *all* journalists, she reminded herself. This one is kind and nice and wants to talk about the horses, not me. She threw the towel over the radiator to dry and pulled on her clothes.

Knowing Miranda was probably downstairs by now, she hastily rubbed her hair dry before attempting to blast it into submission with the hairdryer. After a couple of minutes the dryer started emitting a weird smell and humming. Ella peered down the barrel: the heating element was glowing an alarming, fiery red. She switched it off and unplugged it. The last thing she needed was her hairdryer bursting into flames.

She pulled open the drawer of her dressing table and found a stray lipstick, applying it quickly. It was bright scarlet – left over from one of Lissa's attempts to make her more glamorous and less yokel-like. There wasn't a tissue to hand, so she pulled her old T-shirt off the floor and wiped most of it off with the hem. Sophisticated to the last, she thought to herself, throwing it back onto the side of the bath. It slithered off and landed in a puddle of water.

'Ah, there you are.' Bron, putting a cosy over the teapot, looked up from the kitchen table. Miranda, perched on the edge of one of the rickety wooden chairs, clearly didn't quite know what to do with herself. The space where she might put her elbows or even a notepad was

– as always – swimming with the oceans of crap that floated through their daily lives. Ella lifted the *Farmers' Weekly* and a copy of *Horse & Hound*, and shoved two of Bron's Georgette Heyer novels onto the dresser.

'Sorry I'm a bit late –'

'Oh, don't worry,' said Miranda, her pale blue eyes wide. 'Being early is a very bad habit of mine.' Her cheeks flushed a pretty pink. 'Didn't mean to catch you unawares.'

I bet you did, thought Ella. Classic journalist trick. 'It's fine.'

'I suppose you're not used to having people wandering around the place unannounced.'

'Not really.' Ella sat down opposite her, shoving a wobbling pile of paperwork to one side. She picked up the teapot and shook it slightly, before putting it down again. Her hands were trembling. This was a hideous mistake.

'I've seen far worse, don't worry,' said Miranda, cheerfully. She took out a notebook and put it down on the newly cleared space on the table.

'There's biscuits here on a plate,' said Bron, 'and there's a plug over there, if you need one for your laptop or whatever it is you use.'

She motioned to the wall by the dresser where the dogs lay in a heap on their bed, tails wagging lazily. Cleo raised her head, noticing she was being pointed at, half-hoping for a walk.

'Not you,' said Bron, firmly. Cleo's head sunk back down onto the pillow she was resting on.

Miranda sat back in her chair as Bron left the room with a novel under her arm. She was off to curl up, as was her wont, by the fire in the cosy little book-lined sitting room where she'd lose herself for hours in Regency romance, the light from the log burner filling the room with a warm golden glow. Ella felt a pang of envy.

'This place is so cosy!' Miranda pulled out a pen from the top pocket of her shirt and fiddled with her phone.

'D'you mind if I record our chat? I'm hopeless with shorthand, and it's far easier for me to go back over it if I've got it all here on the phone.'

Ella felt her eyes widening in panic and her throat tightening. Her pulse was racing in her chest. She took an unsteady breath, placing both of her hands flat, palm down, on the table. Exhaling, she realized she was beginning to tremble.

'Are you OK?' Miranda looked at her curiously.

'I'm fine.' She pushed back her chair and made for the kitchen sink, pouring a glass of water. She took a sip slowly and carefully, trying to manage her body's reaction. Panic attacks were rare for her now, partly because she'd learned to recognize the signs and stop them in their tracks. But it didn't always work. Her heart was thudding against her ribcage.

'Would you excuse me for just a moment? I've just realized I've forgotten to double-lock one of the gates.'

She turned, hands by her sides, palms flat against her legs. She was convincing her body that she felt calm.

'Of course, that's fine.' Miranda smiled at her. 'I can't seem to get a mobile reception here. Is there a wi-fi password?'

'Violet1867,' said Ella quickly. 'I'll just be two minutes.'

She closed the door and flopped back against the cold stone of the farmhouse wall outside. The air was sharp on her cheeks.

Come on, she told herself. This is a new start. You NEED this to work. She took another long, slow breath and let the air out, counting to five in her head. Her pulse rate steadied. It was ridiculous that she'd dedicated her life to helping people overcome their own traumas, and here she was hiding from a journalist and trying to fight the overwhelming urge to jump in her car and drive miles away.

'You OK to start?' Miranda, tapping at her phone, looked up with a smile as Ella came back into the kitchen. Ella pulled out the chair, tucked herself in and sat up very straight, allowing as much oxygen as possible to get into her lungs. She nodded briefly.

'Course.'

Miranda tapped her phone again and hit record.

Ella paused, her eyes on the red button on the phone screen.

'You're OK with me recording this?'

'Mmm.' She couldn't trust herself to speak. We need

the money, she reminded herself, lifting up a copy of the local paper and putting it down carefully on top of the heap of bills so that Miranda couldn't read them upside down.

'So, you've got a gorgeous set-up here,' she began. 'And it's your aunt's farm?'

'Mine now, actually.'

Bron had signed the house and land over to Ella a couple of years ago, for a token sum. That way, she'd said, looking unusually serious, if anything happened, she wouldn't be stung with death duties, or whatever they had these days.

'Lucky you.' Miranda looked across the kitchen at the battered red Aga, the flagstone floor and the window which looked out over the valley, the sweeping sky bright blue above the hills. 'This place is *super* sweet.'

'I like to think that when clients come up here they can get away from it all, and find a place of refuge. That's why I came here to –' Careful, thought Ella. It would be all too easy to let things spill out by accident.

Miranda inclined her head a little to one side and raised her eyebrows ever so slightly, questioning.

'To . . . ?' Her pen hovered over her notebook.

Ella was firm. 'For the first clients that came here. That's when I realized that what we had was something very special.'

'And how did you get into equine – therapy? Is that what you call it?'

'I had a psychology degree, and I was doing postgrad

research,' Ella began, cautiously. She didn't add that she'd stopped her research abruptly and never returned to it. 'And then I went to Lancashire, and trained alongside a woman called Maddie who was doing some amazing work with autistic children. I realized that it would be good to work with people who were suffering from emotional upset or trauma, and that the horses have a way of helping people to open up.'

Miranda glanced for a split second at the teapot. 'Shall I?'

'I'm sorry.' Ella took off the cosy and poured tea into the two flowery mugs Bron had left on the table.

Miranda took the milk jug in one hand and lifted it.

She was young, Ella thought, but she was clearly very astute. She wouldn't last long on a local paper before she was off, probably headed for online work or television. A journalist needed to give the impression of a warm nature, of being just like you. That was the easiest way of instantly building a rapport with people. It was a case of being a chameleon. Miranda smiled at her, and Ella thought to herself that she wasn't going to fall for it on any level. She sat up, adjusting the collar of her shirt.

'Milk and sugar?'

'Just milk, thanks.'

'So you use the horses to help get your clients to relax? And then do you do therapeutic work with them on a one-to-one basis? Counselling, that sort of thing?'

'To a degree, yes, it comes out as part of the process. But really the work is about helping people to rediscover themselves. Working with such big animals, getting them to behave in a manner that you've suggested – it's incredibly beneficial. Makes people feel like perhaps they can make the changes they need to in their own lives.'

'Do you find it helps you?'

'Well . . . ' Ella leaned forward, taking a mouthful of tea before looking out through the glass door. She could see Sweetbriar's head snaking forward out of the stable door, peering out to look at the herd in the outdoor arena. There was a muffled clattering as she banged an impatient hoof against the stable door. 'Yes, of course, working with horses was my dream, so I'm very lucky.'

'And do you ride them?'

Ella shook her head.

'Really? What a shame. I can't imagine having all these horses and not wanting to go riding up in the hills here. Aren't you tempted at all?'

'I spend enough time up the hill tending to them in winter.' Ella took hold of a lock of hair that had fallen loose from her ponytail and twisted it absent-mindedly around a finger. 'I don't miss riding.'

'You used to ride, though.'

It wasn't a question. Ella felt a warning chill.

She put the mug down and pushed her chair back, the legs screeching on the flagstone floor. 'Do you want to come and have a look at the herd? If you bring your phone we can chat out there, and I can explain what we do – maybe show you some of the equipment we use?'

'If there's something you want to discuss off the

record, I can always switch the recorder off – I won't quote you on it, but it might give a flavour to the interview? We're always looking for a bit of human interest for these sorts of things.'

'There's nothing,' said Ella, holding the door open. She pulled a jacket, stamped on the back with the business name, from the hook by the back door and shrugged it on. The sunshine was deceptive, and it was still November crisp outside.

'And there's just you and your aunt – Bron, wasn't it?' Miranda was holding the phone, cupping a hand around the microphone to protect it from the wind that was whistling around the side of the barn.

'Us and the dogs,' said Ella, motioning to Bob and Cleo, who were sniffing around the wheels of Miranda's car. On cue, Bob, the scruffy little rough-coated Jack Russell, cocked his leg and peed vigorously against the alloy wheels. 'Oh God, I'm sorry.'

There was a flurry of whickering as the horses jostled forward, reaching out with their noses, hopeful faces in search of treats.

'Actually –' Ella remembered she had a secondary motive. 'Bron's leaving soon for Australia, to visit family for a few months. I'm planning to take someone on to help out. Maybe you could mention that in the article?'

'I'm sure I can fit it in.' Miranda stepped back as one of the horses nudged hopefully at her arm. Ella gave him a look, and he stepped backwards politely. 'So you're a sort of horse whisperer, too.'

'Not exactly.' Ella laughed. 'I use a clicker to train them, so they learn from their first days how to behave if they want treats. It means they respond to my body language – but horses do that instinctively, anyway. Watch this.'

She stepped through the gate, lifting her arms wide out at her sides. The little herd turned, moving along the wall in a fluid motion. She beckoned Tor with an index finger and he stepped forward, ears pricked up, his long forelock hanging in his eyes like a teenager. She lifted the same finger and he paused, still looking intently at her.

'Good,' said Ella, and took a treat from her pocket. She held it out and he took it from the flat of her hand.

'He's my star, this one.'

Miranda stood leaning on the gate, her phone forgotten. The horses had this effect on almost everyone – they were all so beautiful, their long manes and tails shining after their grooming session, their dark eyes kind and curious.

'And you use this to train them?' Miranda motioned to the pile of wooden poles and brightly coloured plastic cones and tubs.

'Yeah. Most of it.' Ella climbed over the post and rail fence, springing to the ground neatly 'So these cones are used to set up a little walking course – it's one of the first things we do in the arena. And these –' she pointed to some wooden steps – 'are used once people are more used to dealing with the horses. We get them to step over them – it's an interesting exercise. If you can imagine, it helps you think about the issues you're coping with and how to step over those. That might sound simple, but it's surprising how people handle it.'

'So if you can get a horse over, you can get over it yourself, that sort of thing?'

'Near enough. The issue is always in the head. We build things up to be so much bigger than they really are.'

You should know, Ella told herself. She'd managed to ride out the beginnings of the panic attack, and her pulse rate and breathing seemed normal again. Only the clammy dampness of her T-shirt, soaked with sweat beneath her coat, betrayed her true feelings.

'And the horses don't mind doing this sort of thing?'

'They love it. They love people, and they develop a real bond with the clients. I've got people who still come back years later just to say hello.'

'So your clients aren't just from Llanidaeron then?'

'Not at all.' Ella shook her head, laughing. The people of Llanidaeron were politely wary about her strange horsey goings-on. They knew she did something to do with therapy, but most of them seemed to think she was some sort of counselling service and the horses were just a bit of a side helping, a bigger version of the soothing goldfish who swum around the tank in the waiting area. The idea of horses delivering the therapy was hard for people to get their heads round. It was nice, in a way, because it meant that the clients she got were already open to trying something new and different. They approached the stables with trepidation but a desire to make changes – that was part of the fun of it all.

'I get clients from all over the place – they often stay overnight at the Lion, and come up for the weekend. It's good because as I'm sure you know, the village needs all the investment we can get.'

'True. And you've no plans to move away or expand?'

'I'm not going anywhere – the farm belongs to me, now. But we're hoping to take on more clients, which is partly why I thought –'

'We?' Miranda said, looking up with interest. 'Is there a Mister Ella in the background?'

Ella had a brief vision of Nick's hand caressing the waist of the blonde girl in the pub at Hallowe'en, and his look of surprise when he saw her.

'Definitely not, no.'

If things had been different maybe he'd have been up here one day, his van parked in the drive, his big feet up on the sofa, a beer by his side and the rugby on – actually, for the first time the thought of all that hit her. As an on-off bit on the side, Nick was great. But actually *living* there? In her house? She hadn't really thought that through. She'd have been compromising herself for the sake of feeling that she ought to be in a relationship. Well – she realized, examining her thoughts more closely – that, and the fact that Bron leaving was going to make for a pretty lonely existence for a while.

'No, there's nobody else. I'm quite happy here with the horses.'

Miranda flicked a glance at her.

'I suppose you must have to be quite – well, sorted? Emotionally, I mean?'

'To do this job?' Ella cast her mind back, thinking of the seemingly scatty Maddie who had trained her in equine therapy, helping her along the way. She too had been through her own painful experience, coming close to death through an infection caught when she was back-packing solo around the world. Lying in a hospital bed in Colombia, she'd decided that when she returned to the UK she was going to do something good and make a difference. And she had: the countless people who had passed through her doors, and the clients Ella and her other protégées had worked with meant that Maddie could feel good, knowing she'd done her bit. But Ella knew she still felt torn, desperate to return to Colombia, where she'd worked with children who had so little that they were delighted with the gifts she'd brought from the nearby city. And Ella, of course, was carrying the scars from her own experience. The physical ones had healed, and the mental ones – well, they'd healed as well as they could. The dreams at night were all the evidence she had now.

'I suppose so,' said Ella. For a moment she felt a familiar stab of guilt and regret at the things she'd said in the past. It didn't seem to matter how many times she worked through it, the feelings still lingered.

She walked across the yard, beckoning Miranda to follow.

'This is the waiting area, and I've got a little room here –' She opened the door to the therapy room, furnished with two comfortable chairs, a side table with tissues, and some black and white charcoal drawings on the walls.

'Those are beautiful.'

'My friend Lissa, she's an artist. Well, she's a teacher, but she likes to come up here at the weekend sometimes and sketch the horses.'

'Does she do commissions? I've got a friend who would love something like that.'

'I'll ask.' Ella smiled. The worst seemed to be over. She pulled the door to and brushed her hands down the front of her jeans, dusting off the horsehair that Tor had left there when he rubbed his head against her. They sat for a moment in the little waiting area, in an awkward silence.

'That would be lovely.' Miranda fiddled with her phone. 'There's just one more thing and then I'll take some photos.' She lifted the shoulder bag she was carrying. 'I've got to be journalist and photographer – everyone's the same in the business these days.'

She looked at Ella, her expression kind and questioning. 'You were in an accident.'

Ella closed her eyes. Leaving it to the last minute, waiting until the interviewee was lulled into a false sense of security . . .

'I was.'

Miranda pushed on, twiddling the pen she was holding between her fingers. She leaned in, conspiratorially.

'Do you feel that doing this work has been the secret to your recovery?'

'I think any kind of work that takes you out of yourself is a good thing,' Ella said, trying to redirect the conversation. 'If you come up here with me, there's a place where you can get a really lovely photo of the yard and the horses all in the outdoor arena.'

They walked in silence up the track. Ella marched in front, fit from daily treks back and forth checking the horses. She could hear Miranda puffing slightly, but didn't let up her pace.

If Miranda had put two and two together, Ella didn't want it going any further. The villagers knew what had happened – they were tactful, kind, never pushing – but it was never a topic of conversation when she was around. And of course in a place like this where life and death was far closer to home, with farming part of the community, it had become part of Ella's past. She knew that some of the older villagers who'd known her years before, when her dad used to drive her across the hills to spend each summer with his sister-in-law, looked at her with concern in their eyes.

Ella had tried to find a balance between her natural inclination to hide herself away, throw herself into the one thing she'd discovered she still had a passion for – the horses – and the realization that it was slightly terrifying to think of another fifty years living alone on the hill, surrounded only by animals. But now, with the threat of bailiffs turning up on the doorstep, she was going to have to make some serious changes.

She stood by Miranda's side whilst she pulled out the big Canon camera and focused it on the farm below. The fields spread out like patchwork, the sheep dotted across them as if made of cotton wool. Smoke curled from the chimney of the cottage like a child's drawing. The whole scene looked, Ella thought, as if someone had taken a primary school painting and brought it to life.

'Perfect,' said Miranda. 'A couple of you with the horses would be great.'

The photos done, Ella's stomach churning with nerves as she waited for Miranda to pipe up again with more questions about the past, she waved her goodbye.

'I'll give you a shout if I have any further questions,' Miranda said, throwing her bag onto the passenger seat. She unzipped her bright red padded coat and folded herself gracefully into the driver's seat. 'I often get home and write it up and realize I've forgotten some minor detail. With luck we'll get it in next week's edition.'

'Thanks.'

Ella held the gate open as Miranda drove through and headed back towards town. Her little red car beetled back down the hill, winding between the high hedges that sheltered the lane. Ella closed the gate and slid the lock across with a comforting clang.

She couldn't help feeling that she'd dodged a bullet

this time, but only temporarily. The sick feeling in her stomach returned, and she ran a hand through her hair before turning back to the farmhouse, glad that Bron was still there – for now, at least.

Chapter Ten

Ella

The sky is dark – no moon, just lowering clouds which have built over the day to a huge crescendo and released themselves – a torrent of fury and thundering rain in the darkness. Ella follows the horse box, radio playing loud enough to drown out the incessant squealing of the windscreen wipers which swing back and forth wildly, pushing what seems like a flood across the glass.

The horse box is trundling at a snail-like 40 miles an hour on the dual carriageway, and a never-ending stream of lights pass by her shoulder as impatient cars hurtle past, desperate to get home to the warmth of their homes. Ella smiles to herself, thinking of her little house by the church, imagining the cats curling themselves around her ankles. The kettle will be boiling and their wet things heaped up by the front door. One of them will have run a bath. She can see it all, and it makes her smile. She pushes the indicator down, echoing the horse box in front, imagining her dad chatting away. She hopes they've got over the land war about who was driving – Dad being a cantankerous old sod was determined it should be him, but Mac, checking the weather forecast on his phone, had

insisted that he was driving. Her dad was so bloody overpro-
tective, a hangover from nearly twenty years of single
parenting. She loved him to bits, but –

'Honestly, Neil, I'll take over. You have a break.'

Ella shakes her head, remembering the argument the two
men had in the car park of the arena. Neil had been driving his
daughter to horse shows since she was a tiny thing, and he
knew what he was doing, rain or shine. Ella, trying to keep the
peace, had put a hand on her dad's arm, telling him he could
relax and listen to the evening play on the radio.

'And you can have a coffee, and a bit of a rest.'

'I don't need a bloody rest. For God's sake, you two – stop
treating me like I'm some old git ready to go out to pasture.'

Mac had winked at her behind his back. The truth was, her
dad was recovering from a minor operation and could do with
the break, but neither of them was going to point that out. He
was a stubborn old sod at the best of times.

'How about we split it?' he'd suggested. 'You do the first
half, I'll take over when we get to Warwick services?'

Neil had harrumphed loudly and rolled his eyes, but grudg-
ingly accepted. Ella knew he loved his new son-in-law and was
delighted that she'd found someone who supported her love of
horses. The idea of Mac taking over, though, was a step too far.
Neil had cheered Ella from her pony club days, taking her to
training camps and specialist instructors, determined to help
her follow her dream of top-level dressage riding. She'd won the
latest competition with Ruby, her huge, beautiful chestnut
mare, and things were looking hopeful for the qualifying round
of the national championships. The other riders had a string of

expensively bred horses, but Ella had managed so far with just Ruby – there was talk of sponsorship, and a promising youngster had been offered to her for the following year. Ella, straight out of university, newly married, working hard at her psychology post-grad and teaching classes on the side, was stretching herself as thinly as she could.

If it wasn't for Mac, she probably couldn't have done it all. They'd met in their first year at Edinburgh University and fallen almost instantly in love. He was cute, kind and funny – and thoughtful, the kind of man who'd bring her coffee at two a.m. when she was trying desperately to get the research notes written up for a project, even though he had work to do the next morning at six a.m. It was that kindness that had convinced Neil this man was good enough for his only daughter, the girl he'd brought up from the age of six. When Ella's mother had died one morning – a brain haemorrhage as she made Ella's packed lunch, crumpling to the ground in a second – they'd pulled together and found a way through. The horses had been the key, bonding them and giving them something to focus on. His sister-in-law Bron's little farm with her Welsh mountain ponies had been a perfect escape for the two of them and they spent every summer there, hidden away from the world.

Ella smiles to herself as they pull off the dual carriageway and onto the little country road that leads home. She imagines her dad turning to Mac, nodding happily, making the same joke about having forgotten something back at the venue and telling him they'd have to turn back. He's done it every time they've gone to a dressage competition since Ella was small.

She shakes her head. The funny little routines and habits that make up family life, the shared in-jokes and silly sayings – they're precious to her. She supposes they are to everyone, but with such a tiny family somehow they seem even more important. They're the threads that hold the family together. She's glad that Mac, who comes from a strangely remote family, seems to have woven himself into their lives. She thinks of him jumping down from the horse box and swinging her into his arms, pushing her wet hair out of her eyes. He's a good man. She is lucky.

The familiar hill is steep and the horse box has slowed now to a chugging 20 miles an hour. The rain hammers down relentlessly and the music is giving her a bit of a headache, so she switches it off.

The road is black and twisting and narrow. The crossroads leading to the hamlet of Brotherton is approaching and the tree-lined roads dip and meander through the fields. Ella sees the lights of an oncoming car before Mac does.

There's a moment when she sees it happening, knows that in a second her whole life has changed, realizes there's nothing she can do. And then there's an unearthly bang, a sensation of flying, and then silence.

Ella woke with a start. She hadn't had the dream for a long time now. She reached over and switched on the bedside lamp, feeling the familiar weight of Cleo curled up at the foot of the bed. The spaniel lifted her head and gave a few hopeful beats of her tail.

'Come here.' Ella reached out, pulling the dog into her

arms. She was freezing cold, the covers trailing on the ground, and she buried her face in Cleo's fur, trying to right herself.

Miranda's questions had awoken old memories. And it was ten years, she rationalized, so she was bound to be reliving everything that happened. She tucked the quilt around herself and took a sip from the glass of water by her bed.

No wonder Miranda had made her feel that way. After the accident, when the inquest was taking place, she'd had her fingers burnt, speaking out of turn to a journalist who caught her off guard. She'd been tearful and completely alone, and the woman had taken her arm, guided her into the corner of a cosy cafe, and probed gently until Ella had told the story of the crash.

The next day the papers were full of her anger and regret about the accident, and it had been the final nail in the coffin of her marriage. Mac, who had spent the last six months living with an angry, grieving, resentful shell, had walked out to stay with friends on seeing the words 'It doesn't matter what the inquest says, I can't get past the fact my husband was driving' in black and white. They were – in part – true; or they had been that day, at that moment. Ella's feelings back then had veered from one moment to the next – if she'd only sounded the horn, warned them in the lorry that there was something coming, maybe she would have saved them. If her dad had been driving, would he – knowing the lorry of old, knowing how temperamental the steering could be and how it had to be nursed home after a long drive – have been able to act more quickly? Mac, furious, had turned on her after weeks of taking Ella's desperate stress on the chin. There was no way anyone could do anything, he'd screamed at her – the truck brakes had jammed, and it was a miracle the other driver had survived. But Ella's dad was gone, killed instantly in the accident, and Ella's pelvis was smashed in the crash, broken in two places. She'd never ridden again. It was anger and regret for all of that that had poured out in the cafe that day, and the loss of control she'd had that day had been the catalyst for every change that had happened in her life since.

Too proud and angry to deal with her husband's bitter fury, she'd got on the train, throwing the barest of essentials into a suitcase. She'd told him to sell the house and that she'd send for her things. *Fine*, he'd said, in a one-word text that made her heart ache all over again with a raw throb that felt like it had been ripped out of her chest.

With her father gone and her marriage in ruins, there had been nowhere else to run but Bron's farm, and she'd been there ever since. Ruby, her dressage horse, had survived the crash but was too terrified of travelling to ever go in a box again. With her riding career curtailed due to her injuries, and feeling somehow that she had to punish herself for what had happened, Ella had given Ruby to Mel, the owner of the stables where she was kept. It was another layer of pain on top of everything that had happened. It felt like a punishment, and somehow she felt as if she deserved that.

After the crash she'd even had a couple of the national papers on her doorstep – the promising young rider, her career ruined. When she lashed out at Mac it caught the interest of the sort of paper that loved a nice middle-England human interest story. There were temporary lights at the junction which had failed, they'd discovered later – the driver of the other car had explained at the inquest that they'd been green, and so had the lights on the other side. Her husband or her father – it didn't matter who had been driving, the accident would have happened regardless. Of course, none of that mattered now, years later. She'd put it to one side, allowed it to become part of the fabric that made up her life. Her darling dad was gone, her marriage over. Her life at the stables was enough. She settled back down against the pillows. Talking to a journalist about what she did now wasn't going to drag everything back up – not in the real world. It was just a case of making her brain understand that.

Chapter Eleven

Jenny

Jenny woke to hear the rain pelting against the window. The wind sounded like it was going to take the roof off the cottage. Lou snored on, oblivious. She pushed the duvet off and found her slippers, heading downstairs to go to the loo. Three thirty in the morning. It was pitch black outside, and the storm had come out of nowhere. She crept quietly across the hall and opened the door, peering in on Hope. She was sprawled across the bed sideways, the covers hanging off. Wind whistled an eerie tune through the window as Jenny tucked her in, pushing a strand of hair back from her face. When she was sleeping she looked just like her mother. Hope stirred, muttering, and Jenny withdrew before she woke up. At this time of the morning Hope could be up for the day if she was roused, and she slept lightly, like a cat.

Jenny tiptoed downstairs, trying to remember which of the ancient wooden steps it was that – *creak*.

She rolled her eyes. Too late. Pausing, she held the banister and her breath, hoping that if the noise of the storm didn't wake the rest of the house, one creaky step wouldn't do it either. Silence.

The kitchen was warm and welcoming. She set the kettle to boil on the Aga before heading to the freezing cold of the bathroom. It had two outside walls, and the radiator did nothing to warm it up. Jenny thought for a moment about the luxury of their recently done-up bathroom back home.

You're here to give everyone a change of scenery, she reminded herself, wincing slightly as the icy cold water hit her wrists. She towelled her hands dry.

In the kitchen, she pottered around in the dim glow of the under-cupboard lights. There was something about waking up at this time of night that made it impossible to get back to sleep, experience had shown her. A cuppa and a chapter of her book might help settle her mind.

Harry had left a new pony book sitting on the table when he'd left last night. Hope had pushed it aside, cross that he was leaving for work again, and it sat upside down, the spine cracking – a book lover's horror. She righted it and smoothed the front cover, placing it at Hope's favourite seat. They'd only been there a few days and she'd surprised them by settling in remarkably well – a little too well, given that she'd twice escaped to the field full of horses up the hill. They'd put a bicycle lock on the gate that led up to the fields, and since then she'd stayed put – although Jenny and Lou were still watching her like hawks. It was exhausting.

Jenny looked down at the cover of the book. *Horses of*

the World. Hope loved to read non-fiction, learning every fact about subjects that fascinated her – fossils and horses had been favourites for a long time now. She'd probably pick it up in the morning, once she was over her unhappiness at Harry's departure. He'd left before the storm had picked up, heading down south for a meeting – another of the countless meetings he seemed to have. Her mouth twitched in a moment of irritation. For a long time after Sarah's death, it had seemed that Harry's way of coping was to throw himself into work. That had been fine, because it slotted in perfectly with Jenny's own coping mechanism. Keeping busy, organizing everyone, never giving herself time to think. She'd had counselling and been told that she should find a way to give herself some *me*-time, but whenever she had time to reflect it just brought back the memories of what she'd lost, and what she'd dreamed of. So it was easier to just keep on going, running the house, trying to keep Hope settled and bring her up as well as they could. Never mind the plans she'd made for their eventual retirement.

'You have to find a space for yourself,' her friend Margaret had said one morning, as they sat at the park watching Hope spinning round and round on one of the rides.

'My *space* is looking after Hope,' she'd replied, slightly irritated. What else was she supposed to do?

'Harry's her father.' Margaret cocked her head to one side and looked at her. They'd had variations on this conversation several times. Lou – working long hours at the police headquarters – had allowed Jenny to take the reins, and Harry seemed happy to step back and let her take over the role of parent. Hope stopped spinning for a moment and stood up, clearly dizzy. She held onto the side of the railing for a moment and then made her way towards the swings. Jenny stood up to help her on and give her a push.

'He's her stepfather.' She lowered her voice, lifting Hope up under the arms and popping her safely onto the swing. Hope held the metal chains and rocked back and forth, waiting to be pushed. Jenny put a hand to her back and she swung gently into the air.

Margaret's voice was brisk, but kind. 'He's her father, Jen. He adopted her – in the eyes of the law, he's her next of kin. Her biological father doesn't even factor into the equation.' She pursed her lips and looked directly at Jenny. 'He's never going to be able to do his job while you're in the way. You need to step back.'

'I'm trying,' Jenny had replied. They'd stood for a while then, not talking, Jenny pushing and Margaret on the other side, making faces that made Hope giggle.

That was a year after her daughter's death, and four-year-old Hope's difficult behaviour was still being put down to grief. Jenny wondered, sometimes, if it was possible for a child to be loved too much, by too many people. She was the only piece of Sarah they had left, after all.

The kettle lid rattled gently, interrupting her thoughts. She leapt up, pulling it off the hotplate before it started to whistle, and busied herself making tea. She picked up her book and settled down on the chair closest to the comforting warmth of the stove. It was surprising just how loud it could be, living in the middle of nowhere. The rain was battering against the kitchen window, the branches of the trees outside creaking eerily in the wind. Jenny shivered, and felt glad that she wasn't alone.

The next time she looked at the clock, three quarters of an hour had passed. She'd been so engrossed in her book – a diary of a woman who'd travelled around South America – that she'd completely forgotten the idea was that she should soothe herself back to sleep. The storm was still crashing outside but, lost in the tale of a trek to Macchu Picchu, she'd been oblivious. She sighed, and closed the book. The wind was whistling through the gaps under the old wooden door. She kicked the draught excluder into place and checked the lock, out of habit. Alan, the man in the little post office shop that sold a bit of everything, had told her that nobody bothered much with locking up around here, but she wasn't quite ready for that sort of relaxed attitude yet. She left her mug in the sink and switched off the light. Perhaps she'd creep upstairs for a bit more sleep.

Chapter Twelve

Ella

'You are not cancelling the flight. Don't be so bloody ridiculous.'

Ella lifted the bag into the boot of the Land Rover and shoved it, hard. She pushed the door shut with a clunk and turned, hands on hips, to face Bron. The wind, which had slammed the feed room door so hard against the stone wall that it creaked away from its hinges and crashed to the ground, had all but disappeared now. All that was left was a stable yard that looked as though a giant had picked it up and turned it upside down. Empty feed bags gathered in corners, leaves turned in whirling, eddying circles. The horses looked out over their doors in mild surprise, ears pricked. But they were more interested in the pile of bags Ella was guarding. 'It's minor storm damage,' she said, firmly.

'The place looks like it's been turned upside down, Ella.' Bron gestured to the stable yard, scattered with tiles that had been blown off the roof of the cottage.

She'd managed to hustle Bron away from the worst of

it, shooing her back inside, telling her that she shouldn't be trailing around in travel clothes getting muddy.

'It's nothing I can't handle.'

'Well, if you're sure . . .' Bron twisted the end of her long plait.

'Completely.' Ella gave a nod. 'Now give me a hand with this case, and we'll get going.'

The narrow road down to the village was strewn with detritus from the storm. Luckily, there weren't any trees down, but the Land Rover crunched over a few lost branches before they turned onto the road that led out of Llanidaeron and towards the airport. They sat in silence. Bron gazed out of the window, and Ella didn't like to disturb her reverie. It was a long time since she'd left the village for anything more than a brief holiday, and – Ella took a deep breath, feeling a wave of sadness threatening to overtake her – Bron was going to be gone for ages. She gripped the steering wheel and headed for the motorway.

'Now I don't want any of that nonsense.' Bron reached across with a finger and wiped a tear that had sneaked out and was travelling down Ella's cheek. Her voice was gruff. 'I'll be back before you know it.'

'I know.' Ella swallowed and squared her shoulders. 'I've got so much to do, I probably won't even notice you're gone.'

'Watch it, young lady.'

'Not so much of the young.' Ella looked up at one of

the huge illuminated displays, where a glowing woman with perfect teeth beamed down, her skin flawless. She'd rushed around getting the yard into some sort of order before they left, and as a result looked distinctly rural, even by her standards. 'Maybe I should buy some of that posh face cream.'

'I'll bring you back some from duty free. Deal?' Bron, who hated fuss, shouldered her bag. 'Now you'd better get back, or you'll end up paying through the nose for parking. You've only got fifteen minutes.'

'I was going to—' Ella began, but her aunt raised a finger.

'No point putting off the inevitable. Now come here.' She pulled Ella into a tight hug, squeezing her hard. 'Your dad would be proud of you, you know.'

Ella balled her hands, pushing her fingernails into her palms. Bron wasn't one for sentimentality, but there was something about getting on a plane and travelling to the other side of the world that made people say things they normally kept inside.

'Love you,' Ella said, giving her a kiss on the cheek.

'You too. Now, shoo. You're cramping my style.' Bron cackled with laughter and turned for the check-in desks. She had a flight to Amsterdam first, before the long journey to Sydney began.

Ella watched as she walked away. Half of her wanted to run after Bron, but the other half felt a mixture of fear and excitement she remembered from her competitive riding years. Whatever happened, she was on her own now. It was time to make things happen. And first of all, she had to work out how the hell she was going to find four thousand pounds, by yesterday.

Chapter Thirteen

Ella

The path by the river was carpeted with leaves in every shade of gold and copper. If this was November, she liked it so far. But, puffing alongside Lissa, Ella was cursing herself for agreeing to keep her company on a training run.

'Bumped into Nick at the Co-op this morning,' Lissa panted, her words appearing as clouds of frozen breath in the air. 'He was asking after you. Checking you'd got home after the party the other night, he said.'

She turned, looking over her shoulder briefly at Ella, who rolled her eyes, breathless, unable to talk. She pulled air into her lungs, feeling them aching. She wasn't used to running and despite the long days of physical work that came with the horses, she was struggling to keep up. Lissa – who normally spent her time parked on the sofa with a pile of marking and a bottle of white – had been training for a few weeks now, and she'd picked up fitness surprisingly quickly.

Ella, who'd never seen her friend running for anything more than the train into Shrewsbury, had burst out laughing when she'd found out.

'I promise you if you keep up the training for four weeks, not only will I sponsor you twenty quid, but I'll come on a run with you.'

Lissa's eyes had sparkled with amusement. 'Deal.'

And so now, here they were.

'Hang on,' Ella said, stopping on the path, bending double, catching her breath.

'Ha!' said Lissa, triumphantly. 'You said I'd never stick to this.' She danced from one foot to the other, cheeks bright pink with the cold, dark curls tied back in a ponytail which bobbed back and forth as she moved.

Ella straightened up and took a long breath in. The air smelled crisp and fresh. The bright chestnut leaves of the beech hedge that lined the river path were tipped with frost, each one outlined carefully as if someone had dipped them in icing sugar.

'I had no idea you were so bloody determined.'

'I am when there's a bottle of gin at stake. Helen the SENCO put two on the table – one for the fastest woman and another for the fastest man. I'm not bloody surrendering that to anyone.'

'Aha.' It all made sense now.

'Come on, slowcoach, the dogs are miles ahead.' Lissa shot off again, leaving Ella trailing behind.

'Can we walk back?'

They'd done three miles, and Ella's legs were like jelly.

'Go on then,' teased Lissa. 'You owe me twenty quid.'

'I'd pay forty not to have to do any more running. I'm

knackered.' Ella whistled to the dogs, who had sneaked under the wooden railing and were sniffing at rabbit holes on the edge of the hill. Bob's little white terrier face was covered in mud, giving him the appearance of an elderly gentleman with a beard. Cleo, the spaniel, danced in circles, her tail wagging so hard that the whole of her back end was swinging back and forth. Ella pulled two treats out of her pocket, throwing them one each, laughing as they caught them in mid-air.

The two friends turned back, cheeks freezing cold, chins muffled in fleece neck-warmers. Lissa was still full of energy, dancing sideways as she looked searchingly at Ella.

'You're OK with the whole Nick thing, then?'

'Yep.'

'I just thought maybe –'

'I don't need a man to have a happy and fulfilling life, Lissa.'

Lissa stuck her tongue out, knowing she was hearing her own words echoed back.

'I'm not saying that.' She fell into step beside Ella, tucking an arm through hers. 'It's just – you know, you don't have to spend the rest of your life alone in penance for what happened – before '

'I know, but . . .'

It didn't matter how many times she heard it. Ella knew it had been an accident that had killed her father. She knew that she'd behaved badly, lashing out at Mac when he'd done nothing wrong, allowing her own hurt and anger to take over like some kind of monster that demanded feeding – and his pain was what it needed. She'd wanted him to feel bad. It was impossible to reconcile those feelings with the way things had been before – it was as if her life had been divided in half. There was before the accident, when she was one person – full of life and joy, madly in love, impetuous, fun. And then there was afterwards.

'You deserve to be happy, Ell. And let's face it, if Nick had been anything other than a convenient shag you'd have sorted things out with him bloody years ago.'

'You don't think I drove him away by being a –'

'Don't even go there. You didn't drive Nick away, he got in his own car and went. And it was *nothing* to do with you. You're lovely, and it's about time you realized that.'

Lissa grinned, poking her in the ribs, and sprinted off.

They dropped the dogs off in Lissa's kitchen, leaving them with a bowl of water and a blanket by the radiator, and headed to the Pink Elephant Cafe for a drink, still in their running clothes.

'All right, girls?'

Connie looked up from behind the counter. She had a duster in her hand, polishing the brand new 1950s-style coffee machine that was her pride and joy. She wouldn't let anyone else in the cafe use it, and liked to show it off to everyone who came in – even if they'd already seen it several times over. Everyone in the village knew they had to make polite noises of admiration before sitting down at one of the rickety, mismatched chairs in the little cafe.

'Watch that, it's delicate!' Connie tutted. A young girl with pillar-box-red hair and a nose ring darted sideways, avoiding a smack on the wrist. She had a Pink Elephant Cafe apron tied round her waist and was holding a cloth, which she had almost used to wipe the surface of Connie's treasured machine.

'You go and sit down, ladies. I'll send Charlotte over to take your order in a moment.'

Even after all this time, Ella still delighted in the lilting sing-song of the Welsh accent. She'd tried over the years to soak it up, but she still sounded resolutely English, no matter what she did.

They sat down at the table by the window.

'You could always try online dating,' said Lissa, in a less than subtle whisper.

'Er, no thanks.'

'Well, Nick was the only eligible half-decent man in the village, and he's off the menu.' Lissa waved the actual menu in the air for emphasis, as if Nick was on there under Quick Bites or Afternoon Snacks.

Ella shook her head. 'I'm not going on bloody Tinder. Can you imagine it here?'

'Oh go on, we could download it and see which of the village husbands are signed up on the sly. You know there's supposed to be a swinging circle, according to staffroom gossip?'

'No way. Everyone would know.'

'Ah, you'd think.' Lissa, who heard everything that went on through the staffroom grapevine, shrugged. She ran a finger down the menu with her eyes closed, stopping and looking to see what she'd chosen. 'Baked potato with low-fat cottage cheese, my arse. I'll have an all-day breakfast, please.' She looked at Ella, expectantly.

'Same here.'

'OK.' The scarlet-haired teenager wrote it down carefully on the notepad. She darted another nervous look at Connie before sidling over to pass the order through the hatch into the kitchen.

'Coming right up,' called Connie, her voice carrying across the noise of the sizzling bacon and hissing steam of the coffee maker.

The cafe was quiet before the lunchtime rush. In summer Llanidaeron was busy with tourists who came to stay in the holiday cottages that dotted the hills around the valley, and over the last few years quite a few of the workers' cottages in the town itself had been bought up, done up and rented out online. But at this time of year the town was dead on a weekday morning, with only a handful of virtuous churchgoers out for the early service. Later on, if the weather stayed nice, it might pick up a bit.

'What's the story with this newspaper interview?'

'I've done it already.' Ella raised her eyebrows, leaning back for a moment to allow Connie to place their coffees on the table.

'You in the news, Ella?' Connie, who prided herself on

being up on all the gossip, put a hand on her hip and waited to hear more.

'Not me.' Ella pulled a face. 'The business. A girl from the *Argus* came and did an interview, part of that local business feature they're doing.'

'I'll have to keep an eye out.' Connie bustled off.

'When's it coming out?' Lissa asked.

'This week, I think. Unless something major happens in the meantime.'

'Not much chance of that round here. You get any photos done?' Lissa ripped open a bag of sugar and tipped it into her mug. 'You should have got her to take a couple of nice ones, put 'em up on Tinder.'

Ella shook her head in horror. 'No, thank you. I was in the background, hiding behind the horses. I doubt I'll even be in them – you know what I'm like in photos.'

It was a standing joke that in every photograph Lissa and Ella took, Lissa would look bright-eyed and beautiful. Her open, smiley face was reliably photogenic. Ella, on the other hand, would inevitably have one or both eyes closed, or her mouth hanging half open catching flies.

'Um, yeah.' Lissa lifted her coffee to her lips and looked at her friend thoughtfully over the top of the mug. 'And did she bring up anything about . . . you know, anything?'

Ella had known Lissa for over a year before she'd told the whole story to her new friend. Lissa, who had watched her own parents' marriage disintegrate in a vicious divorce when she was fifteen, had listened, not judging. She'd told Ella that she shouldn't beat herself up, and helped her to start to believe she should forgive herself for walking away from everything. Ella, lonely and in need of a friend, had collapsed in long-held-in tears and together they'd cried their way through two bottles of red wine, falling asleep on the sofa and waking the next morning to carry on the conversation over breakfast here in the cafe. Lissa was a good friend, and it was a relief to have someone know everything there was to know about her and still stick around. Despite lots of counselling, and the work she did with her own clients, there was still a sneaking, tiny part of Ella which felt secretly that she didn't deserve anyone. That she'd had her chance at happiness, and thrown it away so violently that being alone was all she deserved. Lissa's conviction that she deserved more was a tiny spark of hope which she allowed herself to look at once in a while.

The truth she was beginning to recognize was – she was lonely. And although she'd been shocked to discover that Nick had no desire to settle for her (even if that had been what she wanted), it was a horrible feeling to realize that with Bron gone, there was nobody else to welcome her home at night after a long day at work. Apart from the dogs, she supposed. She'd just have to become an eccentric animal lady. Except – God, maybe that's exactly what she was already. She thought of the glowing woman on the billboard in the airport, and resolved to have a bath with a face mask later.

Connie reappeared, two plates overflowing with food on her arm. Her teenage assistant hovered in the background, looking distinctly uncomfortable. She twisted a lock of brightly coloured hair and chewed on the side of her mouth.

Ella pushed her chair back, giving Connie room to set the plates down on the table. She looked outside. The high street was still quiet, only a dog walker dressed warmly against the cold passing by. She pulled her scarf up to cover her nose, catching Ella's eye through the glass and smiling. It was good to be inside on a day like this, and to be in Lissa's easy company.

'Toast?' Lissa waved a slice under her nose, disturbing her thoughts. 'Penny for them?'

Ella shook her head. Lissa lived her whole life on a sort of bouncy fast-forward. Ella had contemplated asking if she'd like to come up to the cottage and stay for a while when Bron went, keeping her company. But she knew Lissa was happy with her little place in town, walking up the hill to school every morning with an armful of books, trailing back in the evening with her Ikea shopping trolley full of marking. She was only going to be down the road – and the cottage had Merryn's farm just over the footpath and the cottages, and the little row of modern bungalows just below, so it wasn't like she'd be living in the middle of nowhere. The truth was, though – Ella shuddered at the thought – she hated the dark. The dreams that woke her could be scared away with a few moments of breathing, or a potter downstairs for a cup of tea. But knowing that her aunt lay sleeping in her flannel pyjamas a couple of doors down the hall was a comfort.

'I was just thinking about Bron. She's not even gone for that long; but it feels like bloody ages.'

'Any luck getting someone to help?'

'I asked the girl from the *Argus* if she'd mention in her article that we're looking for someone.'

'Think she will?'

'Dunno.' Ella pushed a piece of bacon around the edge of her plate, not looking up. 'She knew something about the crash. It was weird, though, she didn't push it.'

'Probably just as well.' Lissa looked at her with a shrewd expression. 'You don't really want all that stuff dragged up again.'

'No.'

'Does Bron ever talk about it?'

Ella shook her head no, her mouth full of toast.

Lissa looked up, her dark eyes regarding Ella, head to one side. She knew better than to push it too.

Ella had thought long and hard as they'd sweated along the river path, too breathless to talk. The leaves had swirled through the air in front of them. The storm the other day had ushered autumn in with a vengeance. Running was surprisingly relaxing, in an exhausting, sweaty, painful sort of way. It gave her time to think in a way that working didn't. Up at the yard, she was always thinking one step ahead, juggling work and the horses, keeping half an eye on the clock, waiting for clients.

'Maybe I'll do the 10k race with you.'

'Seriously?'

'It wouldn't do me any harm. What's the date of it again?'

'Valentine's Day.' Lissa's expression was mischievous. 'You've got about three months to get your arse in gear.'

'Three months is enough.'

'Right. I'm holding you to that.' Lissa waved a sausage, speared on the end of her fork, for emphasis. 'Reckon you can get some of your clients to sponsor you?'

'I'm not sure that's exactly ethical.'

'Oh come on, it's for the PTA. They're wanting to get a load of equipment for a sensory room. The more we get, the quicker we can help the kids who need it. Plus, it won't do you any harm to get in with the head. I reckon she could have some sway in getting a bit of work sent your way.'

'I don't do children,' said Ella automatically.

Lissa pursed her lips. 'You've got an eff-off massive rates bill you can't afford to pay, and bugger all in the bank. You can't afford to be choosy. And you're good with kids; I've seen you.'

She'd been roped in often enough to help out with Lissa's various fundraising events. And she'd been trained in working with children – but until now she'd made it a policy that she focused on adults.

'It's just the responsibility, and the potential for disaster, and –'

'Shall we try focusing on the positive?' Lissa made a

face. 'You're skint. You need business. And if you're getting someone to help out with the behind-the-scenes stuff, you'll have more time to actually do the work that brings in the money.' Lissa waggled her fork again for emphasis. 'I'll put a word in when we have our next staff meeting. I bet Chris, the head, could help you put in a bid to the LEA. They've got that Pupil Referral Unit in town. It's for secondary-age kids, so you won't have tinies like my little ones under your feet.'

'I thought there was no money.'

'There's never any money. That's education for you. But we manage, somehow. There's probably grants or something. If you don't try, you won't get anywhere.'

'Thanks. That would really help.'

Lissa gave a little nod. 'That's what I'm here for.'

Chapter Fourteen

Ella

Hi Ella, just to let you know there's no space for the feature
this week, so we're pulling it. Will let you know when it's in.
Photos look great though! M

The rest of Ella's email was junk, and people trying to
sell her stuff she couldn't afford. She closed the lid of the
laptop and pushed it back on the table, picking up the
car keys. It was half three on one of those gloomy
November days when it never quite manages to get
light.

'Can I stick this in the window, Alan?'
The little post office and bakery was still open – just.
The bell jingled a warning as she slipped in through the
door. Even late in the afternoon the place still smelled
deliciously of freshly baked bread and warm pastry, and
Ella's stomach was rumbling. She'd been so busy rushing
around the yard sorting out the horses single-handed
that she'd forgotten to eat. It wasn't even a client day. She
was supposed to be catching up on paperwork, but by

the time she'd done everything that needed to be done she was completely worn out.

'And a Cornish pasty, too.' Ella grimaced. *Hashtag clean eating*, she thought. If she didn't get someone to help out soon, she was going to end up keeling over from one too many emergency junk food meals.

'Give us a look.' Alan took the index card out of Ella's hands and lifted the reading glasses he wore on a string round his neck. Given that her plan for a free job ad in the form of the article wasn't going to be happening, Ella had decided to write an advert for display on the shop noticeboard. All that time avoiding press, and now that she actually wanted it the paper wasn't forthcoming. It was sod's law. Meanwhile, she still hadn't found a way to raise the money, and with every day that passed the debt worried her more and more.

'Stable help wanted,' Alan read aloud. 'I think I've got just the person for you, save you a job looking.'

He looked thoughtful as he lifted a pasty from the warmer, placing it in a paper bag.

'Sarah Lewis's daughter Charlotte. She finished school last year and then turned around at the last minute, telling them she didn't want to go to university.'

'Why not?' Most teenagers were desperate to get out of Llani as soon as possible.

'I dunno. Maybe she didn't fancy it.' Alan shrugged. 'You could ask her yourself. I reckon she'd be up for it.'

'And what's she doing now?'

*

'Nothing,' Charlotte said cheerfully. 'Not a thing. You ever tried looking for a job in Llani?'

'Fair point.' Ella smiled at the girl standing in front of her. She had blue hair and an alarming-looking piercing through the middle of her nose. The T-shirt she was wearing proclaimed her to be a member of the Death Cult, and her skin-tight black jeans were really just holes held together with fabric.

'And you've got experience with horses?'

Ella felt she ought to ask. But it was obvious, standing in the yard, that Charlotte had been around them all her life. She'd approached the bad-tempered Sweetbriar with a confident stance, reaching underneath her mane and scratching her in the favourite spot she loved. The mare had given a tiny snort of satisfaction and whiffled gently at Charlotte's shoulder with her muzzle. She was leaning over her shoulder now as Charlotte spoke, eyes half closed in pleasure as Charlotte rubbed soothing circles on the whorl of white hair in the middle of her forehead.

'Oh yeah, I had a pony when I was little. Kept him at Rimmer's yard over there.' She waved an arm in the direction of the hill that curved over the other side of the valley. 'And when I outgrew him – he was only tiny, 12.2, like – I helped out at the stables with the lessons, and Jim let me ride out on treks.'

Jim Rimmer's trekking stable was a hugely successful business. Tourists over the years had found themselves drawn to the idea of setting out across the miles of tracks that led up into the hills, knowing they'd see wildlife and scenery they could only imagine from the back of a car. He was one of Nick's biggest clients, with a farrier's bill that kept Nick in expensive cars and luxury furnishings for his beautifully decorated cottage. Ella gritted her teeth, reminding herself that she wasn't supposed to be thinking backwards, but forward.

'And how about dealing with the phones, keeping the office tidy, that sort of thing?'

'No problem,' said Charlotte, airily. 'I mean, my room at home's a tip, like, but I'm quite good at tidying up stuff that doesn't belong to me. Y'know what I mean?'

Ella laughed. 'Yes. Yes, I do.'

'I suppose I could get Jim to give me a reference, if you need one? I only managed an afternoon try-out at Connie's cafe . . .'

Ah, *that* was why she looked familiar. She'd had scarlet hair the other day when they'd been in having breakfast after their run. She'd probably got on the wrong side of Connie by pressing the wrong button on the coffee machine – or just by going anywhere near it.

Charlotte shifted from one foot to the other. She was clearly good with horses, and she seemed nice enough underneath the myriad of sparkling piercings that festooned her nose and both ears.

'No need for a reference.' Ella's tone was decisive. If Charlotte turned out to be a disaster, she'd address that issue when it happened. 'I can see you've got a knack with horses – if you can charm Sweetbriar, you can pretty much do anything – and you'll definitely brighten the place up a bit.'

A hand went up to the blue hair and Charlotte frowned. 'Oh, I wasn't planning on staying this colour.'

Phew, thought Ella, imagining the expressions on the faces of some of her more conservative clients. It would be a relief if she was going back to something less – startling.

'I'm bleaching it back at the weekend.' Charlotte's nose crinkled as she beamed cheekily. 'I'm going pink for Christmas.'

Chapter Fifteen

Harry

You're not going to sort your life out if you're never there.

My life doesn't need sorting out, bossy.

Right . . .

There was a pause. Harry watched the dots on the screen moving back and forth as his friend Holly composed a message.

Why don't you bin off work and surprise her?

Harry tapped into his phone.

I can't do that . . .

. . . because – he looked at the motorway service area, where he'd stopped to grab a coffee before heading towards another meeting where he'd sit in a stuffy room full of executives looking at a screen full of financial forecasts. There'd be a stack of sweaty-looking chocolate muffins and deflated pastries for elevenses, and he could predict the lunch menu with alarming accuracy.

Far be it from me – in my current skint state – to point out the obv, but you're about to inherit a SHITload of money. You're the only person I know who doesn't actually have to work.

Harry grimaced. His parents hadn't been much cop on the love and affection front – spending most of their time using him as the ball in a never-ending game of ping-pong – but they'd been well off, and with his father's house up for sale now, the reality was that he didn't have to carry on doing a job he'd fallen into by mistake.

All right, fine. One condition.

Excellent. What?

He could imagine Holly sitting at the desk of her little studio, bashing away on the ancient iPhone she'd had for years and refused to update. *It still works, doesn't it?*

Come and see us soon? Jenny and Lou would love to see you and you can have my room. I'll sleep on the sofa.

There was a moment's pause.

Deal x

Hi Kamal – can you cover for me for the rest of today? I'm feeling a bit grim.

It was surprisingly easy to chuck a sickie, considering he'd never done it before. A cheery reply shot straight back, and in the time it took to drink half his Americano he'd gone from dreading another day on the treadmill to ducking out to do whatever he wanted. And what he wanted to do – no matter how complicated that was, with the whole delicate situation of trying to negotiate Jenny's feelings – was spend some time with Hope.

'Hello, you.' Lou looked up in surprise as Harry walked into the sitting room, removing his reading glasses and putting them down. He was leaning over the coffee table, reading the local paper. 'Trouble at t'mill?'

Harry shook his head. 'Decided to take the day off. And I'm working from home tomorrow.'

'I know someone who'll be pleased to hear that.' Lou put his glasses back on.

'Where is she?'

'Nipped to the shop to pick up some eggs, I think.'

'I meant Hope!' Harry laughed. He looked around the room. Jenny and Lou hadn't even been there a week, and somehow they'd managed to make themselves at home.

He ducked his head to avoid hitting it on a beam as he headed for the hall.

'Here I am,' said a small voice.

'Good morning, again.' He'd kissed her goodbye at five in the morning and set off. Now it was half nine – he felt like he'd been gone for hours – and the day had only just started for the rest of them. Hope was still fuzzy-haired in pyjamas.

'Grandma's gone to the shop.'

'So I gather.'

'Can we go to the gold mines?'

'The what?'

'There's a gold mine near here. Look.' She pulled out a leaflet from the basket which had been left by the cottage owners. He scanned it quickly.

'It's not open just now, sweetheart.' The thought of spending hours stuck in a mine didn't appeal. It was only a little white lie . . .

'Oh.' Her face fell.

'Let me get out of these work things, and you get dressed, and we'll go and find an adventure.'

'Where?'

'You can choose.'

'I want the gold mines.'

Lou flicked a significant glance his way.

'Maybe we could go and have a look,' he said, realizing there wasn't going to be an easy way out.

*

165

Jenny had been delighted to see him – he was surprised she hadn't had anything to say about him ducking out of work – and even more surprisingly, she'd been more than happy to let the two of them head off on an adventure to explore the area.

'Don't worry about us,' she'd said, closing the door behind them. 'I'm taking your grandpa for a nice lunch at the Lion, and there's a bridge class in the village hall this afternoon. Maybe we'll give it a go.'

Bridge didn't seem exactly Lou's thing, but Harry let it pass. He made sure Hope was settled in the back of the car, and they headed off towards the gold mines.

The roads were narrow and winding, but thankfully the signs for the gold mines were clear. They spent a lovely morning exploring the mines – despite his previous reservations – and Hope was delighted with the little nuggets of gold she managed to find in the water.

'The man says they're real gold, you know.'

'Does he?' Harry winked at her. Hope had chosen to ignore the part of the talk when they'd explained that the glittering they could see in the silt at the bottom of the water was fool's gold – or iron pyrites, to give it the proper name.

'I'm going to keep it in my box of special things.'

He reached out his hand and she took it, skipping along beside him as they headed back to the car park. 'What else have you got in the box?'

'Mummy's jewels, from when you got married. And a

photo of a horse Grandma gave me. And an ammonite. That's the curly one, you know the one that goes –' She did a twirling motion with her finger.

'I know the one you mean.'

'Grandma said she should look after Mummy's jewels but I took them back out of the box in her bedroom when she was downstairs.'

Harry's eyes widened slightly. 'Maybe we could tell Grandma you're keeping them safe, just in case?'

Hope shook her head. 'She gets worried about stuff like that.'

They reached the car. Harry reached across, checking her seatbelt was fastened properly. He got in, and turned on the engine.

'What d'you want to do now?'

'Hot chocolate?' Hope's eyebrows raised.

'Go on then.' Jenny would probably disapprove, but never mind. And there was a nagging voice in the back of his mind that reminded him that being Hope's parent was about more than just taking her out on adventures and being the village version of a McDonald's dad, plying her with treats in the cafe.

They drove back along the narrow roads, Hope fiddling happily with the tiny pieces of 'gold' she had collected.

They parked in Llanidaeron High Street and made their way to the cafe. 'Hello, young lady,' said the woman behind the counter. Hope smiled shyly and ducked behind Harry's legs, the way she used to when she was much younger.

'You go and sit down over there,' Harry said, pulling out a chair for her in the corner, where she liked to sit. 'I'll find two hot chocolates.'

'Quiet, is she?' The woman nodded in Hope's direction.

'When she feels like it,' Harry laughed. There was a colourful pinboard on the wall, crammed with flyers for all sorts of craft classes and lessons, reiki healing circles, and all sorts of weird and wonderful things. Welsh village life seemed to attract a fair number of hippy types, if it was anything to go by.

'We've got something for all sorts,' the woman said, noticing him reading. 'You don't look like the knit-your-own-yoghurt type, mind?'

Harry shook his head and laughed. 'Not really my thing. I do a bit of carpentry, that sort of thing.'

'We could do with someone to make a cabinet for this wall, if you're after a job?' She squirted cream on the top of the drinks and scattered tiny marshmallows on top.

'Oh, it's not my job,' he said, handing over a note to pay for the drinks.

'Pity.' She handed back the change. 'You two on holiday? The schools all seem to take different holidays nowadays. I can't keep up.'

'No, we're staying at a cottage just up the hill.'

'Oh,' the woman said, and brightened. 'You must be

Jenny's son-in-law.' She reached out a hand. 'We met the other day when she came in for a coffee. I'm Connie.'

'Harry.'

Her face puckered in sympathy. 'Sorry about your –'

He shook his head and picked up the tray with the two drinks on top. 'It's fine.'

'Poor little lamb,' Connie said, looking across at Hope. She was staring out the window, biting on her thumbnail. 'How's she settling in?'

'Not too bad. We've just been to Dolaucothi, to the mines.'

'Is she going to school after half term, or is she staying at home?'

'Home?' Harry frowned.

'Oh, there's quite a lot of the kids round here are home educated. There's a group in the village that meet here once a week, you know.'

'No, she's starting at the village school. She wasn't – Jenny maybe said . . .' He tailed off.

Connie nodded. 'Yes, she said she'd had a hard time of it at school. Poor little chick. Well, the village primary is lovely. I bet she settles in a treat.'

After they'd finished their hot chocolates, Harry and Hope wandered along the high street, trailing in and out of the shops, inspecting the contents of an Aladdin's cave of treasures, poring over the books – new and second-hand – in the little bookshop, and picking up various interesting-looking jars of jam and crusty sourdough bread from the shop. Their last visit was to the post office, where the man behind the counter gave Hope a sweet from one of the old-fashioned jars, and Harry felt obliged to spend some money on something. He picked up a magazine for Jenny and a copy of the local paper for Lou.

'See you again,' called the man as they left.

There was something naggingly familiar about the whole place, but he couldn't think why.

'Have you had fun, darling?' Jenny asked when they arrived back at the cottage. She looked relaxed. She was sitting with her feet up on the sofa, reading a book. Lou always joked that she travelled the world inside the pages, so they didn't have to go anywhere.

'I had a huge hot chocolate *and* we got spicy cheese,' Hope said, waving a brown paper package at her Grandma. 'And Harry says we can go to the cafe again after school next Tuesday and have more.'

'Tuesday?' Jenny frowned up at him, putting her book face down on the coffee table. 'I think we've got to take Grandpa to the hospital for a check-up that day, sweetie. Maybe a different day?'

'No,' said Harry, firmly. 'I'm taking her. There's an art class.' Jenny looked taken aback. He stood firm, and was gratified when Hope gave a decisive nod. Jenny lifted a hand to her hair, touching it carefully, as if checking it was still in place. He'd seen her do it before – an automatic self-comforting gesture, he remembered reading about such behaviours in the paper one Sunday. Jenny liked everything to be done just so, and by that she generally meant her way. It occurred to him once again that actually, perhaps trying to find a way to be more involved with Hope's life could prove a battle of wills.

'Oh, that's fine,' she said, after a moment. 'But what about work?' She lifted up a cushion and plumped it before setting it down beside her on the sofa.

'I'm due some leave. I've told Kamal I'll do a bit from here, dodgy wi-fi permitting, but he can manage without me. It'll do him good to take the reins.'

As soon as he'd emailed, he'd sent a message to Holly, who'd been triumphant and was taking all the credit.

I'll make a slacker of you yet, Macallan.

Her reply had made him laugh. Funnily enough, the one thing he could never be accused of was that – not when it came to work, anyway. When he'd met Holly – Sarah's childhood best friend – she'd laughed in surprise at his formal, neatly pressed work suit. It was a real contrast to Sarah's laid-back hippy look and her own perennial art-student style. At home, Harry was most comfortable in a hoody and a pair of beaten-up old jeans, but he always made an effort to look respectable for work.

'Well,' Jenny said, after a moment's pause. 'That's lovely news.'

Harry couldn't quite read the expression on her face as she lifted her mug of tea.

Chapter Sixteen

Ella

A few days in, and she already couldn't imagine how she'd managed without Charlotte. The yard, which she'd exhausted herself trying to keep tidy as well as keeping up with paperwork, clients, horses and everything else, was now immaculately swept. Charlotte had been with her only a week but she'd already cleared out the waiting area, cleaned the fish tank and placed a vase of flowers on the desk. The consulting room was scented with a lemon and lime aromatherapy blend she'd bought from the health food shop.

The now pink-haired Charlotte was hard at work grooming Tor in preparation for Brian, a retired bank manager who had a lifelong ambition to ride across the American plains on a Western-trained horse, complete with cowboy hat and checked shirt. The only minor setback was his fear of horses. So far his first two sessions had taken place outside the stable door, with an apprehensive Brian standing to one side commenting that Muffin, the small Welsh Mountain pony, was 'surprisingly big, up close'.

Muffin stood with his head over the stable door, waiting. His forelock was long and thick, hanging down almost to his nose, and he tossed his head in anticipation as he heard activity. There was a crunch as Brian's Vauxhall pulled up onto the gravel drive and Charlotte sprang forward to open the gate.

She patted Muffin on the nose on the way past. 'You might make it out of the stable today, if you're lucky.'

There wasn't any chance of that. Ella knew that the next step for Brian was to find the confidence to approach the pony, reach out a hand and discover that he wasn't in fact a savage beast but a perfectly friendly creature. Muffin was used to the routine, and would wait patiently until the client plucked up the courage.

'I've decided to take the bull by the horns today,' said Brian. 'Show him who's boss. I'm not afraid.'

He'd gone for the full cowboy look today and was wearing a pair of suspiciously crisp-looking jeans, clearly straight off the hanger. His checked shirt still had the fold lines from the packaging. It was a relief, Ella supposed, that he wasn't actually wearing a stetson.

He marched across the yard and put his hands on his hips. Looking for all the world as if he was about to draw out his pistol for a shootout at the O.K. Corral, Brian levelled his chin and looked at the pony, who gave a snort of alarm and stepped backwards, his head ducking out of sight so he stood in the gloom of the stable.

'Where's he gone?'

Ella smiled despite herself. She stepped sideways so

they were no longer facing head-on into Muffin's stable, and she could see him visibly relax in the gloom of the box. His neck dropped, and one ear flicked backwards.

'The reason horses work so well in the therapy work I do is that they respond to human behaviour. It's like holding up a mirror.'

Brian turned to look at Ella, listening attentively as always. She'd told him a lot of this when he'd first called to enquire about the work she did, not realizing at that point that Ella wasn't running a sort of desensitizing programme for people with horse phobias, but was in fact a therapist. However, Ella knew that what Brian needed wasn't actually that different to her usual work. There was more to his problem than a simple fear of sharp teeth or flying hooves.

'Muffin relies on a stream of sensory data to sense whether he's safe, or in danger. And he can hear the human heartbeat within four feet. If you're standing there with your hands on your hips, you're making yourself into a shape that looks threatening.'

Brian's arms dropped to his sides. He lifted a hand and scratched his head, looking anxious.

'So he's scared of me?'

'He's not sure what you're up to, and he's not going to hang around to find out. He'll hang back, withdraw into the safety of his box.' Ella clicked her tongue and the grey pony stepped forward, reaching his nose over the edge of the stable door. 'It's OK, beautiful.' Ella stepped forward, extending the back of her hand gently, allowing Muffin to sniff it.

'He's like a dog!' Brian was delighted.

'He's just checking me out, checking what we're up to. He knows you're apprehensive, so he's picked up on that and he wants reassurance from me that there's nothing to worry about.'

Brian stepped forward, echoing Ella's movement, holding out his hand.

'It's soft. I didn't expect his nose to be so soft,' he said, as Muffin gently nudged his outstretched fingers. He took another step forward so he was standing right up against the stable door. Ella noticed Charlotte standing to one side, the broom she had been using held still as she watched with wonder. Brian reached up and laid his other hand gently on the flat of Muffin's neck.

'Hello, there.'

'How does that feel?'

Ella never tired of this first stage. It was marvellous to watch people overcome their fears and anxieties and take a step into the unknown. She had seen collapsing marriages healed by the work she'd done with the horses, and people who had experienced awful trauma finding courage and strength from working with the beautiful, gentle animals here at her yard. It was an honour to be part of it.

'Good.' Brian's face was lit up, his eyes bright with courage. 'I feel good!'

By the end of the session Brian had opened the door

and spent half an hour in the company of Muffin, allowing him to sniff the brand-new jeans and the crisp checked shirt. He'd even picked up a brush and smoothed it through the pony's long, thick mane. The next step would be for him to take Muffin out of the stable and walk around the yard. That would come at the next session. Brian seemed delighted with himself.

'That American trip doesn't seem so much of a pipe dream now,' he said, handing over neatly folded notes – the exact amount, as always.

'I'll look forward to seeing the photos afterwards.'

'You can put one up on the wall in here.' Brian waved at the pinboard, recently re-organized by Charlotte, full of cards and notes of thanks from previous clients. Many of them came back to visit the horses long after their sessions were over. The bonds they made were precious and made Ella's heart swell with happiness. Days like this made all the worrying over money and the trudging up and down to the fields through the mud worth it.

'That was amazing,' said Charlotte afterwards, twisting the lid off a bottle of Coke. Brian had headed off to the Lion for an early lunch, and the afternoon was free because they'd had a cancellation.

'I love the idea of Brian heading out into the Wild West.' Charlotte looked dreamily out of the window. 'One day I'd like to do something like that.'

Ella didn't say anything. Years ago she'd dreamed of a trip out to the States, or of riding across South America.

But that was before the accident and the end of her riding career. Now she kept both feet firmly on the ground. She'd recently had a note from her old friend Mel to say that Ruby, her dressage horse, had been retired; Mel had enclosed a photo of Ruby, shaggy-coated in a winter rug, peering over a wooden gate. They'd worked so hard to get to where they once were in the dressage world. But Ella had filled the space left by her losses with the horses here, and each of them had a special place in her heart. They were family to her. Particularly the beautiful Tor, who had also caught Charlotte's eye.

'D'you suppose . . .' Charlotte ducked her head, breaking halfway through her sentence. She screwed the lid back on her drink and leaned down, shoving it into her rucksack. It was festooned with countless pin badges, scrawled on with black marker pen, and worn away at the corners so that the contents peeked out.

'What is it?'

'I just wondered if you ever – if any of the horses can be ridden?' Charlotte looked up, pulling the woollen beanie hat she was wearing off her pink hair and spinning it around on a finger before shoving it back on. She twisted her mouth sideways, chewing the inside of her cheek.

Ella had suspected the question was coming sooner or later. Not many people – especially girls of Charlotte's age – were content to spend their days with horses on the ground, working with them without riding. The joy – for most people – was getting on, exploring the countryside, feeling the wind in your hair and the sound of hoof beats on turf on a frosty morning.

'It's just – I noticed saddles in the tack room and I . . .'

Charlotte was brilliant with the horses, and the clients who'd met her over the last week had loved her – pink hair and all – saying she brought a breath of fresh air to the place. Ella, who even before Bron's departure had been struggling to keep on top of everything, suspected what they really meant was that they were amazed by how organized and clean everything was all of a sudden.

'Well, it's a while since he's been ridden, but Tor would probably love it as much as you would.'

'Seriously?' Charlotte leapt off the edge of the desk where she'd been perching, almost tripping over her rucksack and falling flat on her face.

'Seriously.' Ella laughed.

'When d'you think – I mean I'm not suggesting now, but . . .' The words tumbled out in a burst of excitement.

'It's been quite some time. A woman from the village was exercising him when her kids were at school, but she was trying to juggle working from home as well and it just sort of fizzled out.'

Charlotte looked in danger of fizzing over, rather than fizzling anywhere.

'Could we do some work with him on the lunge rein maybe? Get him used to having a saddle on again?'

It was surprising how sensible she was for eighteen. She knew her stuff and was already, after just a week, proving her worth around the yard. And now – where

Ella at the same age would have charged in head first, thrown on a saddle and probably been thrown off just as quickly – Charlotte was taking the steady, measured approach.

'Come on, then, seeing as Catherine has cancelled her session.'

By the time Ella had gathered everything they needed to work Tor in the school, Charlotte had groomed his dark coat until it was shining like a fresh conker, the silken threads of his mane and tail glistening in the pale winter sun. They carefully placed the saddle on his back, giving him time to get used to the feel of the girth around his stomach after months of freedom. Tor stood placidly, half-dozing, his nose resting on the rope that tied him to the metal ring on the stable door.

'There.' Charlotte unfastened his head collar, replacing it with the cavesson noseband, which was used for working horses on the lunge rein. 'Do you want to lead him up?'

'You do it.'

'Really?' Her eyes were saucers of excitement. She clipped the long rein onto the ring at the front of his noseband and led him forward. Ella took up the lead. It already felt like Charlotte had been here forever.

She opened the gate and swung it wide, allowing Charlotte and Tor to step through. The sunlight was thin and pale, with no heat in it. She rubbed her hands together, wishing she'd remembered her gloves.

'Just let him have a walk around and get used to the saddle.'

Charlotte walked in a circle, allowing Tor to walk alongside her, extending the long lunge rein every few moments until eventually he was walking in a fifteen-metre circle around her whilst she stood in the middle, turning as he orbited around her. As always, he looked delighted to be doing something – he was bright and easily bored, and the secret to keeping him happy was keeping his mind occupied. Left to his own devices for too long, he'd start fiddling with the lock on his stable door, worrying at it with his teeth until it slid open and then wandering into the yard looking for something to do. Often Ella or Bron would find him ambling about with a grooming brush in his teeth, or causing trouble with the goats. He was a character, much beloved by the clients for his handsome looks and charm.

'Shall I get him to trot?'

'Go on then.'

Charlotte gave the command and Tor sprang forward, toes pointing elegantly, his sweeping tail raised high in the air like a flag. Ella watched, leaning over the wooden gate, as Charlotte laughed in delight.

'He's loving this.' She steadied him back to a walk again, making sure he was listening to her commands, before signalling him back into a smooth trot.

'I don't think you're going to have any problems, somehow.' Tor's ear was cocked sideways, his face a picture of concentration. He was desperate to do something.

Ella felt a pang of envy at the thought of Charlotte jumping on and heading up across the hills on this beautiful winter day. She didn't often allow herself to miss riding, but the feeling right then was so vivid – she could imagine the silence of the countryside and the skeletal trees, the sense of wild freedom as the horse beneath her powered forward into a gallop. Her stomach tightened for a moment with a feeling of regret and loss and she turned away, looking across the yard and over the valley. She'd been told by her consultant after the final visit to hospital that she was perfectly safe to ride, but something had stopped her. Shaking her memories away, Ella focused on Charlotte again.

'Why don't you get on?'

Tor had been trotting obediently around the arena for a good fifteen minutes and his breath was blowing in white clouds from dilated nostrils. He loved working – his ears were pricked and he looked alert and happy. Ella realized that she'd been holding him back, keeping him focused on the ground work he did with clients.

'Are you sure?'

Charlotte's face belied the doubt in her words. It lit up like a ray of sunshine in the biting cold of the afternoon.

'Go and grab a hat – there's a couple in the tack room. I'll keep him walking round.'

Ella watched as Charlotte hurtled across the sand of the arena. She vaulted over the gate, her legs flying beneath her. Ella hadn't expected a horse-mad teenager to have such a natural warmth and maturity when it came to dealing with the clients. She'd been good at working with them – perhaps with time she'd be able to do some client work herself . . . if she was interested.

Meanwhile the hills stood around them, solid and reliable, changing with the seasons. They were rust-red with bracken, the colours muted and dulled by the onset of winter. The trees had all but lost their leaves now, only a lacing of bright colour left hanging in the branches.

Bron had arrived safely in Australia, and Ella was surprised at how much she was enjoying the feeling of being in control without having to double-check everything with someone else. It wasn't so much that Bron expected it – more that she'd never quite shaken off the feeling of being the child in their relationship, even at thirty-three.

'Got it!' Charlotte hurtled across the yard, waving the hat in the air.

'Better off on your head, I think.' Ella, who had been allowing Tor to walk gently on the end of the lunge line in sweeping circles, gave a gentle shake, gaining his attention. 'Here,' she said, and he turned to face her, walking in obediently as she gathered in the long sweeps of rope.

Charlotte was tall enough that the stirrup leathers had to be let down by a good six inches. Her long legs hung low on his sides, her feet almost reaching his elbows.

'He's small, I suppose, compared to the horses over at Jim's place?'

'No, I quite often rode the ponies.'

'But Arabian horses can carry fully grown men and heavy weights on their back.'

'I know, I've read all about them. Did you know they used to sleep in tents?'

Charlotte grinned, tucking a strand of hair back beneath the chin strap of her riding hat.

'Yes.' Tor nudged Ella gently in the stomach, eager to get on. She stepped back, still holding the lunge line, and sent him out again in a wide circle, allowing the rope to feed through her hands until he and Charlotte were orbiting her. She stood at the centre, watching the two of them. It wasn't clear who was the most excited – Tor's ears were pricked forward so sharply that they almost met in the middle, his expression focused. He was an intelligent horse and he took everything seriously. Charlotte, on the other hand, was beaming so widely that she looked like the Cheshire Cat.

'He's like floating on air!'

'He's a good boy, aren't you?'

'I've dreamed of riding an Arab since I was a little girl. This is amazing. Can we trot?'

'Gently.' Ella clicked her tongue. 'T-rot,' she said, and Tor sprang forward, his muscular haunches propelling him, toes pointing delicately.

Ella pivoted on one heel, following his movement, watching the two of them. Charlotte had a natural balance and the years of riding out with the trekking centre ponies had given her a good, solid riding position. She looked perfectly comfortable up there. For a moment a pang of envy overtook her and she could imagine how it would feel to get on, feel the power of the muscular horse beneath her, watch the mane flying in the wind. She could open the gate and set off up the lane, onto the path that led up to the wilds of the hill.

'Can I ride him off the lunge rein tomorrow?'

Charlotte pulled Tor up to a halt, running a hand down the muscles of his neck, ruffling his long, sweeping mane.

'You can have a try now, if you like?'

Ella unclipped the rein from the front of the cavesson noseband, running a hand down the girth to check it was fastened tightly enough. A slipping saddle could be dangerous. But she didn't have to force Charlotte to live in the same world of rules and risks. She'd be fine.

'Take him for a trot around now.'

Charlotte looked confident and balanced, and Tor was walking out, one ear cocked backwards, a sign he was listening to his rider. The silence was broken only by the call of a pair of circling red kites overhead. They swooped down together before hovering silently over the field below, prey in their sights.

There was a crackling of sticks in the hedgerow. Tor leapt sideways, giving a snort of surprise, and stopped dead. He lifted his head high, ears pricked forward, and gave a warning neigh to the herd which echoed in the emptiness. 'What was that, hey?' Ella stepped forward, reaching out a hand to steady him.

Another whinny mirrored back from the distant field. *We're here*, it said, Ella knew. *We are safe*. Tor stood stock still, as immovable as a statue.

Ella followed his gaze. In the hedge, for a fleeting second, she thought she saw the face of the little girl again. For some reason, she hadn't been able to get her out of her head. There was something haunted about her huge, dark eyes.

'Hello?'

The face darted out of sight.

'Hang on,' she said to Charlotte. 'Hop off whilst I investigate.'

Charlotte gathered the reins in one hand and sprung to the ground on feather-light feet. As Ella made her way across to the overgrown hedge by the side of the arena, she could hear the sounds of something moving in the undergrowth.

'Are you OK?' Charlotte called across.

Ella peered in through the spiky branches of the blackthorn bush. It was heavy with dusty purple sloes and as she pushed against the hedge, they pattered to the ground. There was nobody there.

She stepped back, brushing the damp drops of mist that had splashed on her face from the remaining leaves.

'Take off his saddle and give him a brush down and a bit of hay. I'm just going to have a look down the lane, see if I can see anything.'

*

185

In the distance, Ella could see the small figure. She was running, dark hair flying from a ponytail, arms outstretched. The lane was a no-through road, but tractors still rumbled up and down bringing feed for the hill sheep. And then there were the Land Rovers full of men and spaniels, heading up to shoot pheasants in the bracken. The child wasn't safe running about on her own like that.

'Back in a minute,' Ella shouted over her shoulder, slipping through the yard gate and hooking it closed behind her.

The running with Lissa had definitely started to make a difference to her fitness. She caught up with the little girl in a couple of moments.

'Are you all right, my love?'

The little girl stopped and looked at her, her big eyes dark and suspicious. She was dressed warmly in a red woollen jumper and a thick padded waistcoat, her cheeks pink from the cold. There was a smudge of mud on her cheek and a piece of blackthorn twig tangled in her fringe. She nodded, silently.

'Are you lost?'

A shake of the head.

'Where's your mummy and daddy?'

'They're gone.'

Ella felt her eyes widening. What the hell was going on here? It was the same as dealing with a nervous young horse. She had to stay calm, not give the impression of being worried. She knelt down so she was on the same level, looking into the little girl's watchful brown eyes.

'Gone where?'

'My mummy died.'

'Oh, I'm sorry.' Ella felt an ache in her chest and realized she was reacting exactly the way adults always had to her when she was young. The cocked head, the pitying tone. She'd realized early – probably by the time she was around the same age as the little girl standing here alone in the road – that telling people meant she had to deal with their own feelings on the subject. So that much she knew.

'Right, well, I think we'd better get you back to –' She paused for a moment. 'To whoever is looking after you. OK?'

There was a moment when Ella could have sworn the little one looked relieved. She nodded.

'So where is home, then?'

A second later, the answer became clear.

'Hope!'

A woman in her late sixties, neatly dressed, her ash blonde hair immaculately styled, burst out of a gap in the hedge. 'There you are!'

She bent down, enveloping Hope in a hug and looking up, her eyes glittering with tears of relief. 'Thank you.' She stood up, brushing pieces of grass from neat blue trousers. She was obviously not a local – nobody hereabouts dressed that smartly unless they were heading into town to go shopping, or out for lunch.

'It's fine.' Hope's voice was matter-of-fact. 'I didn't do anything – I was just going to look for –'

'Grandpa and I have told you a *million* times, darling. You mustn't just walk out of the house without asking.'

'I was only going to see the horses.' Hope looked at Ella, her mouth twisting as she chewed on the inside of her cheek, anxiously.

Ella smiled at her cautiously. She didn't want to encourage her into absconding from her grandparents' house, but she remembered being eight and horse-mad and sitting by the window of the family home in Aylesbury, watching as the mounted police clipped past on their huge, glossy steeds. She'd longed for a horse of her own. Every patch of grass in town was an imaginary field, each disused garage a potential stable. She'd written stories about the horses she'd own as a grown-up, until one day her father had surrendered and taken a pony on loan at the livery yard outside town. It had been the happiest moment of her life. Ella suspected that her father – lonely from the loss of his wife, and not sure how to bring up a child by himself – had seen the routine of horse ownership as something to hold onto. The excitement of competing each weekend, training for the dressage tests, polishing the tack until it shone, had given them both something they had been missing. Horses had changed her life twice – once when she was young, and again after the crash, when she'd realized that the soothing routine of turnout, stable duties, cleaning up and mucking out was enough to keep her going when everything else had been lost. So she could empathize with Hope, and understand why she'd sneak off to peer through the spiky branches to watch Tor circling round and round.

'I'm so sorry. I didn't realize that there was a riding school at the top of the hill.'

'Oh, we're not actually a riding school.' Ella shook her head.

'Oh –' The woman looked at the logo on the front of Ella's jacket.

'We're not a riding school, but we do work with clients. I'm an equine therapist.'

'You fix horses?'

'No.' Everyone said that, and she smiled despite herself. 'No, we – I work with people, and the horses are part of the therapy. The joy of them is that they're non-judgemental. They take us at face value, and –' She stopped. 'Sorry, I didn't mean to give you a lecture.'

'No, not at all. It's very interesting. Well, anyway. Never mind. Come on, darling, we need to get you back home and into the warm.' She hesitated for a second and then turned, putting a hand to Hope's back to guide her back down the lane. But then she turned back.

'I don't suppose –'

'Why don't you –' Ella found herself saying.

The woman took a step. The little girl – Hope – looked from her grandmother to Ella, her eyes wide with anticipation. Her mouth was pursed as if she was holding her breath.

'Bring her up. Tomorrow, if you're free? Or you could even come today?'

Why am I saying this, Ella was thinking. But she knew the answer – it was written all over Hope's little face. Her eye were saucers of excitement and she was standing very still, her fingers stretched out in a star-shape, as if someone had hit *pause*.

Hope's mouth made a perfect circle.

'Today?'

'Grandpa won't know where we are.'

'Can't you call him?'

'You can always ring from my landline,' Ella found herself saying. 'Mobile reception is terrible here – you've probably discovered that already.'

'Are you sure this is OK? We're not putting you out?'

'Not at all.'

It was lovely to see the delight on Hope's face. Charlotte was happy to take her from one stable door to the next to meet the horses who were inside.

'I'm Jenny, by the way.'

'Ella.'

They shook hands in that very British, slightly awkward sort of way, and stood for a moment in a silence broken only by the rhythmic chomping of Sweetbriar, leaning over her stable door with a mouthful of hay.

'So what brings you to Llanidaeron?' Ella said, as Charlotte called out that she was taking Hope round to look over the gate at the horses in the bottom field. She did a thumbs-up of approval and turned to look at Jenny.

Jenny took a shallow breath, but nodded, her eyebrows raised slightly. She was balanced on the balls of her feet, as if ready to dash to Hope's rescue. She was a woman on high alert. As they spoke, Ella watched her trying to look casual, but her nervous glances in the direction of the field were clear indications of her inward feelings.

'She'd be at school at this time normally, but she's on half days for her first week, just to get her used to it.'

'Oh, so you've moved in permanently?'

'Just for six months. We took a long-term holiday rent, because we all needed a change of scene. My husband is recuperating from a heart operation.'

'Oh, my friend teaches at the school. Lissa Jones?'

Jenny shook her head.

'She teaches the older kids, I think – Hope must be with one of the others. You'll get to know her soon enough, though. The school is tiny.'

'So what exactly is it that you do?'

Ella led her towards the little waiting room and handed over a printed leaflet.

'It's all in there. But basically the secret is that horses are an effective mirror, and they can help us to process our own emotions, and get over the blocks standing in our way.'

Jenny nodded slowly, still looking at the brochure. 'And do you work with children?'

'I can do, yes.'

'Hope absolutely loves your horses. This is the most animated I've seen her in a long time. Her – my – we lost her mum when she was only very young, you see.'

'Yes, she told me. I'm sorry.'

'It's fine.'

Ella noted that, instinctively. 'Fine', she thought – the word that raises flags with therapists everywhere. Usually a pretty good indicator that in fact everything is anything but.

'And you feel that Hope's struggling with her mum being gone?'

Jenny nodded again, vigorously this time. 'Yes, definitely. She was struggling at school, refusing to go in, complaining of tummy aches and all sorts of mysterious ailments. And she tends to be quite – withdrawn.'

'Well, we can certainly do some work, see what comes up.'

Jenny's shoulders dropped in relief and she looked noticeably less tense.

'I'd like that a lot. Yes. Yes, please.'

By the time Hope and Charlotte returned from the front of the farmhouse, where they'd stood watching the horses graze from the fence that divided the woefully untidy vegetable patch from the field, Ella had taken down Jenny's details and made an appointment for an initial consultation. Jenny was just filling in the paperwork when Hope appeared at her side.

'What are you doing?'

'Just some forms and things. Ella says you can come up again on Friday, after school, and we can spend some time here, if you'd like?'

'Yes!' Hope's face was wreathed in smiles and she nodded so hard that her hair flew back and forth.

'Perfect.' Jenny scribbled her signature and passed the clipboard and pen back to Ella. 'We'll see you at two.' She turned to Hope. 'Let's get back to Harry and Grandpa.'

'That was fast work,' Charlotte teased, as the gate clanked shut behind Jenny and Hope.

'Very funny.' Ella shook her head. 'Let's get this lot sorted out early, and you can get off.'

Charlotte hesitated. 'Dad's not picking me up until six, though.'

'Oh God, sorry. I forgot.' Charlotte was doing such a good job, and working so hard, that Ella didn't want to take advantage. 'D'you want a lift? I could take you, if it's easier.'

'I'd rather stay, if you don't mind.'

It wasn't the first time Charlotte had lingered longer than strictly necessary. Left to her own devices, she'd curl up on the floor beside the Aga and read one of the countless equine textbooks Ella had accumulated over the years. Ella got the feeling that if she could make a little space in the corner of the kitchen, Charlotte would be quite happy to stay there permanently.

Chapter Seventeen

Harry

'When are you leaving?'

Harry ducked under the beam and sat down on the bed beside Hope. She was flashing a projector torch beam against the wall, switching it on and off and on and off. She could do that for hours.

'Tomorrow. After lunch.'

'Good,' said Hope, flashing the light on, then off.

Harry had tried to forget that a trip to sign the documents relating to his father's estate was looming. On the plus side, the journey home would be filled with Holly's chat about everything under the sun, from her obsession with celebrity gossip to the latest news on the US election results. Knowing she was coming back made it a bit more bearable. Plus, he thought, he'd have a bit of back-up with the Jenny situation. He'd returned from the supermarket the night before with a mountain of shopping to find Hope completely sky-high with excitement about *visiting the horse lady*. When he thought about it he felt a slight twitch of irritation that once again Jenny was doing what she thought was best, and he was sidelined.

He lay back on Hope's bed and watched the lights flickering. He knew she didn't mean *good* that he was leaving. It was good that she knew *when*. If she knew when things were happening, she could operate within those parameters quite comfortably. Hope liked to know when things were happening. It was one of the things that made her feel safe.

From the moment he'd seen the solemn eyes of Sarah's baby girl that day, he'd felt like he was looking at an old soul. She had blinked and regarded him thoughtfully. He'd never felt comfortable speaking to her in baby talk, so he never had. From the earliest days, as soon as she could toddle, the two of them would go out walking together. He'd tell her the names of all the trees and the plants they discovered, and she soaked them up like a little sponge. He'd loved spending those days with her. Hope's biological father, Mark, had hovered around the edges for a couple of years, popping up now and then, but showing no real desire to be part of Hope's life. When they'd married, Sarah had asked if he'd be happy for Harry to adopt Hope. Mark hadn't objected – something Harry found almost impossible to comprehend – and they'd settled down to an all-too-brief happy time together in their little town house in Norwich.

Now, at eight, Hope knew everything there was to know about the flora and fauna of the Norfolk woodlands, and he felt certain that if she was ever lost in

Thetford Forest she'd be able to find her way back home. Not that he ever intended to try it out.

But she had a wandering habit, which was something they tried to keep on top of, with varying success. The doors in the house were always locked, and the windows. At night, if by chance someone forgot, the perpetually sleepless Hope would sneak off out the front door – not because she wanted to rebel, but because she wanted to examine a particularly interesting tree or piece of fungus she'd spotted when out for a walk that morning. Or any other morning – she had a memory that was astounding.

Moving here to Wales was supposed to have curtailed that, slightly – like moving a cat to new territory. They'd hoped that in unfamiliar surroundings, perhaps she'd want to stay close to home. Early indications suggested that *no* was the answer to that one. He wondered if maybe introducing her properly to *the horse lady* might curb her curiosity slightly, or at least manage it. He had to give it to Jenny, he acknowledged. Sometimes it felt like he couldn't get a foothold when it came to climbing the mountain of parenthood, but she seemed completely confident. It was hard to find a way in around her certainty.

The next morning, before breakfast, Hope insisted Harry go with her to see the horses.

Harry lifted Hope up onto the gate so she could lean across, pointing to the grey mare who grazed warily out of reach. He gave a click of encouragement and pretended to rifle in his pocket for treats, and she lifted her head up and gave a low whicker.

'How did you make her do *that*?' Hope's eyes widened with surprise and wonder as the mare ambled towards them, trying to act as if she wasn't interested. She kept one ear flicked back, listening out for the rest of the herd.

'Hello, beautiful,' Harry said, putting a hand out for the horse to sniff.

'Can I stroke her?' Hope reached an excited hand out, and the mare snorted and took a step back, her long mane flying in the wind.

'She's a bit cautious, I think.' Harry retracted his hand. 'Let's just watch them for a little while.'

He didn't watch the horses. He watched Hope as she gazed at them, fascinated. After a while they headed back down through the empty field and over the gate that led into the tiny paddock that was the back garden of the cottage.

'Now, you mustn't go sneaking up there when we're not looking, do you understand?' Harry squatted down to Hope's level and spoke very clearly and calmly.

'Harry knows all about horses,' Hope said a while later, as she ate a slice of toast.

'Does he, dear?' Jenny looked at him, surprised.

'I used to help a – friend – with them, a long time ago.'

'A *friend*?' Jenny never missed a trick. She cocked an

eyebrow at him as she tipped flour into a mixing bowl. 'I'll have to quiz Holly when she visits.'

'Oh God,' Harry shook his head dismissively. 'It was long before I knew her.'

'Of course. I forget sometimes that you two only became friends through Sarah. It'll be lovely to see her.'

'Even if she is gloating with satisfaction that I've taken some time off work.' He turned to Hope. 'Do you want to do some drawing afterwards?'

She'd shown him the picture she'd done of the horses in the field. It was good to see her expressing her artistic side – something a therapist had encouraged, Jenny said, after they'd spoken to her about Hope's refusal to go to school.

'Well,' Jenny said, clearly trying not to look smug. 'I'm glad you've decided to take some time away from work.'

'It's not time away.' Harry looked across at her. 'I'm working at home on Monday, and taking Fridays off. I'm just going to be around a bit more. Spend some time with Hope.'

'Grandma always knows what she's doing,' Hope said unexpectedly in a solemn voice, which made them both laugh.

Chapter Eighteen

Jenny

'I haven't a *clue* what I'm doing,' Jenny told Lou, as she gathered an armful of fleece gloves, scarves and a hat. Hope was refusing to put any of them on, and was standing in the hall waiting impatiently to go to the stables dressed in jeans and a bright pink My Little Pony T-shirt.

'You'll get cold, lovey,' Lou said, carrying a hoody in one hand, opening the door with the other.

Jenny pressed her lips shut to keep a sigh of exasperation inside. There was absolutely no point trying to have this conversation, no matter how cold the November wind on the side of the hills. 'It's fine.' She picked up the keys and added a cheerful lift to her voice. 'We'll drive up, won't we, darling?'

Hope wasn't paying attention. She was humming to herself, lost in her own thoughts.

'You going to be OK?' Lou put a hand to Jenny's waist and turned her round, gently. She nodded, catching a glimpse of her reflection in the hall mirror. Goodness, she looked old. What she needed was a holiday.

It was Friday afternoon and Hope was itching to visit the horses. Up at the stables, Jenny was invited to take a seat at the side of the indoor school. There was an electric heater, which took the edge off the chill, and she was grateful to discover that while the chairs were hard and plastic, there was a heap of fleecy blankets to wrap around cold knees.

'Here you go,' said the helper – Charlotte, Jenny thought her name was. She passed over a mug of coffee from the machine in the little consulting room where they'd chatted for a while before Ella headed off with Hope.

Charlotte had vibrant pink hair and an alarming-looking piercing through her nose, but her face was kind, and she ducked her head in shy thanks when Jenny smiled in gratitude. 'I'll be outside if you need me.'

Jenny, left sitting alone in the echoing, barn-like space, wasn't sure what she might need but thanked Charlotte anyway. She took a sip of coffee and looked around at the surroundings. This place couldn't have come cheap – she didn't know much about horses, but they looked expensive, and a building like this must have cost a fortune.

There was a rumble as the door slid open and a small grey pony trotted in, snorting loudly.

'They'll be through in a moment,' Charlotte called, closing the door. Jenny tried to stay calm. There was a solid wooden barrier between her and the pony – it was small, and small horses were called ponies, she knew that much – but she felt distinctly alarmed and somehow responsible. She stayed in her seat and peered at it over the top of her coffee mug.

The pony gave another resounding snort and trotted to the opposite corner of the building, standing against the wall and looking at her with suspicious eyes through a thick thatch of hair.

'Here we are,' Ella's voice was such a relief that Jenny sank back in her chair, exhaling audibly. A side door opened, and Ella and Hope stepped onto the soft surface of the indoor arena.

Over the next forty minutes, Jenny sat transfixed. She hadn't really thought about what equine therapy would mean, practically speaking, and when Hope had been fitted with a riding hat she'd wondered if Ella was planning to teach her to ride after all. But the two of them sat on wooden blocks, chatting in the middle of the arena, and eventually the little pony wandered across to see them. It seemed to hover uncertainly for a while, and then eventually stood facing Hope, its head dropped down low. Jenny couldn't hear the conversation that was going on between Hope and Ella, but they seemed happy enough. Eventually, Hope reached out a hand, and the pony seemed to sniff it, and then step closer. A few moments later Ella stood to one side while Hope leaned in, close against the long grey mane, and seemed to soften, as if the tension she habitually carried around had somehow been absorbed.

And then it was over. Jenny braced herself for tears, but Hope walked out quite happily. Jenny realized, as she stood up and folded the blanket neatly, putting it back on the pile, that Hope hadn't looked over at her once. Maybe this really was going to make a difference.

'Hello, Hope!' Mr Taylor, her new teacher, seemed ridiculously young. He had dark hair gelled upwards in spikes and a round, open face. He squatted down to Hope's level.

'Lovely to see you again. Now, your grandma told me last week that you know all about fossils?'

Hope nodded, still holding her hand. Jenny could feel her little palm was clammy with sweat and anxiety. There was a moment's pause.

'What's your favourite kind?'

'I've got an ammonite in my bag.' Hope lifted her schoolbag off her shoulder and made to unzip it.

'Excellent.' Mr Taylor looked up and gave Jenny the ghost of a wink. 'Do you fancy telling me all about it in Show and Tell?'

'Yes,' Hope's face lit up. 'I found it on the beach when we went to Dorset. It's called the Jurassic Coast because . . .'

Hope didn't even look back. With the talent of a born teacher, Mr Taylor had whisked her into the classroom and Jenny was left standing, alone, outside in the empty playground. Maybe, she thought, this was going to work after all.

Chapter Nineteen

Ella

'*Christmas Fair*?' Jenny read the sign Ella was holding. 'Already? It's only November!'

Ella had popped into the cafe to do a favour for Lissa after another training run. Pink-faced and still out of breath, she swiped at her damp forehead with the back of her hand.

'I know. Apparently it's to do with term dates or something. I think they're planning to get it out of the way before December gets started. We'll be celebrating new year in December at this rate. Can I pin this on the board, Connie?'

'Course you can, love. Can I get you anything? Drink? Cold shower?' Connie cackled with laughter at her own joke.

'I'm fine. Need to get back to the yard, I've got more clients this evening.'

'Can we come and see the horses again soon?' Hope was dressed in a grey school pinafore with a green cardigan. She looked up from the picture she was colouring.

'Next Friday,' Jenny reminded her. Hope nodded, her ponytail swinging.

'Muffin is looking forward to it.' It was lovely to see Hope beaming at that. She'd had a second session already, and it was rewarding to see just how much of an effect it was having. There was a noticeable difference in the way the little girl carried herself – she looked less haunted around the eyes, and younger, somehow. Ella crouched down to look at the picture and was rewarded with a gap-toothed, shy smile.

'How are you getting on with Mr Taylor?'

'He's nice. And he paired me up with Megan so I have someone to play with at break. It's much nicer than my other school.' She popped the lid off a yellow pen and started colouring intently, tongue between her teeth in concentration.

'Hey, Ella,' Connie called over from behind the counter. 'Did you see you're a cover girl?' She winked at Jenny, including her in the joke. 'Your fifteen minutes of fame.'

She approached with a copy of the *Mid Wales Argus* in her hands, and laid it flat on the empty table beside them.

'Nice photo of you.' Connie pointed. 'That won't do business any harm. Make sure you send them all down here for a coffee afterwards, won't you? And don't forget us when you're famous.'

Along the top of the paper, just under the title, there was a colour photo of Ella and two of the horses. Somehow Miranda had manage to capture one where instead of looking stiff and formal, her nose was wrinkled in laughter, eyes shut, and Tor nudging at her pocket for a treat. The Welsh Horse Whisperer, the text said. Never mind that it wasn't *strictly* accurate . . .

Feeling nervous, Ella turned the pages. Inside was a lovely, positive article which was bound to do the business the world of good. Not a word about anything untoward. She pulled a face to herself, feeling slightly guilty at just how cagey she'd been with Miranda. Maybe she'd send a box of chocolates or a card or something, just to say thank you. And God, maybe this would bring in the clients – and the money – they needed.

'Will we be seeing you at the Christmas light switch-on tomorrow?' Connie turned, picking up a cloth to give her beloved coffee machine a polish.

'I'll be there,' Ella nodded. 'I'm manning the PTA mulled wine stand.'

'Lissa got you roped in again?'

'Something like that.' Ella turned to Jenny. 'I think I mentioned my friend to you before – Lissa Jones, who teaches at Hope's school?'

'We met, actually. She seems lovely. Hope, you liked Miss Jones, didn't you? She's got lots of energy.'

'You're telling me.' Ella motioned to her running kit. 'She's got me training for the fun run as well.'

'How's the training coming along?' Connie called over her shoulder as she headed back to the till, where a customer was waiting.

'Slowly.'

'Are you sure you won't join us for a bit?' Jenny offered.

She looked like she would appreciate the company, and Ella hesitated for a moment. Charlotte was holding the fort, excited that she'd been offered the chance to sleep over in the spare room of the farmhouse.

'If you really don't mind, that'd be lovely. Can I have a latte, please, Connie?'

'Can I have the iPad now, Grandma?'

Jenny rummaged in her bag and pulled out an iPad complete with a tangle of wires. Hope plugged herself in, the colouring abandoned, and sat back, watching a cartoon on the screen.

'Modern children,' Jenny said, as if by apology.

'I think we all need to zone out after a hard day. How's she getting on at school?'

'Good. I've been surprised, actually.' Jenny lowered her voice. 'It's been difficult –' Jenny shook her head and poured tea into her cup and added milk, stirring absent-mindedly for a moment longer than she needed to, considering she hadn't added sugar. 'Well, I mean it can be, sometimes. Hope's –' She paused for a brief second. 'My son-in-law – he works away quite a bit.'

There was a charged silence.

'He's not here at the moment. He's dealing with his father's estate. It's all been a bit – up in the air.'

Jenny fiddled briefly with the shirt cuffs that peeped out below her navy cardigan, straightening them. She frowned and looked up.

'It's difficult, you see. When Sarah – when Hope's mum passed away, it was hard for any of us to know what to do for the best.'

There was another beat of silence. Hope was staring out of the window now, watching the workers who were heaving the huge fir tree into place for the Christmas light switch-on.

Jenny continued. 'It seemed easier to just pick up the reins. I'd been a mother before, and when Sarah was having treatments, I'd been looking after Hope. So it just carried on.'

This happened more often than not. Clients would come to Ella with one issue, and it would take a while before the real problem would reveal itself.

Jenny fiddled with a little paper packet of sugar.

'And now?'

'Oh, I'm not saying I want to step back,' said Jenny, quickly. 'Just that I feel sometimes that – well, with Lou's heart scare, life can be very short, and you never know, and . . .' She tailed off and took a drink, replacing the sugar in the bowl in the middle of the table.

'Yes, it can.' Ella looked at Hope.

'I'm sorry, I've no idea why I'm telling you all this stuff.'

'It's fine. I think it goes with the territory. That, or I just have that sort of face.'

'Well, I'm grateful to you for listening.'

The conversation shifted then, to Jenny's plans to get Lou involved in village life and keep his mind off work, and her mission to sign up for the yoga classes at the church hall.

'You could always sign up for the mini fun run? It's only a mile.'

'I'm too old for that sort of thing.'

'I tried that excuse on Lissa. Didn't have much luck.'

Ella glanced up at the clock. Time had slipped past, and she'd left Charlotte up there alone for long enough.

'I'd better get going.'

'Oh gosh, I'm sorry I've held you back.'

'You haven't at all. It's been lovely to have a chat. See you soon?'

When Ella headed back up the road, she drove past the cottage where Hope, Jenny and Lou had settled for the next few months. Jenny was bending over backwards to make everyone else in her family content, but she didn't seem particularly happy herself.

Chapter Twenty

Harry

Sure you don't want me to come?

Nah, you can meet me after for lunch though. My shout.

Deal. (It'd have to be, I'm skint)

Harry smiled at Holly's text. She was never anything but, and he said as much in his reply, laughing to himself as he hit send and tossed the phone onto the passenger seat before switching on the ignition and putting the car into gear.

Nothing new there then . . .

There was always something a bit eerie about the Norfolk Broads in the depths of winter. Mist never quite lifted, but hung around the edges of farm buildings, wraith-like, giving the place a haunted feeling.

The roads were deserted, too. In summer the place was thronging with tourists and the roads choked with cars, but as Harry drove along the familiar route to Burnham House he felt as if he was the only person for miles.

The house had been standing empty since his father's death, and he hadn't been back. Hadn't wanted to, in fact, and if he could have got away without going there and sorting through his father's neatly organized belongings, he would have. As it was, there was a furniture clearance company coming the next morning. All he had to do was sort the place out, and then the estate agents would take over. He'd been back at work for a week and although his intention had been to sort the house immediately, he'd been putting it off.

He turned the key in the lock. The house was huge, imposing and solidly grey. In another setting, surrounded by trees, it would have made a cosy vicarage, with flowers in the window and a garden filled with roses and children playing. But for as long as he could remember it had been a huge, empty mausoleum. The house had been in the family for three generations, and Harry felt a vague sense of guilt that he wasn't keeping it on. But his life was with Hope, and right now she was living with her grandparents in a cottage two hundred miles away in deepest, greenest, wettest Wales. At least the drizzle wouldn't come as a surprise, he thought, looking out at the relentless dripping. It seemed to be damp all year round here.

With a lunch date sorted, Harry had a goal to aim for. Whoever bought this place would be delighted with it, probably. A vision of his mother popped into his head.

He was tiny, his legs swinging under the chair as he sat drawing at the huge, scrubbed oak kitchen table. His mother was leaning, head in her hands, with her elbows on the silver hotplate covers of the Aga. She'd stood like that for a long time, he remembered. And then she'd gone. The next thing he knew she'd moved out, and he'd become a parcel that was manhandled back and forth between the two of them, waiting patiently while they bickered over who was having Christmas Eve and birthday, never asking him where *he* might like to be. It was no wonder he'd been so desperate to escape.

He turned the key in the lock and stepped back to look for the last time at Burnham House.

Holly was waiting in the corner of the Saddlemaker's Inn when he walked in. She pointed to the log fire with an impish grin. 'Got the best table,' she said, doing a thumbs-up sign. 'I haven't ordered anything yet. Was worried you might bail out and I'd be screwed because I haven't got a bean.'

'Bloody hell, Holl.' Harry shrugged off his coat and hung it on the rack that stood in the corner, right behind their little two-person table. 'D'you need me to lend you some? Give you some, even?'

She shook her head. 'It's fine.' She twiddled with the long string of beads she was wearing for a moment before letting go so they clattered on the tabletop.

Holly was incredibly proud, and perennially skint. He

picked up the menu and scanned it quickly, knowing perfectly well what he'd be having.

'D'you want –' he began.

'Sausage and mash and extra peas and apple crumble and custard?' Holly laughed. 'Yes. The usual.'

Waiting at the bar to place their order, he turned to look back at her as she fiddled with her phone. She twirled one fair ringlet around her finger absent-mindedly and screwed up her mouth sideways in a thoughtful pout, leaning forward to scrutinize something on the screen for a second. Then she caught him looking, stuck out her tongue and pulled a face.

It crossed his mind – not for the first time – that it wouldn't be hard to fall for Holly. It would make everything work. As Sarah's best friend, Jenny and Lou were fond of her and had known her for years. Hope adored her. She was funny, sweet, kind –

'What'll it be, love?'

'Gin and tonic and a half of Guinness, please.' He'd parked the car outside Holly's place. By the time they'd had lunch and walked round to pick up her stuff he'd be fine to drive.

'I've never been to Wales,' Holly said, a forkful of mashed potato paused in mid-air. 'Or maybe once, when I was little.'

'It's beautiful.'

'I still can't believe Jen just upped sticks and moved you all to the back of beyond on a whim.'

'Not really a whim, is it?' Harry scratched his chin. 'She's had itchy feet for years.'

'Yeah, I know, but it was visiting the rainforests of Costa Rica and drinking rum in Cuba she was after, not a wet winter in Wales, surely?'

He shrugged. 'I guess you've got to take it where you can find it.'

'Cuba, Wales . . . yeah.' Holly pulled a face. 'I can see how you'd go from one to the other. They're basically the same.'

He didn't say anything for a moment. There was the fleeting thought again. Maybe if he – should he be trying to settle down? Maybe if he and Holly actually did make a go of something, Jenny and Lou could head off and do something with their retirement. Holly wouldn't have to worry about money, as he'd have the inheritance, and –

'Penny for them?' Holly poked his arm with a fork. 'Oi.'

He shook himself and took a drink. They'd had one drunken encounter that they'd agreed to put to one side and forget about, not long after Sarah had died. That had been years ago – fuelled by far too much gin, their shared grief and the weird urge to cancel out what had happened by proving they were still alive, somehow. He glanced at Holly once again and she looked up, meeting his eyes for a moment that felt –

Strangely uncomfortable, is what it felt. Whether that was because he was worried his thoughts were written all over his face, or because he was trying to figure out if maybe they could have feelings for each other, he wasn't sure.

They finished the meal and headed back to the car.

'Bloody hell, you weren't joking when you said it was in the middle of nowhere.'

'Nearly there.' Harry indicated and turned off the main road, up into the hills.

'Is that nearly there, or "we've got another half an hour of this" nearly there?' she teased him.

He pointed to the sign.

'Welcome to Llanidaeron,' she read, mispronouncing it. He'd done the same when they first arrived, but Jenny, who'd been put right by Connie in the little tearoom, soon corrected him. The language looked beautiful, but even though all the signs were in Welsh as well as English, he still struggled to work out how to pronounce any of them.

'Oh, this is pretty!' Holly jumped out of the car as soon as he pulled up at the gate. Dark had fallen quickly – the drive had taken a bit longer than expected thanks to traffic, and he was surprised to see the cottage in darkness.

'Not sure where everyone is.'

He'd been expecting a rapturous welcome for Holly from Hope, and Jenny to be bustling about, welcoming her in, taking their coats. Instead the garden was lit by the automatic security lighting, but the cottage itself looked deserted. Fortunately he had a set of keys. He unlocked the door and ushered Holly in. Turning on the kitchen light, he spotted a note on the table.

Gone to Christmas Light ceremony. Come and join us if you get here in time! Jx

'Oh wow, it's even got an Aga.' Holly parked her bum on the rail and beamed with happiness.

He waved the note at her. 'You don't fancy going back out to the village tree-lighting ceremony?'

Holly lifted her eyebrows and inclined her head towards a bottle of red wine sitting on the worktop beside the kitchen sink. 'We could . . .'

'Great minds.' He passed it over. He didn't take much persuading. He knew Jenny was keen to involve herself in village life, and she'd been telling him happily on the phone yesterday how she'd had a good chat with the woman who owned the stables, as well as Connie from the cafe. But it was cold, and dark, and he'd just driven 250 miles. 'There should be glasses in the cupboard up there. I'll get our bags in – you stay here, it's freezing.'

'Are you having fun, darling?' Jenny looked down at Hope, who was gazing at the still-dark Christmas tree with expectation.

'When are they turning on the lights?'

'Soon, I think.' Jenny turned to Lou. 'What time did they say?'

'Six thirty, the poster said.'

The air was filled with the scent of mulled wine and buzzing with the excited chatter of children, all wrapped up in scarves and hats against the cold. Jenny had said hello to Ella, and met her friend Lissa, the two of them standing at the fundraiser stall stirring a huge vat of steaming, spiced mulled wine. Hope had shyly taken a gingerbread cookie – but hadn't said a word until Charlotte had come along, her fringe peeking out from a black beanie hat.

'Your hair is red!' Hope's face lit up with delight.

'For Christmas,' Charlotte had nodded. 'D'you want a mince pie?'

Hope shook her head no. 'I don't like raisins.'

'Me neither.' Charlotte bent down to Hope's level. 'I only like the pastry bits.'

As if to demonstrate, she bit the lid off a pie, shoving it all in her mouth in one go. Hope giggled.

Lou had pottered off to talk to Alan from the post office about something or other and Jenny stood, watching Hope watching Charlotte, and realized that she felt content. It was such a rare feeling that she stood for a moment, waiting to see if something else was going to take over – worry, or concern for Hope, or nervousness about Lou. But no, she was standing in the little main street of Llanidaeron, where despite the fact that she hardly knew a soul, people were smiling hello and jostling gently for position to see the tree light up, and she felt oddly at home. They'd lived in Norwich all their married life, but there was something lovely about this little place – perhaps because it was exactly the sort of village she'd wanted to live in when she was growing up.

'How are you settling in?' Lissa leaned across, raising her voice to be heard. 'Are you excited about Christmas, Hope?'

Hope nodded, shy at seeing Miss Jones outside of school.

'Yes,' Jenny nodded. 'I think we've landed in the right place.'

'I think Llani's got magnetic qualities,' Lissa said in her lovely accent. 'I tried to leave once, you know, but I got drawn back in. You'll never get out of here now you've come.'

That wouldn't be the end of the world, thought Jenny, smiling to herself.

'Look, Grandma!' Hope tugged her arm. A group of teenagers gathered by the tree, and in front of them a gaggle of much smaller primary school children.

'Oh Christmas Tree,' they began to sing.

Hope joined in with the countdown afterwards.

'Ten, nine, eight,' she chanted, clapping her hands in time. 'Four, three, two –'

And with a wave of light, the tree was sparkling on every branch with hundreds of tiny silver-white lights.

'Jingle Bells . . .' began Lissa, behind them, and everyone soon joined in. Lou smiled broadly at her from across a sea of people. He was standing by the edge of the road, chatting happily to Alan, his back straight, shoulders tall.

All those years of old-fashioned policing hadn't left him. He'd mentioned something about Alan wanting help to set up a Neighbourhood Watch scheme, after there had been a couple of break-ins over the summer. Jenny had been dubious, but – she noticed him heading across.

'Alan's offered to buy me a drink so we can have a chat about this idea,' he said, ruffling Hope's hair. She was holding her hat, despite the cold, but at least she'd conceded that she'd wear gloves and a scarf.

What kind of drink, Jenny wanted to say. She bit it back, aware that the last thing he needed was her policing his every move. But it was hard. Harder than he realized. Watching him wheeled out on a stretcher and seeing him wired up to machines had brought back the cold feeling of dread she'd worked so hard to try and get over after Sarah's death.

'Can I borrow your man for a quick – no-alcohol – beer?' Alan said, joining them.

Jenny flicked a glance at Lou and tried to arrange her face into a relaxed, yes-that-sounds-lovely smile. 'How will you get back?'

'I'll give him a lift up the hill,' Alan said. He rubbed his jowly face, thoughtfully. 'I had a bit of a scare a few years back myself. I stick to the soft stuff as well.' He smiled at her then, deep trenches forming in his jowly cheeks, and Jenny picked up Hope's hand.

'Oh, I'm sorry to hear that. But yes, that sounds lovely.'

'Good stuff.' Alan gave an upwards nod. 'Shall we get off before all the seats in the Lion are taken?'

Lou leaned across and murmured in her ear. 'I'll be fine,' he said, gently. She felt his lips grazing her cheek and turned, smiling. 'Have a lovely time.'

'Can we stay and watch the lights for a bit longer?'

'Yes, we can,' Jenny said, remembering what she'd been told about offering Hope options to make it easier. 'Or we can go and see if Harry and Holly have arrived?'

That did the trick.

'Are you two off?' Ella offered Hope a marshmallow that she'd been toasting on a wooden skewer. 'Do you want this?'

Hope frowned thoughtfully. 'I might.' She reached out a cautious gloved hand and took it, but made no attempt to eat it. 'We're going back to see Holly,' she explained.

'That's nice,' said Ella, smiling. 'Is Holly your friend?' She looked at Jenny for clarification. Jenny shook her head. 'Friend of the family. We all love Holly, don't we, darling?'

'Ah,' said Ella. She lifted a finger, as if to say she'd say no more on the subject.

'See you soon then, Hope.'

They waved goodbye to Ella and Lissa, and after one last look at the sparkling Christmas lights, headed back to find the car.

'Holly!'

'Hello, beautiful face.'

Harry watched as Hope leapt into Holly's arms and she spun her in the air.

'We saw Christmas lights and I got a marshmallow stuck on my coat, look.'

Hope pulled forward the fabric, showing a smeary circle of pink goo. She swung her legs, still in Holly's arms.

'Let me take that, honey.' Harry reached across and Holly, reading his mind, put her down on the edge of the table. He unbuttoned her coat and went to the kitchen sink, picking up a sponge to try and remove the sugary mess.

'Can I show you my bedroom? You could sleep in my bed with me. Where's Grandpa?'

He turned to see Jenny walking into the room. She opened her eyes in an exaggerated gesture of horror which made him laugh. Holly took Hope by the hand.

'Why don't you show me your room, sweetheart.'

'I can do that if you like,' Jenny indicated the coat that was in his hands.

'It's going to need a wash. How did she get a marshmallow stuck to her?'

'Oh, the girl from the stables was working on the stall with one of the teachers – everyone seems to know everyone here – she gave her a toasted marshmallow at the end of the night.'

'And she didn't eat it.'

'She wanted to save it until we got home. You missed the tears in the car park. Have you two eaten? There's soup in the warming oven.'

'We've had some, thanks.'

Harry checked the pockets of Hope's coat, removing a wizened conker, two fidget toys, a yo-yo, a plastic horse and a couple of large stones. He put them on the table.

'Holly looks well.'

Harry picked up the stones and turned them around in his fingers. Jenny's tone was curious, but there was something – after the thoughts that had passed through his mind today – that made him feel uncomfortable about that statement, where in the past it wouldn't have given him pause.

'Hope's glad to see her.'

'Lou's gone off for a drink at the Lion with his new friend from the village,' Jenny said, carrying on, oblivious. Maybe he was overthinking all of it. Maybe signing over the house, and all the stuff that came along with that, was making him go a bit odd. He filled up his wine glass and another for Jenny and handed it to her, silently. Perhaps he just needed to sit down and stop thinking for a bit. He closed his eyes and listened to the sound of Hope giggling at something Holly had said. Was the answer to everything right in front of his nose?

Chapter Twenty-one

Ella

Ella put Tor back in the stable and stood back for a moment in the yard, watching as Brian and Carol chatted outside the waiting room. It was another ice-bright day. The horses' breath clouded from their nostrils as they hung over the stable doors, peering to see what was going on. Sweetbriar clattered an impatient hoof against the door.

'That's enough, madam,' Charlotte laughed, reaching up to fasten the head collar around her neck. 'I'm going to stick her in the outdoor school for a sec so I can clear this properly.'

'There's a haynet up there, I think.'

'Cool.'

Charlotte hitched up her jeans and picked up the lead rope. She leaned across to Tor and scratched him on the forehead where his hair whorled outwards like a Catherine wheel. He whickered hopefully as she moved away, unbolting Sweetbriar's door and leading her across the yard. They dodged the puddles, which were fringed with sharp-edged ice from yesterday. Brian and Carol were chatting happily, laughing together. It was such a change for them both. They'd arrived wound up and apprehensive with their own issues to overcome, but the therapy was working its magic.

Ella watched as Carol pushed a hair back with her hand and ducked her head. Was she *flirting*?

Brian caught Ella's eye. 'I'm going to need a Stetson, not one of these,' he said, motioning to the protective riding hat he was fastening on his head.

'I'd stick with the hat if I were you,' Carol said. 'You don't want to fall off halfway across the wilds of Montana and end up with a head injury.'

'Right,' Ella said cheerfully, before either of them spiralled into their respective worries. 'Carol, same time next week?'

She nodded, jingling her car keys, and gave Brian a shy smile. 'Good luck.'

'And Brian, I'll be with you in a moment, OK? Ready?'

'As I'll ever be.' He winked at Carol, who giggled.

Ella tended to leave a gap between clients so they didn't have to make awkward conversation, but somehow Brian and Carol had ended up coming on the same day. Carol's tendency to hover after the session, coupled with Brian's habit of turning up half an hour early, could have been a problem, but they seemed to be getting on surprisingly well. Last week, Ella had found them sitting in the armchairs in the waiting room, both sipping coffee from the little machine on the desk.

Charlotte had decorated the waiting room with a little

pine tree in a pot, and on the desk were several Christmas cards from clients and ex-clients alike. All of them were filled with messages of hope and happiness.

'You should frame all these, then you can look at them when you're having a bad day,' Charlotte had observed earlier, shuffling them around to make space on the desk.

Ella waved goodbye to Carol and turned to Brian. They were going into the indoor school today to do some work with Echo, who was taller than Muffin but by far the gentlest horse they owned. Brian baulked slightly on opening the door.

'Bloody hell, he's massive.'

Rather than rushing to say anything, Ella held back and waited. After a few moments, Brian stepped forward. Echo dropped his head low to the ground and stood surveying him, one ear cocked forward in interest, the other flopped back. He was comfortable – but what Brian did next would set the tone for the session.

Brian dropped a hand low to his side, extending it palm out, as he'd learned to do with Muffin. Echo took a step forward, and his nostrils flared as he sized up the situation. Brian took a step. Echo paused, as if to give him space. And Ella watched as man and horse slowly met in the middle of the school, both looking calm and relaxed.

'He's not so big close up.' Brian turned to her, beaming. Echo put his nose into his palm and rested it there for a moment, his eyes soft and peaceful. That was the ultimate sign. Horses could read unspoken body language so well that if Brian had been trying to cover up his worries with bravado, Echo would have kept his distance.

'OK,' Ella said, unable to suppress a huge grin of triumph. 'Let's get to work, shall we?'

'Was that Brian *leading* Echo back to the paddock I saw earlier?'

Charlotte spoke through a mouthful of crisps, her chin in her hands. They were sitting at the kitchen table having a late lunch. The dogs were lying under the table in the hope of scavenging some crumbs, but Charlotte dabbed her finger on the table and collected them, shoving them into her mouth. Probably with a side helping of cat fluff and dust, Ella thought, pulling a face.

'Yes.' Brian had led Echo all the way out, chatting away quite happily. It was wonderful to see how quickly he was coming on. 'He's doing really well.'

The newspaper article had gone online as well as in print, and there had been a steady stream of new bookings coming in, which was making a huge difference. When she'd spoken to Bron by Skype the other day it had been lovely to tell her that they were doing well, and to really mean it. It was such a good feeling to know that she'd managed to make a difference. She put her misgivings about spending Christmas alone to one side, along with her worries about money. Bookings were beginning to come in, and it looked like maybe – just maybe – she might find a way through.

'And Carol's doing really well, too.'

'Did you notice –' Charlotte raised a knowing eyebrow. 'There was a bit of flirtage going on?'

Ella put a finger to her lips, smiling. 'Shush.' She widened her eyes. 'Yes. Brian's arriving earlier and earlier, and Carol's hovering afterwards.'

'Your first stable romance?'

'I doubt it, somehow. Brian was talking about some woman from work he'd met, and I think Carol's still getting over her horrible ex.'

'He's nice, though, Brian.'

Ella nodded, pushing her chair back to stand up. They had an afternoon free, and countless little jobs that had been waiting to sort out. A builder from the village was coming to look at the mortar that was crumbling away on the side wall of the foaling stable.

'Nice,' Charlotte continued, thoughtfully. 'And rich. I wish I could go to Montana and ride around for a month.'

'Well, keep this up and maybe you might be able to.'

'Get rich working with horses? No chance.' She snorted and pointed to the ever-present heap of paperwork on the table. 'Talking of which, there's a bill there from Nick. He popped in when you were in the school with Carol.'

Ella picked it up and tore the envelope open. She'd managed to duck out of his last visit to trim the horses' feet, asking Charlotte to supervise, saying she had to pop to the big supermarket to get some paper for the printer. She'd stayed out of the way for a couple of hours, having a coffee in the little drive-through McDonald's outside, and yet she'd still managed to pass his van on the way back up the lane. He'd pulled into the passing place and waved as she edged the Land Rover past.

There was nothing going on between them, but she still felt super-awkward about bumping into him. Logic stated that it would get worse the longer she left it.

She took a deep breath.

'I might just nip down this afternoon, pay him and get it sorted.'

Charlotte looked alarmed. 'You can't do that.'

'Whyever not?'

'I've just remembered –' Charlotte's hand flew to her mouth and her cheeks stained pink. 'I booked Hope in for an hour at two. I completely forgot to tell you. I saw the diary was empty and I remembered you're trying to get more bookings and Jenny asked if we could fit her in for an extra session.'

'It's fine.' Ella took advantage of Charlotte's pausing to draw breath. Now she had a perfectly valid excuse to carry on avoiding Nick.

Later that evening, Ella sat at the kitchen table. Charlotte – who had taken to staying over whenever possible – was under a heap of blankets and dogs by the fire, watching some of Ella's ancient training DVDs.

She pushed open the laptop and clicked on the Skype icon, hoping that tonight was going to be a night when the wi-fi behaved itself. There was no accounting for it

– some days it worked perfectly well, others trying to get a connection was impossible.

The familiar tone rang out, and she shoved in the earbuds and clicked *answer*.

'Hello, my love!' Bron's face came into view on the screen. The sound was delayed, so her mouth moved a little out of sync with her words. Their chats were always the same, though, and Ella was getting used to the strange echo effect.

'Evening –' Ella looked up at the clock – 'or should I say morning. What time is it with you?'

'Eight o'clock,' said Bron, smiling. 'And it's 24 degrees already. Going to be a scorcher today, I reckon.'

'Nice for you. The rain started this afternoon and hasn't stopped yet. I've had to juggle a load of wet horses and a feed delivery. Charlotte's still defrosting in the sitting room.'

'I'm glad you've got company. She seems to be working out well.'

'Really well. Couldn't manage without her. Even if she did book me in for a session with Hope this afternoon and forget to tell me about it.'

'Ah,' Bron raised her eyebrows, laughing. 'How's it going? How are you enjoying working with a little one?'

'She's lovely.'

Ella had taken Hope into the arena with Muffin in the winter afternoon darkness, letting her groom him, not asking anything of her. Jenny had sat up on the chairs at the edge of the school, drinking coffee and reading a magazine, wrapped in a fleece. She'd come dressed for the occasion the last couple of times, rather than in the smart jacket she'd had on the first time they'd met. She seemed to be relaxing into country life, and so did Hope.

'We went to see a haunted house with Holly,' Hope said, as she shoved Muffin's mane over to one side of his neck, and begun brushing the underside.

'A *haunted* house?'

'Yes.' Hope nodded solemnly. 'There were seventeen ghosts in it.'

Ella waited. Hope brushed, the plastic curry comb swishing through Muffin's long grey hair.

'How do you think Muffin feels about having his hair brushed?'

Hope frowned.

'I think he likes it. Look, he's got his eyes half closed. That means he's sleepy and relaxed.'

Hope leaned her face against Muffin's mane and sniffed it. 'He smells all warm and of biscuits.'

She carried on grooming him. Ella had noticed what might not be apparent to outsiders – Muffin's calm and relaxed state was a sign that Hope was feeling peaceful. The therapy was working.

'It sounds like you're doing some really good work with her,' The picture on the laptop screen stuttered for a moment and Bron's face froze midway through a word, her eyes closed. The sound carried on. 'You're not over-doing it, though?'

Ella stared at the screen and it resolved itself, coming back to life. 'No, definitely not.' She was exhausted, if she was honest with herself; but the money coming in was enough to satisfy the council with a payment, along with a promise that more was to come in monthly instalments. But Bron didn't know that, and she wasn't going to bring it up.

'Isobel's doing well. I was going to get her on to say hello, but she's still in bed, the lazy moo.' Bron laughed. 'And we've got Christmas dinner all sorted. Shrimps on the barbie, and all that.'

'You are not.' Ella listened to the rain thrumming on the windows. It was getting louder, and tomorrow was going to be hard going at this rate.

'Not quite,' Bron laughed. 'But we're having lunch with some friends from across the street. Are you spending it with Lissa?'

Ella shook her head.

'Lissa's got a family thing on.'

'Oh, Ell. You're not going to be all on your own? I feel terrible now.'

In the background, Ella could see the sun stretching out through the French windows of her aunt Isobel's bungalow. She longed to step through the screen and into the picture, give Bron a hug and sit down on a sunbed with a cool drink.

'Ell?'

'Sorry, I was just daydreaming.' She watched herself smiling in the corner of the screen, knowing Bron would be checking anxiously for signs she was miserable or not coping – and she was neither. 'Actually, Hope invited me to go down to the cottage to have Christmas dinner with her family.'

There was a pause as the news travelled, and then Bron pulled a face.

'How does Hope's grandma feel about that? What did you say her name was? Jessie?'

'Jenny.' Ella laughed at Bron, who had a thing about names 'I tried to back out of it, because there's nothing worse than a child inviting you somewhere you're not wanted, but Jenny insisted. Said she'd ordered a massive turkey from the butcher and they'd be glad of the company.'

'So it'll be the four of you for dinner. Maybe you could make one of your nice pavlovas for pudding?'

'I was thinking that.' Ella eyed *Nigella Christmas*, which was already lying open on the kitchen table. She'd been contemplating what to make by way of a thank-you. 'But there's six, not four – Hope's dad is there, too. And his girlfriend, as far as I can gather.'

'Nice,' said Bron, with an expression that suggested the opposite. The screen froze once again, leaving her looking like she'd sucked a lemon. Ella laughed.

'You've gone all funny,' Bron's voice said, staccato. 'This picture's not –'

The screen went black.

Unable to make a connection, the computer said.

A message flashed up a second later on the chat box.

Sorry, this thing's gone to buggery. Talk soon! Xxx

There was a banging at the door and a crash as Lissa swung in, soaked, her hair hanging in wet rat's tails around her face. The dogs had leapt off Charlotte's sofa and hurtled through, their tails wagging furiously.

'If the mountain won't come to Mohammed, etc.,' she said, holding a bottle of wine and an overnight bag. 'I've brought my marking.'

'So what's the story?' Lissa put her feet up on the little coffee table, wiggling her toes in fluffy socks. She held out a hand and Ella put a glass of red in it before collapsing onto the sofa beside her friend, and switching off the television. The fire was burning merrily, and Charlotte – who hadn't been taught by Lissa, but who'd only just left school and so couldn't see her as anything more than the slightly terrifying Miss Jones – had made herself scarce and headed upstairs to have a bath.

'I think I've freaked Charlotte out.'

'She'll get used to it.' Ella swallowed half a glass of wine in one gulp. God, she was tired.

'Is she staying here all the time now?'

Ella shook her head. 'Not officially. But her dad can't get over to pick her up in the evenings, and I get the feeling she's quite happy to totally lose herself in horse world. I was the same at eighteen. If I hadn't gone to uni, I'd have worked in a yard.'

'I think life in her house is pretty full-on, from what I could gather when she was at school. Lots of siblings. She probably enjoys the peace.'

'It's nice having her around.' Ella shifted in her chair, feeling her back aching. 'I want to have a word with her tomorrow, see if we can make it more formal. She can get accommodation as part of the package – we'll give it six months, see how it goes.' She stretched. 'I need a massage or something. I feel like I'm falling apart.'

'Getting old, that's what it is.'

'Watch it, you.' Ella swatted her, laughing. 'All this extra work we're getting is wearing me out.'

'Ooh, that's the other thing I wanted to talk to you about. You'll never guess what happened. I was in a meeting with the head of the Pupil Referral Unit, and you came up in conversation.'

'I did?'

'Well, I brought you up,' Lissa grinned. 'Sort of crow-barred you in, but he didn't seem to mind. He's got two years' worth of funding to do something different with the kids at the unit, and I sort of threw your hat in the ring.'

Ella got up and threw another log on the fire, watching the flames die down and then rise up as the silver birch bark caught alight. If she could get an ongoing contract, she'd have a guaranteed income coming in. It would make all the difference. No more balancing clients with bills and keeping her fingers crossed that the two would meet in the middle, somehow.

'Ell?' Lissa broke into her thoughts. 'You don't mind, do you?'

'No, it'd be amazing.' She realized that she meant it. All this time she'd avoided working with children, and Hope had changed her mind.

Lissa beamed and raised her glass. 'Bloody hell. I thought I'd completely screwed up.'

'The opposite.' Ella touched her glass to Lissa's. 'So what's happening besides that?'

'Well . . .' Lissa looked coy, and hid a smile behind the edge of her wine glass.

'Well?'

'I had a very nice coffee date with the hot single dad from the PTA. You know the one at Hallowe'en – the one with the beard?'

'You did *not*.'

'Did too.' Lissa grinned. 'We were discussing fund-raising possibilities for the school.'

'That doesn't sound like a hot date.'

'Yeah all right, but it's a start.'

'Anyway, you can't go getting off with a parent. It's against the rules, or something.'

'Not if they're not one of my pupils,' Lissa said, reaching across and tipping more wine into their glasses.

'That sounds like seriously dodgy ground.'

'No, I mean, literally not a pupil. His eldest got a music scholarship for St Jude's.'

'So why's he still on the PTA?'

'He signed up to be the chair in September. Well, I think he was guilted into it. And then the scholarship came up, and he's tried to leave but nobody's willing to take it on.'

'So you took him for coffee to seal the deal.'

Lissa's eyebrows flashed upwards for a second. 'No, I'm hoping dinner next week'll do that.'

'You are impossible.'

'You love me for it, though.'

'I do. How are you feeling about the Christmas lunch extravaganza at your dad's place?'

'Hideous. I feel really bad for you too, leaving you in the shit.'

'Oh don't worry, I've been invited to have Christmas lunch with Jenny and Hope.' Ella pulled a face.

'OK, and you're quizzing *me* about ethics?'

'Oh, it's fine.' She'd said yes to Hope without actually thinking it through. But she'd decided that actually, there was nothing to say she couldn't have lunch with them. It seemed fair enough – and she'd only be there for a couple of hours at most, then she'd head off back to do evening stables. It would be fine, she told herself, not for the first time. Nothing could go wrong.

Winter at the stables was so busy that the weeks leading up to Christmas passed by in no time at all. Brian and Carol carried on meeting 'by accident' for a coffee each time they had a session. Charlotte branched out into riding several of the horses, and they were flourishing on it. Ella felt a secret pang of envy, watching her schooling Tor in the early morning sunshine.

'Don't you ever wish you could just jump on and head up across the hill?'

Charlotte was angling to be allowed to ride Tor outside the confines of the indoor arena. On a day like this, Ella could understand why. The air was crisp, the sunlight filtering in thin, pale rays through the hedge. She laid a hand on the frost-covered wooden gate and felt the sensation of the cold beneath her fingers. Riding – at one with a horse, across the hills, where the animals ignored her and she could see deer up close and red kites flying overhead – was the thing that had always made her feel most alive. Her chest ached with longing, but –

'I've told you before,' and her voice was slightly sharp, despite trying to modulate her tone. 'I can't ride.'

'Oh God, I'm sorry, I didn't mean –' Charlotte turned Tor away across the school and Ella felt an immediate pang of guilt.

'I know.' Her tone was conciliatory. 'I tell you what, one day, between Christmas and New Year, I'll walk the dogs up the hill and you can hack out with me – if you're not busy?'

'Oh my God. I'd love that.'

'Consider it an early Christmas present.'

The joy on Charlotte's face was enough for Ella to know she'd done the right thing.

Chapter Twenty-two

Harry

Harry, Jenny and Lou sat together, watching Hope opening her presents with the uncontained joy that only an eight-year-old can. She had been entranced by the bite marks in the carrot she'd left out for Rudolph, and was determined that she was going to keep it in the freezer forever as a happy memory. Right now she was upstairs, clearly more than a little bit over-excited, watching one of her favourite Disney movies on her iPad. It was only half past nine, and Harry was so tired that his eyeballs throbbed. He wondered if he could sneak off to bed for an hour before lunch, but decided he'd better give Jenny a hand with the cooking instead and let her have a rest.

'I'll do the veg and make the potatoes,' he said, firmly, steering Jenny away from the baking hot Aga.

'This thing has a bloody mind of its own,' she said, sitting down at the kitchen table and putting her head in her hands.

'It's just a case of getting used to it.'

'It's been ages,' said Jenny, despairingly, 'and I still haven't tamed it.'

She looked hot, and tired, and cross. Harry wondered if the shine of rural life was wearing off a little bit. He thought about her lovely house back in Norfolk with its kitchen, range cooker and double sink. It was her pride and joy. Maybe renting this place for six months had been a bit excessive.

'That –' Harry lifted up the door and slid a pan into the warming oven, 'is pretty much average for a meal cooked on an Aga. I grew up with one.'

He had, that is, until his mum had left. He'd been ten years old when she'd moved out of the huge, draughty house that sat like a ship in the middle of the Broads and into a centrally heated, all-mod-cons bungalow on the edge of Thetford. The first thing she'd bought was a microwave. He'd loved the half of the week he spent at her house, where – freed from the shackles of that bloody monster (the Aga, she meant, he thought) – she let him eat ready-to-heat dinners every night after school.

'You sit down.'

Jenny flopped onto a kitchen chair, and he poured her a glass of Bucks Fizz. 'Here, have that. It'll perk you up.'

'Are you joining me?'

'Not yet.' He made a strong black coffee and pottered around the kitchen, organizing plates and serving dishes.

'What time are we expecting our *mystery guest*?'

It had delighted Hope so much that she had *a secret surprise* – as she'd called it approximately five hundred times already that morning – that Jenny had agreed that yes, they could keep the identity of their lunch guest a secret. Harry didn't let on that he'd overheard her telling Lou in a stage whisper loud enough to be picked up in the next village that *the horse lady was coming for Christmas dinner.*

'I said midday. You've done a good job of keeping up the pretence.' Jenny smiled up at him.

'I'm dying to meet this miracle worker.'

'Can't believe you've not met her yet. She only lives up the lane.'

'I know –'

He knew exactly why he hadn't. He could have taken Hope up the other day when she went for a session after the last day of school, but he'd cried off, saying he'd go to the supermarket instead, pretending to himself he was being helpful. The truth that he didn't like to admit was that he felt a bit put out that Jenny had – once again – muscled in. He'd scaled back work, was trying his hardest to be there for Hope, but it wasn't as easy as all that, finding a way in.

Lou was dozing on the sofa, worn out by their supremely early morning. Harry settled down by the fire after he'd finished sorting out the kitchen, and with Hope curled up in the crook of his arm, read her stories from her new book until he dozed off and she crept away, finger to her lips, giggling conspiratorially with her Grandma.

The knock at the door woke Harry. He jumped up from the armchair with a jolt, catching sight of himself in the mirror. His hair was standing on end, his jaw shadowed with stubble. And he had bags under his eyes big enough for a transatlantic flight. He rubbed his face with his hands, yawning so widely that his jaw cracked, and braced for impact. He could hear Hope scampering across the slate floor of the hall to answer the door before anyone else could.

'That'll be our visitor,' said Jenny, appearing from the kitchen with a tea towel over her shoulder.

She opened the door into the hall and he heard voices – excited chatter from Hope, and –

He looked and saw a dark-haired woman bent low over a picture Hope was holding. Her hair was loose and tumbled in waves over her shoulders, and he couldn't help noticing the curve of her waist and hip in the clinging turquoise top she was wearing with her jeans. She straightened, and turned to say hello.

'Harry, this is Ella.'

Chapter Twenty-three

Harry

There was a moment of silence which seemed to last forever. Her hazel eyes widened, the freckles on her nose
standing out as she first went ghostly pale, and then a
faint blush stained her cheeks. She raised a hand as if to
cover her mouth, then dropped it again, arranging her
face into one of polite greeting.

'Ella, this is Daddy. He's good at cooking and he says
he won't burn the turkey like Grandma keeps doing with
all the dinners since we lived here.'

Hope giggled, and took his hand.

'Shall I take your coat?' Jenny lifted it from Ella's
hands and hung it on the peg by the stairs. 'Would you
like a drink?'

Nobody seemed to be aware of what was happening.
He couldn't find the words to say what needed to be said.

The blood was thrumming in his ears, drowning out
Jenny, who was still chattering away. Ella was standing
frozen to the spot as well, her dark eyes huge and her lips
parted as if she, too, was trying to find the appropriate
response.

He felt as if he was standing outside of his body watching the scene. There he stood, his mouth hanging open wordlessly. His T-shirt was untucked, and his hair was mussed up from where he'd been asleep on the sofa, completely oblivious to the fact his whole world was about to be spun on its axis once again.

'Come on, Daddy. We can show Ella the baking kit I got from Santa.'

His daughter's voice broke the spell and he looked stupidly at his hand as Hope darted forward, tugging him towards the kitchen door.

'That sounds – lovely,' said Ella, her voice faint.

Hope clapped her hands in delight and danced on the spot.

'I'm so excited you're here. Ooh! Can I show you the book I got about horses? I've been drawing pictures of them and learning all the points of the horse so you can test me. I know them almost all by heart already.'

'Take a breath, sweetheart,' said Lou, appearing in the hallway at last. He reached out a hand to Ella and shook hers. 'Very nice to meet the famous Ella-from-the-stables at last. I have to confess I was expecting someone – older.'

'Lou.' Jenny gave him a sideways look.

'What?' he said, mildly. 'Hope said she was *quite old*.'

'She is,' said Hope, matter-of-factly. 'She must be at *least* twenty-five, and that's really old.'

Thirty-three, Harry found himself thinking. Birthday the nineteenth of October. He still hadn't uttered a word.

'Anyway, can you come up and see the horse book now?' Hope tugged at Ella's arm.

She smiled. 'I'd love to.'

She caught his eye for the briefest moment, and he felt a maelstrom of emotions churning up, threatening to boil over. But he could see Hope was on the verge of over-excitement – and he was the adult.

He tipped his head slightly in a nod of welcome.

'Nice to meet you, Ella.' There was a tiny inflection in her name which nobody in the room but her would catch. She looked down at the floor, avoiding his gaze. He turned on his heel and headed back into the kitchen, closing the door behind him.

Harry swore under his breath as a splash of boiling hot goose fat splashed on his arm while he rearranged the trays in the Aga. The turkey was out and resting, covered with towels, on the worktop.

'Ella has the patience of a saint,' Jenny said, walking into the kitchen.

She pulled out the drawer and started counting cutlery for the meal, piling it on the table beside them. Each tiny metallic clatter set his nerves on edge a little bit more. He felt like he was going to explode. If the place had any mobile reception, he'd text Holly and say – what the hell *would* he say? He'd dropped Holly back at the station a couple of days before – she'd stayed longer than expected; weeks, rather than days – because (there have to be some perks, she'd said, rolling her eyes) being self-employed, she could. Nothing had happened between them. He'd thought, watching her laughing with Jenny and Lou one lunchtime as they sat in the Lion pub, that it would have been the simplest thing on earth. Hope adored her. She was part of the family. She was the link that would have kept Sarah alive, in a strange way. But Sarah was gone, and no matter how easy it would have been, he'd realized that it wasn't the answer. He still wasn't sure what was.

They'd had a lovely time together with Hope, and she'd headed home on the train, giving him a kiss and hug goodbye that had left him standing on the platform wondering. Holly was hardly the sort of person who'd be sitting around waiting on the off chance he was going to make a move. And he hadn't, because something had stopped him. And now – this.

He shook his head. He'd placed his hands flat on the marble-effect worktop, trying to find some sort of balance, but it wasn't working. What the hell was she doing here?

'Right,' said Jenny cheerfully. 'That's the cutlery sorted. I'll set the table here, shall I?'

The cottage was so small, and it seemed to be shrinking. Right now she was upstairs with Hope, but in a moment she was going to emerge and the walls were closing in on him.

'I'm just going to nip out the back for a sec, get a bit of fresh air.'

'Course, love,' said Jenny. She looked up at the clock.

'I thought we could eat at two-ish. D'you think the veg will all be ready by then?'

'Yep.'

If she was surprised at his brief response, she didn't say anything.

He closed the back door behind him and leaned against the centuries-old wall of the cottage. This place must've seen some dramas in its time. Think, think – there had to be a way to deal with this. What would Holly say? She knew – through Sarah – about his previous marriage. It hadn't been a conscious decision to keep it from Jenny and Lou, but it just hadn't ever come up. And then time had passed. How was he supposed to casually drop into the conversation the fact that they'd inadvertently invited his ex-wife for dinner?

Ella was still as beautiful as ever. He allowed himself a moment to recall the long hair hanging down her back, brushed out as it never was when she was working with the horses. She'd been dressed in slim-fitting dark jeans and a light green embroidered top that set off her eyes. She hadn't changed at all.

She looked just as she had the day he'd walked into the newspaper shop, still thinking there might be hope of reconciliation, and seen the words trapped behind the local newspaper billboard in six-inch-high letters.

*WIFE NAMES HUSBAND AS CULPRIT IN
DEATH CRASH*

The old feelings curled up tightly in his stomach. He realized that he was standing with his hands by his side, his nails biting into his palms and his pulse pounding in his ears.

How could he be so stupid? How could he forget the damage she'd caused with her careless accusations, the whispers and pointing at work, long after the hearing had found that the crash was nothing more than a heart-breaking series of coincidences. *No smoke without fire,* people had said. *If he didn't do it, why did his wife leave him?*

And now – after he'd rebuilt his life, patched up his heart, spent hours in therapy – she was here. It was like some sort of sick joke on the part of the universe.

He released his fingers, stretching them out, feeling the points of pain in his hands where the nails had been pressed hard into his flesh.

His instinctive reaction was to walk back in there, tell Ella to get the hell out of this house and close the door behind her. But if he did that, he'd traumatize Hope, who was showing real signs of progress – she was happier in herself, more confident, and she was sleeping much better. The horses were helping her to relax and express her feelings. No, he'd have to take it a bit slower than that. He had no idea what Ella's next move was going to be, but he was ready for it. He wasn't going to let it spoil Hope's day. He'd be the perfect son-in-law to Lou and Jenny, and the kindest, most attentive father to Hope that he could possibly be. And as soon as the last mince pie was eaten, he'd open the door, see Ella out, and find a way to make sure that nobody in the house ever saw her again. There was no other way.

Chapter Twenty-four

Ella – and Harry

Upstairs, Ella was trying to listen to Hope explaining a very long and complicated joke she'd invented about fetlocks and forelocks, whilst also trying to hold her mobile up to the skylight in Hope's bedroom so she could send a text message. There was one bar of reception, and if she could just get the angle right, it would . . . *swoosh*.

'Thank the lord,' she said out loud. It had sent. Calls tended to work, but messages were a different thing altogether. Now all it had to do was reach the intended recipient, and she could escape. And my God, did she need to escape. Her heart was thumping so hard in her chest that she'd felt it must be obvious to everyone in the room. She'd walked in, already apprehensive, and –

She'd often thought about bumping into her ex-husband in the street, or in a bar one day. It had been a long-held daydream. She'd be smartly dressed and articulate, cool and in control. Definitely not in muddy jodhpurs with unbrushed hair. Thank God she was at least reasonably respectable today, having recycled the outfit she'd worn for a Christmas Eve-Eve drink at the pub with Lissa and some of her workmates from the school.

In the daydream version of events, she'd tell him she was sorry for the way she'd behaved, that she knew now that her reaction was one grounded in an unbearable pain – emotional and physical. That she'd been grieving her father and the riding career she'd dreamed of since childhood. That if she could turn back time she'd take back every hurtful word she'd said, and –

'Which lord are you thanking?' Hope's voice was clear and inquisitive.

She shook her head, returning from the fantasy world where she could organize everything just so and the man she'd once married wasn't sitting downstairs.

'It's just a saying.'

'But why did you say it? There isn't a lord here.'

Ella didn't have the brain capacity to explain. She was twisting a lock of hair in her fingers, trying to work out how on earth she could get through the meal if Lissa didn't return the rescue call. What if she'd turned off her phone for the day in one of her mad digital detox missions she'd been reading about in *Glamour* magazine? Or what if it sat, ignored, while she played Monopoly with her family and they drank their way through the crates of fizzy wine that Lissa had bought to lubricate the occasion?

'Do you mean the lord like Jesus?' Hope carried on

fiddling with the plastic horse figures. 'Do you believe in angels?'

The thing she'd learned about Hope was that her insatiable appetite to know more, read more, absorb every bit of information like a tiny little eight-year-old sponge meant that every single new word was catalogued and filed away in her astonishing brain. She had a vocabulary far beyond her years.

'Why were you sending a message?'

'I was just checking on the horses.' The lie resolved itself in her head, and she tried it out loud. 'In fact, one of them isn't feeling very well, so I might have to go straight after we've had Christmas dinner.'

'Awww.'

'I know.' She gave what she hoped was a sad smile. 'But the horses can't tell us when they don't feel well, so we have to listen to them by watching what they're doing. That's why we have to stay close.'

Hope nodded solemnly. Even after a few short weeks of working with the horses, she had developed an empathic bond with them.

'My bedroom is nice, isn't it?'

'It's lovely.'

It was low-beamed with sloping ceilings, and a little pine bed sat in the middle, flanked by matching wooden drawers and a dressing table which was piled high with plastic model horses and Hope's drawing and painting kit. Ella's stomach swooped with nerves. She'd messaged Lissa:

MASSIVE SOS I need a rescue call.

That ought to do it. They'd had the deal for pretty much as long as they'd known each other. Ella had barely ever used her side of the bargain, but Lissa was forever getting into bad dates and using her friend as an excuse to bail after the first drink. It was time to call in the favour.

'Are you two all right up there? Ella, can I get you a drink?' Jenny's voice floated up the wooden stairs of the cottage.

'That would be lovely, thank you.'

'Let's go and see if we can have some of the nice Christmas stuff. Grandma's bought lots of bottles of *ginger beer*.' Hope looked as if she'd have been happy enough with Christmas if she'd had nothing else.

Harry's face felt incredibly odd. It was as if it was formed out of plasticine and he couldn't quite get it to work properly.

'Would you like a drink?' he said stiffly, as Hope towed Ella by the hand into the kitchen. He took off the oven gloves he was wearing and hung them precisely on the rail of the Aga before opening the fridge, avoiding eye contact. In the little utility room, he could hear Jenny and Lou bickering good-naturedly about the turkey and where to carve it.

'Yes, please,' said Ella, with feeling. 'But only a tiny one. I'm driving.'

'Me too, please, Harry.'

He turned away, opening still-unfamiliar cupboards to find the champagne glasses. They were in a box, still wrapped in their protective packaging from the move. He opened them and busied himself with unwrapping and carefully washing and drying each one. The air was thick with words unspoken and he still couldn't bring himself to look at her, or even speak directly to her. How could she be here? It didn't make sense.

'That's not ginger beer,' Hope said, as he twisted the cork off a bottle of Mumm he'd been given as part of a corporate award package. He couldn't stand the stuff, and for some reason at this time of year it was handed out left, right and centre. Jenny wouldn't drink on her own, and Lou was of course on a strict diet following his heart trouble, so the cupboard in the cottage was groaning with bottles.

'No, it's not ginger beer,' he said, grimly. He poured the champagne into a glass and handed it to Hope.

'Give that to your friend, darling.' He turned away as Hope carefully passed the glass to Ella, and busied himself pouring drinks for everyone else.

The grandmother clock on the wall whirred in the silence, clicked the hour, and chimed two o'clock.

'What shall we drink to?' said Hope, echoing the phrase she'd heard adults saying. She held up her champagne glass of ginger beer and beamed at him. His heart melted and he smiled back at her, raising a matching glass of ginger beer.

Ella looked across at him fleetingly and the warmth in his heart chilled again instantly. He fixed her with a look which he hoped summed up everything he was feeling. God, he was so angry.

'Christmas!' sang Hope, loudly. 'Let's drink to having a nice Christmas.'

If Jenny or Lou noticed the chilly atmosphere, they didn't say a word. Dinner was served, the food was apparently delicious, and if anyone noticed that he served himself the smallest portion of everything and pushed it around his plate without swallowing a mouthful, again nothing was said. Hope ate four roast potatoes and then asked for a raw carrot, which she gnawed on 'like a reindeer'.

Ella seemed to be coping admirably, he noted. How could it be that she of all people owned a thriving equine therapy business? Jenny and Lou had been asking questions about it all the way through the meal, and he'd had to grit his teeth and nod politely in all the right places. He'd had to turn the snort of disbelief into a cough when Jenny proudly explained that Ella was a real inspiration for Hope. The idea of Ella providing therapy to traumatized people was almost impossible to imagine.

How could someone so utterly unforgiving possibly work as a professional in the counselling industry? He remembered with a stab of bitterness how she'd looked the day he'd seen her for the last time – and the things she'd said to him.

He noticed she kept checking her phone. Probably

looking for an out, he thought. But the reception here within the stone walls of the cottage was so hopeless that there wasn't much chance of anything making it through.

Eventually, after the main course, she excused herself to go to the loo. Hope hopped down from the table to assemble some Lego character she'd been given. Lou sat back and stretched – he still got tired in the afternoons, and they'd all been up for hours. He'd be off for a nap in a moment, and the pudding could wait until later.

As Harry got up to clear the table he noticed that Ella had barely touched a thing on her plate, either. He swept the leftover meal into the bin with grim satisfaction.

Call me. SOS. Help.

The bloody message wouldn't send. Ella had locked herself in the downstairs loo of the cottage, which was absolutely freezing, the stone walls damp with condensation. She held the phone up to the tiny window, but nothing happened.

Come on, she said to herself, think, *think*.

Perhaps I don't need to actually get a message in front of them for this lie to be feasible. They probably don't even care. They're hardly going to check the text for evidence. She tipped her head forward, resting her forehead against the cool glass of the mirror above the sink. This was like some sort of awful Christmas nightmare. Lissa still hadn't answered her bloody phone, and Ella had been in the loo so long it was starting to look awkward.

She pulled the chain and then ran the taps to make it sound like she'd been using the bathroom, then stopped midway across the room to stare at her phone in a studious manner, as if someone had just sent a message. It felt completely staged and artificial. She'd never been any good at drama at school and she could feel a blush prickling the back of her neck and creeping up her cheeks. Harry would know she was lying, if he remembered her as well as she remembered him – a strange sensation of nervousness fluttered in her stomach – but she couldn't let that stop her. He must want her gone as much as she wanted to be out of there.

She set her shoulders back and stepped into the kitchen, her voice coming out slightly higher than normal. She tried to sound just the right balance of casual and concerned.

'Oh Jenny, I'm so sorry to cut this afternoon short. I've had a message from Charlotte to say that one of the mares is looking a bit uncomfortable. I think I'd better go up and check her.'

Charlotte wasn't even there. Oh God, there went another lie.

'But we haven't had the Christmas pudding yet.' Hope's little face dropped. 'It's got flames.'

Ella squatted down to her level to look her in the eye. 'I know, Hope, and if I can get back I will –' *God, please don't strike me down for telling lies to a child* – 'but I need to make sure that Sweetbriar can be the best mummy she can for her foal.'

It was night-time dark outside already. If Jenny looked out she'd see that the lights at the farm were off, and put two and two together and start asking where Charlotte was and why she was up there in the dark.

'My mummy died.' Hope looked at her, steadily. Her eyes, Ella realized, were not the same chocolate brown as Harry's but instead a greener brown, ringed with dark circles.

'I know, sweetie. I'm sorry.'

'It's not your fault.' Hope pursed her lips thoughtfully and continued, 'We'd better make sure Sweetbriar doesn't die. Can I come?'

Ella shook her head. She looked up briefly and saw Harry standing, arms crossed, a nerve jumping in his cheek. His face was thunderous.

'Not today, but maybe very soon?' If she made it out of the door without Hope's tears falling, it would be a miracle.

'Tomorrow?' The little girl's lower lip was beginning to wobble.

'Sweetheart,' Jenny put an arm around her grand-daughter's shoulders and squeezed. 'How about we let Ella get back to check on the horses, and then we can work out some good dates and write them down on your new calendar?'

Hope nodded. She loved to know what was happening and when, and a huge laminated wall planner had proved one of her best Christmas presents. She'd already instructed Harry to hang it on the wall over her bed and gathered a load of stickers to decorate it.

'Shit.' She banged her hand on the steering wheel. 'Shit, shit, SHIT.'

The bloody Land Rover, temperamental at the best of times, whined and then went dead. She turned the key again, knowing perfectly well what was going to happen.

Bollocks, bollocks, shit. Ella leaned her head against the window, soaking her face with condensation.

Maybe if she just tried again after a moment.

There was a knock at the window

Afterwards, Harry had no idea why he'd been the one to say 'don't worry, I'll sort it'.

He curled his fingers around the keys, feeling their familiar weight. Was it because he wanted to make sure she was out of the way, so they could enjoy the last hours of Hope's eighth Christmas without him having to avoid Ella's eye or bite back angry comments about the past?

'I'll give you a lift.' His voice was stiff and formal.

'It just needs a jump start.' Ella had turned to look up at him from inside the battered Land Rover.

'Have you got jump leads?'

She'd shaken her head. 'They're in the barn.'

Maybe it was because – with her belted into the car – he could tell Ella, without having to look her in the eye, which felt dangerous, somehow, exactly what he thought of her. His jaw ached. He ran a hand across it and heard it cracking.

Ella reached back and picked up her long waxed coat from the back seat of the Land Rover.

'It's fine, it's only a walk up the hill.' She zipped it closed.

He shook his head. 'It's pouring with rain. Let me take you.'

'It's fine.' Her voice was tight with tension.

'It's a good ten-minute walk uphill.' He was getting soaked now, standing here arguing the toss with her. Water dripped down the neck of his shirt.

'OK. Fine.' She sounded defeated.

'What's happening?' Jenny appeared under an umbrella, the rain battering down and running on rivulets off the ends.

'Land Rover won't start. I'm going to give Ella a lift.'

'I said it was fine, but Ma – Harry insisted.' She flushed slightly. Bloody hell, she'd almost given the game away. He wasn't Mac. He was Harry – Hope's father. And someone she thought she'd left long behind in her past.

'Let's go then.' He knew it sounded curt. Jenny shot him an odd look. If he wasn't careful he'd have more explaining to do when he got home, and he was definitely not in the mood. What he wanted was a tumbler of whisky and a good hour staring into the flames of the log burner, trying to work out what the hell had happened and exactly how he felt.

Hope burst out of the door in her socks, running across the gravel towards Ella, who had climbed out of the Land Rover.

'I don't want you to go.' It was a wail, more than a sentence.

'Ella has to check the horses, sweetheart. I'll be back in five minutes, I promise.'

Hope twisted her mouth sideways, chewing on the inside of her cheek – it was something she'd always done when she was anxious. He bent down, pushing a strand of wet hair from her cheek.

'And if Sweetbriar is OK, will you bring Ella with you so we can play games and watch *Frozen* again?'

He closed his eyes briefly. He was torn between his own desperate need to get her out of the way, and the desire to do whatever it took to make his beloved girl happy.

'Pleeeeeease?'

He flashed her a brief smile, nodded and closed the door.

Chapter Twenty-five

Jenny

'What on earth's up with Harry?'

Back in the warmth of the cottage, Jenny settled down beside Lou on the sofa, picking up her mug of coffee and wrapping her hands around it. Hope was sitting on the armchair, her legs sprawled out over the sides, a pair of noise-cancelling headphones on. She was humming to herself and playing some sort of game on her iPad.

'Christmas effect.' Lou picked up the *Radio Times* and looked at the page, which he'd marked with highlighter pen.

'There's a thing on about reindeer in the Arctic Circle. Hope might like that. Shall we watch it?'

Jenny shook her head. 'She needs a bit of downtime. She's quite happy there.'

It was hard to work out how she could be a grandma when she still felt about eighteen inside. Her knees didn't, mind you, and neither did her back. All that bending up and down tending to the Aga (which she'd dreamed of for so many years, and refused to admit to Lou had turned out to be a huge, intractable lump of iron) had left her feeling stiff as an old ironing board. She'd have a bath later, when Hope was settled and Harry was back.

Hope shifted in her seat, so she was lying on her back on the seat of the floral armchair with her legs up against the back. It was one of her favourite positions – Jenny smiled, remembering it had been one of Sarah's, too. She felt, privately, that the reason she'd coped so well with Hope's particular needs was because her daughter was cut from the same cloth. It was easy to deal with Hope's mercurial moods, her strange fascinations, her need for space to do her own thing, because the apple hadn't fallen far from the tree. It was – her stomach clenched with the familiar hollow feeling of grief – as if she'd been left with an echo of Sarah.

She looked up at the photograph on the mantelpiece above the wood burner and smiled sadly. Living after the death of a child was a burden she'd managed to carry for five years now, but God, it was hard. So hard sometimes that grief would hit her with a wave that felt like she'd been struck in the back of the legs with a heavy axe, and her knees would just buckle underneath her. Once, when Sarah was only just gone, she'd crumpled onto a wooden pallet in Ikea of all places and wept desperate, gulping sobs – all because her beloved darling girl wasn't there to laugh about the ridiculous names of the products with her.

A tear rolled down her cheek, and she pushed it away with a finger. She'd hoped, secretly, that perhaps moving somewhere different would mean that this year the memories would let Hope have the sort of Christmas she should have – not one where she found Grandma weeping over the sprouts, or switching off the Festival of Nine Lessons and Carols on Radio Four on Christmas Eve because it reminded her all too painfully of the mince-pie baking sessions she and Sarah used to share.

The trouble with Christmas, it turned out, was that there was something about the familiar rituals that just drew attention to the loved ones who were no longer at the table. Perhaps that's why Harry had been so out of sorts – inviting someone he hadn't even met before to join them had seemed like a kind gesture by Hope. She'd been so touched by that that she'd dismissed all the other concerns around inviting someone into an occasion which always seemed to bring her emotions to the surface. The thing was, grief didn't fade away slowly year on year. It swelled up and burst out at the most unexpected and inconvenient of times.

Poor Harry. No wonder he'd looked so uncomfortable, shoving his dinner around on the plate and grunting monosyllables when they tried to engage him in conversation with Ella. She hoped he hadn't thought they were trying to set him up with her. She'd been wondering, in fact, if there was something more than friendship going on with him and Holly when she'd come to visit. It was probably wishful thinking, hoping that he'd end up with

Sarah's best friend. She'd been reading too many romance novels in the bath.

'Nice car.'

Ella finally spoke when she buckled her seatbelt. She didn't turn to look at him, but faced directly ahead.

'Thanks.'

He mirrored her movements and sat there for a moment in the dark, strapped into his seat. His heart was banging against his ribs so hard that he was sure she could hear it.

He switched on the ignition, and realized with a sigh of irritation that the inside of the car was fogged up with condensation after the temperature had dropped. This bloody car, he thought. He switched on the air conditioning and waited.

'What –' she began.

'I –' he said, at almost the same moment.

They both stopped, and an excruciating silence fell again. Harry reached down into the door pocket, desperately hoping there was a cloth or something he could use to clear the windscreen.

'Do you want me to just walk?' Ella said, quietly.

'Hardly.' His voice was a rasp.

'Look, there's no *horse crisis*. You know that, right?'

He flicked a glance at her profile in the darkness. It was lit softly by the outside lights of the cottage and in one brief, snatched look, he took in the features he'd tried so hard to forget.

He swallowed. 'I suspected as much.'

Ella's shoulders dropped slightly. 'I wouldn't have come if –'

He'd expected anger, and she seemed – regretful. She gnawed on a thumbnail and gazed out of the passenger seat window.

The windscreen was half cleared now, at least. If he crept up the lane, he'd be able to manage it – if he leaned forward and peered. But the idea of beetling up the hill like an elderly gent taking a day trip felt humiliating somehow, so he put a foot gently on the accelerator and revved the engine slightly, hoping to warm it up.

'I had no idea you'd be here.' Ella's words tumbled out, breathlessly. 'How was I supposed to know that of all the men in the world, *you* would be the father of the little girl who moved into the holiday cottage down the lane?'

She'd turned to look at him now, tucking a strand of hair behind her ear.

'I moved here to get away. I moved to Bron's house where nobody would find me and where I could start all over again.'

Harry put a hand to his head, dashing his forehead with his palm. No wonder the place had seemed naggingly familiar. He'd visited Bron's house with Ella when they first got together, spending a rainy weekend by the fire, only dashing out to pick up supplies. Bron had been away on a training course somewhere, and they'd enjoyed playing house and dreaming that one day they could live in a house like that. He shook his head and groaned.

'What is it?'

'I was stuck in traffic when Jenny sent me directions. She was supposed to be –'

'Moving to a different cottage in another village. I know.'

He'd worked so hard to get Ella out of his head and here she was, sitting in his bloody car.

'Llan-something, she said.'

'Everything's Llan-something in Wales. It means town.' Ella gave an ironic laugh.

The windscreen was clear, but they still hadn't moved.

He shook his head again, in disbelief, and pulled the car out of the driveway.

'This is it,' said Ella. The security light shone brightly in their eyes as he swung into the wide entrance of the farm, and in a moment Harry realized where he was.

'I remember now.'

She nodded.

'And you live – here?' He leaned forward, looking at the whitewashed cottage which sat on a ridge of slate. Inside – even with the car doors shut – he could hear the frantic barking of dogs.

'Ever since the –'

And in that second it flashed back into Harry's mind. He saw the headlines and remembered that the woman sitting in the car with him was the same person who'd gone to court and said that she couldn't remember what happened, but that she thought it must have been his fault the lorry crashed. Must have been his fault her father had died instantly. Must have been his fault the other driver had life-changing injuries and she broke her hip. He felt a twist of anger.

'You've been here all this time, and you never once wanted to get in touch and say sorry?'

'A million times, Harry.' Ella's voice was flat.

'You tried to *destroy* me for something I didn't do.' He could hear the blood rushing in his ears again. 'I didn't do it.'

'I know.'

It took a moment to listen. A moment to absorb what she'd just said.

'I blamed you, Harry, because it was easier than accepting that sometimes accidents just happen.'

'But the inquest said –'

'It said there was a fault in the traffic control system. Nobody could have helped what happened.'

He ran his hands through his hair, leaving it standing on end, giving a huge sigh.

'But you said to the paper it was my fault.'

'I told a journalist I couldn't help blaming you.' She looked at him, directly. 'And I will regret that for the rest of my life.

'You'd better go. Hope's waiting down there for the rest of Christmas.'

'She wants you there.'

'I know.'

'She's talked about you non-stop for weeks.'

Ella smiled. 'She is a lovely girl.'

'I know.'

She went to open the door, and he was surprised to find himself saying the words.

'Ella?'

She turned, the car door half-open. She looked at him as if to say *go on.*

'Would you . . . I know it's a lot to ask. But I'd stay out of the way. It's just – it's so nice to see her engaged with another person. We've had trouble getting Hope to talk to strangers at all, and she seems to genuinely want to spend time in your company.'

'I don't think so, Mac.'

Their eyes met for a second. Nobody had used that nickname for him since their divorce.

'You bloody well owe me,' he exploded, banging his hand on the steering wheel. Something in the intimacy of that moment had opened a floodgate. 'Fuck, Ella. You put me through hell.'

She dropped her head again. 'I know.'

'Come back. It doesn't matter about us. They don't know. I just want –' he ran a hand through his hair, realizing it was soaked – 'I need Hope to have a good day. I'm trying to get things right at last.'

'At last?'

'I've been pretty useless. She deserves better.' He

watched her chewing on her lip, and knew then she was undecided. 'Please?'

'OK.' She opened the car door and got out.

'What are you doing?'

'Getting the jump leads.'

She ran across the yard to the barn and slid open the heavy wooden door. A light flickered on in the gathering dusk, and she emerged a few minutes later. 'OK.' She clicked her seatbelt fastened once again. 'Let's do this.'

'What will I say?' Ella stood on the doorstep of the cottage, biting her lip.

'Tell them it was a false alarm. They don't have a clue about horses.' Harry turned the doorknob and they stepped inside.

'About –' she stumbled over the word. 'Us. I meant about us.'

Harry shook his head. 'Nothing. Not now. God, not now.'

'Ella!' Hope gave a little shriek of joy and did a dance of excitement on the mat. 'You came back!'

It was lovely to see her so animated. When she compared the Hope of now to the frightened shadow she'd caught hiding in the hedge just a couple of months ago, it was hard to believe she was the same girl.

'Will you sit next to me? Grandma's making hot chocolate with cream and marshmallows and we're going to watch *Frozen*.'

'I'd love to.'

Jenny dropped a hand on her shoulder as she headed for the kitchen. 'I'm glad you could come back,' she said, giving her a warm squeeze.

'Me too.'

'Me three,' chirruped Hope. 'Which one is your favourite, Ella – Elsa or Anna?'

'I don't know. I've never seen *Frozen*.'

'You've *what*?' said Harry. He looked at her with his dark eyebrows raised in surprise. 'I thought everyone in the whole *world* had seen *Frozen* at least five hundred and forty-seven times.'

'Five hundred and forty-*eight*, actually,' said Hope, giggling.

Ella shook her head. 'Well, if you two are the experts, perhaps you could fill me in.' She moved along the sofa a little so there was room for Harry to take his place beside a delighted Hope, who sat between them like the filling of a particularly happy sandwich.

'I might nip off for a quick post-prandial snooze,' said Lou, directing a wink at Ella. 'I've seen this film more times than I care to admit.'

They sat by the light of the fire together and watched the film in contented silence. Jenny popped in once, to deliver a cup of coffee to the adults, but disappeared straight afterwards. Ella was surprised at how natural it felt to be there.

Chapter Twenty-six

Ella

It was two days after Christmas, and Ella was standing in the stable yard, hands on hips, trying to work out where to begin. She'd slacked off for a couple of days and, with Charlotte on a surprise trip to Disneyland with her grandparents – slightly at odds, Ella thought, with her rainbow-haired, many-piercings appearance – there was nobody but her to get everything done. And the yard looked a bit like Lissa's house, only with tangles of haynets instead of discarded tights lying all over the place. She'd been glad to get home after the shock of Christmas Day. Spending time with the horses was the company she wanted – they didn't ask anything of her, and she needed the headspace.

The clatter of the gate opening alerted her and the dogs at the same moment. Hope was there, crouched on the ground, laughing as both dogs prostrated themselves on the floor to be tickled.

'I'm sorry.' She heard Harry before she saw him. He stood in the gateway, one hand on the post. He rubbed his jaw, looking uncomfortable. 'We were supposed to be going for a walk up the hill, and –'

'And I said we should come in so Harry could see the horses. Can I show him?' Hope's voice was clear and carrying, and – confident. How could Ella resist?

'Of course.' She spun round, mainly to give herself time to gather her thoughts, and headed back towards the yard where the horses were waiting. There was a clatter of hooves and a shuffling of straw as they peered over their stable doors to see who had come to visit, and what the likelihood was of some extra treats. Little Muffin, hearing Hope's voice, pierced the air with a high pitched whinny.

'Help yourself.' Ella tried to smile, but she knew it didn't meet her eyes. Harry held back, looking just as uncomfortable as she felt. Hope, oblivious, ran towards Muffin and threw her arms around his neck, burying her face in his long mane. She watched Harry's face soften then and he stepped towards Hope, putting a hand on her shoulder.

'So this is the famous Muffin.'

Hope nodded. Muffin nudged hopefully at her arm, looking for treats.

'Very nice to meet you, Muffin,' said Harry, solemnly. He caught Ella's eye for a moment, then looked away in an instant, turning back to look at the pony.

She busied herself, picking up a broom and carrying on with the tasks she had set herself for the morning, but it was impossible to work. She felt painfully aware of

Harry's presence, and conscious as well that Hope might pick up on her tension. She didn't want to undo all the progress they'd made.

'I'm going to put the kettle on,' she found herself saying. It slipped out almost before she knew what she'd done. 'Would you like a coffee?'

'That would be great,' said Harry.

Inside, she set the kettle on the hotplate of the Aga to boil and busied herself gathering everything onto a tray to take out to the stables. Hope could have some apple juice, and there were probably some chocolate biscuits left over somewhere. She pulled open the cupboard. Marmalade, the stable cat, was dozing inside on a pile of tea towels.

'You should be out earning your keep,' Ella tutted at him. He opened one lazy eye and gave a small chirrup of agreement before going back to sleep.

Ella carried the loaded tray outside and set it down on the top of a bale of wood shavings. 'Here you are.'

'Ooh, biscuits,' said Hope.

'Coffee?' Ella lifted the cafetière. It kept her going on winter days – it was double-walled against the cold, so she made a huge pot mid-morning to sustain her until lunchtime. Charlotte preferred to drink vast quantities of Diet Coke, swigging it from a bottle which was never far from her side.

'Thanks.' Harry's eyes met hers briefly as he took a sip. It was only then that she realized she'd handed it to him black, without thinking, knowing how he took it.

'Oh –' she added. 'There's sugar there. I mean, if you want it.'

'I don't,' said Harry. He gave a grim smile. 'Can't stand the stuff.'

Ella, who knew that, too, hid her face behind her mug and took a sip of too-hot coffee, which made her cough.

'Of course.'

'Can I have another biscuit?'

Hope was so cheerful and happy. Ella passed the packet over. 'Have two.'

'So –' Harry cleared his throat. 'Equine therapy.'

Ella nodded.

'How does it work, exactly? I was thinking of the stuff they do with Riding for the Disabled, but it's not that, is it?'

'Everyone thinks that.' Ella reached underneath Sweetbriar's mane and scratched her neck, smiling as the mare reached forward, nudging Harry on the arm. She was grumpy at the best of times, but now, heavily in foal, her mood was only alleviated with continual attention. Ella carried on rubbing the mare's neck.

'If you're trying to get a horse to do something and you're too nervous, or aggressive, they just won't do anything. So if I'm working with adults, I get them working through a course of obstacles. They have to get the horse to follow them.'

'On a lead rein?' Harry looked interested.

'No, at liberty. Free.'

'How do you do that?'

'Trust,' Ella said. She glanced down at the concrete floor, pushing a piece of straw with her toe. They'd strayed into uncomfortable territory.

'So if I want Muffin to do something with me, I have to use my body language to show him,' said Hope.

'Of course,' said Harry, with a slightly-too-hearty laugh. 'That sounds very interesting, darling.'

'The thing is,' Ella continued, realizing as she did that the spiel she used to explain the therapy to potential clients was leading her down a dangerous path, 'horses are non-judgemental. They don't care about your past, or what's going on in your life today. It's easier to open up around a horse and share your problems.'

Harry dropped a hand on the top of Hope's head. 'Right, my lovely, we should let Ella get on. I'm sure she's got lots to do.'

'Awww,' said Hope, twisting away and casting a hopeful glance at Ella through her long lashes. 'I don't want to go yet.'

'I tell you what,' Ella found herself saying. 'Why don't we show your daddy what we do with Muffin?'

She had no idea why she'd said it, but she felt an overwhelming urge to prove herself, somehow, to Harry. To show him that what she did made a difference to people. And to apologize, somehow, for what had happened in the past. It would take more than that, but perhaps it might be a step towards showing him that she wasn't the same person any more. He looked surprised at her offer, but Hope was predictably delighted. She stood back, allowing Hope to fasten the rope onto Muffin's head collar and take the lead, walking beside him towards the indoor arena.

'She looks so confident.' Harry held back, walking parallel to Ella.

'Muffin is a good teacher.'

Harry raised his eyebrows, but didn't reply.

Chapter Twenty-seven

Harry

Hope walked along in front of them, carefully holding onto the lead rope with two hands. As they reached the sliding door of the indoor school she stopped and Muffin stood beside her, waiting patiently. Harry stood back, watching, not interfering. This was exactly what Hope had needed for so long.

Ella went ahead then and slid the bolt, pushing the heavy door open.

Hope marched around the yard with the same confidence he'd always admired in Ella when she was younger and working at the dressage yard in her spare time. She would have huge, seventeen-hand-high performance horses following her around like pet dogs. It made sense that she'd gone into work like this, combining her love of horses with her fascination for psychology and human behaviour.

And although he was still full of anger towards her, he had to admit that she seemed to adore Hope. He stood back, watching them from the side of the indoor arena, while Ella led her around on the back of Muffin, patiently explaining how to sit up straight and reminding her to use her hands and legs to gently guide the pony where she wanted her to go.

'Can I have a ride on my own?' Hope said, as they approached him.

'I don't know, my darling. Can she?'

'If you're happy to let her, she's more than capable. I wouldn't let her at this age without a parent's permission.'

Their eyes met and for a moment something hung in the air.

'Just walk round once, then. And remember to keep those hands super gentle.'

Hope's face scrunched up in absolute joy. She set off, talking to Muffin, concentrating hard. Muffin, who knew the drill, walked very slowly and carefully around the outside track of the arena, aware that he had precious cargo on his back.

'She's got a natural talent.'

'And a good teacher.' Harry looked at Ella for a moment and she dropped her gaze, looking at the floor.

He found himself filling the silence. 'I met Sarah – her mum – when Hope was three months old.' It felt uncomfortable, somehow, bringing Sarah and Ella together in a conversation. It was as if he was introducing them, or something. He rubbed the back of his neck as he continued. 'We got together around the time my mum died. We met at the – she was having a check-up at the oncologist.'

Ella glanced across at Hope, making sure she was OK.

'And after – after – well, I didn't think I'd meet anyone else.'

Ella shifted from one foot to the other, gathering her hair up in a bunch at the back of her neck before letting it fall. And then she looked up at him, steadily, with the eyes he remembered so well. She'd barely changed.

'She was incredible. Kind. You can see it in Hope.'

Ella smiled, and together they watched as Hope carefully negotiated the far corner. Muffin was taking his job incredibly seriously and they were moving just above the speed of a snail.

'Anyway,' he said, and the words tumbled out, 'she died, and Hope was only three. Her dad had been pretty much out of the picture from the moment she was born, and he was happy to sign over parental responsibility to me.'

'But Jenny and Lou are looking after her so you can work?'

'It's – it was – it's –' he stammered. 'That was sort of the theory, but –'

'You don't have to talk about this if you don't want to,' said Ella, gently.

He shook his head. 'I do. It's just – well.' He dropped his gaze to the floor. 'I've always worked away a lot. And after Sarah died, I – it just seemed like maybe me being around wasn't the best thing for anyone. I need to try and undo the mess I've made of being her father.'

'You haven't made a mess, as far as I can see. She loves you very much.'

And he loved her to the moon and back, as they said every bedtime. The trouble was – and he knew this, even if he couldn't say it out loud – he was frightened to let himself be there for her completely. Frightened he'd mess up being a parent, like his father had done. Jenny and Lou had taken over so *competently* that it felt, a lot of the time, as if there wasn't any space for him. And Hope was their only link with Sarah. How was he supposed to find a place for himself in all of that?

He took a step back and pulled out his phone, distancing himself. It felt so natural to talk to Ella, but he had to remember that she wasn't the person he used to know. When they'd finished the session he hurried Hope home, leaving Ella standing in the yard with a confused expression on her face.

Chapter Twenty-eight

Jenny

Jenny and Lou were wrapped up in scarves and hats against a sideways wind. They made their way along an almost-deserted high street, heading for the cafe. The space between Christmas and New Year seemed to stretch out forever, and they'd left Harry at home with Hope, watching *Frozen* for the millionth time. He'd come home in an odd mood, but Hope was full of excitement, telling them how they'd been to the stables and she'd been allowed to ride Muffin. Harry had been monosyllabic, clearly not wanting to discuss it.

The air was icy on Jenny's face, but it was better than another afternoon sitting at home watching repeats on television and helping herself to the chocolates Lou couldn't eat.

'No other bugger is out in this,' grumbled Lou.

'You're supposed to be getting out and about, the doctor said, and so that's what we're doing.' Jenny pushed the door open and inhaled the welcoming warm scent of freshly baked cakes and coffee.

'Bloody freezing out there,' said Connie. Jenny smiled

to herself. She'd never get tired of listening to the Welsh accent. If they stayed – she allowed Lou to pull her out a chair and sat down, unbuttoning her coat – she'd like to try and learn the language. There'd been something in the Sunday magazine supplement the other week about learning a second language being good for keeping the brain active. She hadn't shared her secret hope with Lou yet – but she'd surprised even herself with how fond she was of the quirky little village.

'What'll it be?' Connie asked, coming over with a pen and her little notepad. 'Or do you need a minute?'

'I'll have a ham toastie and a cup of tea, please. I wasn't sure you'd be open.'

'Oh God, I can't stand this dead time between Christmas and New Year. I'd rather keep busy.' Connie brushed down her apron in a brisk manner.

'And I'll have a vegetable soup and a wholemeal roll,' Lou rolled his eyes in a long-suffering way. 'And *no* butter.'

'How are you feeling today, Lou?'

'Not too bad, thanks.'

'How's it going with Alan and the Neighbourhood Watch meeting plans?'

'Good, thanks.' Lou sat back in his chair.

Jenny took a sharp intake of breath. She could predict what was coming next. She'd been on the verge of asking Connie when the Welsh language evening course she was running would be starting again.

'Police cuts,' he began, 'That's the problem.'

'You know what, Lou, I completely agree with you,' said Connie. She pulled up a chair from the neighbouring table and sat down. 'Now what we need to do is take matters in to our own hands. We don't have a local bobby any more, and I've always thought Neighbourhood Watch was a bit nosey-parker-like, but –'

'Times have changed.' Lou finished her sentence.

'They have that.' Connie gave a decisive nod. 'Ffion Jenkins from the primary school had her bag nicked out of her car last week. That sort of thing never used to happen around here. We've got a bloody crime wave on our hands.'

'Well, let's hope it's not quite at that level yet,' said Lou. Jenny hid a smile, bending down to look in her handbag for a tissue. She felt torn. She loved Llanidaeron and the beauty of the countryside, and she'd even fallen for the cottage she hadn't chosen. It was wonderful to see Hope settling – and even Harry seemed happier. He'd taken her back up to Ella's stables again. In fact, everyone seemed to be finding little moments of happiness. If Lou got caught up in this Neighbourhood Watch scheme, he might well find that he enjoyed life here after all – but at the same time, she felt a tightening in her stomach. What if he pushed himself too hard and ended up in hospital again?

'Anyway –' Connie was still talking, she realized – 'I'd better get your food on and stop talking.'

'Just give me a shout and let me know when the first meeting is.'

Jenny looked at her husband beadily as Connie bustled away. He had the expression on his face of a man who knew he'd been caught out.

'It's not work.'

She shook her head. They'd been through so much together in – it seemed almost impossible to believe it, but it was forty-four years they'd been married. Next year was the big wedding anniversary. If he didn't work himself into the ground.

'I don't want you overdoing it,' she said warningly.

Lou put a hand on hers and another beneath her chin. He lifted her face up, gently, so she was looking directly into his eyes.

'My darling. I love you. I love you so much I'm sitting in the back end of bloody nowhere and all my golfing mates are off on a trip to Portugal this week and I could be there. I love you so much that I will do whatever – whatever – it takes to make you believe that I have absolutely no desire to pop my clogs for a long time yet.'

Jenny swallowed. She could feel her chin wobbling slightly and the last thing she wanted was to start weeping in Connie's tearoom. She nodded against his hand.

'I know.'

'I've got to do something. If my suspicions are correct, you're secretly hoping I'll fall for this place and want to stay.'

She tried not to laugh. He knew her far too well. He curled his hand under her hair, around the nape of her neck, and leaned over, surprising her with a kiss.

'I adore you, and I have every intention of being around for a good long time to come. We've got Hope to think of, for one thing.'

'Here you are,' Connie slid a tray between them. 'Nice to see a bit of romance.' She gave them a wink and made herself scarce.

Jenny busied herself with stirring her tea before asking, 'D'you reckon something's going on with Harry and Holly?'

'I don't know –' Her husband paused for a moment, spreading low-fat spread on his wholemeal roll and pulling a face at it, before taking a mouthful and grimacing at the taste.

'I think there's definitely a bit of chemistry there, don't you?'

Lou thought for a moment.

'She's coming back over for a visit in January, isn't she?'

'Mmm.'

'I know you,' he said, chuckling. 'That "mmm" has a double meaning.'

'I could be wrong. It would be nice, though, don't you think? If he ended up with Sarah's best friend?'

'I dunno. Is it nice, or is it a bit close to home?'

Jenny shook her head, tutting. 'For goodness' sake, you. I think it's high time Harry found himself someone else. It's been far too long.'

'Well, whatever's going on, I'm glad he's hanging around for the rest of the week. I wasn't expecting that.'

'No, he's normally off like a shot.'

Jenny felt a bit guilty. It wasn't that Harry didn't love Hope, but she suspected that he felt somehow that he had to play second fiddle to them as grandparents. The truth was, however, that both she and Lou considered him to be just as much a part of Hope's life as if he'd been there at the conception. More than could be said for the waste-of-space sperm donor (she smiled to herself at that, remembering that was the name Sarah had always given him).

What she hoped Harry realized was that Hope *needed* him to be a major part of her life. The trouble was that you couldn't force someone to get over their own fears and step into a role, and over the last five years since – since Sarah – Harry had definitely had his own demons to fight.

But hopefully that was all in the past now. He seemed to be enjoying spending time with Hope. Harry worked hard – far harder than he needed to – and she'd watched Lou doing the same thing, working himself into a heart attack and intensive care. She was glad Harry had changed his hours – and hopefully his outlook on life.

Oh, there were so many things to worry about. She took a mouthful of tea and closed her eyes. Maybe she should try and get along to that yoga class on a Tuesday night in the village hall. She needed to switch off a bit.

Chapter Twenty-nine

Harry

Harry had offered to take Hope for her therapy session while Lou and Jenny had lunch out with some friends they'd met in the village. They seemed to be fitting in more socializing than they'd ever done back home in Norwich.

He'd been surprised to discover that Ella had clients in the holiday season. He told himself he was taking Hope along because he wanted to see a full session, after the brief one he'd seen the other day. Hope, delighted, had put on her new jodhpurs and riding coat, and was waiting at the breakfast table at six thirty, hours before they were expected at the yard.

Ella waved goodbye to a client and led the chestnut colt past and back to the stable to put on his rug. Hope was up next, and Charlotte came to take her through to the barn.

Harry stood waiting in the little office. A photograph caught his eye and he stepped forward, looking at it in detail. It was Ella, dressed formally in white jodhpurs and long black tailcoat, competing in a dressage championship with her beloved Ruby.

His stomach lurched, and he reeled back and out into the fresh air.

The crash had been so violent and so – final. Back then she'd given away everything to do with horses, even passed on her promising competition horse. He remembered her deathly white face in the hospital where she'd lain, recovering from her broken hip – she'd told him then that she'd have nothing to do with horses, nothing to do with her old life.

It had been months before he'd stopped trying to get her to see him. Months of passing messages via friends, begging for the chance to make her understand that he was sorry, that there was nothing he could do, but that if he could turn back time he'd have done anything – *anything* – to stop the crash. He'd gone over it again and again. The inquest had stated clearly that it was just an unfortunate and tragic accident – a failing of the traffic control system.

And he'd put all that to one side, in the end. Realized that sometimes in life you don't get to say you're sorry, or explain your side of the story. He'd closed off the piece of his heart where his feelings for Ella had resided, and resolved to live the rest of his life without opening it.

'I'll just be a moment.' Her voice made him jump. She strode past, carrying a heavy winter rug over one arm, and disappeared into a stable.

Charlotte popped her head out of the barn. 'Hope's

been grooming the ponies for ages now. I don't think Muffin has ever been so clean – or so happy. Come and see.' Harry headed over to the open barn door.

'Daddy, I'm going to stay here *all* day.' Hope looked up, Muffin's long tail in one hand and a brush in the other.

He laughed. 'I'm not sure Ella will be happy to hear that.'

The pink-haired Charlotte edged her way out of a stable door as he said that, a pitchfork balanced on top of a wheelbarrow full of dirty straw. He stepped backwards, letting her past. The wheel on the barrow squeaked painfully as Charlotte manoeuvered round him.

'She's fine with me,' Charlotte said over her shoulder as she headed for the muck heap. 'She's being my little helper, aren't you, Hope?'

'I'm not little,' said Hope, indignantly. 'I'm *almost* nine, actually.'

'My *big* helper.' Charlotte grinned.

'That's better.'

'Ready when you are,' Ella called, from outside in the yard. She appeared in the doorway a moment later. 'Now, you remember we're taking Echo today?'

Hope's face fell.

'But I've brushed Muffin.'

'I know,' said Ella calmly. She bent down to Hope's level. 'How about you take Muffin, and we'll bring Echo in later?'

There was a moment when it looked like it could go

either way. Hope glanced at Echo, who was tied up outside the stable, his shaggy grey coat neatly groomed by Charlotte.

'OK.'

Harry caught Ella's eye and mouthed *phew*. She smiled back, and for a second he felt like he was back in his old life. Then she turned away, beckoning Hope to follow her. He stood in the doorway of the barn, watching as Hope walked alongside his ex-wife, who was somehow the person who was putting his daughter back together. He shook his head.

It was a revelation to watch Ella working with Hope. They were playing a game of hide and seek with Muffin. Charlotte would hide, while Hope hid her eyes in Muffin's long mane. Then they'd set off together, looking behind piles of plastic barrels and various other obstacles that had been set up beforehand. Hope was shrieking with laughter, and Charlotte burst into fits of giggles every time she was found. Meanwhile Muffin took it all in his stride, his little legs trotting alongside Hope as she led him confidently around the arena.

'She's opened up so much.' Ella turned to him briefly as the two girls made their way back up from the other side of the school.

He shook his head, smiling. 'It's hard to believe it.'

'OK, Charlotte,' Ella said as she came closer. She tipped her head towards the side of the school.

'We're going to get Echo now, Hope.'

Hope stiffened and looked up at him for confirmation. He nodded, hoping it was encouragingly, and crossed his fingers behind his back. He really wanted this to work. But Ella had explained that all the therapy work they'd done so far had been with Muffin, and this was a new level.

'I tell you what, while we're waiting, why don't you hop on Muffin for a little ride around.'

'Without a saddle?'

'Yes.' Ella helped her onto his back. 'You and Muffin are good at talking to each other. You'll feel him moving underneath you. Do you see?' Muffin shifted sideways as Ella lifted a finger and Hope's face registered surprise.

'It's a bit wobbly.'

He watched Ella lay a hand on the side of her leg, steadying her. Hope sat up straight, gaining confidence and finding her balance.

'Can we go round?'

'Of course.' Ella lifted up the strap that hung around the pony's neck. 'Hold onto this, or you can hold onto Muffin's mane.'

Hope gave a little nod, her face serious. He watched the two of them as they chatted and laughed all the way around the perimeter of the school.

By the time they'd come back round, Charlotte had returned with the much bigger Echo. He came straight over and leaned over the wooden barrier, nudging Harry for treats.

'I haven't got anything, old boy.'

'He's a greedy sod,' said Charlotte, laughing.

Ella helped Hope to slide off Muffin's back and passed the lead rope to Charlotte. Once the pony had been led out through the door, Ella let Echo's lead rein loose so he was able to move about freely. It was surprising to see the difference. Hope stood, biting her lip, looking at Echo through a curtain of hair. He regarded her through his forelock, echoing her.

'What do you think Echo is thinking?' Ella said gently to Hope.

'I think he's wondering where Muffin's gone.'

'How do you think that feels?'

Hope scuffed the surface of the arena with her toe before she spoke. 'I think he might be a bit cross.'

'A bit cross,' Ella echoed.

'I think he's missing Muffin.' Hope's little chin lifted then, and she looked at Echo for a moment. He took a cautious step towards her.

'He looks very nice after you brushed him with Charlotte, doesn't he?'

Hope nodded. 'He's got soft hair on his legs.' She took a couple of steps forward and put her hand out. Echo reached forward, stretching his neck, and sniffed her gently. 'His whiskers are tickly.' She giggled.

They carried on in this vein for another ten minutes or so before Charlotte came back to collect Echo, the hour being up.

'Can I help you take him back?' Hope was eager.

Charlotte looked over at Ella, who was rolling up the

long lead rein they'd used earlier. Ella nodded in Harry's direction. 'If it's OK with you?'

He agreed with a smile, and stood watching as together they led Echo out of the ring. Then he left the school and headed for the little waiting room, money in hand. Before long Hope and Ella appeared there too.

'Harry, can I go and help Charlotte put the food in the buckets?'

'If it's OK with Ella.' They were so cautious with each other, skirting around politely, careful not to cross the line at any moment.

'Fine by me.'

He handed over the money and pocketed the change she gave back. Her hand touched his, and he had to stop himself from jumping backwards at the heat of her fingers on his icy cold hands.

'I'll just wait here until she's done.'

'Do you want a coffee?'

'If it's OK.'

Ella rolled her eyes then, and laughed. 'Of course it's OK. That's what the machine is for. At least when I remember to buy refills, that is.'

'So.'

'Yes.'

She looked at him over the top of her mug.

Ella took a deep breath.

'Look. We might as well get this out in the open now.

Then we can get on with what we're supposed to be doing.'

'What's that?'

'Helping Hope.'

He looked down, shifting his mug so the handle aligned with the edge of the desk. 'Yes, of course.' He nodded.

'A lot of water has gone under the bridge since – before.' Ella looked at him steadily. One of the dogs padded into the room and started drinking noisily from the water bowl, and she shook her head, laughing. 'Kind of hard to have a serious conversation with a spaniel in the room.'

Sensing she was being talked about, Cleo made her way over and laid her head on Harry's lap. He ran a hand down her silky ears.

'We're not the same people we were before,' Harry agreed. 'I mean, I've got Hope.'

'And I've got this place.' Ella nodded.

He remembered the connection and how she'd ended up here. It felt too intimate to ask her when she'd come back to Bron's place – but looking at the photograph stuck on the pinboard of Ella and Bron, arm in arm, squinting into the camera on a sunny summer day, he wondered what had happened. Should he ask?

Ella followed his gaze.

'She's not dead,' she said drily. 'If that's what you were wondering.'

'I wasn't.' He was.

'She's in Australia, discovering herself. And staying with her sister.'

'Discovering herself?'

'Bron's spent all her life here. I think she's having a sort of delayed gap year, enjoying making new friends, seeing new sights.'

'I met people like that when I was travelling.' He leaned forward, putting his chin in his hand and looking at her. He liked the way she echoed his movements, her eyebrows raised in question.

'Where did you go?'

'Anywhere I could.' He hoped they weren't straying onto dangerous ground. 'After –' He stopped.

'Look, if I'm working with Hope and you're living down the lane, we'll have to find a way to communicate.' She looked at him directly, her hazel eyes steady. 'I know I said it the other day, but I'm sorry. I treated you terribly, and I shouldn't have. It wasn't fair, and I wish I could take back what I said.'

He shook his head. 'And I'm sorry for what happened.'

'OK.' She laughed briefly, which surprised him. 'It's taken a lot of therapy to get to that place,' she explained, before adding, 'I always thought I'd have to just let it go. I never thought you'd turn up on my doorstep and let me have closure. It's not the way things happen, as a rule.'

'I think the fact that I ended up on your doorstep might've been a certain small someone giving us a nudge,' Harry said. She went slightly pink then, and he cleared his throat and drank some more coffee. There was another silence then.

'Anyway.'

'Anyway. You were saying?'

'Travelling. Colombia, Costa Rica, Mexico. I saw the Panama Canal in action – it's huge. And then I went all over Australia.'

'Did you take a gap year or something?'

'No, I just did contracting work for a while. Saved up a load of money, and my parents gifted me some as well; I took a few months off, travelled until it ran out.'

'And then you met Sarah?'

'Yes. Well, then mum died, and I met Sarah. On the same day, weirdly enough. They sort of adopted me, and Jenny and Lou were so kind and welcoming, and Hope was so sweet. It just seemed like it was meant to happen.'

A nerve in her jaw twitched slightly and she swallowed.

'That's lovely.'

'And then Sarah got sick, and – well, here we are.'

He realized that he'd been talking constantly about himself, and Ella hadn't given anything away.

'And you?'

'I didn't do anything.'

He frowned and lifted an arm, indicating the stable yard, and the fields which swept down the valley outside the window. 'All this?'

'I ran away. I came here, I hid in Bron's cottage, and I worked with the horses. Eventually I trained as an equine therapist. I spent my inheritance from Dad on the indoor arena and sorting out the stables.'

'It's pretty amazing, Ella.'

She ducked her head. 'Thanks.'

He was relieved that Hope and Charlotte reappeared, just at the point where the silence between them was growing unmanageable.

Later, as he was walking back down the lane with a worn-out Hope, she looked up at him.

'She's nice, Ella, isn't she?'

'She is, darling, yes.'

'You're friends.'

He wouldn't go that far, yet. But he realized, surprising himself as he spoke – 'I'd like to hope we might be, yes.'

'Good. Then we can go to the stables lots and lots.'

Chapter Thirty

Ella

'I can't believe you ducked out of New Year's Eve.' Lissa cocked an eyebrow at Ella.

'Here you go, love,' said the barman, sliding two sets of cutlery rolled in paper napkins across their table. 'Grub won't be long.'

The Lion was packed out. Alan from the post office waved at them from the bar, lifting his drink in greeting. Sally was behind the bar, looking unruffled as ever despite the crowds. It seemed like everyone had decided to cheer up the most depressing week of the year – the first week of a grey, wet January – with dinner out.

Lissa sat back against the green leather of the little booth and lifted her chin to look at Ella appraisingly. 'So what's the story?'

'It's nothing, really.' Ella poured her Indian beer from the bottle into the glass, watching as it foamed up and spilled over the edge. She caught the foam with a finger and licked it away. It tasted metallic.

'Let me get this straight. I wake up half-cut on my

mam's sofa on Christmas Day to find everyone singing 'Do You Want to Build a Snowman' at the telly, and there's a text message saying SOS.'

Ella nodded. 'False alarm.'

'Right.' Lissa rubbed her forehead. 'And the second *get me out of here* was another one? And when I text asking what's the story, you're all "oh it was nothing, everything's OK . . ."'

Ella pulled a face.

'And then you're "ill" on New Year's, but well enough to go running two days later?' Lissa snorted. 'Come on, spill. Something's going on . . . or is it *someone*?'

Ella sat back against the cushioned leather. 'OK. You're not going to believe this, but . . .'

'Bloody hell.'

'I know.'

'And is he still hot?'

'Lissa!'

'All right, someone had to ask it. And it was probably going to be me, realistically speaking. I've seen the photo, remember. D'you reckon he'll be doing the school run? I can check him out.'

'He's my *ex-husband*.'

'Shut up.' Lissa tore off a piece of naan bread and wiped her plate with it. She'd wolfed down her chicken jalfrezi while Ella had been filling her in, and Ella's plate was pretty much untouched.

'I'm not saying I'm after him, I'm just curious to know

what the Great Love of your Life looks like in person. You going to eat that?'

'He's no such thing,' Ella protested. 'And yes, I am.'

'Right then, get on with it, or I'll nick it.' She reached over as if to demonstrate and pinched a pakora from the edge of Ella's plate.

Ella took a mouthful of the cooling food and realized that she wasn't even remotely hungry. She hadn't been, if she was honest with herself, for most of the week. Harry had popped up almost every day, because Hope wanted to see the horses. She'd been so happy with Hope's progress, and seeing how well she was getting on with Charlotte, that Ella had put her reservations to one side, and despite herself, she'd found it was surprisingly un-awkward having him around, considering.

'Oh hello!'

The hand dryer had given up the ghost completely, so she was wiping her wet hands on her jeans when she walked straight into Lou.

Lou touched the collar of his polo shirt – an old habit, Ella guessed, from years of working in a shirt and tie. He looked relaxed and happy.

'Nice to see you. Curry night seems to be a popular one. We should have booked a table.'

'I bet they'll squeeze you in,' Ella said, looking over her shoulder. Lissa was peering, eyebrows raised in interest.

'The woman behind the bar says if we wait ten

minutes, that family over there are going.' Jenny appeared, putting her bag over her shoulder.

'Is it date night?' Ella said, kissing Jenny hello. She smelled of expensive perfume and hairspray, her ash blonde hair neatly blow-dried. Ella felt scruffy by comparison, dressed in her usual skinny jeans and a grey shirt she'd picked up from the top of the washing basket.

'Funny you should say that,' Jenny exchanged glances with Lou. 'What are you doing, have you eaten already?'

'I'm just with a friend over there,' Ella said, motioning to Lissa. 'We've had dinner already.'

'Oh that's a shame,' Jenny said. 'You could have joined us.' Just then the waiter came over to tell Jenny her table was ready. Ella waved them goodbye and headed back to the bar.

'So,' Lissa was nothing if not persistent. 'What's he like, your Harry?'

'He is *not* my Harry. In fact, as far as I can gather, there's someone in the background back in Norwich.'

She'd heard enough about Holly to piece together a picture of her – Harry hadn't mentioned her much apart from in passing, but Jenny and Hope had talked about her often enough that Ella had worked out there was something going on, even if they hadn't.

'All right, fine. Not your Harry. What does he do?'

'Business consultancy or something. One of those jobs that sounds good but you've no real idea what they actually do.'

'What did he do when you were together?'

'He was working for a social media company.'

'Bit of a weird leap. Mind you, business consultant. He must be loaded.' Lissa waggled her eyebrows hopefully. 'And he's single?'

'Lissa.' Ella fixed her friend with a warning look. 'Widowed, remember. Hence the lack of mother for Hope.'

'Shit, yeah.' She looked cast down for a moment – but only a moment. Her face brightened. 'Still, he's been widowed for ages. How long is he supposed to be in mourning?'

'Dunno.' Ella had wondered that herself. Sarah had been gone for five years – longer than she and Harry had been married. And yet he was still living with her parents, seemingly single, and apparently not exactly moving on with his life. Not – she pulled a face to herself – that she was doing a great job of that, either . . .

'So how's the love life going?'

Lissa gave a grin. 'Not too bad.'

'Is that it?'

'Oh Ell, he's lovely. I keep expecting him to turn into a frog but honestly, I think he's a – an actual nice man.'

'Get out.' Ella nudged her with an elbow. 'Do you think?'

'I know.' Lissa's eyebrows shot up briefly. 'And you know what they say about nice boys . . .'

'I'm not sure I want to know.'

Lissa burst out laughing. 'Buy me another drink and I'll tell you.'

*

Later that night, having caught a lift back up the hill from a local farmer, Ella made her way around the yard doing the last checks of the stables. She was slightly regretting that last glass of wine, but she couldn't go to bed until she knew all the animals were safe for the night. The dogs darted around, disappearing into the darkness out of the pools of light cast by the stable yard floodlights. Horses arched their necks over the doors, hopeful of a last handful of treats or a scratch under the mane. Ella checked each one, making sure their water buckets were topped up and that they all had some hay in their nets.

Charlotte was still awake. The light was shining from her bedroom window. Ella wondered if she'd carry on staying there once Bron came back – if Bron came back. On Christmas morning she'd looked so brown and happy – and so much younger. There was a sparkle in her eye that Ella hadn't seen in a long time, and for the first time she'd allowed herself to contemplate the possibility that her aunt might decide to stay out there for longer than she'd originally planned. Everything seemed to be changing. At least she'd have Charlotte to help.

She closed Lido's stable door and looked through the passageway between the barn and the stables. Her gaze drifted, somehow, down the hill. The sky was clouded over, so the stars and moon were hidden, and the darkness was thick and black. At the bottom of the hill she could see the lights of the village glowing softly, and if she looked at the sleeping cottage below she could see a light shining through one of the skylights. Hope was sleeping in there – or more likely, from what she'd gathered, not sleeping. She wondered if Harry was sitting in her bedroom with her, chatting and telling her stories.

Harry was, in fact, balanced at the end of Hope's bed, sending some end-of-week emails. The mobile phone reception in the village might be hopeless, but thankfully the broadband was pretty decent. He'd rejigged a few early January meetings – most people clearly feeling the same way as he was, there hadn't been many objections – and he planned to hang around at home with Hope for a couple of weeks.

'If you don't mind,' he'd said to Jenny, as she wrote a shopping list at the kitchen table.

'Mind?' she'd said. 'I would be absolutely delighted. Watch out, though, or Lou will have you roped into this Neighbourhood Watch meeting next week. He's in cahoots with Alan. There are *posters*, you know.' She'd laughed.

Hope was curled up under the covers, her head balanced on an impossible tower of stuffed animals which looked incredibly uncomfortable. She was almost asleep, but asserting every few minutes that she absolutely could not sleep at all. The spaces between assertions grew longer, and the resolution in her voice lessened, and in the end she began to snore, gently.

Harry closed his laptop and sat for a moment, watching the covers rise and fall as she slept. His heart was overflowing with love for her. Watching her come into her own with Ella's horses was a revelation – and the prospect of tearing her away and back to Norwich was painful. The long-term plan was that he'd buy a house near Jenny and Lou, so she could still be part of their lives. But he couldn't see Jenny being happy to let go any time soon. Realistically, he couldn't carry on living indefinitely with Hope's grandparents. There was only one problem.

He stood up, switching on the night light and switching off the main one, and quietly closed the door to Hope's room. He paused on the stairs, looking out of the window and up the hill. He found himself wondering if Ella was awake, too.

As he climbed into bed, exhausted, his last waking thoughts were of her.

Will you marry me?

He looked in the mirror and mouthed the words. They sounded frankly ridiculous. How the hell did anyone ask it with a straight face?

He knew what he had to do – had the ring, which he'd saved up for and bought with the money he'd earned in the summer after graduating.

She'd been working at a competition stable yard in Berkshire and he'd travelled down every weekend to see her, sleeping in the tiny, rickety caravan she'd been allotted. It was freezing cold even on warm nights and every morning they had to shake their clothes to get rid of the earwigs that crept in through the cracks in the doorframe. But it was their first attempt at living together properly. She'd work all day, coming home filthy and exhausted. He'd drive to the supermarket in Windsor and buy ingredients, cooking on the two-ring gas stove and chopping salad on the folding table, which became their bed by night.

In the evenings they'd sneak to the shower block when nobody was around and he'd watch as she scrubbed the dirt from her body and shampooed her hair to wash out the straw and sweat and dust. Her bottom curved beautifully – toned by hours in the saddle – and inevitably he wouldn't be able to resist. He'd reach out, offering to soap her back and she'd turn and grab his wrists, pinning him against the wall, laughing, and kissing him as the water ran on, drowning the sound of the other workers banging on the door, waiting to get in.

Now summer was over and he knew – absolutely, with a certainty he'd never felt about anything before – that he wanted to spend the rest of his life with Ella. There was nobody like her.

'Harry!'

Through the fug of sleep he felt a hand shaking his shoulder, urgently.

'Harry.'

He turned around.

'Can we go to the stables now? I'm ready. Look.'

Hope was standing, dressed in her warmest clothes, her cardigan buttoned up the wrong way, and her wellington boots on. He peered at the clock.

'Sweetie, it's half past five.'

'I know.'

'It's pitch dark.'

'It says in my horse book that you got me that if you like horses you have to be prepared to get up early, even on weekends.'

He groaned, rubbing his eyes, and sat up. He laced his hands together and folded them behind his head, stretching until various parts of his body cracked alarmingly.

'I think that's if you have a horse of your own, Hope, darling.'

'Oh.' Her face dropped for a moment. 'But Ella said I could treat Muffin as if he was my own, so that's almost the same.'

'I suspect Muffin is probably still asleep. You wouldn't want to wake him up, would you?'

Ella scrunched her little mouth sideways in thought. 'I suppose not.'

He looked at the clock again. One day, one blessed day, Hope might need more than a few hours of sleep. He had no idea how Jenny coped with it when he was away at work. At least he could give her a bit of a rest – he'd noticed she was looking pretty frazzled. Trying to keep everyone happy was Jenny's thing, and it didn't seem to leave her much time for herself. He pushed back the covers.

'OK, let's do a deal. You creep downstairs as quietly as a tiny little mouse, and I'll get my socks on because the kitchen floor is freezing. And then we'll make pancakes and Nutella for breakfast.'

Hope's eyes turned saucer-shaped. She put a finger to her lips.

'Like a very tiny mouse.'

'The smallest, quietest mouse in the world.'

He watched as she crept out of the room. When she'd gone, he ran a hand through his hair and looked for a second at his reflection. He looked knackered – the shadows under his eyes matching the three-day stubble on his jawline. In his grey T-shirt and checked flannel pyjamas, he looked like the before shot of one of those dads on the kids' TV makeover show Hope liked to watch. At this rate he was going to go back to work – as he always did – more tired than he was before the start of the holidays.

Harry hovered at the gate to Hillside Farm. He could see the flash of pink hair in the distance that was Charlotte, already at work in the midwinter dawn. It was quarter to nine, which was the absolute latest he'd managed to extend his pancake-making delaying tactics, and Hope was hopping with excitement as he slid open the metal catch. Bob and Cleo hurtled towards them, barking with excitement.

'Look, Harry,' Hope giggled. 'Cleo looks like she's twerking.' She wiggled her bottom to demonstrate and he burst out laughing.

The dogs heard the gate before Ella did. Pulling her hair into a ponytail, she stepped out of the cottage and into the yard, yawning.

Harry grimaced and lifted a hand in greeting. 'I'm so sorry,' he said.

'Why? What have you done?'

'Well, I'm sure you've got loads of work to do, but Hope was very keen to see Muffin and –'

Ella smiled. 'Come on then, young lady. Let's go and say good morning to Muffin.' She sneaked a look at her reflection in the kitchen window as they made their way across to the yard towards the barn. Thank God she'd actually had a shower and brushed her hair.

'Actually, I don't have any clients today. I try and give myself a couple of weekends off in the month, or I end up working seven days a week if I'm not careful.'

'Oh?' Harry looked surprised.

'Since the article in the paper we've been getting busier and busier. I can't wait to tell Bron that we're actually in the black.'

'Ella, that's brilliant.'

His voice cracked with emotion. Ella glanced over at Harry. He hadn't shaved. She felt an unfamiliar sensation in her stomach. She turned away before he caught her staring at him.

They stood watching as Hope shot straight off in the direction of the barn where Muffin was probably still flat out, snoring. He was the laziest pony she'd ever known.

'I'm going to take the dogs for a –' she motioned to their leads, not saying the word – 'do a bit of paperwork, that sort of thing. It's all glamour around here.'

'Could we come?' Harry sounded hesitant.

'With the dogs?' Cleo and Bob were circling already. She hadn't even said the word *w-a-l-k* in front of them, but they were already impatient to get going.

'OK,' she smiled. 'You get Hope and I'll just grab the whistle for the dogs. Charlotte can do morning stables.' She looked back. 'If you're ready now, that is?'

'We've been *ready* since half five this morning.'

Up on the hillside, with Hope creeping around amongst the dark red bracken looking for fairies, Ella blurted out the words she'd been trying to say.

'Harry.' It was hard to say his name. She swallowed before continuing. 'I want to apologize.'

'For what?' He lifted an arm and waved back at Hope, who was now carrying two huge bracken leaves as wings and running in circles with the two dogs joining in delightedly.

'For divorcing you for unreasonable behaviour.' She pushed back her hair, which was blowing in her face, and turned to look at him. 'When I was the one who was a complete nightmare.'

'You'd lost your dad.' She startled when he caught her hand for a second, holding it for just long enough for the heat of his touch to shoot right up her arm, jolting her with surprise. He let go and she stepped back, surprised at her reaction. A pheasant whirled up, chuntering with surprise, as Hope emerged from a thicket of bracken, waving her arms and laughing, the dogs in hot pursuit.

'You've lost your parents too.'

'Yes, but –' His voice was low. 'You know what mine were like. You were your dad's whole world. And – and he was yours.'

She bit her lower lip and looked down at the rough grass. It was freckled with moss and broken up with rough grey stone which jutted out on a little ridge beneath their feet. Some tiny voice inside her said *so were you*. She pulled out the whistle, stepping away from him and turning to look down the hill.

'Cleo, Bob,' she called. She whistled the dogs back with three clear bursts. They hurtled towards her and lay on the ground, tongues lolling.

'I wish Hope was as obedient,' Harry laughed. 'When she was little she used to run off in the park and all the other parents would say "Don't worry, she'll come back" – but she wouldn't.'

'Anyway,' Ella said, determined to clear the air again – she realized she seemed to be doing quite a lot of that – 'I just wanted you to know that I know I behaved like a complete dickhead.'

He grinned at her then. 'Nothing new there, then.'

'Watch it, Macallan.'

Chapter Thirty-one

Harry

'Have you got your PE kit?'

Hope waved a drawstring bag in the air from the back seat of the car. 'Grandma reminded me.'

'Brilliant.'

He pulled the car in on the side street behind the primary school and climbed out, opening Hope's door. Jenny had been surprised when he'd insisted she stay at home with a late breakfast while he did the school run, but he was trying to make space in his life for the little moments like this, instead of putting all his focus on quality time with Hope. He'd been doing some reading online, and an article he'd read said it was important to spend as much time as possible doing the seemingly boring stuff, because that's when the interesting conversations happened. So far, he hadn't noticed much in the way of interesting conversations, but maybe Hope's monologue on the subject of her favourite cartoon and the intricate details of Class Three's social structure was it. He didn't really have anything to go by.

'Morning, my lovely,' said the teacher on the gate. 'I see you've brought your daddy with you today.'

Hope nodded. 'But he isn't staying for school.'

The teacher was looking at Harry intently. She smiled at him, and for an uncomfortable moment he wondered if he'd got something stuck on his teeth or in his hair. She was very pretty, with dark curls and skin, and precise freckles dotted across her nose. She smiled at him again, widely. 'Lovely to meet you at last.'

'You too,' he said, politely. He could have sworn Hope's teacher was male, but maybe he'd picked up the wrong end of the stick. He leaned down to give Hope a kiss goodbye and she darted off, too-big rucksack banging against the back of her coat. He headed back to the car with the slightly uneasy feeling that his every step was being watched.

After dropping Hope off, he wasn't sure what to do with himself. What did being a full-time parent actually involve? What would Jenny be doing now? He thought ahead to the end of the day, when he'd have picked up Hope and they'd be home, and they'd have dinner together. Perhaps he should make a trip to the supermarket and make her favourite meal.

He realized with a sinking feeling in his stomach that he'd spent so long working and away from family life that he wasn't sure what it was. She was growing up so quickly.

'Hello again,' said a familiar voice behind him in the queue at the little supermarket. He turned, heart bashing against his chest. Ella was standing there, hair tied in a high ponytail, her face pink with exertion. She was wearing a pair of trainers and running tights that emphasized the length of her leg and the curve of her hip. He glanced away, rubbing at his forehead.

'Hi.'

'I've been running,' Ella said, and then she laughed, gesturing to her clothes. 'I mean, obviously.'

'I'm just – getting some shopping.' He groaned inwardly. This was ridiculous. 'What're you doing –?'

'It's only five weeks until the fun run. I think I'm going to be finishing miles behind everyone at this rate.'

The woman on the checkout started bleeping the groceries. 'You doing this school run, lovey?'

Ella pulled a face. 'More like a walk, I suspect.'

'I think she's better than she thinks she is,' Harry said. 'I know her of old. She underplays her talents to lull the opposition into a false sense of security.'

'I know the type,' the woman teased. 'Eight pounds forty, love.'

He hovered for a moment after paying, wondering if it was obvious to Ella that he was waiting to see what she was doing next.

'Hope's doing really well at school.' He fell into stride beside her as they headed out to the car park.

'She's doing really well, altogether. I'm amazed, really.'

'You're just being modest. You must see this all the time.'

'It's different with adults. They've got more layers. Hope – well, she was under there all along, waiting for us to find her.'

He stopped at his car, holding his keys in one hand. 'I feel like this place has been the making of her.'

'I know. Lissa – my friend, she's a teacher at the school – was telling me she's doing really well at school, too.'

'She's the teacher?' It fell into place.

Ella nodded, opening her bottle of water and taking a drink.

'I think I met her this morning.'

'You'd know if you have. She's quite – direct. She said she'd be looking out for you.'

He nodded, thinking of the teacher's stare. 'I think that's the one.'

The sky was clouding over.

'Anyway, I'd better be getting back.'

'D'you want a lift? It's a long walk up the hill.'

'Run.' Ella raised her eyebrows.

'Haven't you done a run already?'

'Yeah. It was a bit ambitious. I thought I'd run down, round by the river, and back up. Only now I've stopped, and with that overhead –' she gestured to the darkening sky – 'I don't really fancy it much.'

He pressed a button and the car doors unlocked. 'Let's go, then. I won't tell if you won't.'

'So apart from your plans to become the running champion of Llanidaeron, what else are you up to this week?'

'I've got two clients this afternoon –' Ella looked straight ahead, giving him the chance to glance at her face in profile. She had a smudge of dust on her cheek, and he gripped the steering wheel, realizing he had the urge to reach across and brush it away.

'Adults?'

'Yes. Carol and Brian. They're not together – yet.' She flashed him a look of amusement. 'But they come as a package. I have a suspicion that I've inadvertently acted as Cupid.'

'That's sweet.'

'It's certainly unusual.'

He cleared his throat. 'But no children?'

She shook her head. 'Not yet. I'm waiting for final clearance on a contract with the LEA. When that comes through, I'll be a lot busier, and I'll be working with teenagers from a PRU – Pupil Referral Unit – nearby.'

'That's amazing.' He pulled the car to a halt outside the farm, wishing they could carry on talking.

'I know. It's thanks to Lissa, really – she got me out of a hole just when I thought we were in real trouble.'

'You're making a difference to people.'

'I hope so. I feel like I've . . . I want to give something back.'

He tensed. 'You do. I mean, you are.'

Ella ducked her head. 'Thanks.'

'Right,' he said, reluctantly. 'I'd better let you go.'

Ella climbed out of the seat and then paused for a second, leaning back into the car. Her hair was curling in tendrils that framed her face, and the smudge on her cheek just added to her appeal.

'I'm going to a farm sale at the weekend.' She chewed on her lip. 'I don't suppose you and Hope fancy coming, do you?'

Harry glanced over his shoulder to see if Hope was settled comfortably in the back of Ella's battered old Land Rover. She looked a bit put out, because she'd been under the impression that Harry was taking her to buy a farm.

'It's not the farm they're selling,' Ella explained, changing gear as they climbed the steep hill. 'It's the equipment. Sometimes it's because the farmer's retired and moving on, sometimes they just have a bit of a clear-out. It's a chance to pick up tools and bits and bobs, but more than that, it's a chance for everyone in the farming community to get together and have a catch-up.'

Harry glanced at her. She was dressed in a pair of jeans and dark brown knee-length boots. She had a green rugby shirt on, and her hair tied back. The only jewellery he'd seen her wearing was a pair of tiny gold stars in her ears. They were there today, as always. When they'd been younger the only thing she'd worn was her wedding ring. He wondered where it had gone. He still had his, strangely enough. He'd kept it, even after the divorce, boxed away at the back of his desk. He didn't think Sarah had ever known – but she wouldn't have minded. She wasn't that sort of person.

What he realized now, seeing Ella, was that the feelings for her had been stored away, like his wedding ring. Not gone, not forgotten, but – stored. Carefully. All he had to do was keep them there, despite the fact that they kept trying to sneak out. If he could just padlock them away, he could have a really good friendship with her. And that would be better than nothing. If that was the best they could get, then that would do.

'Here we are.'

'It's not very far away,' Hope observed. 'We've only been driving for twelve minutes.'

Ella laughed. 'I know. I don't go to the far-away ones, because I can't stay away from the horses too long. But this one might be interesting because Daffyd Jones, who owned the farm, used to breed Arabian horses years ago. I thought he might have some stud books I've been looking for.'

'What's a stud book?'

'It's like a . . .' He watched Ella cock her head sideways, thinking. 'Like a list of all the parents and grandparents and great-grandparents of a horse.'

'Like a family tree?'

'Yes. That's a much simpler way of describing it.'

'We had to do a family tree at school once.'

No wonder Hope found school stressful. She hardly had the traditional nuclear family.

'We did one of them too,' Ella said, turning round to look at Hope. 'It was really tricky because I got sad because I wasn't sure if I was supposed to put my mummy on it.'

Hope, who was sucking on a finger, nodded solemnly. 'That's the same as me.'

'But you do,' Ella said, and she gave a smile that made his heart want to burst open. 'Because your mummy is always your mummy, even if she's not here any more.'

'That's what Daddy says.' Hope's eyes were wide with surprise.

'Then Daddy is very clever.' Ella turned to look at him, and the expression on her face was unreadable.

'Shall we get you out of the car, pickle?'

His voice was so hoarse that it was almost a whisper.

They left the auction in the barn a while later.

'I'm relieved we've managed not to accidentally lift an eyebrow and end up buying an old tractor.'

'D'you think that happens often?'

Harry grinned.

'Would you like a hot chocolate?' Ella turned to Hope. Babs was there – as she was at almost all the farm sales – with her little catering van, selling hot drinks and delicious burgers stuffed full of onions and mustard that slipped out and spilled down the front of your top.

'Coffee for me, please,' said Harry. Hope nodded.

'You go and have a look at the old toys and stuff, then, and I'll bring it over.'

There was a whole table full of old cast-iron toys and wooden animals, most of them dating from the middle of the last century. They were boxed up in old-fashioned wooden fruit crates, and had probably been there since Daffyd Jones was a boy growing up on the farm. Now he had a lung problem, and with nobody to take over the farm, he and his wife were selling up and moving to a bungalow in Beaumaris on the island of Anglesey, where his brother lived.

'The sea air's supposed to be good for your lungs,' he was telling all and sundry. Ella privately suspected that he was trying to convince himself, more than anyone else. Farming was in his blood, and it was going to be a wrench to leave this beautiful old stone farmhouse with its views across the valleys for even the most up-to-date centrally heated bungalow in the middle of bustling, touristy little Beaumaris.

She'd fallen in love with Wales in the years she'd been living here and couldn't imagine living anywhere else now – despite the fact that almost every day had a bit of rain. Without it, she knew, the place wouldn't be as lush and green and beautiful as it was. And she loved the feeling of isolation.

'Two hot chocolates, love, and a coffee. Milk and sugar are on the table there.'

Ella took the drinks and went over to the table indicated, then headed back to where Hope and Harry were playing with a battered old red London bus.

'Reminds me of that trip we made to London that time.' Harry took the polystyrene mug from her hands. 'D'you remember?'

She closed her eyes for a second.

'I remember.' She opened her eyes and found that she was looking directly into his. Her cheeks burned hot and she ducked her head, tucking a strand of hair behind her ear in a self-comforting gesture.

'Here you are. You can have the whole box if you want, my lovely. Tell your mummy and daddy they can have it for a fiver?'

The auctioneer's booming voice broke the spell. Ella recoiled, her face flushing scarlet.

'We're not –'

'She's not –'

'Can I have it?' Hope was oblivious to the tension the auctioneer's casual comment had caused. She looked at Harry. He stuck a hand in the back pocket of his jeans and pulled out his wallet, leafing out a fiver and handing it over. The auctioneer dumped the box unceremoniously into Harry's arms. Ella was looking anywhere but at him, and the atmosphere was distinctly uncomfortable.

'I think maybe we'd better get back,' Harry said, lifting his wrist to check his watch, then dropping it when he realized he wasn't actually wearing one.

Ella nodded. 'I think so, too.'

They drove home in silence. Hope sat on the back seat, singing along to the radio. Harry stared out of the window. His jaw was rigid with tension.

'I'll drop you back at the cottage, shall I?'

'I think so. I've got some work to do.'

'But Harry –' Hope looked unimpressed – 'you said we could go and say goodbye to Muffin.'

'I think Ella's got lots of work to do, sweetheart, and so do I. Another day, OK?'

There was a moment while she contemplated her response.

'OK.'

'Thanks for the lift,' said Harry stiffly, as Ella pulled up outside the cottage.

'It's OK.'

'Bye, Hope.' Hope waved at Ella briefly, but was more interested in showing her grandma the box of delights she'd come home with.

'Your grandpa is going to love these. They look like the toys we played with when we were little.'

Ella looked in the rear-view mirror as she pulled away, ready to give a wave. But Harry had turned his back to her and was walking back into the cottage.

'You OK?'

Charlotte collapsed in a heap on the sofa and flicked on the television. Ella was sitting in front of a dead fire, in gathering darkness, still wearing her coat and her boots.

'Fine.'

'OK,' said Charlotte, looking dubious. 'It's just you went out looking like this . . .' She pulled a goofy face and did an exaggerated thumbs-up. 'And you've come back looking like –' she reversed the face and put both thumbs down – '*that.*'

Ella puffed out a long breath and hefted herself off the sofa.

'Just a weird sort of day. I think they're right when they say you can never go backwards.'

'Like sharks?'

Ella frowned.

'They have to keep swimming or else they'll drown.' Charlotte pressed the remote control button rapidly. 'I think it's sharks, anyway. There was a thing about it on television the other day. I saved it. D'you want to watch?'

'I think I might pass and have a bath.'

Ella reversed out of the room, pulled off her boots, and headed upstairs.

Back at the cottage, Harry was pacing up and down in the tiny kitchen.

Jenny, wisely, wasn't saying a word. Something had clearly happened, but whatever it was, it wasn't going to be helped by her sticking her oar in. She carried on chopping carrots for shepherd's pie and tried to focus on the play she was listening to on Radio 4.

Harry sat down at the table.

'I need to nip down to Norfolk for a couple of days and sort out some work stuff.'

'OK.' She carried on chopping and didn't turn around. She suspected there was more chance of getting whatever it was out of him if she didn't pry. 'Good idea.' She slid the carrots into the saucepan, where they started to sizzle gently with the already sweating onions. 'You should invite Holly back up to stay for a few days. Hope would like that.'

'You know what – I might just go this evening, get it over with.' Harry stood up. 'I'll get my stuff.'

'Now?' She spun around then, surprised.

'I might as well. Sooner the better.'

'What about Hope?' This felt like a return to the old Harry, who disappeared out of their lives with little explanation for days at a time. She knew her tone was disapproving, but she couldn't help herself. 'She's not going to be very happy about this. I don't know, Harry.'

'I've got to do this, Jen.'

'I'm sure you do. I just don't think you're doing Hope any good. She needs you in her life consistently, not just disappearing on a whim whenever you feel like it.'

'There's more to it than that.' He turned and left, knocking a chair sideways as he did so. It wobbled on two legs for a moment and toppled over as he pulled the door closed behind him.

'Bloody hell.' Jenny banged the chopping board down on the kitchen worktop unnecessarily hard. It didn't help.

'You all right, love?'

Lou pushed the door open and stood in the doorway.

'Fine. No, actually, I'm not bloody fine.'

'What's the matter?'

'Harry. Hope. All of this.' She indicated the kitchen

323

table, strewn with the detritus of preparing dinner and Hope's latest Lego creation and the half-read Sunday papers, and leaned back against the sink, putting her head in her hands.

'Do you never feel like you'd like to just run away?'

Lou surprised her by chuckling, making his way across the kitchen, and taking her in his arms.

'Yes. Let's go.'

She looked up into his bright blue eyes and laughed. 'We can't do that.'

'We bloody well could, you know. Harry's more than capable of looking after Hope without us.'

'But Sarah –'

'Sarah's not here, sweetheart.'

The words still had the power to twist a knife in her heart. She swallowed tightly. 'I know.'

'And what I've noticed since I've been around a bit more is that Harry's desperate to be a father to Hope, and we're standing in his way.'

'Not tonight, we're not,' she replied, bitterly. 'He's buggering off to Norfolk on a whim.'

'Well, maybe it's time we made it clear that things are going to start changing.'

He put a hand on her cheeks, cupping her face gently. 'I don't think for one second Sarah would expect you to put your life on hold. In fact, I think you know damn well she'd be bloody furious to think of you doing just that.'

Jenny bit her lip and nodded. Maybe it was time to start making some changes.

For a start, Jenny decided, splashing her face with water, she'd go and have a long soak in a hot bath later, and finish the book club book. She'd been invited to join the group that met once a month in Connie's cafe after hours, and somehow with Christmas and everything else, she'd barely managed to get halfway through. There wasn't enough time to do anything. Sometimes she remembered the plans she and Lou had had years ago. They'd always said that when they retired, they'd pack a rucksack of belongings and a passport each, and head off round the world. But that was before. Then Sarah got sick, and Hope needed looking after, and . . . well. Maybe Lou was right. It was time to start thinking about making some changes – even if just thinking about them made her heart feel like a lead weight.

Chapter Thirty-two

Ella

'Shh.'

Lissa pulled a face at Ella.

They were lying side by side on yoga mats in the school gym hall. The floor smelled exactly the same as her gym hall had twenty years ago: of dust, and sweaty feet, and industrial cleaning fluid. It was as far removed from the tranquil surroundings of an ashram in Bali as you could possibly be, but the instructor was taking things very seriously indeed. Following a lecture on the importance of vegetarian eating for a pure spirit, they'd manoeuvred themselves into a series of positions which suggested to Ella that while she might be fit from all the work she did at the yard, she was far from flexible.

She'd dragged Lissa along to yoga, telling her it was bound to be good for stretching out their running muscles. So far, it had felt more like being back at school with a particularly strict teacher.

It didn't help that Lissa couldn't stop bloody talking, so they kept being shushed and glared at. They moved into another position, following the instructor's lead.

'So are you going to tell me what happened?' Lissa continued talking, legs akimbo. She was *trying* to whisper.

'I'll tell you afterwards. I'm worried if we get into trouble she's going to tie us into pretzel shapes and throw us out of the window.'

Ella hadn't been to a yoga class since university. Back then, she'd been a bit of a fitness fanatic, working out all the time to make sure she was as strong and flexible as she could be to enhance her prospects as a career rider. Back then, she'd had her life mapped out.

And then everything had changed. She'd somehow thought that after the accident there wasn't much point in doing anything other than ticking the box and doing the rehab exercises the physio had given her. They still left her stiff on one side, and all these years later she still hadn't tried riding. But with Charlotte riding now, and her fitness coming on because of the running, something was happening. She'd had several dreams in which she'd been riding and woken up, startled by her subconscious.

The longer she left it, the more nerve-wracking the thought of getting on a horse had been. Eventually she'd convinced herself that she was happier doing ground work and leaving the riding to other people. Working with clients meant she spent plenty of time with the horses, and Charlotte was more than happy to help with the exercising. But Hope's enjoyment of riding had caused Ella to start questioning herself. She missed it. She missed the feeling of being able to saddle up, gallop across the moors and see the wildlife that wouldn't come near her if she was on foot.

There was something unsettling about Harry coming back into her life that had shaken up all sorts of things she'd resolved to forget about. And there was something about the almost-silence of yoga, even in a gym hall, that was giving her a chance to think about the things she liked to keep locked away in a box in her head.

They switched position again. The instructor moved between them, gently correcting Ella's posture with a guiding hand on the small of her back. 'Beautiful,' she said to Lissa, who stuck her tongue out at Ella as the instructor turned away.

She hadn't seen Harry since the farm incident, and when Hope had come for her therapy session, it had been Jenny who had accompanied her. Apparently Harry had had some family business to deal with, but Ella couldn't help thinking that this wasn't the only reason for his absence. Ella had been busy with clients – the New Year often brought with it a flurry of bookings from people who had made resolutions, and the article in the local paper had had surprising results. She'd managed to pay off a good chunk of the rates bill, and the council were off her back for now. Things seemed to be bobbing along relatively peacefully. That was one good thing, at least.

She'd also finally been awarded the school contract, after what felt like a million forms and phone calls.

Dealing with the paperwork involved in working for the local authority was taking up her evenings. She was grateful, though, to have something to keep her mind busy, and it stopped her from thinking about Harry and what he was up to.

It had been easy to fall into a familiarity based on an old life – but the truth was, Ella thought, she didn't really know Harry any more. In the intervening years, he'd travelled, met Sarah, become a parent – and lost his wife. Maybe it wasn't that easy to pick up a friendship . . . or anything more. He seemed so closed off.

And of course she couldn't ask Jenny what she thought. She'd been cautious and bitten her tongue several times when she'd been on the verge of asking how he was, or whether he was around.

'And gently roll over into corpse pose,' the instructor intoned. Ella blinked hard. She'd been lost in thought for so long, she'd forgotten what she was meant to be doing.

While everyone else in the class had been having a spiritual experience, she'd been spring-cleaning the contents of her brain. She switched position obediently, and tried not to fall asleep. The room fell silent, broken only by the faint sound of what would be politely described as a gas emission. Lissa snorted with laughter. They'd been discussing this before the lesson, and Lissa had just won the bet. She'd insisted that she'd never been to a yoga class where someone didn't let out at least one. Ella kept her lips pressed together to stop herself from giggling.

'Did you think Zen yoga thoughts when you were doing that?' she asked Lissa afterwards in the changing room. She pulled off her T-shirt and fished in her bag for her top. The room was packed with women in various stages of undress. It was a strange feeling to be back in a school changing room. She was having flashbacks to PE with Miss Stuart, who had forced them to do long-distance running in the pouring rain.

'Did I buggery. I was thinking about last night's hot date with James.'

'The PTA dad?'

Lissa nodded, beaming. 'Come on, get changed and I'll tell all over a pint.'

Sitting in the pub half an hour later, Lissa looked genuinely happy. After a tempestuous year of hearing the never-ending saga of her playing cat and mouse with the married head of the English department at the secondary school, Ella was relieved her friend looked so straightfor-wardly happy.

'And you're going out for dinner again tomorrow?'

'Yep.' She clinked her beer bottle against Ella's wine glass. 'Told you I was going to do this year differently.'

'You're not bloody joking.'

'No more messing about with married dickheads.'

'I'll drink to that.'

'And what about you?' Lissa leaned forward, her chin in her hands. She surveyed her friend thoughtfully.

'Dunno.'

Lissa wasn't going to settle for vague mutterings about seeing what happened, or giving it time. Ella scanned the room, playing for time. As she did so, her eyes landed on Nick, who gave her a wink of hello and raised his pint slightly.

How she'd actually contemplated a proper relationship with him was beyond her, especially now.

'Is Nick still with that girl from the Hallowe'en do?'

'Stop changing the subject.' Lissa looked at her directly. She lifted the wine glass out of Ella's hands and placed it firmly on the table.

'I've known you long enough to know there's more to this than you're letting on.'

'More to what?'

'Stop stalling. What's the story with you and Harry?'

Ella felt her shoulders sagging, and she sat back in her chair. She picked up one of the sodden bar mats and started peeling it apart.

'There is no story.'

'Last I heard, you were getting on like a house on fire.'

'Ish.' She thought about the day at the sale.

'And then?'

She sighed. 'And then someone mistook us for Hope's parents, and he freaked out, and I felt awkward, and – here we are.'

'And you've cleared the air, being a qualified counsellor and all that, yes?' Lissa's tone was teasing.

'No.' She shifted in her chair. It was as simple – and difficult – as a short conversation, and yet Harry's frosty demeanour when she'd dropped him off at the cottage had made it impossible.

'That was a bit awks the other week, wasn't it? How

about we pretend it never happened and carry on getting reacquainted?' Lissa did a terrible impression of Ella's English accent.

'That would be the logical solution, yes.'

They both laughed. Logical solutions were lovely in theory, but real life didn't work out quite like that.

'Hello, my lovely, how's it going?'

Bron's face on the laptop screen looked bronzed, about ten years younger, and happier than Ella had seen her in – well, forever.

'Good, thanks. But how about you? You look like you've gone native.'

'I love it here!' Bron beamed. 'Who knew the lack of responsibility could be so good for a person?'

'I wouldn't know.' Ella pulled a face. 'I'm in the middle of sorting out an apprenticeship for Charlotte so we can arrange training, I've got paperwork for this PRU application coming out of my ears, and Lissa's got me roped in to this running thing in my spare time.'

'Doesn't sound like you have much spare time,' Bron chuckled.

'It's pretty thin on the ground.'

'How's Sweetbriar doing?'

'Grumpy.'

'Good to know. I'd be worried if she was anything but.'

'She's not due for another four weeks, and she's so bad-tempered I daren't let anyone near her. I've put her

332

in the foaling box round the back of the yard, just in case she tries to take a bite out of any unsuspecting clients.'

'How's your littlest client coming along?'

Ella could see her own face in the corner of the screen lifting with animation when she talked about Hope. 'Really well. I can't believe the difference in her. She's loving school, she's chatty, she's made a whole gang of little friends –'

'And her dad?' Bron cocked her head sideways, knowingly.

'He's fine.'

'I'm not taking that from you. Don't flannel me with *fine.*'

'He's – I'm – well, it's a bit weird.'

'Darling, what do you mean by weird?'

Ella told her the whole saga, explaining what had happened at the farm sale, and telling her that since then Harry had kept a low profile.

'It's as if he remembered everything, and –'

'Realized he'd been burned once?'

'Exactly. And I feel shitty because I wish we had the chance to sit down and talk about what happened, and I could tell him it made me feel uncomfortable too.'

'It's such a tiny little thing. Funny what triggers people, isn't it?'

Ella nodded mutely.

'You know, the thing is, darling, sometimes people come into our lives for a reason – and go back out again.'

'I know.'

'They're going back to Norfolk, though, aren't they?'

'I think so.'

The thought of it made Ella feel faintly sick. She said her goodbyes to Bron and sat in the kitchen for a long time, alone, thinking. She'd made the rookie mistake of tangling up the personal and professional strands of her life, and now she was paying the price.

'Bloody hell, you weren't joking when you said you'd been working at it.' Lissa was doubled over, head between her legs. 'I've got a stitch.'

Ella stood up with her hands on her hips and felt her heart thudding against her ribcage. Running had turned into an addiction. She loved the feeling of pushing herself, and the strength growing in her legs as a result of challenging herself to make it to the top of the hill without stopping.

'I never thought I'd see the day.' Lissa stood up, wiped the sweat off her forehead.

They stood in companionable, exhausted silence on the brow of the hill, looking across the valley. It was early on a Saturday morning, and a haze of mist hung over the village. Smoke lazed from the chimneypots of the houses. It was an idyllic scene.

'Can you imagine leaving all this?'

Lissa shook her head, swigging from her water bottle at the same time. She wiped her mouth. 'You're not trying to tell me something?'

'No. Just thinking about Bron on the other side of the world, and Jenny and Hope and –' She tailed off.

'And?' Lissa's eyebrows arched upwards.

'When they applied for Hope's school place, did they say it was only temporary?'

'It doesn't work like that. You're either in, or you're out. They'll have to reapply for her place when they go back to wherever it was they're from – Suffolk, was it?'

'Norfolk.'

'That's it.' Lissa stretched her arms over her head, then lifted a foot to stretch her quads, putting a hand on Ella for balance. 'Why d'you ask?'

'Just wondering.'

'You've been spending quite a bit of time with them, haven't you? I mean, above and beyond work stuff?'

'They're neighbours. And Hope loves spending time with the horses, and Charlotte. She's making such good progress.' Ella smiled, remembering Hope's last visit and how she'd happily climbed on Echo, all her previous fears forgotten.

'And Jenny probably enjoys the company, right?' Lissa's tone was arch.

They started walking back down the hill.

'I don't suppose it's been a hardship spending time with your good-looking ex, either.'

'I've not seen him for ages. Besides, there's nothing going on there.'

'Didn't say there was.' Lissa nudged her, and broke

into a jog. 'Come on, last one back's buying the drinks next time we go out.'

Ella was grateful for the peace in the yard that afternoon. She pottered around, tidying up, and spent a bit of time giving the increasingly pregnant and grumpy Sweetbriar some attention, brushing out her mane and tail until they shone like pale golden silk threads, and adding an extra layer of straw to her bedding to make sure she was comfortable when she lay down to rest her legs, tired from the extra weight she was carrying.

Then she grabbed a bag and her keys, and nipped into the village.

'All right, stranger?'

A hand on her shoulder as she withdrew money from the cash machine made her jump. She spun round to discover Nick standing there, the familiar twinkle in his eye.

'Hi.'

'Haven't seen you for ages. You been avoiding me?'

Ella shook her head. 'No, just busy.'

'I hear you've got a contract to work with the kids from Greenhill School?'

It wasn't possible to sneeze in this village without someone ten minutes later reporting you'd been rushed to hospital with flu. 'Who told you?'

'Little bird. Well, Lissa actually.'

Bloody hell, Lissa was such a blabbermouth sometimes.

'I've done some work with kids that have come out of

there myself. My last apprentice – remember Joe? He came from Greenhill.'

She nodded, remembering a slight, wiry boy who'd helped Nick out for while a couple of years back.

'Anyway,' he said, giving a nod. 'Just wanted to say I reckon you'll be perfect for it. Hope you get it sorted.'

He gave her a slightly awkward pat on the arm, and ducked his head. 'Don't be a stranger, all right?'

Ella laughed. 'Hardly likely. I've got you booked in for three weeks' time to do their feet.'

'Cool. See ya.'

Nick raised a hand and strode off. She stood watching him make his way down the high street. The thing about living in Llani was that you had to accept that whatever or whoever – happened, you were going to be bumping into the same people for the rest of your life. There was no hiding from the mistakes you made, or the bad decisions you might choose on a night out.

The delivery truck parked beside her pulled away and she turned, hitching her bag up on her shoulder as she went into the post office.

'Hello, my love, what can I get you?'

'I need some of those big A4 envelopes.'

'Have a look on the shelf over there.' Alan pointed to the jumble of things stacked up underneath the newspaper stand in the little post office shop. She moved a bag of elastic bands, several battered boxes of stickers, and a brightly coloured pre-school magazine that had fallen down from the rack.

'You looking forward to this fun run?' Alan rang up the price on the till. It gave her a flutter of nerves and excitement every time she thought about it.

'You know what –' Ella smiled, handing over a ten pound note. 'I am. Weird as it might sound, I am.'

Chapter Thirty-three

Ella

Hope was so keen to learn more that Ella had softened after the girl's last therapy session and said that she could come up and have a ride on Muffin.

'It's not strictly my remit,' she explained to Jenny, 'But if you don't mind, Muffin is as bombproof as they come, and Charlotte's more than capable of taking them round the school on a lead rein.'

'I don't mind at all,' Jenny had smiled, putting a hand on Ella's arm. 'You've worked wonders with her. With all of us, in a funny sort of way.'

'Bring her up tomorrow,' Ella said, touched. 'I've got an hour and a half free between clients. We can fit in a mini riding lesson.' Hope was the first child she'd worked with, having always been adamant that she only wanted to work with adults. Her time with the little girl had changed all that, and she couldn't wait to get involved with helping the children from Greenhill School. She was so pleased at the difference Hope's therapy had made. That was the only reason, she told herself firmly. Nothing whatsoever to do with Harry, or how he looked when he saw his daughter's growing confidence.

Nothing at all.

'Ready?'

Hope nodded. She was sitting up very tall in the saddle, her body encased in a protective vest, helmet fastened securely. She was wearing a pair of brand-new purple jodhpurs and a dinky pair of riding boots.

Ella had the long rein clipped to the noseband of Muffin's bridle. It meant the pony could trot around in circles, and Hope could enjoy the sensation of being in control, but with someone on the end of the rein in case anything went wrong. Not that anything *could* go wrong with the stolid little pony underneath her.

'Are you absolutely sure you don't mind me leaving her here?'

Lou was in bed with a cold, and none of them relished the prospect of telling Hope her ride was going to be put on hold. It was now, or next weekend – and Ella remembered being eight well enough to know that a week felt like a lifetime.

'I'd call it man flu,' Jenny confessed, jingling her car keys, 'But after his heart scares, I daren't make a joke.' It was a sign that she'd unwound in the last couple of months that she was able to even attempt to crack a joke about anything to do with Lou's health.

'You get to the chemist before it closes. I promise you, she'll be absolutely fine.'

Ella stood back and watched Charlotte as she encouraged Hope to practise her rising trot on Muffin, keeping her hands steady on the reins and her back nice and straight. She had a lovely, natural position.

Hopefully when they headed back to Norfolk, Hope could keep riding. Jenny had confessed, while Hope and Charlotte were tacking up Muffin, that she secretly half wished they could stay in the area. 'Even Lou has made some friends here, and he's so much more relaxed than he used to be,' she'd sighed.

Ella didn't ask how Harry felt about it, and Jenny didn't offer. He was nothing to do with her, and their brief friendship had fizzled out. It wasn't surprising, really. What had happened in the past was hard to get over. She'd hoped privately that maybe they might be able to build some bridges, but – she closed her eyes, remembering the farm sale – it seemed that wasn't going to happen. She had to accept that.

'I'll take over in two seconds,' Ella said. 'Just want to move this rug. I'm putting a load of stuff in to get repaired, and this has been on my list for blooming months.'

The stable rug with a broken strap had been hanging over the edge of the school for so long that it was covered with a layer of dust. Ella picked it up and shook it. Something large and buzzing flew out from underneath and she dropped it, shuddering.

'Ugh.'

'What is it?' Charlotte called over.

'Bumblebee or something.'

It happened in seconds. Ella looked up and Muffin gave a squeal, kicking out a back leg as he jumped sideways. Hope almost slid off the saddle and Charlotte grabbed her thigh, steadying her. And then Muffin gave a snort and leapt up as if he'd had an electric shock. Hope was catapulted out of the saddle and crashed to the floor in a heap, one leg bent awkwardly beneath her body.

Hope.

Ella dashed through the gate and sprinted across to the two girls. Hope was white-faced and silent. Charlotte was holding Muffin, looking stricken. The pony was wild-eyed, his nostrils flaring pink and his flanks heaving.

'I don't know what happened.'

'It wasn't Muffin's fault,' Hope said in a small voice.

Ella dropped to her knees and reached out a hand to reassure her. 'What's happened?'

'I don't know. We were only walking. Something happened and Muffin spun around and jumped and Hope fell off and –' Charlotte started to cry.

Ella looked at Hope's pain-blanched face. 'Where does it hurt, my lovely?'

'My leg is sore.'

And Ella noticed then that the leg underneath her was lying at an unnatural angle. She felt bile rising to her mouth and put a hand up, shocked. Adrenalin started pumping through her body. She could feel her heart racing, but she had to keep calm. She pulled off her puffa jacket and laid it over Hope.

'You're being very brave,' Ella told Hope, taking her hand. Hope's eyes were huge. She bit her lip and nodded. Ella noticed a tear pooling in the corner of her eye. It spilled over and trickled over her nose and down to the ground.

'It wasn't Muffin's fault,' she repeated.

'Oh, darling.' Ella squeezed her hand. 'I'm going to call an ambulance. Charlotte, can you just –'

Charlotte looked from Hope to Muffin and back.

'He's fine. I'll tie him here.' Ella took the reins and looped them through one of the rings on the wall.

This was why they still had a phone installed in the school, as well as one on the yard, and in the house. She spoke quickly, explaining the situation.

'We'll be with you as soon as possible,' said the call handler, calmly.

Ella puffed out a breath and bit her lip. No sign of Jenny. She picked up her mobile and keyed the numbers in on the landline. No response – just the three short beeps that indicated no signal.

She ran back and dropped down to her knees beside Hope. 'Don't worry, my love. The ambulance will be here in a moment and when they come they'll give you something to stop it hurting.'

Hope closed her eyes for a moment. She was being incredibly brave.

*

'What's happened?'

Jenny dropped her bag as she caught sight of Hope lying on the ground. She ran across the school and flung herself on the floor, almost knocking Ella out of the way. 'Darling, are you OK? Are you hurt? What happened to you?'

Ella shifted position, allowing Jenny to take her place, cradling Hope's head.

'We're not sure.'

'What do you mean not sure? Did she fall off?' Jenny's eyes were drawn to Hope's leg and she turned to Ella, eyes steely. 'How did she get hurt?'

'I'll take Muffin back to the stable,' said Charlotte, looking at the floor. She scuttled off and took him by the bridle, leading him slowly out of sight.

'Hello?'

Just at that moment, a green-clad paramedic popped his head around the door of the school. 'What have we here?'

'My granddaughter has been injured. She needs help.'

'That's what we're here for,' said the paramedic. 'Come on, Ali, we've got an injured young rider in here.'

Hope caught Ella's eye and tried to smile.

'Hello there, young lady.' The paramedic put his bag down on the soft surface of the school. 'What have you been up to?'

'It wasn't Muffin's fault,' Hope said again, her little face tight with pain.

'Usually isn't.' He raised his eyebrows. 'Have you been trying acrobatics on horseback?'

They administered a painkiller and got Hope onto a stretcher. She looked like a broken little bird as they carried her out and to the doors of the ambulance.

'Don't worry, we'll get her to hospital and have her back on horseback in no time.'

Hope smiled drowsily at this.

'OK, who's coming for a ride?'

'I'm her grandmother.' Jenny stood with a protective hand on Hope's arm.

'Hop in, then,' said the paramedic.

'Do you want to go as well?' Charlotte chewed her lip, looking at Ella.

'One person only, I'm afraid,' said the quieter of the two paramedics. She typed something into her phone and looked up. 'Right, let's get this little one off to the hospital. You're lucky you caught us on the way back from a shout. Not often we're on the scene that quickly.'

'Thanks,' said Ella.

'Oh –' Jenny mouthed in concern. 'Can you tell Lou? Let him know what's going on?'

'Of course.'

'Tell him there's macaroni cheese in the fridge if he wants dinner and that he's not to worry about tidying up because I'll sort it later and he's to remember his medication –'

The paramedic put a hand on her arm. 'Don't you worry about that. It'll get sorted.'

The ambulance headed back down the lane. Ella turned her thoughts to the pony who was still standing inside the school, tied by his reins to the wall. True to his usual gentle nature, he hadn't moved an inch and looked at her through his long mane, whickering a gentle welcome when she walked in.

'What's happened to you, my lovely?' Ella looked at him for a moment, scanning him all over for any obvious signs of injury. There weren't any that she could see, so she began very slowly and thoroughly running her hands over his body. When she reached his near hind leg he raised it quickly, flinching. She looked closely and saw a swollen, raised area on the soft skin of the inside of his thigh.

'Oh, sweetheart.'

Muffin kept lifting the leg up, clearly uncomfortable. Ella got the torch from her phone and shone it so she could get a closer look – she could see the tiny puncture mark. She remembered the buzzing as she'd moved the horse rug earlier: poor Muffin had obviously been stung by whatever angry insect she'd dislodged. No wonder he'd jumped in shock. Ella thanked goodness it was Muffin – another horse without his calm nature would have reared or even bolted, which could have caused even worse injuries for Hope.

'Come on, little one. Let's get you settled.'

The next client was a regular, and Ella could have hugged her when she took it in her stride when Ella apologized and asked if they could reschedule.

Muffin's bite was bathed with some soothing lotion, and Ella added a sachet of painkiller to a handful of food for him as she sorted out the buckets in the feed room.

'I could do this if you wanted to get to the hospital and check on Hope.' Charlotte had apologized countless times, and couldn't seem to grasp that she hadn't done anything wrong. She was clearly in shock. She hadn't stopped talking the whole time they'd done the afternoon feeds and checked over all the horses, making sure they had hay and water.

'I want you to go to the hospital.'

Ella wavered. 'I do need to check on Lou.' She'd driven down the lane after Jenny and Hope had disappeared in the ambulance, only to find him half asleep on the sofa in front of a football match. 'I'm not sure he's taken in what's going on at all. But I'm not sure about leaving you, either.'

'I'm fine. Just a bit spooked.' Charlotte looked more like herself when she said that, rolling her eyes. 'I'll watch telly and have some chocolate. Sugar's good for shock.'

'Ring me if there are any problems, OK? I'll be as quick as I can.'

'Tell Hope I'm sorry I wasn't paying attention.'

'It's not your fault, Charlotte.'

Ella shuddered, thinking about what could have happened.

During the fifteen-minute drive to the hospital, her mind was working overtime. It wasn't Charlotte's fault, no. It was hers. Poor Hope. If Ella had been holding the lead rein, maybe she could have stopped Hope from falling. Her logical brain said otherwise, but she couldn't help it.

She tapped her fingers on the steering wheel with irritation as the driver in front inched along at 25 miles an hour in a 40 zone. There was no way of overtaking on this bendy stretch of the road that looped around the edge of the hillside. '*Come on*,' she muttered to herself, '*come on*.'

The car took a left and she put her foot down, speeding away from the junction. Driving at the speed limit after proceeding at snail's pace for three miles made all the difference. She indicated right and drove down the hill to the outskirts of town, towards A&E.

She pulled a parking ticket out of the machine and drove forward into the car park as the barrier lifted.

Chapter Thirty-four

Ella

'I'm looking for a little girl – Hope? She came in earlier with a riding injury.'

The receptionist frowned. 'Is she a relative of yours?'

'Friend.'

'I'm sorry, she's in cubicles. Relatives only. You can wait here if you like, or come back later?' She looked down at her screen and typed a series of numbers on the keyboard.

'But I can't –'

'Sorry, love – if I let everyone through there, we'd be in a worse state than we already are.' She indicated the swinging doors. Through the window Ella could see people lying on trolleys in the corridor and harried nurses rushing past. One popped a head out.

'We're jammed in triage. Can you change the waiting time for non-emergencies to two hours?'

The receptionist tutted. 'Or tell them to go to their GP.'

The nurse raised her eyes skywards. 'Don't get me started.' She stepped back, and the door swung closed.

'I'm really sorry. I didn't mean to get in the way.' Crestfallen, Ella turned to leave. She didn't know what else to do. Fishing in her pocket for change, she felt her mobile vibrating and pulled it out.

Not much signal in here. Tell me when you arrive.

Jenny.
She gave a sigh of relief and tapped in a reply.

Here now. Where are you? I'm in reception.

A couple of moments later, Jenny popped her head out of the swinging door where the nurse had been previously. She beckoned to Ella to come in.

The receptionist looked up.

'She's with me,' said Jenny.

'On you go.' The receptionist gave a curt nod.

Hope was lying, a tiny shape, her eyes closed, on the hospital trolley. They were in a side bay which had been an offshoot of a corridor at one point, but which had been commandeered as an overflow.

'They've had a look at it. We're waiting for a call from X-ray, but the doctor says it's obviously a fracture. It's strapped up just now.'

'I'm so sorry,' Ella began. Jenny put a hand up, finger raised in warning.

'Not in front of Hope.'

Ella nodded acknowledgement.

'Can I get you anything? Tea?' Ella suspected it might help.

'I would love that.' Jenny gave a polite smile. She perched on the edge of Hope's trolley.

'OK. I'll go and find some.'

'Here we are,' she said a few minutes later, turning the corner into the little bay.

She stopped dead. There was no sign of Jenny, or of Hope's trolley.

Instead, standing in their place, dressed in a suit, his tie in hand and top button undone, looking absolutely furious, was Harry.

'She's gone to X-ray.'

Ella stood stock still, holding the two cups of tea in front of her. Steam rose, curling up through tiny gaps in the lid. Her chest was rising and falling rapidly.

'I said I'd wait here and let you know where they'd gone.'

'I'm so sorry, Harry.' Her voice was almost a whisper.

'What the hell were you thinking?'

'She was with Charlotte. I was only gone for a few minutes.' Ella knew how pathetic it sounded.

'She could have been killed.' His eyes were blazing with anger, his mouth an angry line in his face. He pushed a hand through his hair so that it stood untidily on end.

The blood was rushing in her ears. She felt ice-cold,

then clammy. Her back was trickling with sweat from the heat of the hospital ward. 'It was –'

She closed her mouth and looked at the floor. What was she going to say? *An accident*? *A split second*?

She swallowed, the back of her throat tasting bitter.

'I think now I'm here, it would be better if you just left.'

The coldness of his tone stayed with her all the way home in the car.

'Will you give Hope my love?' she'd asked, turning to look at him once before she slunk out of A&E. Harry had nodded briefly, not quite catching her eye.

She checked on Charlotte when she got in. On finding her fast asleep on the sofa with the dogs, she pulled a blanket over her and closed the sitting room door, gently.

Ella sat alone, hugging her knees, her back against the Aga, long into the night.

Chapter Thirty-five

Jenny

Jenny had just settled down on the plastic chair next to Hope's bed in the cubicle when there was a rustling and the sound of the curtain being pulled back. 'Just in here, I think.' A nurse popped his head in, smiling at her. 'Someone here to see the patient.'

'There you are.' She put a warning finger to her lips and motioned to Harry to close the curtain. 'Did you catch Ella?'

He nodded briefly, his face expressionless. 'I told her we could take it from here.'

He had a teddy bear tucked under his arm. If he hadn't stopped at the hospital shop to buy that, he might have been there five minutes earlier. She clenched her teeth. 'You're here now, that's what matters.'

'I was on the way back when you rang.' He fiddled with the cotton sheet that was draped over Hope, who was drowsy. She mumbled and stirred, opening her eyes and then screwing them closed again against the stark white of the hospital light.

'Here we are,' Jenny kept her voice deliberately light

and cheery. She stood up quickly and looked down at Hope's pale face. Her skin had a greenish cast.

'Daddy?' Hope peered behind her, looking for Harry.

'I'm here, sweetheart.' There was an awkward scuffle of chairs and bags as Jenny stepped back so he could take her place.

'How did you get here?' Hope tried to sit up, but the weight of the cast pinned her down.

'Magic,' said Harry, smiling. He leaned over and kissed her on the cheek, brushing back the damp tendrils of dark hair that were sticking to her forehead. He whispered loving words in her ear and a tentative smile broke through.

'I'll go and see what happens now. I think it's something to do with crutches.' Jenny wished Lou was there. It seemed ridiculous. All she'd ever wanted for her Sarah was a partner who'd treat her kindly and make her happy. All those years battling to have a child of her own – so many losses when she and Lou first married, to a point where their GP had taken him to one side, gently, and suggested that perhaps they could consider adopting a child, or fostering. She'd always dreamed of a big, unruly family with a table full of rowdy children. But when she finally became pregnant – miraculously – and Sarah was born safe and healthy, Jenny felt she'd been given a chance of happiness, and that she'd be greedy to try for any more.

It seemed unbelievably cruel that Sarah's life had been cut short, so she hadn't had the chance to know her own little girl. And today they could have lost Hope. Jenny closed her eyes for a second, squeezing them tightly, trying not to think about all the things that could have happened.

There didn't seem to be any nurses to ask. She caught a woman in pink scrubs and asked if she knew what was going on.

'Sorry, I'm just taking a short cut to resus.'

'Don't worry.'

A handful of staff were gathered around a computer station in the corridor. Jenny stepped towards them hesitantly. They were all so busy and she didn't want to get in the way.

'Excuse me, I'm just trying to find out about – my granddaughter's in a cubicle –'

'Let's have a check.' A tall, gangly-looking man clicked the screen. 'Chrissy, do you know what's happening about cubicle four?'

'Just waiting for crutches, I think.'

'I don't think she's up to walking just yet,' Jenny started to say.

'Don't worry. We've got chairs out there in reception. Pop her in one of them when you're ready and you can wheel her out. Just bring it back afterwards.'

'Oh. Thank you.' Jenny grimaced, feeling the prickle of tears.

'You all right, my love?'

She shook her head and blinked hard. 'Just a long day.'

'They all are, in here.' He flashed her a smile and turned back to the screen.

'I've brought you a chair so we can get you safely to the car.' Jenny wheeled the chair into the cramped cubicle.

'That's lucky. We've just been delivered these –' Harry raised a pair of tiny grey crutches. 'Hope had to hop out of bed and try them for size, and she did very well, didn't you, darling?'

Hope nodded. The painkiller she'd been given must have taken effect, because she looked much brighter.

'Well done, sweetheart.'

Jenny gathered up her handbag, and the tissues she'd left sitting on a shelf, and straightened her coat. 'Shall we get you home, then?'

'Grandma,' Hope said, looking up at her from the chair as they headed out into the darkened car park, her dark eyes serious, 'is Muffin OK?'

'I think – yes,' Jenny corrected herself. She didn't have a clue, but Hope's state of mind mattered more than a small white lie about the pony that had caused this in the first place. 'Yes, I'm sure she's fine.'

'He,' said Hope. 'Muffin is a boy pony, not a girl. And where's Ella? You said in the ambulance she'd be following us.'

'She's gone,' Harry cut in, before Jenny had a chance

to speak. His face was an expressionless mask, but when his daughter turned to look at him, he shifted it into a kindly smile.

'Perhaps she needed to check on Muffin.'

'Yes,' said Harry, after a long pause. 'That was it.'

They drove Hope home, sliding her carefully into Harry's car so her leg could stay propped up on the back seat. The shock – or the painkillers – had knocked her out, and when they got home in the darkness she was fast asleep. They carried her inside. Lou was waiting.

'Ella helped me make a bed up on the sofa. I think we'll have to keep an eye on her down here until she gets that temporary cast off.'

They lifted Hope onto the sofa and tucked the covers in. She stirred slightly, moaning in her sleep.

'Poor little one,' Lou said, bending over and stroking her forehead.

'Have you eaten?' Jenny couldn't help fussing. She looked at the mantelpiece for his medication, checking it had been moved. 'I left macaroni cheese in the fridge.'

'Had some soup, had my pills. I'm fine.'

'Soup?'

'Ella brought it down. She came down to let me know what was happening, then popped in on the way back from the hospital. She looked pretty shaken up.'

A noise of disapproval escaped from Jenny's nose. 'She shouldn't have put my granddaughter on a dangerous horse, then, should she?'

'Oh, come on,' Lou chided her. 'Is this the same fluffy

pony I've been hearing Hope rhapsodizing about for the last two months? The one that's transformed her?' He made a shoo-ing motion. 'Off you go. Take the weight off your feet. I'll make you a cuppa and you can calm down.'

'I'll do it.' She stood her ground, blocking his path to the kitchen. 'You stay here with Hope.'

Harry paced up and down the kitchen like a caged animal, throwing his suit jacket onto the table. It slipped off and onto the floor.

Jenny swooped down and picked it up, shaking it gently and hanging it on the back of the chair. She picked up a kitchen cloth and wiped the work surfaces, rinsing the soup tin Lou had left sitting on the side, placing it in the recycling basket. Then she straightened the tea towel and wiped toast crumbs from the Aga surface into her cupped hand and ran them down the sink, wiping the sink afterwards.

Harry crashed down onto a chair, putting his head in his hands.

'I should have been there.'

'You can't be there every second.'

'What the hell was Ella thinking? How did it happen?'

'I don't know. I wasn't there.'

He looked up sharply. 'Where were you?'

'I left her with Ella and Charlotte. I had to pop into town and pick something up.'

'Charlotte's a *child*.' Harry looked at her accusingly.

'She's eighteen, Harry. She is an adult in the eye of the law.'

'I don't care what she is. Ella should have been looking out for Hope, and she didn't do her job.' He looked ahead stonily, his jaw set. 'I've a good mind to make a complaint to someone about this.'

'You can't do that – she's just got a contract from the local authority for a really big job.'

'I don't care.'

'She's been good to us – to Hope.'

'She's irresponsible and she risked my child. Why the hell shouldn't I?'

'I think you're over-reacting.'

Jenny reached into the fridge and opened a bottle of white wine, tipping a generous amount into two glasses. She pushed one towards Harry. He took a long draught and put the glass back on the table. She didn't wish Ella harm – Harry's reaction underlined that.

'It was a mistake. Not even that. An accident.'

Harry pushed his chair back with a screech and stood up. It crashed back against the tiled floor and spun for a second. His hands were on the edge of the table, his knuckles white. His shoulders rose and fell as he tried to breathe and calm himself.

'There's a whole lot more to it than that.'

'What are you talking about?'

'An accident.' He gave a bitter laugh. 'I could write the book on *accidents*, and so could Ella.'

'Ella?' The kitchen was uncomfortably silent. The

clock ticked loudly over the window, and when Jenny swallowed it seemed to echo around the room.

'Ella.' He said the name on an exhalation of breath and pushed himself away from the table, spinning around and pacing across the room again.

'I don't understand.'

'No.' Harry looked up at her then, his eyes dark. 'There's a lot about my ex-wife I don't understand, either.'

Chapter Thirty-six

Jenny

'Hope's woken up and she's a bit teary.' Lou blundered into the room, knocking the door against the fallen chair. He made a face and stooped down, picking it up and setting it back against the table. 'What's going on here? Are you two having a party?'

'What is it?' Jenny sounded snappish, she knew, but of all the times for Lou to come wandering in –

'She's asking for you, Harry. It's probably just the shock, or the painkillers wearing off a bit.'

'I'll deal with her.' Harry turned on his heel and walked out of the room.

'Everything OK?' Lou's eyebrows lifted.

Where the hell would she start?

'Fine.' She gave him a look he recognized after decades of marriage, and he withdrew, closing the door behind him. She poured more wine into her glass with an unsteady hand and set it on the table in front of her.

Whatever the hell was going on, there was more to it than just Harry's anger about Hope's broken leg.

Ten minutes later he walked back into the room, closing the door.

Jenny looked up and asked with a raise of her eyebrows what was happening next door.

'She's asleep again. I'll sleep on the armchair beside her tonight.'

She slid the wine bottle across the table, and he emptied his glass in a mouthful before tipping in some more.

'I didn't know what to say.' His voice was low. He licked dry lips, and she watched him swallow, closing his eyes.

'I thought –' She scanned her memory, spooling back over every encounter they'd had since Christmas Day, when he'd met Ella for the first time. Or what she thought was the first time. 'I don't understand.'

He shook his head and stood up, pacing back and forth again. The kitchen wasn't big enough for his long legs – at over six feet tall, his dark hair brushed the wooden beams on the low ceiling as he strode back and forth, brows drawn together in a frown of concern. Twice he stopped as if to speak but then shook his head, banging closed fists against one another.

'It was a long time ago,' he began, and his voice was quieter still, as if he was dragging long-buried memories back from deep beneath the surface.

'You knew Ella before Sarah?'

He nodded.

'But she never said. She – Sarah told me everything.'

He flicked a glance at her, and she inhaled sharply.

The old, familiar place in her chest where the sadness resided gave a dull throb.

'But –'

They'd always been so close. More like sisters, everyone said. Everyone said that about their daughters, but with Sarah it was true. They'd shopped and lunched and laughed together. For God's sake, she'd chosen to stay in the town where she'd grown up. And all those long hours talking when she lay in a hospital bed while life-saving poison was dripped slowly into her veins. Sarah had made her promise she'd do everything to look after Hope and her darling Harry. Jenny felt her stomach contracting and she pulled away from the table, wrapping her arms around herself. It suddenly felt chilly in the usually cosy kitchen.

Harry sat down at the table opposite her.

'She wasn't keeping it from you. Don't blame Sarah.' His voice softened as he said her name. 'I didn't want you to know. I didn't want anyone to know. I couldn't . . .'

And it all spilled out.

'We were in an accident. Her father was killed.' Harry looked down at the table again, and when he looked up his eyes were dark with bitterness and regret. 'She blamed me.' He dropped his eyes again and steepled his fingers, pressing them together hard so the skin turned white at the tips of his fingers. He closed his eyes and she noticed a nerve jumping in his cheek.

'An accident?'

'It was . . .' He began again, haltingly. 'There was an

inquest. She couldn't believe – couldn't let herself believe – that something that awful just happened. To us all.' His shoulders crumpled then, and he dropped his face into his hands.

By the end of the long, sorry tale, Jenny had moved around and was sitting with an arm around his shoulders.

'My God, Harry.'

'I know. I just didn't want – couldn't bear the thought of you thinking it was my fault.'

'But you know it wasn't your fault.'

'Sarah helped me understand, yes.' He smiled at her, and wiped away a tear. 'And then when she got sick again, I felt like maybe I was just destined to mess things up.'

'But you're an amazing dad to Hope.'

He shrugged and made a face. 'I've been away working half the time.'

'She loves you more than anything, you know that?'

He nodded. For a moment he looked like a broken child, and she wanted to scoop him into her arms and tell him everything was going to be OK. She wrapped her arms around him. 'I'm sorry you've carried all this.'

'I'm sorry I – we – I'm sorry you didn't know.'

'I understand. But why didn't you tell us when Ella turned up on the doorstep? We could have cut ties with her. The last thing I would have wanted was for you to feel uncomfortable.'

He shook his head again and reached forward, spinning

the wine glass around in his hands before taking a mouthful. He pulled another face.

'I could see how much Hope wanted to be around her.'

'But that's why the atmosphere was so weird.'

'Yeah.'

She started to laugh. 'Lou and I thought there was a bit of chemistry going on, especially after there was nothing going on with you and Holly.'

He looked up at her sharply. 'Me and Holly?'

She shrugged. 'You're a young man. We – well, we wondered. My God, we couldn't have been more wrong.' She reached across and tipped the last of the wine into their glasses. 'About all of it. I think we're going to need another bottle, at this rate.'

They sat in silence for a while.

All that time Ella had spent with them and not said anything. Jenny had thought they were friends. Ella had talked about the importance of honesty and explained that the horses reflected back your feelings and the truth. Jenny scoffed at her own naivety, and at Ella's deception.

'So let me get this straight,' Lou said later, as they lay in bed, side by side, staring at the ceiling in the near-darkness. The room was illuminated by a full moon and the shadows of the trees danced on the walls.

Jenny reached out her hand, finding his. She held on tightly. She was wretched, worn out by the day's events. Hope was fast asleep, her leg carefully propped up and surrounded by pillows. They'd given her some more pain relief, and Harry was sleeping on the chair beside her.

'*Our* Harry was married to Ella. They divorced when her dad was killed. Not a word about it to us when he and Sarah got married –'

She should be furious at Ella, and yet somehow – was it the wisdom that came with having made more than her fair share of mistakes in the last sixty-odd years? She could see how easy it was to make a bad judgement, and one that could have ended in tragedy. Life wasn't black and white.

'Sarah knew,' Jenny pointed out, 'and I don't suppose it was really any of our business.'

'No.' Lou shifted slightly and pulled the covers up. 'It's cold, isn't it?'

The wind rattled the window panes, as if to make a point. Outside, the sky was bright with stars and the hills echoed with the sound of a clear winter's night.

'Anyway. The only thing that's a bit odd about the whole thing is that neither of them said a word to us.'

'I know.'

'How do you feel?' Lou's voice was kindly. After his years in the police force he was pretty much unshockable. This was a minor hiccup to him.

Jenny pinched the bridge of her nose, and thought.

'I feel – a bit *cheated*, somehow.' She sighed. 'As if one of them should have said something. I don't know. Awkward, perhaps.'

'Hmm.'

'I don't know why, though. It's not our place, is it?'

'It's hard when you're a parent, letting go. Trusting they'll do the right thing.'

'Maybe they felt all that stuff was best left in the past.'

Jenny thought about the last time she'd seen Ella and Harry together at the stables. They'd been laughing about something as Hope sat on the floor watching Muffin snooze beside her. They'd looked comfortable – close, even.

'They certainly didn't look like a couple who'd been through a bitter divorce, did they?'

Lou pulled her in close, wrapping her in a hug. 'Perhaps we're not as switched on as we like to think we are.'

She yawned.

'I think perhaps you're right.'

Lou was asleep in moments. Jenny lay there for hours, watching the silhouettes of the trees outside dancing against the curtains, and thought not just about what she'd learned about Harry and Ella but about the day's events. She'd considered herself indispensable and thought she was doing the right thing stepping in to care for Hope, but when the chips were down it was Harry that Hope wanted. Which was exactly as it should be, of course – but that didn't stop it from being painful. It wasn't a very pleasant feeling to realize that you were somewhat redundant.

Chapter Thirty-seven

Harry

'I want Grandma. I don't want to do a wee with you here, Daddy.'

Hope had woken up grouchy, hungry and irritable. Pre-caffeine negotiations over loo visits were the last thing he needed.

'Grandma's not up yet, darling. How about I just put you on the loo and I'll wait outside and you can call me when you're done?'

She gave a grudging harrumph as a reply. This was going to be a long six weeks of recuperation. He averted his gaze as he stood on the landing, not looking up the hill at the white farmhouse with its plume of smoke.

'Can we go and see Muffin?' A small voice called through from behind the bathroom door. And then – 'Finished.'

'We can't go right now, Hope. You've only got a temporary cast on, for one thing.'

He scooped her up in his arms and carried her downstairs before returning for the tiny pair of crutches they'd been given.

*

Making breakfast, he scanned his work messages. He'd been working from home as much as possible, but there was a meeting in Paris at the beginning of the week that he couldn't skip. He'd been working on the proposal for the best part of a year, and they were expecting him there to go through it. He puffed out a sigh of exasperation. If he could just get that out of the way, he'd work it out from there.

'How are you feeling this morning?'

Jenny came into the room wrapped in her dressing gown.

Hope looked up from the sofa. 'Daddy says we can't go and see Muffin until I get my leg fixed. Can we go to the hospital today?'

Jenny ruffled her hair. 'Sorry, sweetie. They said we've to come back tomorrow.'

'About that . . .' Harry began. 'I'll get you some cereal, sweetheart. You wait there.' He handed Hope her iPad and the television remote.

'What's up?'

He raised his eyebrows at Jenny, ruefully. 'You mean besides the wine head from last night?'

She picked up the two glasses and the bottle from the table and put them beside the sink. An unspoken moment of communication passed between them.

'I think our main priority right now has to be making sure that Hope is happy and healthy.'

'I agree.' He poured cereal into a bowl, and added milk. 'I'm going to start by giving her this.'

And then, he thought, we can discuss the fact that I've got to get on a flight to Paris first thing tomorrow and Hope's going to miss school and all the positive steps we've taken have been set back because Ella messed up. He tensed at the thought, and then pasted on a smile. He headed into the sitting room to give Hope her breakfast.

'She's a lovely girl. Tragic what happened to her,' Connie said to Jenny, lowering her voice. She settled her elbows on the counter, ready for a chat. Jenny shifted from one foot to the other, feeling uncomfortable. She'd only popped in to the cafe to pick up one of the iced gingerbread men Hope loved, and somehow Connie had brought the subject round to Ella and the accident.

'Poor little love.' Connie shook her head

Jenny considered herself to be scrupulously honest. It made her feel uncomfortable to think that Ella had got to know her, and not felt comfortable enough to admit the truth about her relationship with Harry. But he was her son-in-law, and neither had he. Thank God Hope's leg wasn't in a fit state for her to be going anywhere, let alone the stables. It was going to be a different matter once they'd replaced the cast with a lightweight one, but they'd have to deal with that problem when it arose. In the meantime, she decided, she'd keep her head down.

'Hope will be missing a few days of school, then?'

'Yes, just until we get the permanent cast on.'

Connie leaned in further still, inviting a confidence. 'I've always thought horses are bloody big beasts to be doing therapy with, if you ask me.'

Jenny moved back almost imperceptibly. 'It was an accident.'

'Hmm,' said Connie. She shook out a cloth and pursed her lips. 'I hope the council don't get wind of it and change their mind when she's just about to have all this new business coming in.'

'Honestly, it was just one of those things.' Now she was making things up on the spot. She'd no idea what had happened, and wouldn't until she spoke to Ella. 'It could have happened any time.'

'That's what I mean,' Connie said darkly. 'Bloody big beasts. You wouldn't get me near one of them if you paid me.'

If there was one thing Jenny knew, it was that village gossip spread like wildfire. She didn't want to be responsible for causing any more harm. Whatever had gone on in the past, she wouldn't be party to anything that could mess up Ella's future.

'How much longer have we got you here?'

'Just over a couple of months.' She could tell Connie to the day, if she wanted. She and Lou had lain in bed that morning talking seriously about what was going to happen next. Neither of them was as keen to get back to their old house as they thought they might have been, and they'd had an email from the letting agency saying that the family who were renting it might be interested in keeping it a bit longer. They hadn't been able to find a house they liked, apparently. If they'd had the same conversation a day earlier, it would have been cut and dried. They'd have happily stayed longer – but it wasn't just about them. Hope needed to be settled somewhere, and it was increasingly clear that it was time for Jenny to cut the apron strings that tied grandmother to granddaughter and let Harry step into his role as father. It had taken long enough.

'Seems a shame, when you're all settling in so well.'

'Mmm.' Jenny picked up the paper bag of cookies and put it in her handbag. 'We'll have to see what happens.'

The words sounded hollow to her ears, and she suspected from Connie's expression that they didn't ring true with her, either. The truth was plain to see. She walked down the high street, past the deli and the bookshop, waving hello to Alan through the post office door, and into the little car park. The village of Llanidaeron had settled inside her and made itself at home.

Chapter Thirty-eight

Ella

Ella swept the entire yard. She'd barely slept and she knew that Jenny and Hope, Harry and Lou must be home because she'd – she was slightly ashamed of herself – had a look to see if she could see their cars through Bron's bird-watching binoculars, telling herself it was just so she could know they were home safely. But she hadn't heard a word.

Perhaps she should just ring Jenny and ask, but there was another part of her that wondered what Harry had said, and *why* she hadn't heard anything. She made a deal with herself. If I haven't heard by three, I'll call.

She put the broom away in the feed room and checked her email.

Sending this from the staffroom because there's no bloody chance you'll get a text in time. What's the story with Hope? Rumours flying around the school that she was attacked by one of your horses. If you want me to do some damage limitation, speak now. Liss x

Shit. Ella thought fast. If this got back before the final paperwork was signed, she could lose the contract. She needed to move quickly. She scanned the calendar on the wall and made a spur-of-the-moment decision.

I'm going to have an open day this weekend. If you spread the word, I'll get some posters printed off and stick them around town, and put a note up on the village Facebook page.

You're a bloody genius. I'll come up after school and see you. Big kiss. xxx

Ella typed quickly:

Hillside Farm Equine Assisted Psychotherapy
Ella Waters BSc (Hons) MSc Dip.EAP
OPEN DAY
Saturday 21st January, 12–3 p.m.
ALL WELCOME

That ought to do it. Now all she had to do was hope against hope that Charlotte was down to work on Saturday and hadn't made any plans to go off and have something pierced or shave half her hair off, or something. That, and get the place – and the horses – looking spotless. She had to show everyone that her horses weren't child-maiming monsters, and that she ran a professional therapy practice.

*

Ella worked at warp speed for the next few days. Lissa came up after school in the evenings and baked a load of cookies for the visitors ('If nobody turns up, it's a win,' she said cheerfully. 'We get to pig out on chocolate chip cookies and a load of Prosecco.')

She took all the horses in on Friday and kept them stabled with rugs, to minimize the chances of any of the greys lying down in something awful and getting covered with green poo stains. Charlotte worked like a trooper, polishing all the leather of the head collars and making sure Tor's tack was gleaming. She was angling to do a ridden demonstration, even though it bore very little relevance to the afternoon's events.

Several clients had volunteered to come along and act as horse handlers; they'd heard about the accident and wanted to show their support. And Brian and Carol – separately – offered to help too, each promising they'd bring along some extra bodies to make the place look busy.

'Not that it won't be,' Carol had said, comfortingly.

'I really appreciate this,' Ella said.

'You've changed my life,' Carol smiled. She'd driven to the shop and bought flowers for the office, and was arranging them neatly in a vase. 'If I hadn't come here, I wouldn't be the person I am now. I love this place. And the horses.'

Ella felt a rare smile reaching across her face. She'd been almost numb with worry. She hadn't heard anything from the local authority, and Lissa kept telling her that no news was good news. She also still hadn't heard a word from Jenny, or Harry. She'd dropped in with a box of chocolates, a pony magazine and some flowers, but Lou had answered the door. He'd thanked her, in his gruff, kindly way, but hadn't asked her to come in. All she knew was that Hope was doing fine, and that she was back at school (that thanks to Lissa's updates) with a brightly coloured cast on her leg, which was the envy of all her new schoolfriends.

But she couldn't think about Hope, or Harry, now. She had to concentrate on getting everything perfect for the open day. She didn't want all the good work she'd done to fall apart, and Bron to return – if she ever did – to a failing business.

Chapter Thirty-nine

Harry

Harry sat on the plane, gazing out of the little window at the lights sparkling below as they circled, waiting to land. He shifted in his seat.

'Sorry,' said the woman sitting next to him, automatically polite as he knocked her leg.

'My fault.'

She smiled and looked at the printed-out report he was reading. 'No rest for the wicked, is there?'

A smile curved at the corner of her mouth. They had another twenty minutes to landing and he couldn't face conversation – his mind was spinning.

'Something like that.' He cleared his throat and looked down at the papers, frowning as if concentrating hard.

The truth was, he wasn't taking them in at all. In the days since Hope's accident, he'd spent long hours awake running over everything in his head. It was glaringly obvious. Whenever he and Ella were near each other, bad things happened. He thought back to his childhood. When his mother had moved out, he'd overheard an argument in which his mother had shouted angrily that if they hadn't had children, they might have stayed together, but that when he came along, everything changed. The words had settled deep within him, until he met Ella. When he fell for her, and went home to the warmth of her house and her lovely, kind-natured dad, he'd felt that perhaps there was a space for him. Bron had come to visit and filled the house with delicious food. The whole place had felt safe and welcoming. It couldn't have been a bigger contrast to the echoing, silent cavern that was Burnham House.

And then everything fell apart, and he was alone again. After the accident and the divorce, his parents' sympathy took the form of money. He was told to take some time off, travel and see the world. The unspoken message had seemed to be *and don't bother us*. So he hadn't.

Then Sarah took his hand that day at the hospital. Small and dark and freckle-nosed, she wouldn't take no for an answer. She pulled him into her family and into her life, and he was happy to be towed along. It seemed safer to keep the truth of what had happened in the past in a box, separate from his new life. But the truth was –

The moment he'd seen Ella in the hall of the cottage on Christmas morning replayed itself in his head. The way she'd looked when she'd stood up and turned around. The expression on her face – not anger, not resentment. It was something else. Something different. Something –

He shook his head. The truth was that no matter what he might feel, those feelings were dangerous. Hope had suffered a broken leg, but it could have been far worse. It wasn't a coincidence that Ella had come back into his life – it was a warning.

The email from the solicitor had arrived yesterday, when they were having a break from a meeting that had dragged on interminably. His head was pounding and his A-level French was flagging. He'd headed out into the cool stone of the corridor. The building was in the centre of Paris, and he'd found himself looking out across an early evening skyline that was achingly romantic.

Dear Harry,

There are some final details regarding the sale of your father's property which require signatures. I can have these sent to you by special delivery if needed, or you can pop by, soonest.

Yours, etc. . . .

It could have waited, but he wanted it done. Harry ducked out of the meeting, handing over the reins to the eager – and more than capable – Kamal. After landing at Heathrow, he hired a car to drive north, cutting through the rolling green of Essex and up to the fenlands. The road seemed to go on forever, the miles counting down one by one, until he turned into the centre of town. The ornate, old-fashioned clock tower of Downham Market marked home.

He parked the car and made his way up to the beautiful building that was home to Donald Jenkins, who had been the family solicitor for years.

'Sorry to spring myself on you first thing,' Harry said. He towered over the little desk that was set to one side in a room which had – once upon a time – been the drawing room of a very fine town house. Now – and for as long as the furniture had been there, which looked like the early 1970s – it was the home of the redoubtable Donald Jenkins, a tall, thin man who looked like a crane bird in a suit. Harry always half-expected him to pick up one long, spindly leg and hold it, folded, in mid-air. Since they'd last met he'd lost even more hair, so all that remained was a faint memory, circling a bald patch which reached almost to his ears.

'Wasn't expecting you to drop in *quite* this quickly,' Donald said. He picked up a pile of letters and riffled through them briefly.

'Can you deal with these, Peter, and bring us through a pot of tea?'

The young man behind the desk – probably only eighteen or so – nodded and smiled, nervously.

Harry signed the paperwork and passed it back to Donald.

'Well.' He looked at Harry over his glasses. 'You've got a quite considerable nest egg now, even after inheritance tax. Any plans?'

'I think I might give up work,' he said, surprising himself.

You about?

About as in – here?

As in – put the kettle on.

Harry smiled to himself as he stood on the front step of Holly's little cottage. There was a crashing from inside as she threw herself down the stairs, and pulled the door open with a beaming smile.

'What the bloody hell, Macallan. Why didn't you tell me you were coming?'

Harry loosened his tie and put it down on Holly's little round pine table. It slithered off some newly bought frames and landed on the floor. She handed it back.

He shook his head. 'Bin it.'

'You what?' Holly held it at arm's length, as if it were a snake.

'Put it in the bin.'

'It's not that bad.' Holly curled her lip. 'Bit boring, if you ask me.'

He reached across, laughing, and took it out of her hand. 'I didn't.'

With a fluid movement he reached across, tapped open the bin, and dropped it in, on top of a mess of eggshells and left over baked beans. He closed the lid.

'OK.' Holly sat down. 'We're going to need to take this from the top.'

'D'you fancy a drive out to my dad's place, and I'll tell you the whole story?'

Holly looked at the picture frames. 'I'm meant to have them at the Country Kitchen for their art sale tomorrow.'

'Don't worry.' He made to get up. 'It was just an idea.'

'No.' She shook her head. 'I'm in.'

As they made their way down the drive of Burnham House, Harry realized they were effectively trespassing. The house wasn't anything to do with him anymore, and he'd already said goodbye.

'Bloody hell, I forgot how massive your dad's place is. I mean, was.' Holly grimaced. 'Were you not a *tiny* bit tempted to keep it and do the whole Lord of the Manor thing?'

'Not even slightly.'

'I so would. I'd have millions of dogs and make it an art collective and turn the big sitting room into a gallery.' They got out of the car. 'Actually, I wouldn't. That would mean people, and I can't be doing with people. I've realized I'm quite happy with my own company.'

They headed around the back of the house, down the lawn, and through the hedge into the vegetable garden. He'd paid a gardener to keep it up after his father died, so the soil stood, bare and hopeful, waiting for spring.

There was an old metal bench where he'd sat at weekends when he was small, watching his mum weeding carefully, thinning out carrot seedlings and earthing up potatoes. It was rough with rust, the paint bubbling and flaking away. He sat down.

'OK.' Holly sat down beside him. 'What's going on?'

'Nothing. Except I've handed in my notice, I've no idea what I'm going to do next, and Jenny and Lou are about to head back to Norwich – and I've got to work out a way to tell them I'd like to start living my own life.'

'You mean, you and Hope?'

He nodded.

'About bloody time.' Holly blew upwards so her fringe puffed up in the air.

'You don't think –' He paused for a moment, thinking.

'I think – now you're asking, and I've been biting my tongue for bloody ages, if you actually want to know – that you've all been skirting around each other trying so bloody hard to do the right thing that you've ballsed it all up.'

'Cheers. Break it to me gently, why don't you?'

'I've tried that numerous times with you *and* Jenny, and neither of you take a blind bit of notice.' She snapped off the end of a dried-out piece of bindweed and started tearing it into tiny pieces, dropping them on her lap. 'Sarah would go bloody mad if she saw the state of you lot. Jenny's always been prone to interfering, and she doesn't know when to let go. Never did. You're too nice for your own good, and Lou's been so busy working himself to death to avoid grieving for Sarah that he didn't even notice what was going on.'

'All right, agony aunt extraordinare, so what do I do now?'

'You go back to Wales, and you hang out with Hope, and you do whatever it takes to keep the smile on her face that I saw there when I came up before Christmas. That's the happiest I've ever seen her. You know why that is, don't you?'

'Why?'

'Because –' Holly took a moment and then swallowed, as if she was thinking about what to say. 'Because Ella is good for her. For both of you.'

They drove back, closing the gate on Burnham House for the last time. Holly was still staggered, shaking her head in amazement.

'Of all the stables in all the world . . .' she repeated, in a Humphrey Bogart voice.

'Very funny,' he said drily.

'You've got to admit it's a bit unlikely.'

'It might be, but it's bloody happened. And I've no idea what the hell I'm supposed to do about it.'

Chapter Forty

Jenny

Jenny paused for a moment, her hand on the iron gate of Hillside Farm. Her stomach was churning, but she felt certain she was doing the right thing.

She took a deep breath, swung the gate open, and stepped onto the gravel.

'Two secs!' said Charlotte, who was tying a balloon to a bucket full of water and half-hidden by a hedge, before looking up. 'Just got to – *oh* . . .'

She flushed a bright scarlet, which clashed terribly with her newly purple hair. 'How's Hope doing?' She bit her lip, brows pressed together in concern.

'Not too bad, thank you.'

'I'm really sorry. I'm so sorry. I didn't mean for it to happen.'

Tears brimmed on her thickly mascaraed lashes and then started to fall down her cheeks.

Jenny stepped forward, putting an arm around Charlotte's shoulders. 'It's not your fault, my love.'

Charlotte sniffed and swiped at her eyes. 'But I was with Hope.'

'And you were doing what you were supposed to, weren't you?'

'Yes.' She wiped her nose with the sleeve of her fleece. Jenny reached into her bag and pulled out a tissue, passing it to her.

'Well, accidents will happen. I understand what happened.'

'I thought you were going to sue us. That's why Ella's doing –' she waved her arm to indicate the stable yard, which was a hive of activity – 'this.'

'*Sue* you?' Jenny shook her head. 'Hardly.'

'Ella's in the stables. Do you want me to go and get her?'

'I'll go.'

The yard was immaculate and there was a horse looking out of each stable door. They were all gleaming and bright-eyed.

'Hello.'

Ella looked up from her position on the floor, where she was squatting down, bandaging the leg of a pretty grey horse. When she saw Jenny her eyes widened.

'Jenny,' she said. 'I just need to –' She wrapped the bandage round again and secured it with some tape, biting the end off with her teeth.

She stood up. The stable smelled of the sweet last-summer fragrance of the hay, and the unmistakable scent of warm, dry horse. The grey horse lifted an experimental foot as if trying out the bandage, then walked in a circle before settling down to eat.

'Hope would like that,' Jenny smiled.

'How is she?' Ella fiddled with the packet the bandage had been in.

'A bit frustrated and cross, but fine.' Jenny put a hand out, feeling the smooth edge of the stable door. It had been worn over years to a satiny finish and she traced a finger along it, thoughtfully. 'I just wanted you to know she's OK.'

'I wondered if you'd come up for the open day.'

'Open day?'

'It's today. Twelve until three. I wanted a chance to show that we . . .' She tailed off.

Jenny didn't need her to say any more. It wasn't hard to put two and two together.

'We've got wheelchair-friendly facilities, if you'd like to –'

For a second Jenny wavered. Hope would be delighted. She could picture her face.

'No.'

Ella gave a small, flat smile. She flicked her eyes upward, meeting Jenny's for the first time. 'I'm truly sorry –' she began.

'I am, too.' Jenny looked at the girl in front of her. If they were moving back to Norfolk, they were going to have to rip the plaster off at some point. Hope's broken leg was a natural – well, a natural breaking point. She swallowed, thinking of the angry little girl she'd left sitting, unable to move, on the sofa. 'For all of it.'

*

387

The open day was a success. Carol and Brian, dressed in matching checked shirts and Stetsons – which were, Charlotte hissed under her breath, either beyond sad or beyond cool, she couldn't work out which – served teas and coffees to a stream of visitors. Some ex-clients had come to offer support, and Ella was particularly touched that the head teachers of both the primary and the secondary school took the time to visit and have their photograph taken for the Facebook page, telling everyone who'd listen what a brilliant service Ella offered. She suspected Lissa had had a hand in that, but Lissa – handing out leaflets detailing the services they provided – simply looked enigmatic.

'Nothing to do with me. It's clearly your natural charm that's brought them up here.'

'Whatever it is, I'm bloody grateful.' Ella pulled her into a hug and had to squeeze her eyes tight to stop the tears from falling. They could wait for later.

Jenny smiled, watching Hope as she determinedly shuffled backwards up the stairs on her bottom. With the heavy temporary plaster cast off and replaced with a much lighter fibreglass one in a very fetching shade of purple, she was much happier and able to get around – albeit in a rather unusual manner – independently.

And independence mattered a lot to Hope. She knew her own mind, like her mummy had. Jenny glanced across at the framed picture on the mantelpiece.

'What would you say to all this?' she murmured.

Sarah's happy, open face smiled back at her. She didn't need to ask. The answer was obvious. If spending time with the horses made her darling Hope happy, then that's what she'd be doing. She wouldn't be sending agonized glances up the hill to the stables, and doing everything she could to distract an unconvinced Hope with assurances that they'd sort something out very soon, darling . . .

'I still don't see what the problem is,' Lou had said. 'You're not being unfaithful to Sarah – and for that matter neither was Harry. If you ask me, you're both getting worked up about nothing. Take the girl to see the horses. She's pining for them.'

He'd pulled on a jacket – it was an unseasonably sunny day, with the future hint of spring in the air – and set off to stroll into town. Yes, he chuckled, gently. Not too fast. And yes, he'd call her to get a lift home later, and no, he wouldn't try walking back up the hill or anything silly like that.

She smiled to herself, remembering the conversation. She'd thought it impossible that Lou would find a space for himself in the village, and yet he was the one off making friends and fitting in.

Spending time with the horses – and it had been a revelation to discover that Harry was easy and comfortable around them, too, although she understood now why he was so familiar with it all – had changed them all as a family. It wasn't just the practical equine therapy work – just being around the animals seemed to bring huge benefits. Perhaps when they went back home, they could see about finding another stable where Hope could take part.

She looked around the little cottage sitting room. Over the last few months it had begun to feel like home, despite having been thrust upon them. The shelves were stacked with their books and Hope's drawings were tucked along the mantelpiece next to her mum's photograph. The stone floor beneath the rush mat had been swept neatly earlier, and the fire was glowing. The holiday agency had sent an email asking her to get in touch, and she was hovering, one foot in one country and one in another. Lou had settled, despite the odds, and he was healthy and happy. If they went back home to Norfolk, they could return to their old life, their old friends; but would they be back to all their old problems?

She looked again at the photo of Sarah, and made up her mind.

Chapter Forty-one

Ella

'Can I ride Tor now?' Charlotte was waggling his bridle at her, dancing in front of her. Sometimes it wasn't hard to imagine her as a pony-mad little girl.

It was half past two and a few visitors were still hanging around, chatting to the horses, or making an extra plastic cup of wine last a bit longer. A couple of children around Hope's age were doting on Muffin, feeding him handfuls of grass they were tearing up from the lawn. They'd laughed as Ella did a demonstration with Muffin and Tor, leading them herself through a series of obstacles, explaining what she was doing to a group of visitors who sat on the benches by the side of the indoor arena.

'Go on then. I'll tell the others you're going to have a ride round on him and they can come in and watch you two show off.'

'Yes.' Charlotte did a fist pump and swooshed off with the bridle in hand. 'Come on baby, it's time to shine.'

Watching Charlotte cantering around the school on Tor, Ella felt a tightness in her stomach that she didn't recognize. It took a moment before she realized the sensation she was feeling was – envy. She'd sent him away to be trained by an expert, promising herself that one day she'd get on his back and get over her fear of riding, but two years had passed and she was no further forward.

'Charlotte!'

She spun round, recognizing Hope's voice immediately.

'I thought I'd bring her up after all,' Jenny said, with a shy smile.

'Hello, little one.' Ella beamed as Hope clattered across the wooden floorboards of the viewing area on her crutches. She was surprisingly speedy.

'Grandma said I could come and see you and Muffin and have some more lessons.'

Jenny's eyes met hers. 'Really?'

Jenny nodded. 'If you'll have us.'

'I would love that. But I thought you were going back?'

Jenny shook her head. 'I think we've found home.'

Charlotte eased Tor to a walk and rode him over. He reached across to Hope, sniffing at her crutches with interest. Hope patted Tor's neck.

Ella left them there chatting whilst she headed out with the last few stragglers, handing them information leaflets and closing the gate behind them. She sighed with relief and headed back to the school to join Charlotte, Jenny and Hope.

'If it's OK with you, I'd like Hope to carry on where we left off.'

'How do you feel about that, Hope?'

She nodded, but bit her lip. 'Good, but I don't think I want to ride Muffin.'

Jenny laughed. 'You can't ride Muffin, darling, you've got a broken leg.'

'I know,' Hope said, her face solemn. 'I mean, I don't want to ride him after that.'

'Why not?' Charlotte, still sitting astride Tor, pushed back her riding hat and looked at Hope with curiosity.

'Because,' Ella said, gently, 'sometimes if you fall off, or something scary happens, it's quite hard to get back on.'

Charlotte's eyes met hers then in a moment of understanding. She slid off Tor's back and stood by his side, holding his reins.

Inside, Ella felt as if every muscle in her body was screaming *no* at the same time as her mind was saying *yes*. She reached out her hand to take Tor's reins.

'Can I borrow your hat?'

Charlotte nodded and Ella fastened it on, clipping the chin strap carefully in place.

Jenny looked puzzled. 'What's going on?'

Ella gathered the reins in one hand, and took the stirrup in the other. The yoga exercises had opened up the stiffness in her hip, and running had given her the strength in her legs to swing herself onto Tor's back without any trouble, even after all this time. She took an unsteady breath and slipped her right foot into the stirrup, looking at them from the familiar, yet alien viewpoint. Tor's ears pricked in front of her, his long mane shining as he arched his neck, jingling the metal of his bit.

'Sometimes,' Ella looked at Hope and smiled, 'if you fall off, it's quite scary to think of getting back on.' As she spoke, she felt herself relaxing. 'It's a very long time since I've sat on a horse, Hope. Years and years.'

'Aren't you scared you might fall off like I did?' Hope looked back at her, wide-eyed.

'A little bit.' Ella, now in the saddle, shifted her weight and Tor responded instantly. He was still warmed up and she pushed him forwards into a walk, feeling him swaying beneath her. It felt like forever, and no time at all. 'But I think if we don't do things that are a bit scary sometimes, we won't ever try anything.'

And she pushed Tor forward into a soaring rockinghorse canter, his mane flying out with every stride. Her body moved instinctively with his and she laughed aloud in sheer joy, circling him back towards the others for a moment and then back across the school in a figure of eight. She hadn't forgotten a thing. It felt like it always had – like she was born to ride. Turning Tor back once more, she steadied him to a walk, sliding off his back almost before he'd come to a halt.

Harry was standing, his arms around Hope, watching her with an unreadable expression.

'I –' Her throat was dry, and the words wouldn't

come. Her legs carried her towards them, Tor walking obediently by her side.

'Hope tells me she's looking forward to riding Muffin when her leg gets better.'

Hope balanced on one crutch and did a thumbs-up, grinning gappily at them. 'I might be a little bit scared but it's OK, isn't it?'

Harry wrapped his arms around Hope, but his eyes looked directly into hers. 'Definitely.'

'I'll just take Tor back to the stable.'

She led him out through the sliding door, ignoring the fact that her inner thighs were already aching and her legs felt like jelly. She opened Tor's door and led him in, lifting the side of the saddle and unfastening the girth, sliding it off his back. She turned to balance it on his door.

'I don't blame you,' Harry said. He took the saddle and lifted it over the door, waiting while she undid the bridle and ruffled Tor's mane in thanks. Tor gave a gusty snort and turned to investigate his hay rack.

Harry opened the stable door for her, the saddle over one arm, and she slipped out, leaning against the wall to hold up her wobbly legs.

'I wanted you to know. I don't blame you for Hope's accident.'

She looked into his face briefly, seeing nothing there but kindness. 'Thank you.'

'Like old times,' he said, indicating the saddle. There was an awkward pause while they both remembered the days when she'd ride Ruby and he'd be there waiting afterwards.

He turned away first, clearing his throat.

'Daddy, do you think maybe one day I could have a pony of my own? Like Muffin?'

Hope made her way across the yard, her bright purple cast finished off with a brightly coloured stripy woollen sock.

'I like your colourful toes.'

Hope waggled her leg. 'It's to stop me getting cold feet. I've got lots and lots of pairs. Grandma bought them.'

'Well?' Hope looked at them as if they were all incredibly forgetful.

'What?'

'Can I have a pony like Muffin?'

Ella watched Jenny and Harry exchange a sideways look.

'We'll have to see what happens, sweetheart,' Harry said.

'I think we'd better let you get on,' Jenny said, patting Tor cautiously on the nose. 'And now I think of it, I believe Lou's out without a key. He didn't know we were going out.'

Ella closed the gate behind them and turned to Charlotte, who was leaning against a wall, checking her phone. Despite the lack of signal, she lived in hope and was perpetually waving it around in the hope something might get through.

'Come on, you. We can finish off the biscuits before evening stables, and then I'm getting in a bath and never getting out again.'

They headed into the house, closing the door on the last light of the afternoon.

Ella could see Bron's face, but couldn't hear a word she was saying. Her mouth was moving and she was gesticulating.

'I can't hear you,' Ella said, for the third time.

'. . Sorry, the microphone was off.'

They were still chatting on Skype regularly. Ella was amused by the changes in her aunt. First some plaited bracelets appeared on her wrist, and then a silver ring. And another the next time. She seemed to be embracing her youth again.

'D'you like my hair?' Bron pulled her long plait over her shoulder and Ella peered at the screen, realizing that the underside was streaked with magenta which wove through the plait like a ribbon.

'Amazing.' She pushed her own hair back, seeing how untidy it looked in the little box on the screen, and she laughed. 'You look like you've gone native. Turned into a surfer dude.'

'Funny you should say that,' Bron raised her eyebrows, mischievously. 'I've been taking some lessons.'

'In *surfing*?'

'Yes.' Bron raised a warning finger. 'And don't you start with the *don't you think you're a bit old for that sort of thing* with me, young lady.'

'I wasn't going to.'

'Good. Because I've got something I want to ask you.'

Ella suspected she knew what was coming.

'How would you feel about me staying out here for another few months?'

She looked back at her aunt's much-loved face, and smiled. 'I think you should stay as long as you like.'

Bron's face lit up. 'I'm very glad to hear that.'

'You're not missing everyone back here too much? And the rain and the mud and –'

'No, Isobel's keeping me busy. And I've –' She paused for a moment and looked away. 'Well, I've been spending some time with a friend I've made.'

'Ah,' said Ella, laughing. In all the time she'd known her aunt she'd been resolutely single, maintaining she had no time for men or any of that nonsense.

'So who is he?'

'*He* isn't anyone.' Bron twiddled with the end of her plait and looked down for a moment, waiting for the words to sink in.

'. . . *She* is Meg. My surfing instructor.'

Ella put a hand to her mouth and started to laugh in surprise.

'There's a photo of her on my phone, here, look.' Bron lifted up her phone to the screen and Ella could just make out a picture of her aunt, smiling with her arm around a tall woman with grey-streaked blonde hair. They looked perfect together.

'You don't mind?' Bron bit her lip and frowned.

'Mind?' Ella shook her head. 'Why would I mind?'

'Well. It wasn't exactly the done thing when I was growing up. It seemed easier to just stay single and focus on putting all my energies into the farm and the horses.'

'Oh, Bron.' Tears sprang to Ella's eyes. 'I'm sorry.'

Bron shook her head. 'No need. Maybe next time I'll bring Meg along for a chat.' She looked proud, and strangely shy.

'I'd love that.'

Bron waved goodbye and reached across to switch off. Ella blew a kiss as her aunt's image disappeared from the screen.

Ella did the last round of checks alone, leaving Charlotte in the farmhouse watching television. Her wet hair was knotted up in a loose bun and she pulled a fleece over her pyjamas, slipping her feet into wellies.

She looped a rope around the horse's neck and led him out of the paddock and into the stable by the indoor school. He'd rolled, trying to relieve the itch that came with the beginning of his winter coat shedding, and she picked up a brush to remove the worst of the mud that was clinging to his back.

As she swept the brush along in long strokes, she thought back to the years when she'd been growing up and had come here to visit with her dad. It had never occurred to her once that Bron might have been lonely, or that she hadn't been alone by choice.

And then when she'd arrived, broken and devastated by the split and the aftermath of the crash, she'd been so wrapped up in herself that Bron had been like a comfort blanket. She'd given her love and support to Ella unconditionally, and now – away from the demands of the farm and the horses – Bron was getting that back.

It was a relief to know that she was happy.

Chapter Forty-two

Ella

'Morning,' a voice came over the top of the stable door. Brian peered down at Ella. She placed Lily's foot down on the floor gently and stood up, pressing her hands into the small of her back and stretching. She needed a long bath, or a massage – or both. She'd been riding in every spare moment she could find since the open day, and her body was protesting – in a good way. Everything ached, but she was getting stronger and fitter. Just as well, because the fun run was only a day away. She'd been slacking off a bit on the running, and hoped she wouldn't let the side down after everything.

'You ready for your final session?'

He bobbed his head sideways with a wink that almost hid the nerves. 'Ready as I'll ever be.'

'Reckon we'll have the time of our lives out there,' Brian said, as he swung his leg over Tor's back and landed gently in the saddle. He'd gone from being too scared of horses to go near them, to leading several of the horses through courses of obstacles, and he'd asked if she would give him a chance to try riding before he booked himself in for some lessons at Jim's riding school across the valley.

'Don't forget, their tack is a bit different to what you're used to. You'll be more comfortable, I should think.' She adjusted his stirrups. 'Western saddles are built for sitting in all day.'

'I don't know about that.' Brian looked uncertain. 'Think we're hoping for a bit of time for shopping and eating and that sort of thing.'

'We?'

'Did Carol not mention it?'

Ella looked up at him in surprise. 'No.'

'She's coming with me. We're going to Calgary, now, in Canada. We can do a bit of sightseeing, a bit of riding, a bit of time together . . .'

'Brian, that's lovely.' Ella smiled as they headed towards the outdoor school. 'I'm so pleased for you.'

'You should put it on your literature.'

'Put what?'

'Something about it being a good way to meet people.'

She laughed. 'That's not exactly the done thing – I think you two are a bit unusual.'

'Well, we've got you to thank.'

'You've got yourselves to thank. You did all the work.'

The next morning Ella woke early. Even when there was a 10k run to do, the horses still needed to be fed, turned out to graze, checked over and mucked out.

'I'll do that,' Charlotte said, taking the wheelbarrow out of her hands. 'You go and get your stuff on.'

They'd closed off the main streets of the village and lined them with bunting, which flapped wildly in the wind. The shops were decorated with pink and red hearts for Valentine's Day, and Babs was there with her catering van, handing out delicious-smelling burgers. Ella's stomach groaned at the thought. She'd had porridge with banana for breakfast, as recommended by Lissa's running magazine.

'You ready?'

'I was born ready.' Lissa did a power pose and spun round.

'Please don't ever say that again.' Ella shook her head.

'Sorry. I was reading a thing online last night that said you were supposed to visualize yourself doing well.'

'I'm visualizing myself at the finish line having a burger.' Ella's stomach rumbled again.

'I'm thinking about dinner tonight,' said Lissa, dreamily.

'Another hot date?'

Lissa made a face. 'I feel like a proper grown-up.'

'You are a proper grown-up. Half your class is over there waiting to cheer you on, look.'

Lissa turned and saw a group of children with a banner in their hands. It had COME ON MISS JONES written in large, smudgy letters.

'Oh my God.' She clapped a hand to her mouth.

'If they'd only added a comma, that would have been sweet, instead of faintly pornographic.'

'You two all right?' Connie caught them both doubled over with laughter.

'Absolutely.' Lissa looked at Ella, and they started laughing all over again.

'Welcome to the first annual Llanidaeron Fun Run,' boomed Alan's voice over a loudspeaker. Ella turned to Lissa in alarm.

'First? We're doing this again next year?'

'Bollocks to that. We've done our bit.'

Ella reached out and gave her a high five as a klaxon sounded and the run began. They settled into a steady pace and she found herself enjoying it, waving to friends from the village as she turned down familiar roads, high-fiving children who were sitting on the church wall waving flags.

'Go on, Ell,' Nick shouted, grinning. He was standing outside the Lion with a group of his mates, all with pints in their hands.

'You should be bloody doing this,' she laughed, breathlessly.

'Next year. I'll let you two try the course out first.'

'Cocky bastard,' said Lissa, through gritted teeth. They'd turned up the hill through the woods.

'Bloody hell,' Lissa slowed down as the gradient started to hit.

'You OK?'

'Fine.' She sounded puffed but kept up her pace.

*

Before they knew it, they'd done the full circuit and were heading round past the old market hall to the finish line.

'Go on, Lissa,' shouted a voice from the sidelines. Ella turned, seeing the bearded face of James. Lissa blew him a kiss and turned to Ella, eyes wide. 'Oh my God.'

'What is it?' It was sweet that he'd come out to cheer her on – not least because, the village being what it was, it meant everyone would know about their budding relationship by sundown.

'I look like a sweating tomato.'

'Shut up.'

They crossed the finish line together, holding hands raised in triumph.

'Not bad for someone who swore they'd never run unless they were being chased by a bear.' Lissa took one of the cups of water offered and poured it over her head. She reached out and downed the contents of a second cup.

'I only did it for the gin,' said Ella, laughing. 'You did say there was gin at the end, didn't you?'

'I'll buy you one tonight. A double. You bloody deserve it.'

'You both do.' Harry's voice made her startle. She turned around to see him standing there holding Hope's hand.

'We came to watch you running,' said Hope, raising both hands in a cheer.

'Hang on a minute,' said Ella, looking down. 'Where have your crutches gone?'

Hope waggled her leg. Her cast was now topped off with a black protective boot. 'They said I could have this instead so I can walk, and I don't have to keep the crutches.'

'Really?'

Harry nodded, dropping a protective hand onto Hope's shoulder. 'Apparently putting weight on it helps with recovery. I'm having to remind someone that doesn't mean she can run a marathon in the first week, though.'

'Hey,' said Lissa, turning round. 'Look at you, Hope. Nice boot.'

Hope ducked her head and blushed. 'Thank you, Miss Jones.'

Harry suppressed a laugh. 'I saw you had a cheering squad out on the course today.'

'Shh,' said Ella, giving him a look and trying not to giggle. 'They worked Very Hard on that banner.'

Lissa slid a look at Ella and her eyebrows curved upwards for a brief second.

'Nice to see you again, Harry.' Lissa tugged Ella by the hand. 'See you at school after half term, Hope. We'd better go and collect our medals.'

Chapter Forty-three

Harry

When Harry offered to walk down to the village that evening and pick up a couple of things from the shop, the sky was clear, the light fading away. It was peaceful walking down the lane in the dusk, the air echoing with birdsong from the hedgerows that towered above his head on both sides. It was like walking down a tunnel, from which he'd emerge, cross the stone bridge, and then turn right and head down into town. A cyclist – head-lamp flashing - nodded briefly as she turned her bike up the lane, the sound of her gears crunching as she braced herself for the long climb towards Penruthin.

The window of the little bookshop was lit dimly and he paused for a moment to look in, remembering the first day out when he'd taken Hope shopping for books. Everyone had been quiet over dinner tonight, and he'd wondered if it was for the same reasons. Neither Jenny nor Lou had seemed surprised to hear that he'd decided to give up work and have a bit of a break to spend some time with Hope. He'd noticed a brief exchange of glances between them, but he didn't push it. Jenny had simply said – stacking the dishwasher afterwards – that they needed to have a talk about what was going to happen now. She'd made it clear from the start that if it was up to her, they'd keep the cottage on for another six months. And Lou had surprised them all by putting down roots and finding himself a place in village life – although, when Harry thought back to his long career, it wasn't really a surprise that he'd done so. Hope was desperate to stay where her beloved Muffin was, and where she could help out at the stables and be around Charlotte, who she idolized.

'The ball's in your court, lad,' Lou had said, half-joking. But it was true that the only thing stopping them was him. Could he settle down here, knowing Ella was half a mile away, living her life? She'd seemed keen to rush off after the run – with her teacher friend obviously in on the joke.

They'd got on well before the mix-up at the farm sale, when someone had mistaken them for a couple. Maybe they could find their way back to that, if nothing else.

'So d'you think we make a nice couple?'

Lissa beamed across the table at Ella. She was trying her hardest to keep her hands to herself, but it was clear that she and James were made for each other, and the spark between them wasn't going to be extinguished by polite conversation over curry at the Lion Inn. The plan had been that they'd have a late lunch to celebrate finishing the run, but when they'd bumped into James and he'd somehow ended up joining them, lunch had some-how trailed into dinner, and Ella had immediately started thinking of excuses to leave. She had deliberately daw-dled slowly back to the table after popping to the loo, and even so she'd returned to find them with eyes locked in a gaze, hands entwined, murmuring to each other.

She scratched her head. There had to be a way to make an excuse and leave – but Lissa knew her too well for any lines about horses having colic, or sudden text messages.

James went to the gents and Lissa sprawled across the table, starry-eyed.

'Isn't he lovely?'

Ella laughed. 'Yes.'

'And he's really funny and sweet, too.'

She nodded. 'And kind. And most importantly –'

They both said in unison, 'He's not a dickhead.'

Lissa blew upwards, so a tendril of dark curly hair lifted, then fell back down on her forehead.

'He is not a dick. He's a genuinely nice man. And a nice dad. My *God*, I've kissed a lot of bloody frogs.'

Ella looked at her reflection in the mirrored wall of the pub. Her hair was plaited back off her face following a quick shower at Lissa's place, and her face was still faintly pink from exertion.

'Liss?'

Her friend snapped shut the lipstick she'd reapplied and used a napkin to blot her mouth. 'Mmm?'

'Look, I know you wanted me to have a lovely

bonding meal with you guys, but would you mind if I sort of –'

'Buggered off?'

Ella laughed. 'Yep.'

'You don't want to stay for the main course and then go?'

She shook her head no.

'I'll tell James you didn't fancy third-wheeling it and you left in a huff.'

'Ha ha.' Ella caught the collar of her coat with a finger and lifted it up over her shoulder. 'Tell him I've got a horse with suspected colic, or something.'

Lissa gave a knowing grin and held out her hand, palm up, for a high five. 'Deal.'

'See you later, Ella, love,' Andy the barman called as she swung open the doors.

'See you.' She raised her hand in a wave. Outside, she paused for a moment on the doorstep and fastened her coat, realizing that the sky had clouded over. The first drops of rain hit her face as she stepped out into the Lion car park.

Her stuff was at Lissa's house, and there was no way she was going back in and interrupting Love's Young Dream to pick up the keys. There was nothing for it, she'd have to start walking, and get in a hot bath when she got home to recover.

The rain was coming down in huge, heavy splattering drops by the time she turned at the telephone box and made her way through the houses and onto the lane that led out of the village. She could feel it beginning to soak through the seams of her coat, her shoulders and elbows feeling damp and uncomfortable. The street lights were on, but with the skies clouded over there was no moonlight. She'd have to walk up the road in the pitch dark. It wouldn't be the first time, but still. There were times when she cursed living in a village with no public transport and an extremely sporadic taxi service – and Huw the taxi driver was at least three pints down in the Lion, so he wasn't going anywhere this evening.

The first rumble of thunder was faint in the distance. Maybe she'd make it back before it started properly. She sped up a bit, puffing as she tried to hold the collar of her coat tight against her neck. It was even darker now, and she reached into her pocket for her phone to use it as a torch.

'Bollocks.'

There was a snort of laughter from somewhere behind her, and she spun around in the gloom.

'Ella.'

She recognized the voice straight away.

'Hi.'

He was standing in the old stone bus shelter, his collar turned up against the rain. He raised his hands skywards in a hopeless gesture and smiled, surprising her. His hair was soaking and he raked it back from his forehead.

He nodded to the bags at his feet.

'I thought I'd pop to the shop, give Jenny and Lou a bit of time to have a chat.'

'I went to the pub to have dinner with Lissa and her new boyfriend.'

Harry pulled a face. 'Awkward.'

'Hmm.'

Ella could hear her heart thumping against her chest and put an unthinking hand up, pressing down as if to steady it. She took a breath in.

His eyes dropped to her hand briefly, and then he met her gaze.

'I wanted to talk to you. To apologize.'

'You didn't do anything wrong.' She felt her cheeks burn, remembering the sight of Hope lying broken on the ground. 'I could have lost everything, and it would have served me right.'

'That was never going to happen.'

'But it would have been fair.' Ella pushed her hair back behind her ear and looked at him, lifting her chin. 'After everything, it would have been fair.'

'After everything?' His voice was gentle.

'After the accident. After – after Dad died.'

'Ella, what happened was awful, and we were both very young. We made mistakes.'

She nodded. 'I only wish I could make it OK.'

'You don't have to make it OK. It just is.'

A gust of wind blew a splatter of raindrops from the edge of the shelter and Ella jumped forward to avoid them, realizing as she looked up that she was now so close to Harry that she could feel the warmth of his hand which – if she reached out her little finger – she could touch.

As if he could read her mind, his fingers found hers and he lifted her hand, taking it between his. 'You're cold.'

She nodded.

'I am, too.'

He stepped towards her at the same moment as she moved and she allowed herself to be wrapped – like a long-forgotten memory – in his arms. She closed her eyes, realizing as she did that she could feel his heart thudding just as loudly through the layers of his clothes.

'Ella,' he said, into her hair.

She pulled back, looking up at him.

'I need you to understand something.' His voice cracked as he spoke.

'When I saw you riding, it reminded me of you – before. And of us. I want to be happy.' He lifted a hand to her cheek, tracing his finger gently down the side of her face, looking at her with a love she remembered so well. 'I want you to be happy.'

'I am.' And she was in that moment, she realized. Even if nothing else happened, this brief moment in the rain had recalibrated everything. She thought of Bron with her arm around Meg, smiling in the sunshine.

A crack of lightning flashed overhead, lighting up his face so she could see the stubble on his jaw and the lines that grief and time had etched around his eyes. She reached a hand up to touch them with a finger. 'I am happy.'

'I want –' He caught her hand and ran a thumb gently down her wrist, sending a crackle of electricity through her body to rival the lightning. It was the smallest of gestures but she realized that if she was going to act, it should be now.

'I do, too.' She lifted her mouth to his, curling a hand around the back of his neck.

'Do you remember that first Christmas when I came to stay, and Bron was baking in the kitchen?'

Ella swung his hand as they walked up the lane in the darkness towards the cottage.

'I do.' She smiled to herself.

'I think she'd be pleased to know we've called a truce, don't you?'

He stopped, pulling her round to kiss her once again.

'I tried,' he said, his mouth close to hers, 'to stop loving you. Tried harder than I have tried anything.'

'Me too.'

Epilogue

'Turn her before the last fence and push her into canter.'

Hope, determination on her face, gave a shout of delight as Muffin soared over the jump.

'Well done, darling,' Bron clapped, turning with delight to smile at Meg. They were leaning on the edge of the outdoor arena in the sunshine, having been press-ganged into taking the role of jump stewards.

'Can you make it bigger, Bron?' Hope pushed her riding hat up and scratched her freckled nose. She was grinning from ear to ear.

'I'll do it.' Charlotte rushed forward. She was making the most of her time at the yard before she headed off to Gloucestershire to university – a couple of years later than her parents had expected, but she was off to work towards a degree in Equine Science.

'Not too high, Charlotte. I think maybe we should do a few more training rounds before you start aiming for the Horse of the Year Show,' said Ella, laughing.

The sunshine was warm on her back as she paused for a moment, watching. Eighteen months had passed, and Hope was on her long summer holiday. She still loved the little primary school. Coming home each night to ride her own pony helped too, of course. Harry's time was spent helping out at the stables, dealing with the paper-work, and of course enjoying his time with Hope.

'Where d'you want this, Ella?' He was carrying a crate of flowers they'd bought from the garden centre to make the place look good for the brochures they were having printed.

She turned and made her way across to him, leaving Hope in the capable hands of her two great-aunts.

'Can I just,' she stood on tiptoe, planting a kiss on his mouth, 'give you this?'

He pulled her close. 'Is it an IOU for later?'

'Could be.' Ella smiled.

'Have you heard from Jenny and Lou?'

She nodded. 'An email. They were in dock, having mojitos on the city wall of Colombia. Next stop was the Panama Canal, I think she said.'

Jenny and Lou had bought another cottage in the vil-lage in the end, selling up their home in Norwich to the family who'd been renting it. They were delighted to take over the house they'd fallen in love with. With Harry home all the time, and Hope happily settled with her new stepmother, Jenny confided to Ella that while she missed so much close contact with her granddaughter, she loved being able to spoil her and not worry so much about the day-to-day things. Meanwhile, Bron and Meg had settled on the Gold Coast of Australia but travelled back to Wales in their winter to spend time with Ella, Harry and their growing family.

Hope was looking forward to a trip to Disneyland

with them at Christmastime – the whole crew. She might not have a conventional family, Ella thought, but between them there was a huge amount of love. When she went into Hope's bedroom to tidy up or put away washing, she'd always take a look at Sarah's photograph and smile. Jenny had assured her that Sarah would definitely approve of the way things had turned out. It felt good to have Hope's mother's blessing, somehow.

'Come and watch,' Hope shouted across to them. She'd wheedled Charlotte into raising the height of the jump and was flying over a fence almost as tall as she was.

Harry stood behind Ella, wrapping his arms around her, dropping a kiss onto the top of her head.

'Let's hope these two –' he patted the round shape of Ella's stomach, laughing – 'don't have such a taste for adventure.'

She squeezed his hand. 'I suspect they might.'

Acknowledgements

To everyone who has waited patiently for this book while I went off and wrote two Y.A. novels – thank you. I am lucky to have such lovely readers, and chatting to you all online makes this work lots more enjoyable (even if it makes me less productive!).

To the writing friends who keep me (relatively) sane: The Prime Writers gang, The Literary Hooters and the Millionaires – thanks for making me laugh when I should probably be working. There's a bit of a theme here. Love and thank you to Ella Risbridger, who could see what I was trying to write when it was still a muddle.

To my family – and the children, and the animals – thank you for putting up with writing Rachael, aka the scruffy and grumpy version. I love you all.

To my editors Louise and Caroline, and everyone at Macmillan who helps turn my scribbles into a real live book, thank you!

Amanda Preston, agent extraordinaire – I am enormously lucky to have you, and your combination of cheerleading and (gentle) arse-kicking is exactly what a writer needs. Thanks also to everyone at LBA for being the best agency (with the most stairs . . .).

And to my lovely husband Ross – oh yes, that's what we were meaning to tell you all – thank you for everything but especially the tea and the baths. And the tea. And for pointing out (frequently) that no, I don't need to hire a skip and declutter the whole house, I need to do my edits.

Wildflower Bay

This little island has some big secrets . . .

Isla's got her dream job as head stylist at the most exclusive salon in Edinburgh. The fact that she's been so single-minded in her career that she's forgotten to have a life has completely passed her by – until disaster strikes.

Out of options, she heads to the remote island of Auchenmor to help out her aunt who is in desperate need of an extra pair of scissors at her salon.

A native to the island, Finn is thirty-five and reality has just hit him hard. His best friends are about to have a baby and everything is changing. When into his life walks Isla . . .